"*The Vanished* illuminates the murky details of art provenance in fascinating snippets of Nazi theft history. Putman's legal expertise shines in this compelling and intricately plotted romantic suspense. Highly recommended!"

—Colleen Coble, *USA Today* best-selling author

"Sometimes small towns hide the greatest secrets. In this taut, sophisticated story, Cara Putman builds the tension beyond legal issues swirling around the provenance of European works of art to the highest level of intrigue and danger linked to underworld thefts and long-hidden family secrets. *The Vanished* is a highly satisfying first installment of Putman's new Secrets to Keep series. Welcome to the world she's created and the characters who live there!"

—Robert Whitlow, best-selling author of *Double Indemnity*

"Once again, Cara Putman has hit a home-run thriller in *The Vanished*! I enjoyed every tightly written page and hated to see it end."

—Carrie Stuart Parks, best-selling author of *Relative Silence*

"Cara Putman has once again created an exciting cast of characters. I was immediately drawn in by Janae and Carter's unique chemistry. This is one story you don't want to miss."

—Rebecca Hemlock, award-winning author of *Fury in the Shadows*

"Cara Putman weaves an incredible tale of art stolen and lost, intriguing legal battles, and history just screaming for us to dive into it in *The Vanished*. My nerdy little reader heart kicked into high gear, and I couldn't put this one down!"

—Kimberley Woodhouse, best-selling author of *The Secrets Beneath* and the Alaskan Cyber Hunters series

"I didn't know I needed a slow-burn suspense novel until I read this one. The pacing is perfectly tuned to the romance, making you want to read as quickly as you can. It will also have readers looking up history and art. Bravo!"

—Kari Trumbo, *USA Today* best-selling author

"*The Vanished* by Cara Putman has everything a good book should contain. A gripping story of deceit, dishonesty, and two people willing to fight for change as they also fight for each other. Great read!"

—Lenora Worth, author of *Disappearance in Pinecraft*

THE
VANISHED

SECRETS TO KEEP

The Vanished

The Accused

The Targeted

We Three Kings: A Romance Christmas Collection

by Crystal Caudill, Cara Putman, and Angela Ruth Strong

SECRETS TO KEEP

THE
VANISHED

CARA PUTMAN

KREGEL
PUBLICATIONS

The Vanished
© 2024 by Cara C. Putman

Published by Kregel Publications, a division of Kregel Inc., 2450 Oak Industrial Dr. NE, Grand Rapids, MI 49505. www.kregel.com.

Published in association with Gardner Literary, LLC. www.gardner-literary .com.

The persons and events portrayed in this work are the creations of the author, and any resemblance to persons living or dead is purely coincidental.

Cover design by Faceout Studio.

Library of Congress Cataloging-in-Publication Data
Names: Putman, Cara C., author.
Title: The vanished / Cara C. Putman.
Description: Grand Rapids, MI : Kregel Publications, 2024. | Series: Secrets
  to keep ; book 1
Identifiers: LCCN 2023042929 (print) | LCCN 2023042930 (ebook)
Subjects: LCGFT: Christian fiction. | Detective and mystery fiction. | Novels
Classification: LCC PS3616.U85 V36 2024 (print) | LCC PS3616.U85 (ebook)
  | DDC 813/.6—dc23/eng/20230920
LC record available at https://lccn.loc.gov/2023042929
LC ebook record available at https://lccn.loc.gov/2023042930

ISBN 978-0-8254-4804-1, print
ISBN 978-0-8254-6364-8, epub
ISBN 978-0-8254-6363-1, Kindle

Printed in the United States of America
24 25 26 27 28 29 30 31 32 33 / 5 4 3 2 1

To My Family

When I started this journey to publication, I hoped to write one book, but it was a dream that was precious and hard to share. Thank you for never laughing and always supporting me even when it meant I had to sit at the computer and ask for five more minutes rather than do fun things. Here's to celebrating forty books together.

Chapter 1

WHAT HAVE I DONE?

The thought pounded through Janae Simmons's mind as the wheels melted beneath her Mazda SUV's tires. The sun lingered above the horizon in its downward descent as she drove through Kedgewick, Virginia, a breeze ruffling her hair through the cracked windows. Her belongings were packed into boxes and suitcases that stuffed her vehicle's trunk, back seat, and passenger seat. The last ten years compressed into the smallest space possible.

Coming home had felt like a good idea in the face of a case gone horribly wrong. But now she wound her way along the final miles, wheels racing away from the hustle and bustle of Philadelphia to the gentler pace back home in Kedgewick, where she'd grown up. Now she second-guessed the decision that led her back to the small town located at the edge of the Blue Ridge, the bedroom community of the Washington, DC, metro area.

After leaving the quaint town behind, the drive morphed into gently rolling hills on a road laced with trees that were covered in the vibrant jewel-toned hues of autumn. Coming home should have felt as peaceful. Instead, unsettled and ready to turn around, she signaled and turned left off the highway and onto the county road that led to her parents' home. She considered detouring to her grandmother's house, testing the response to her return inside the thick stone walls of the centuries-old abode. Instead, she followed the lane back along the horse pastures to the estate that sat on the hill—the stables, barn, schoolhouse, and pavilion nestled around it.

Where there should be peace, a small, panicked voice inside warned that abandoning her safe job was a colossal mistake . . . even if that job sucked the life from her.

Normally, she'd discuss life changes with someone, but this time she'd made the decision on her own after some thought and moments of prayer. Even her parents didn't know she was visiting—much less staying.

She'd live with the result.

Janae fought the tremble that coursed through her, refusing to give in to the fear that pricked her as she drove under the sign of a stylized horse at the entrance to the driveway portion of the road. After parking near the schoolhouse, she stared at her parents' two-story home, the oak tree standing sentinel to the left of the front door ablaze in yellow and orange. Had her best option really distilled down to escaping home to her old room? Even if it was for a short season until she found an alternative, it still meant stepping into her past where everyone knew the old, practically perfect Janae.

They didn't know the new one who had lost her latest client millions of dollars in a botched settlement effort.

She forced herself to reframe the option. Maybe starting over in her hometown wouldn't redeem that mistake, but it would allow her a fresh beginning.

"To move forward." The whispered words did nothing to calm her nerves.

The cardinal-red door opened, and her mother stood framed on the threshold. Willowy with salon-inspired color, Mom drove into Purcellville for her calling as a speech-language pathologist at one of the local elementary schools. She poured her care and love into her kids each day, which earned her the adoring recognition of her young clients. Anonymity evaporated when she worked with small fry, making her recognizable everywhere.

Janae opened her car door and met her mom halfway down the sidewalk, feeling the warmth of the hug cut through the chill kissing the October air. "You shouldn't be out here without a jacket, Mom."

"I couldn't wait another minute to hug you." Her mom squeezed her again, then slipped to her side, and they walked up the half dozen steps together. "It's good to have you home. But this feels sudden. You sure you're all right?"

Janae forced a nod and refused to give the moisture in her eyes a path out. "I needed a change."

Her mom eyed the car, and Janae could see the moment she took in all the containers. "There's a story in those boxes."

"Not really. Just coming home for a bit. I needed to get away from Philadelphia and the lifestyle there."

"Well, your room is always ready if you need a place to land." She tightened her hold on Janae for a moment. "And I'll enjoy every moment while you do." She released Janae and followed her inside, then hurried to close the door with a shiver. "The meteorologists can't decide if we're going to get a dusting of snow or a mere freeze this week."

"Must be nice to have a job where you can consistently"—her mom joined her for the last words—"be wrong."

They laughed, and Janae felt something release inside her. Then Mom led her down the short hallway past the living and dining rooms to the back with the open kitchen and family room. The island and its unique stools had been her favorite spot from the moment they moved into the house when she was in eighth grade. It was magic to watch her mom pull hot chocolate chip cookies out of the oven after her days at school. They'd sit on the stools, drink their milk, and eat cookies while Janae chattered about her friends and classes. She smiled as her mom pulled a cookie sheet from the oven.

Mom noticed and brushed hair from her forehead with a shrug. "Guess I was missing you this afternoon. It feels right."

Yes, it did.

Maybe retreating home would be okay. At least for now.

Mom set a plate with two cookies and a small glass of milk in front of her, then turned and picked up an envelope from the counter. "I received strict instructions to give this to you as soon as you arrived."

"Wait a minute. How did you know I was on my way?"

"You know one of the ladies from church works at a law firm in town. She might have slipped word to me the moment she heard a rumor you were taking a job here."

"And you didn't say anything?"

"Figured it was your story to tell. Kiddo, Kedgewick is still a small town."

"I guess it is." Janae took a bite of the perfectly gooey cookie while eyeing the envelope. "What is it?"

"I have an idea but didn't open it for you."

"You've always said it was a mother's prerogative."

Mom rolled her hazel eyes that mirrored Janae's. "When you were sixteen, yes. Not now that you're twenty-nine."

"Gee, thanks." She dusted her fingers on her jeans and then picked up the envelope. After opening it, she pulled out an embossed cardstock invitation. "A gallery opening?" She looked at her mom. "Who sent this?"

"It arrived by courier. Seemed fancy." She shrugged and tapped the envelope. "I don't know for sure who sent it, but that opening is all anyone can talk about. It's invitation only, and the first show launched by the new director at the Elliott Museum of Art."

"The one at Monroe College?"

"Yes, he's some hotshot from Atlanta."

"If he was really a hotshot, he wouldn't be here."

"Says the woman who's come home."

"That's the key. It's home for me." And it wouldn't be for this man. "Well, it seems very mysterious and out of character for Kedgewick."

"Maybe it's from one of your high school or gymnastics friends."

"Maybe." She glanced at the date again. "It's for tonight? I can't possibly go."

"Sure you can. Rest, clean up, and go be part of the event of the fall."

"I don't have anything to wear."

Mom arched an eyebrow. "You have a car packed with things. You have something."

Janae squared her shoulders and lifted her chin. "Mom, I love you. But I did manage to run my own life for the years I was at college, law school, and in Philly."

Mom cocked her head, hazel eyes sparking. "Then why are you back now?"

"Because you and Grandma need help." And she needed a break from her high-pressure, unrelenting associate position. Much as she loved the law, it was a demanding taskmaster. And she'd been run ragged at the large litigation firm. She pushed off the memory of just how broken she'd become in the process of trying to keep up and earn a partnership.

"If you think I needed you to give up and move home, you should leave now."

"That's not what I meant." Janae didn't have the energy for this conversation. Not after the long drive. Not when she wondered if she'd like the small firm that had offered her a job. The lead partner's son hadn't been a great human being in high school, and the apple didn't fall far from the tree. However, she didn't have many options in Kedgewick. The idea of starting her own firm had caused a near panic attack and forced her from that option quicker than she could letter *not on your life* in her journal. "I've gotta unpack so I can find the dress for this shindig you think I should attend."

Mom came around the island. "I'm sorry. I want you to be happy and that requires being back for the right reasons."

"Well, I already quit my job, so I'm here for the near term. Probably longer."

"Grab the box with your dresses, and I'll get one ironed while you rest and freshen up."

An hour later, she kissed her mom on the cheek. "I'd better hurry or I'll be late. Not the kind of entrance I want to make. Night." Janae opened the door and slipped out before her mom could fire another barrage of tips and reminders about all the ways life had changed since she left Kedgewick.

She spent the short drive into downtown Kedgewick clearing her mind and steeling herself for the night. If she pretended she were about to enter the courtroom rather than an art gallery, maybe it wouldn't feel so excruciating to wonder what the people who knew her as a teen thought of her now. It shouldn't matter, but she'd left Kedgewick all those years ago to get a fresh start, and many might delight that she'd returned. And now she found that the in-your-face antagonism of the courtroom was preferable to the hidden barbs of "friends." Still, part of her wished she were parking near the courthouse rather than on the edge of Monroe College. The courtroom had become her second home in the five years since law school. She hadn't darkened the doors of Monroe College's museum since finishing an art appreciation paper during Thanksgiving break of her junior year at Purdue. It felt like a lifetime ago, but the Virginia-limestone facade of the three-story museum sat unchanged, with couples walking up the steps and across the covered portico to the double doors. Now she was headed to some fancy event here—something she'd never done before. Light spilled from the museum each time one of the large front doors opened.

Did she want to do this?

Did it matter?

She took a deep breath and slid from her car. She teetered across the museum's parking lot on high boots she never should have bought. Fashion should give way to comfort, but sometimes you had to look the part. Tonight was that night, but she hoped she hadn't leaned too close to *Legally Blonde* style. It wasn't the look she was going for.

Several people walked up the stairs to the front of the Elliott Museum of Art, and white lights twinkled over the threshold, illuminating the way. Janae allowed a bit of space, then climbed the rest of the stairs. The wind fought her grasp on the heavy door, seeming to push the door firmly so she couldn't yank it open.

When it finally relented, she stumbled into the foyer of the museum, balancing on boots with too narrow a heel for stability on the slick surface.

Someone grabbed her elbow to steady her, and she felt heat flush her neck.

She quickly righted herself. "Thank you."

"Welcome." The rich baritone should soothe, but instead she stiffened, embarrassed anyone had seen her utter lack of grace.

Put her on a balance beam, and it could be magic. Put her in heels, and she was a stumbling oaf. Then her gaze traveled up until it collided with eyes the bright color of an Italian sky in midsummer, and for a moment she lost her sense of place. His brows quirked as a question filled his eyes. "You all right?"

Janae blinked and pasted on her professional *I-rule-the-courtroom* smile. "Of course. Just here to enjoy the art." Wow, that was articulate. Everyone should hire her to represent them based on that display of oral brilliance.

"Then you're in the right place. I hope you enjoy the exhibit." He stepped back, and she acutely felt the moment he let go. "If you need anything, ask." When he turned, she noted the way his suit perfectly draped his form.

A woman stepped around the ticket kiosk, pulling her attention away. "May I take your coat?"

Janae fought back a shiver but nodded, hoping her hot pink cashmere sweater and brown skirt would keep her warm as she strolled through the galleries. She'd likely be underdressed, but it had been the best she could do on an hour's notice—her dresses had been too wrinkled for even her mother to salvage. "Thank you." She removed the coat and handed it over, accepting the claim ticket in exchange. "Any particular place you'd recommend I start?"

The young woman startled, her red lips forming an O. "No one's asked. Most start in the gallery to the right, but the best painting is through the one on the left. I don't know what it is, but everyone stops and absorbs it."

"Thanks. How will I know which one?"

"You'll know." She took a step closer. "It's where you'll find the new director. He's worth a look even if you don't like art. He was just here, but every fifteen minutes he drifts back there. Oh, wait. You just spoke with him." The college student giggled and then straightened and approached the couple who'd just entered.

Janae headed in the direction the young woman had indicated. It wouldn't hurt to start with the best piece and work out from there. Long ago these halls were familiar, but she hadn't visited recently. She stood in the doorway and watched couples and individuals, some standing in front of art, considering it, others appearing aimless as they flowed around the room. High school art class was the last significant time she'd spent here other than for that one college paper. She hadn't truly valued art until she'd taken an art appreciation class in college. That had ignited an understanding of how art developed over time, while also giving her favorite artists whose work she could look for whenever she visited a gallery. Maybe she should have started by asking the gal at the entrance where to find the museum's Pissarros.

Nerves jittered through Carter Montgomery as he observed a couple wander past without noticing an exquisite painting by Thomas Gainsborough. He'd found it sitting in a small conference room and decided the painting of an English woman from the 1780s was a perfect addition to the exhibit his predecessor had created on Women in Art. It had felt like a light touch, adding his mark to the gallery. Very few would ever recognize it that way, but he hadn't expected people to walk by without seeing her at all.

However, one woman stood transfixed by another painting in the collected works.

The elderly woman with silver coiffed hair stared at a Paula Modersohn-Becker painting on loan for the exhibit, a piece that had reappeared from a private or state collection in the last few years. The Expressionist painting of children had pulled the tiny, birdlike woman into its orbit, and she hadn't twitched. She looked frail enough that she might break at a touch. Yet there was something granite in her slightly stooped posture and the way she didn't move. She barely breathed. An oasis in the slow swirl of others moving from painting to sculpture or standing like small islands talking, waiting to be seen rather than to see.

The painting was nice. Lovely in a way. While Modersohn-Becker had an exquisite touch, she wasn't as well-known as Vincent van Gogh and others from her time. The museum owned more popular paintings than this one on loan, and around the corner were two additional famous paintings on loan from other museums—a Donatello and a Raphael.

What about this painting had arrested her attention so completely?

"She hasn't moved in fifteen minutes." Ariel Sharp, his young, inherited assistant, came and stood next to him. "If I didn't know better, I'd wonder if she'd died."

Carter cut her a sharp look. "Be careful."

"She's as old as the mountains around here."

"And worthy of respect." Before Ariel could say anything else that annoyed him to the point of firing her regardless of who her daddy was and what the board thought, he strode toward the elderly woman. He made a bit of noise as he approached so he didn't startle her. "You like this one."

"Yes." There was the faintest hint of an accent lacing her word. European? Maybe.

"What about it captured you?" He was always curious to know what attracted people's attention.

The woman placed a hand at her chin and tilted her head, making her even more birdlike as she continued to gaze at it. "This painting was a gift to my grandmother on the event of her fortieth birthday."

That was . . . unexpected. "Really? That's incredible."

"Not as incredible as the fact this painting was stolen from my family, and I long for the day it returns home."

His mind whirled as he considered how to respond. A claim like that was far-fetched. And to drop it in the middle of an exhibit—like she discussed the weather and how wonderful the sun felt—was startling and left him floundering. "Why don't we set a quiet time to meet?"

"Why not now? I have already waited seventy years, and my family has waited even longer to find and recover this piece of our heritage."

He gestured to the gallery beyond them. "Right now I have too many guests to give you the attention your story requires."

"I understand." The words whispered from her, causing him to lean close. He felt the gravitas that infused them. Made the simple words firm and unyielding. And from such a small, unassuming person.

"I look forward to it." Noting others watching them, he gave her a half bow.

She turned toward him for the first time, a sad tilt to her fuchsia-colored lips, the color feathering out through her wrinkles. The edges of her eyes turned down, reflecting the weariness of her sloped shoulders. "Until then."

He walked away, careful not to flee, feeling her gaze and those of others in the room. What had just happened? He wasn't sure, but he needed to find an attorney for the museum.

Chapter 2

JANAE TOOK A LEISURELY PATH down the broad hall, noting each work and stopping when something caught her attention. It might be the colors, the subject, or the brushstrokes. She hadn't made time for such immersion while she worked eighty hours a week.

That was something she could change with the return to Kedgewick. Something she could reset.

Eventually she left the hall and entered the gallery and took in the paintings displayed in heavily gilded frames, noting one on the far wall. Standing next to an older woman was the man she'd encountered at the entrance. The director? She should look away but was intensely curious about what the unlikely pair discussed. If her gaze traveled to the man more than the small woman in an elegant coat dress, who could blame her? There was something compelling about him.

Maybe she stood there longer than she thought, because the next thing she knew someone sidled next to her.

"You might want to quit ogling the new director." Margeaux Robbins's teasing tone didn't stop Janae's embarrassment from flaming her skin.

"You're not supposed to call attention to it." Janae gave her a quick side hug, noting how thin her lifelong friend felt.

"I'm glad to see you noticing." Her friend waggled her eyebrows.

Was Margeaux eating? They had spent hours together in the gymnastics facility growing up, forming a tight bond, and there had been seasons Margeaux had struggled. Janae forced her attention away from her concern. "Why aren't you watching?"

"Because I joined the museum's board of directors last month, and that makes me his boss." She wrinkled her nose in a way that reminded Janae of every time her friend got ready to take the floor. Margeaux was a dynamo when she tumbled, and somehow doing that nose wrinkle had helped her release tension before competing. Taller than the average gymnast by a good six inches, Margeaux had channeled her power into a beautiful blend of grace and pure strength that lightly kissed the floor rather than pounding it like a stumbling elephant.

"Congratulations. I hadn't heard."

"Thanks. I haven't posted it anywhere yet. It could be a lot of work, but it lets me send invitations like the one you received."

"I wondered who it came from. Thanks."

"Sure. I wanted one friend here, and since you thought you might come back to town . . ."

"It was a big might."

"You're here." Margeaux grinned at her.

"Show off."

"Just like being right."

"There is that." Janae looked around. "You've always liked spending time here."

"True."

Janae noted everyone already holding long-stemmed glasses. "Looks like your people are waiting for you."

"I don't know about that, but I should pretend I'm an extrovert for the next hour or two."

"No pretending needed." Not when Margeaux managed to find common ground with most people in a matter of minutes. It was what made her a professor who easily connected with her students. But her departure would leave Janae to work her way around the fringes.

Margeaux leaned over and gave her a quick air kiss. "I'll keep an eye out for you. I think Chloe plans to stop by too."

"It would be good to see her." Janae hoped her return meant she'd spend time with her childhood friends, but everyone had their own lives. "Go do your thing. I'm fine." And she would be. She had to be, because the alternative meant the move from the high-pressure firm to home had been the worst decision of her life.

A waitress walked by, black apron over a crisp white shirt, holding a tray of glasses. "Would you like one? Prosecco is on the left and sparkling grape juice on the right."

Janae lifted a white grape juice. "Thank you."

Glass in hand, she walked through the foyer into the first gallery on the right. This one was filled with Virginia artists, none internationally known, but the landscapes captured the best of the state she loved. The older woman had moved in here and now stood in front of one. Janae couldn't help overhearing when a tall man approached her.

"Mrs. Seeger, do you have a moment?"

The woman didn't turn toward the man. "You are?"

"Jarod Shaw, attorney-at-law."

Janae should move but couldn't. Maybe she could learn something from the way he approached people. She took another sip of her sparkling juice and continued to study the landscape before her.

"I know your family's history and would like to help you reclaim what is rightfully yours."

"I do believe that time has passed, young man." There was no irony in her voice even though the man had to be in his early forties. "I did all I could to put forth a claim fifteen years ago."

"But did you know where your family's paintings were then? The ones on display here?"

"What do you mean?"

"Maybe we can talk somewhere private." He handed her his card. "Next week I can come to you. I think we can make something happen now."

"I'll call you."

21

"I look forward to it, ma'am." He melted into the crowd, leaving the woman fingering his card before she slipped it into her clutch.

Before Janae could be caught staring, she moved to the next painting. Then she strolled past several more, nodding to a couple she recognized from when she visited her parents' church. She paused in front of her favorite landscape, a scene of the Shenandoah Valley in the full color of fall. Approximately four by six feet in the frame, it was a painting she could stand in front of for hours, and she had in fact done that on a dare in high school.

"Like what you see?"

The woman next to Carter startled, then seemed to force herself to still, as more bubbles floated to the top of her fluted glass. He glanced at her out of the corner of his eyes, noting the understated perfection of her outfit. She looked like she was ready to cheer on the latest hunt, except for the brightness of her sweater, but somehow she pulled it off. There was an easy elegance to her style, yet she didn't seem quite comfortable standing in his museum.

My museum. Carter had to grin at that thought. He'd worked long and hard to reach this point in his career. In fact, he'd reached it years before his plan or peers had predicted, even with the disaster he'd experienced at his prior job. His one regret was that his older sister wasn't here to see this success. Charlotte had always encouraged his dreams, and his breath still caught in his chest at the reality he'd never see her again.

He glanced around without really moving and noticed Stanley Dukes, the chair of the board and his former colleague, staring at him. There was something in his gaze that set Carter on edge. All was going well with the gallery opening. There were plenty of guests and donors enjoying the evening. Why was the man studying him?

Then a man in a blazer sidled next to Stanley, and the silver-haired man moved into the next room with him.

Carter refocused on the woman next to him, who had stayed silent. "I'm Carter Montgomery, the new director here."

"I'd heard there was a new one. Congratulations."

"Thanks."

Her chin tipped up to meet his gaze six inches above her, styling him as a giant next to her petite frame. She held out a slim hand, nails neatly trimmed but free of polish. "I'm Janae Simmons, attorney-at-law."

He bit back a snort at the way she said it. "Nice to meet you, Janae, attorney-at-law."

"That was pretentious, wasn't it?" She took a quick sip, and he noted the way her hand trembled. "I'm newly back in town and not sure how to explain who I am, and everything feels wrong. It all comes out jumbled or snotty." She clapped a hand over her mouth and rocked her head side to side. "I need to stop, don't I? I'm babbling now."

"Actually, I find this"—he ran a hand up and down in the air— "adorable."

She grimaced. "That's not exactly the aura I was going for." Her shoulders slumped like someone had pricked a hole in her balloon. "Events like this are tricky. I'm a hometown girl, but I've been gone more than ten years. So everyone who believes they know me is wrong. Well, other than one of your board members." She clamped her lips together.

He quickly pivoted back toward the art before she could read his face. Had he met anyone quite like her? Carter hadn't had this much fun engaging with someone in a while. She came across as natural and unaffected, a combination that piqued his interest.

"You can look again."

He couldn't hold back the guffaw, not quite the reaction he wanted others to see, as they turned to stare. He was new in town and an outsider, so no one wanted to know him in this tight-knit community. Best to move the conversation to more artistic territory. "Which is your favorite?"

"Of these?" She glanced around the gallery. "I'm really not much of an Impressionist girl. I prefer Italian art from the 1300s."

He almost believed her until he noted the faint twitch at the side of her perfect mouth. "Now that is interesting. I find most people seem drawn to masters like Manet and Monet."

"I personally like the ones where the people are dancing across the canvas on tiptoe. Give me some good old Agnolo Gaddi or Paolo Veneziano. Add a little gold leaf for color and I'm hooked."

"You've been to the national gallery recently."

"Guilty as charged. Even took the tour."

"And no interest in Raphael or da Vinci?"

"They're so . . ." She paused as if searching for the right word. "Common."

"Ah yes, nothing to seeing the only da Vinci in the western hemisphere."

She mimicked the woman who'd been talking to him earlier, tipping her head to the side as she studied the Pissarro. "Nothing at all."

Chapter 3

THIS MAN GIVING JANAE HIS full attention? A surreal yet wonderful experience. Why would he do that when there were so many important people here? She didn't know, but she was deeply enjoying their repartee. She took a sip of the sparkling grape juice, letting the fizz tickle the back of her nose before she swallowed.

Carter wore a dark navy suit, red-striped shirt, and blue-and-red-check bowtie. It could have looked ridiculous, but somehow the fit made him seem more artsy and unique rather than eccentric. She decided she liked it better than those of the stuffy attorneys she'd spent her time with before. She yanked in the thought. She'd barely made it to town and two hours ago hadn't known about this event. She did not need to let her thoughts wander to what might be possible with a man she'd just met.

She needed a redirection. Fast. "Which is your favorite?"

His eyebrows shot up. "Person?"

"No, though you could tell me." She tapped the glass lightly against her lips as she searched the room. "I was thinking along the lines of paintings. Surely one holds a special place in your heart."

"That's like asking a parent who's their favorite child." He shoved his hands in his pockets and her heart dropped at his words.

"I'm sorry. That's probably too personal." Surely he couldn't have kids. He was too young, and a quick glance at his left hand would fill in the important detail. Though maybe not. Not everyone cared about getting the wedding before the children. Guess she was an old-fashioned woman at heart.

"No, it's a good one for me to consider." He pulled a hand free and pointed at a landscape. "That one is my favorite because I'd swear the Blue Ridge still looks like that even though it was painted over a hundred years ago when Georgia O'Keeffe spent her summers here." Then he shifted toward the one with five children that the elderly woman had soaked in. "This one is so different, yet there's something animated and energetic even as the children sit on that beach without faces we can clearly discern."

"It is unusual."

"Sort of like the O'Keeffe. People forget that she lived in Charlottesville at the UVA campus for a series of summers. She painted more than large flowers and stark southwestern art. I love how unexpected her perspective was of the campus and mountains. She favored watercolors here, a medium she strayed from later because it wasn't perceived as real enough for a true artist."

"I get inspired by Instagram and YouTube videos, but can barely get anything but a blob of gray when I attempt watercolors."

"Look at hers and you'll see what I mean about the detail she added while working in that medium."

A young woman approached, dressed in a skintight minidress that looked very out of place among the more elegant dresses most women wore. "Carter, one of the board members is looking for you. Said something about needing to discuss something."

"Thanks, Ariel." He turned to Janae. "I'm sorry. I have to leave."

"I should probably circulate anyway. It'll be good to let people know I'm back and can solve their legal woes." She clapped her free hand over her mouth again. "Why do I keep saying the first thing that pops into my mind?"

"I must bring out the best in you." The edge of his mouth tipped in an adorable hint of a smile.

"Something like that." She took a final sip of the juice and then looked around but couldn't see a safe spot to deposit the glass.

"No need to frown. I'll take that for you since I need to check on the other galleries after I find this elusive board member."

"You don't need to—"

"I insist. But first . . ." He reached into the inside pocket of his jacket and pulled out a square business card, which he extended to her. "I find the museum may be in need of an attorney. Could you have your assistant call in the next morning or two to set up a meeting?"

Of course she would. Once she had an assistant and a dedicated office. Landing the museum as a client could give her needed clout as she established a reputation in town and talked to others about letting her work for them. "I arrived in town today but will reach out in the next couple days." She paused as a thought flitted through her mind. "Does the museum use the university's attorney?"

"Not for items like this. The general counsel has deferred every art-related matter to us. He's insisted it's outside his area of expertise. I can confirm with him if you prefer."

"That would probably be best and give me time to get settled."

"That should be fine." He looked around at the hubbub. "It'll take a while to get everything sorted, but I would like to connect about this, since I anticipate he'll continue to ask us to handle all art-related matters."

"Of course." She exchanged the card for the glass. "Thank you."

"The pleasure has been mine." He paused as if waiting for her to give him one of her cards.

She gave a small shrug. "Need to get new cards." She could only hope Ashley and Ashby would have some ready for her when she arrived Monday.

He nodded. "I'll look forward to hearing from you." Then he followed Ariel from the gallery.

Monday, October 24

Butterflies fluttered aggressively in Janae's stomach as she steeled herself for her first day at a new law firm. Ashley and Ashby filled the role of a small-town Virginia fixture. She remembered the original Ashley and Ashby as overweight, seersucker-clad old men who'd scared her as a child. Now her best option was walking through that door and working for their sons. Mark Ashby had gone to school with Janae's mother and had assured Janae they'd have work for someone with her skills. However, the way he said it made her think he didn't believe she had skills. After all, what could she learn in the big city that would have value in good ole Kedgewick?

Guess she'd demonstrate exactly what she could offer.

She straightened her bright red peplum suit jacket over its matching skirt, then opened the door and strode into the reception area.

A mousy woman with teased hair grimaced at her. "Can I help you? We don't open for another fifteen minutes."

Janae paused, a bit taken aback, because this wasn't her mother's friend whom she knew well from church, the one she'd talked with when setting up the position. "I expected Caroline Stone. She asked me to arrive now to get set up."

"Caroline is out for several weeks with an emergency. I'm filling in for her."

"Oh." Janae puffed a quick breath as she recalibrated, and then held out her hand. "I'm Janae Simmons, the new attorney."

"Who?" The woman's brow furrowed as if she couldn't understand what Janae had said.

"The new associate. Mark hired me." Well, she supposed it was a joint decision, but Ashley's first name escaped her in the haze of change. "He and Mr. Ashley." And Caroline, but that didn't seem worth mentioning right now.

"They didn't say anything to me." She pursed her hot pink lips, the lipstick already bleeding past her lip line. "Let me call back." Her voice dropped but Janae still caught the next words. "And see what they say." She swiveled slightly as if to block Janae from hearing anything.

Janae bit back the urge to say something that wouldn't help the woman's skepticism. Why hadn't the receptionist done the bare niceties and given Janae her name? Even for a temp she'd done a poor job. Janae would mention something if it wasn't her first day.

The woman had to have an inflated sense of the value of the firm.

Seriously, why would someone come to town and pretend to work for them? She'd have to be extremely desperate.

Maybe she was.

Janae took in the chairs that had probably been used since the 1970s, the vinyl cracked and repaired in places with colored duct tape that didn't match. A fake mimosa tree stood in a corner, the dust coating its leaves visible from where she stood. *Men's Health. Popular Mechanics. Sports Illustrated. Wired.* The magazines spread across the laminate console table dated from at least a year earlier. The issues hinted that old and middle-aged men were the firm's primary clientele.

The vibe of the space suggested the owners had stopped trying sometime around the end of the last decade, if not earlier.

Everything about her standing here felt like a bad idea, but she didn't see other options. The other attorneys in town said they didn't need anyone, but if she wanted to volunteer, they'd gladly find work for her. She'd had to decide whether to laugh or cry.

Saturday she'd felt like the belle at a ball, and now she felt like the forgotten stepsister.

The receptionist cleared her throat. "Yes, sir. I'll send her back." She hung up and then looked at Janae. "I guess it's your lucky day. He seems to think you should work here, though I have no idea why. We didn't have a new client last week."

"Maybe I'll bring them in." After all, the museum director wanted to talk.

The woman studied her and then shook her head. "Doubt that."

So they wouldn't be best friends. Janae squared her shoulders and straightened her posture. "Since we'll be working together can you tell me your name?"

"You won't be here long enough to need it."

Janae felt the words like a punch. So much for collegiality. "Where am I headed?"

"Second door on the left. I've got to warn you. The only room they can put you in is the storage room. It's overflowing with files."

"I'm used to stacks of files when working on discovery."

"Well, some of those go back at least a dozen years. Good luck." She shook her head. "You'll need it." The phone rang and she picked it up. "Ashby and Ashley."

Did the woman even notice she'd reversed the order of the partners? The original Mr. Ashley had to be rolling in his grave over that misstep. The receptionist took her temporary status seriously.

The woman shooed her back even as she kept talking.

No time like the present to see what she'd gotten herself into.

Three hours later, Mark Ashby hadn't stopped talking, his hands resting on the obnoxiously striped, gravy-stained tie spread over his rotund middle.

As he paused for air, Janae quickly spoke. "Do you have anything for me to work on?"

He pushed to his feet and then looked at his watch. "I suppose you should see where you'll sit, and then I have to head to the Rotary meeting. Time to remind everyone we're ready to serve their legal needs. It's chicken-fried steak day down at the diner. The best one if you ask me." He eyed her. "Looks like you could use some of that. Put some meat on your bones."

"My bones are fine and none of your concern." She stiffened as her pulse sped up. What was he thinking making statements like that? This was moving from a questionable decision to a terrible one.

He took his time looking her up and down. "It is if you're too weak to work." He brushed past her through the door, and she refused to shudder. "Follow me."

She released a breath. At least he wouldn't make her walk in front.

One partner in Philadelphia had delighted in seeing how far he could push his assigned associates before they would quit. Complaining was never an option because no one believed the young women, at least no one who could do anything. If Mark was anything like that partner, she knew where his attention would focus.

They'd barely walked ten feet down the hall when he stopped.

"Here you go." He pushed open a door and reached inside to flip on a light switch.

Janae's mouth opened and she couldn't push words out at first. It was even worse than the receptionist had indicated. A desk was shoved into the far corner of the room with a computer and monitor on top of its surface. To get to the desk and chair, she'd have to squeeze between banker boxes piled against two walls in a double row. On the other wall a table was tucked with more boxes towering over and under it. Even more stacked around and in front of the table.

"This is what I left Philly for?"

"No one asked you to come home, Janae Simmons. But we're glad to give you this space and twenty-five dollars an hour to do paralegal work. If you get your own clients, we'll bill your time at a hundred fifty dollars an hour and pay you fifty."

She sputtered. "Are you serious?"

"As a dog wrestling a bone from the ground." His expression dared her to leave.

"You'll be making one hundred dollars an hour on my time." At least. Angry tears formed but she blinked them back. He was right that she wouldn't find other options without heading closer to DC. At least not quickly. This ugly reality was exactly why she'd left the small town behind and never looked back until now. The niggling concern she'd made a mistake threatened to overwhelm her.

The only thing that was more overwhelming was the risk of failure if she didn't stay here and do all he asked. Because fail was what she would do if she went out on her own. If she couldn't remember to file the correct documents on time when she had the support of a massive infrastructure, there was no way she would on her own.

And she couldn't look like a failure in front of the people who'd already watched her leave.

She shook loose of the thoughts. "How can you expect me to get anything done here?"

"You're an enterprising girl. You'll come up with something." Then he tipped an imaginary hat at her and left.

Chapter 4

INHALING DEEPLY, CARTER IMAGINED THE caffeine racing through his veins on the strength of the espresso's scent alone. He'd about stopped at Flo's Diner but remembered in time that it was the day the Rotary Club descended. They could kill a person's enjoyment of a good meal with the way they carried on about assisting the community and how wonderful they were. He'd rather experience their greatness than hear about it each week. And it was country-fried steak day too. The fried food sounded comforting and good, but instead he'd grab a panini from Java Jane's.

The dark wood and dim lights always made him think of a hip cocoon that one could sink into and take a deep exhale while also sipping the nectar of the gods. The house roast was the perfect combination of robust and smooth.

The line was short, only three people in front of him, and he let his thoughts wander as he waited his turn. When he reached the counter, he couldn't hide a grin. It was his favorite barista, the one who always gave him an extra squirt of whipped cream for good measure. "Hey, Ellie. I'd like my usual with the best panini you have today."

She ducked her chin as if she couldn't find the courage to meet his gaze. That was different from her usual. "Regular meat or extra, Dr. Montgomery?"

The barista should be in one of her college classes now if he remembered correctly, but she stood behind the counter in her red apron and a white shirt that always carried dots from espresso gone astray.

He waited but she didn't meet his gaze. "What kind of sandwich is it?"

Her cheeks turned red while she looked at the cash register as if she'd never seen it before. "A ham and Swiss with spicy mustard."

"Regular's fine." He reached down and grabbed a package of jalapeño kettle chips from the basket. "I'll take these too." He waited for her to look at him. "Don't you have a class now?"

"Not today."

He arched a brow and she finally grinned. "Promise. I'd be in class if I needed to be."

"It's still the best place you learn the material."

"For some people." Her feisty grin was back. "Really, class got cancelled, and Adora needed someone to cover a shift. It worked out." As Ellie finished ringing him up, the door opened, and the bell tinkled. He shifted to see who had entered. It was the woman from the gallery show. "That'll be fourteen dollars and thirty-seven cents."

He handed his credit card to Ellie and then pivoted to watch the petite woman approach. "Janae, right?"

The woman looked around as if expecting he was talking to someone else. Then she shook her head. "I don't know why I'd think there's another Janae." Her smile didn't reach her eyes, which held strain. "It's good to see you."

He slid his card into his wallet and then slipped it in his back pocket. "What did you think of the exhibit?"

"It's good. An interesting exploration of the role women played in Expressionist and other styles of art." She clutched her purse strap as if waiting for someone to dash by and try to steal it. "I almost sound like I know something about art, but I enjoyed returning to the museum and seeing the new paintings."

"Changed much?"

"I'm sure it has in places, but nothing that left me wishing for what used to be."

"Your drink's ready, Dr. Montgomery. Extra squirt of whipped cream like you love."

Janae's eyebrows rose. "Doctor?"

"Guess I forgot to mention that Saturday."

She shook her head. "This town is full of surprises."

"There is a college here. I'm not the only PhD running around." He shoved his hands in his pockets. "It's pretty normal for museum directors and curators to have advanced degrees."

"I don't know why it caught me off guard. It's been an odd Monday." She stared at the menu board for a minute. "I haven't been here before. Any recommendations?"

"The Miel. It's a latte with cinnamon and honey."

"Interesting choice. I'm more of a straight latte person."

"Dr. Montgomery?" He shifted his attention and noticed Ellie still holding his mug. He took it from her with an apologetic glance. "We'll let you know when your sandwich is ready. I can even bring it to you."

"Thanks, Ellie." He glanced at Janae, who was still considering the menu. "The panini's also a good choice if you haven't had lunch yet. Try the daily special."

She nodded but didn't meet his gaze, the little furrows at the top of her nose illustrating that something bothered her.

"And if you'd like company, I'll be at the table over there. We can talk about the museum's legal needs or anything really." Why had he offered that? He wasn't sure, but he found he didn't mind the idea of her joining him as much as he might have thought. Spontaneous or not, it had a nice appeal and was a contrast to the solitary way he usually spent his time.

"Th-thank you." Janae looked away as she stammered the words.

"Of course." Not waiting to see if she'd respond, Carter tipped his mug in a silent salute and then walked to the round wooden table that sat in a corner, separated from the other customers by a ring of empty tables. After he sank onto a hard wooden chair, he sighed at the first sip.

Perfection. Whoever roasted the beans needed a raise. He tried not to study the counter to see whether Janae would join him, because then he couldn't be disappointed if she didn't accept his offer.

Still, he felt the letdown when she slipped out the front door with her to-go cup. Had she taken his recommendation? It didn't matter, but he was curious.

Carter knew he shouldn't expect anything from her, but he'd hoped she'd join him. That would have been better than another lunch by himself. Time to build his network. He'd done it while getting his PhD, and he could again.

The problem was, he'd lived in Kedgewick for four months and still didn't feel like he'd transitioned to calling it home. That required more than having a nodding acquaintance with a handful of people beyond those he worked with and the few he knew at his nephew's elementary school. He couldn't count on Andrew and his work for personal connections.

He could find an ally or two on the board. A church would help too. That's where people got to know the real person . . . if he risked it. His sister, Charlotte, had known the real him but then found herself embroiled in an art fiasco involving an Italian crime family. Now she was gone, killed in the shoot-out at an art gallery in Indiana, and he had Andrew, hopefully safe from anyone who might have a lingering vendetta.

Could anyone really hide in today's technology-infused world?

If they couldn't, moving here was nothing more than a diversion.

A handsome man close to her age had invited her to stay, and Janae took the coward's way out. She was too embarrassed to try to explain the mess that was her current existence at Ashley and Ashby. She couldn't bring a client to that—not yet. So she slipped from the building without the courage to meet his gaze.

Instead of heading back to the law firm, she strolled around the block. The town hall and jail sat in the middle, with the county courthouse located a few miles away in Leesburg. The town hall was a modern monstrosity, replacing the original building that had burned down the year Janae joined the world. With a stuccoed exterior, it didn't match anybody's idea of a stately building. Instead, it looked like it was left over from the former Soviet Union.

The wind snaked down her neck, and Janae tugged her coat collar up with one hand, balancing the drink in her other. Maybe strolling wasn't her best idea. She shouldn't catch a cold her first day on the job, but she also couldn't go back to that dreary hole-in-the-wall office. Not yet.

She didn't see how she'd have anything worth doing for the rest of the day. She couldn't imagine a firm less prepared for her arrival, but she should at least see if they were willing to give her real work, since her morning had involved listening to Mark and she imagined the afternoon would crawl by in the closet trying to get the computer to work. Without log-ons for the legal software, which Mark hadn't given her, she couldn't do much other than surf the web. That was not what she'd gone to law school to do, and without a purpose, it felt like a waste of her time. At the same time, without an idea of the type of cases they'd give her, she couldn't proactively prepare for anything.

Her thoughts drifted back to the man she'd left at Java Jane's. She'd noticed the way he interacted with others Saturday night. It had contained the same respect and concern she'd noted when he'd conversed with her.

She really had been a fool not to join him even if she couldn't talk about her job yet.

She almost turned around and headed back, but he'd probably ignore her if she did.

Actually that wasn't fair.

They might not have spent much time together, but she'd seen enough to discern he was a kind man.

Feeling stuck to the pavement, she forced her feet to move toward the firm, but then found the door locked. There was no note or sign to indicate when the office would reopen. This was lax even for a small town like Kedgewick, and a quick call confirmed the receptionist didn't wait inside to take a call or unlock the door. She shivered and shoved her hands in her pockets, wondering which of the open shops she should slip into while she waited. Chapters and Sips Bookstore sat on Main Street between Val's Boutique and A Second Chance Antiques. If it were warmer and she had better shoes on, Janae could head to the W&OD Trail and spend the lunch hour walking its path. Instead, after another look around, she entered the bookstore.

The bell over the door welcomed her as she stepped into the warm atmosphere of a shop filled with shelves of volumes, some new and others familiar, the mix of old friend and fresh acquaintance. And this shop was scented with orange and cloves from a diffuser by the door.

"I'll be right with you." A voice floated from behind the shelves and displays.

"Chloe?"

"Yep." A small woman stepped around a table, arms loaded with books. "Janae?" She startled and almost dropped the pile. She quickly shifted them onto the edge of the table, then squealed and opened her arms. "I didn't know you were back in town."

"Arrived over the weekend." Janae wasn't prepared to tell one of her high school friends about her life.

"Really?" She gave Janae a tight squeeze and then dragged her back to the counter. "Come have a seat and I'll make you a chai latte. It's my favorite and a specialty." She wrinkled her nose at the coffee Janae still held. "Java Jane's is fine, but wait until you have this chai."

"How long have you worked here?"

Chloe shrugged as she pulled something from a small fridge under the old-fashioned counter and then poured it into a mug. "I don't really work here."

"You're giving a good impression otherwise."

"I'm only helping out a friend. It's not full time but helps pay the bills."

"You've always been quick to help."

"Guess it's who I am." Chloe grinned, but it didn't reach her eyes. "How long has it been?"

"Probably two or three years. The law firm kept me busy."

"I wouldn't know about that. I'm still finding my way."

"I bet your debt load is lighter than mine. Seven years of higher ed added up."

"You won every scholarship you applied for. And have your parents." From anyone else that would feel like a weird statement, but Chloe had always eyed Janae's family as the goal. Chloe had grown up with a single mom who couldn't be present much, so Janae understood her desire. And the move to the horse farm must have seemed golden compared to the cramped apartment Chloe and her mom shared. Chloe shook her head as if returning from her thoughts and then frothed the liquid in the mug. "Sorry. Tell me what brings you in."

"I'm locked out of Ashley and Ashby."

"Why would that matter?"

"I started working there today."

Chloe gasped and then grasped her arm. "Run. You do not want to work for them."

"Considering the door's locked right now, I can't get inside." Janae watched her old friend. "Why would you tell me not to work for them?"

She paled, a difficult feat when she already had porcelain skin. "It's nothing." She dumped the liquid in a to-go cup and put a lid on top before sliding it to Janae. "Just be careful."

Janae nodded, and then her phone rang. By the time she looked up from the screen, Chloe had disappeared.

Chapter 5

WHEN JANAE REACHED THE OFFICES of Ashley and Ashby the next morning, she fought to keep a positive perspective. She'd worn jeans and a sweatshirt, planning to deep clean her office that masqueraded as a storage closet. The prior night, as she sneezed through dinner with her parents, she'd known the wells of dust hiding in all that paper made it impossible for her to work without dramatic changes. She hadn't gone to law school for three long years to have this be her future. The small succulent she carried wouldn't do much to change the space, but it was a first step to making it her own.

At least until Mark Ashby walked an old woman who looked slightly familiar by her in the hallway. His eyes widened and his posture stiffened as he spied her.

Had he forgotten about Janae already?

The woman looked at her with open curiosity, but Mark hurried her past and Janae rolled her eyes. Nothing like being completely obvious. Maybe he didn't appreciate her more casual dress, but she wouldn't wear a suit to clean her hidden office. She'd need to dry-clean her red suit thanks to being in that nasty space the prior day.

Why had he offered her the position?

He didn't have a thing to gain from misleading her into thinking she had a place to land when she didn't.

Maybe she should follow that older woman right out the door after her early meeting and then keep driving until she returned to Philly. It was a three-hour drive. She could make a quick stop at home and then walk into her old firm by noon, ready to pretend she'd never lost her mind. If only she hadn't failed her last client in such a spectacular way. No one in Philly would let her move past the moment she'd filed a motion to dismiss in the wrong case. And then it had worked, dramatically ending the multimillion-dollar recovery claims of the firm's most important client. The firm would recover, but she wouldn't. So she'd left. Before they fired her.

Now she sorted boxes until her jeans and sweatshirt were covered with dust and her face flushed from the exertion. She couldn't make decisions on what stayed or got shredded, but she could use the record retention standards of her old firm to make a first pass at what should happen to the files.

She noted many of the names on them. Mansur. Crowe. Roskha. Seeger.

As she had with the others, she rifled through the Seeger file looking for any original court orders. Nothing but some paperwork and letters related to art, but a quick scan didn't show clearly what the firm planned to do. Then she paused as the name tickled at something in her memory.

Wasn't that the name the attorney Jarod Shaw had used to address the woman at the museum? Could it be the same family? It might make sense since he had mentioned helping her reclaim something. They had stood in an art museum, so he could have meant art.

She grabbed the box and took it to the receptionist. "Who is that woman Mr. Ashby is with?"

The woman looked at her and mouthed something as she pointed at her headset.

Janae sighed and walked the files back to her closet. She set the box next to the door and got back to work.

After another sneezing fit, she looked at her watch. She needed a break from the dust, and it was about lunchtime, so she pulled out her phone and dialed a number she knew by heart.

When a slightly quavering voice answered, Janae spoke. "Hi, Grandma. What are you doing for lunch? Can I bring some soup by?"

"Why, Janae, that sounds perfect."

Thirty minutes later she pulled into the driveway of the two-story stone house her grandparents had called home for more years than she had been alive. The green tin roof somehow merged modern with the stone walls that had stood since 1745. If it were a warmer day, she and Grandma would sit on the rocking chairs on the long front porch for lunch and conversation. Instead, Grandma stood inside the entryway, wearing teal nylon pants and a sweatshirt that had snowflakes embroidered on it and hung from her small frame. One look at Grandma, and it was no mystery where Janae had inherited her petite size.

The chance to spontaneously head to Grandma's for a quick lunch was one reason moving home was the right call. Grandma was eighty-seven, and Janae knew she wouldn't live forever. Philly had kept Janae from coming back as often as she'd hoped, and she didn't want to miss more moments with her favorite human.

Janae held up the bag. "I picked up the broccoli cheddar soup from Flo's."

"My favorite."

"I know." She leaned in to give Grandma a hug, feeling the frailness of her bones. "After we eat is there anything I can help with before I go back to work?"

"Ashley and Ashby." Grandma shook her head, then closed the door. "Were you that desperate?"

"Grandma." Heat climbed Janae's neck as they moved to the kitchen. "We should eat while it's warm."

"I have a microwave." But Grandma followed her and pointed to the wooden table. "Everything's set." And it was. Placemats rested against the wooden table and underneath bowls and spoons. Napkins and glasses filled with iced tea completed the arrangement.

"You're my hero. You know that, right?"

"Pshaw. You need to get out more. I only set the table. Let me get some crackers."

A minute later both sat on creaky old chairs, crockery bowls filled with the warm soup in front of them. Janae carefully placed her feet in front of the storage tubs Grandma had stacked beneath the table. She remembered so many times she'd sat at this table, Grandma on one side and Grandpa at the other. She sighed, missing him with intensity.

Grandma set her spoon down and reached for Janae's hand. "You okay, kiddo?"

"Yes." Janae gave a quick nod that felt like a bobblehead. "Just missing Grandpa."

Grandma swallowed and blinked a couple of times. "Me too." She glanced around the kitchen with its exposed walls and cheerful clutter. "This place feels empty without him."

"He always believed in me."

"Sure did. Why wouldn't he?"

"Because sometimes I don't."

"We all have days like that. That's why God gives us grandparents to cheer us on in our dreams. Grandpa was always so proud of you."

Janae closed her eyes and let the words soak into her soul. "I don't know that he would be now."

"Whatever happened in Philly to send you running here wouldn't matter to him. It doesn't matter to me. I'm just glad you're back where you belong."

"But what if I don't?"

"You'll never belong at Ashley and Ashby. What a firm." Grandma snorted and shook her head. "They fired Caroline for getting sick. Can you imagine?"

"I can. Wait, they fired her?"

"Yep. I moved my work the next day." She shook her head. "Such a mean thing to do."

The laws wouldn't protect Grandma's friend since it was such a small employer. Janae forced a brightness to her tone as she changed the sub-ject. "Tell me what you've been up to."

Quiet conversation flowed as Janae let the moment sink over her. *Yes, this is why I moved.* This moment might not last for years, but it made the changes matter. Janae hadn't simply been running from her mistake. She'd been running toward something.

An hour later when Janae returned to the law firm, the receptionist had piled Janae's items, including the little succulent, in a box on one of the tired vinyl chairs. The sad pile looked ready to topple from the box with a hiccup. "Mr. Ashby said to tell you that he wouldn't need your help after all."

Each word struck like a sharp rock tossed carelessly at her, hitting with force.

"He can tell me himself." What a coward, but he would talk to her.

Janae headed to the hall, but the receptionist stood and blocked her path. "He's in court."

"No, he isn't. He's spending the whole day in his office."

"Something came up. Emergency hearing of some sort." The woman waved a hand vaguely.

"Sure." Janae wanted to growl but decided that wouldn't add to her professional image. "Can I at least confirm this is everything?"

"You worked here less than two days. It's everything."

Janae longed to stare down the woman, but instead she collected the box without a glance inside, feeling awkward and foolish. "It's been a pleasure."

"I'm sure." Then the phone rang, and the woman returned to her desk to answer it.

Janae headed from the office, holding the small banker box. As she pushed through the door, she realized she'd never learned the recep-tionist's name. The woman had refused it, and she'd been holed up in that stupid closet too long to keep trying to break through the ice.

Cara Putman

Driving to her parents' empty house would feel too much like admitting defeat, so she deposited her few sorry possessions in her Mazda, then closed the door and headed on foot down the square. There was something settling and beautiful about the historic downtowns so many Virginia towns maintained, and Kedgewick's was vibrant.

Some shops had changed, and others were the same from the last time she lived in town. Java Jane's was new. Val's Boutique was old and the source of many enjoyable shopping excursions with her high school besties. Main Street's Chapters and Sips was new. The Happy Cow Ice Cream Shoppe was old but with Froyo and popcorn added to the menu, if the display accurately reflected the products.

In a couple of blocks filled with sunshine yet a gentle bite of cold, Janae found herself back in front of the Elliott. She considered the facade, taking in the banners that hung on either side of the entry. One advertised the gallery opening she'd attended. The other highlighted community programming days. She scanned the QR code on the sign and then scrolled through the list. The museum hosted all sorts of regular events from tours to preschool workshops to something for those with memory issues. It was a sweet series that served the larger community and Monroe College campus.

She climbed the steps and walked inside. Many of the museum's exhibits were free and open to the public, with a rotating series of special ticketed galleries and shows.

When she'd attended the opening, Janae hadn't wandered to observe what had changed in the time since her last visit. Today she'd explore and discover what she could.

Walking through a museum had layers she hadn't known to appreciate as a high school student. Then she'd attended because a teacher or her mother required it. Now she strolled the gallery with the insights gained in her art appreciation class, which allowed her to see the depth of skill used to create the old paintings, the cartoons that underscored many, and on up. The artists needed talent to know which mediums and paints to use in each project. Pigments. Brushes. Canvases. Stretchers. So many details created the masterpieces that hung on the walls. Even the choice of frame mattered. She remembered reading about a man who invested in antique frames in the 1920s and '30s before donating them to a European museum, creating the trend of setting old masters in frames that would match their date of painting. He'd believed the frames should add to the experience of the art. All the details were fascinating.

"I see you're back."

Janae jumped at the deep voice and turned to spy the museum director standing nearby. She quickly looked away, hoping he wouldn't hold her actions at Java Jane's against her. "I didn't hear you come up."

"Didn't mean to be stealthy." He extended his hand, and she shook it. "It's good to see you again."

"Thank you." She tugged lightly to loosen his hold on her fingers. "I had some free time and wandered by."

He glanced at her. "Looks like you were working hard and earned the break."

Her cheeks heated at his comment. She hadn't changed but instead wore the clothes from her morning spent cleaning that nasty storage closet. "I was busy this morning." She ducked her head, then decided to address her rudeness. "I'm sorry about yesterday. Your offer to join you was kind, and I wish I'd accepted."

His lips twitched, but she noted a faint relaxing in his stance. "Apology accepted. Maybe I'll offer again."

"I'd like that." An awkward silence fell as she waited, but he didn't extend a second chance. When he shifted, hands at his side as he scanned the room, but stayed silent, she hurried to fill the space. "Before the opening, it had been quite a few years since I walked the galleries. I'm calling this my reacquaintance tour."

He laughed and it was a warm sound. "Nice turn of phrase. What would you like to see?"

"Nothing in particular. I wandered in unintentionally." She turned back to the nearest painting. It looked like—yes, it was—a painting by Jackson Pollock. "I'll admit I don't quite understand how this is considered art, when I could set up in my parents' backyard and create a similar arrangement of random black splotches on white with a red slash."

"But did you? Think of it?"

His simple words settled over her. "No, you're right, I didn't. And probably never would."

"That's the hidden genius of the painting and what makes art special. There's a creative magic that happens when artists take mediums and reimagine them. The art hanging in here is from creatives who actually did what the rest of us might but don't. Then there's the da Vincis of the world who are pure geniuses."

"No one will accuse me of that." She cleared her throat to get rid of the wistful tone that crept in. "Know anyone who needs an attorney?"

"Other than the museum? Things not work out?" Small lines creased the outer edges of his eyes as he watched her.

"So it seems. The firm wanted cheap labor to clean out a disgusting closet." She clapped a hand over her mouth. For all she knew Dr. Montgomery attended a civic organization with one of the partners. The way her luck ran, that would be the case. "Sorry. I'll be fine."

"It's always disappointing when things don't work the way we planned or dreamed."

"Exactly. I can't say it was my dream to return to Kedgewick, but I know it's right for this season." Now to figure out what else was right. "Don't worry about me. I'll be fine. After all, I can live in my parents' basement the rest of their lives. Who doesn't dream of that?" She sighed, and then shook her head and chuckled. "Just call me Meg Ryan from *You've Got Mail*."

Dr. Montgomery looked like he'd draw blood as he bit the corner of his lip to keep from laughing. "A good one."

"It is. Sorry, I'm kind of ridiculous right now." She slid her hands in her back jeans pockets. "At least I know God has a plan even if I don't."

"Sometimes he even lets us in on it." He looked distant.

Hmm. There's a story there. But she wouldn't push.

Instead, she took a step back. "Give me a couple days to create a plan before I call to hear about the museum's legal issues . . . Unless you need a quicker resolution?"

He shrugged. "I don't know. It's odd, someone suggesting a lawsuit is coming."

"That can happen. Kind of like testing the waters."

"Well, it's testing my sleep." He rubbed a hand along his jaw, and she noted the purple under his eyes.

"We could meet now if it helps. I can at least listen and make suggestions." She could always figure out logistics later.

"It's all right. Another few days shouldn't matter." He shook his head. "Time to get back to work. Good to see you, Janae."

"Thanks." The word trickled out in a slow blur. Then she glanced at her watch. It was that or watch him walk away. And with all the chaos and unknowns in her life, she did not need to add a crush on the cute PhD exiting the gallery.

Chapter 6

"*CARTER, THERE'S BEEN AN ACCIDENT. Your sister didn't make it.*"

Carter jolted up in bed, the old memory lacing his nightmare. The fourteen months since Charlotte's death hadn't eased his pain.

It had been three months since he'd had this dream, but he knew from experience he wouldn't easily return to sleep. Not until he slipped into Andrew's room, confirmed his nephew slept in the nest of stuffed animals he called his stuffies or cuddle pets.

Whatever he called the menagerie, Andrew surrounded himself with them in a precise order before settling in for the night. The next night they repeated the process. Now nine years old, Andrew didn't look like the lost eight-year-old who had arrived at Carter's door after the devastating loss of his mom. The casket had been closed, and Carter had intentionally not seen her before it was. He wanted to remember Charlotte as the vibrant big sister who liked to boss him around, even if she was a bit wild in her youth.

Carter moved down the hallway toward Andrew's room and paused outside.

Monthly checks arrived from Charlotte's designated trustee for Andrew's care, but the money would never replace the boy's mother. Carter wasn't sure how Charlotte had been successful enough to create the endowment as a secretary who'd wanted to be an artist, but he was grateful for the financial help. Keeping Andrew in clothes and meeting the other needs of a boy was a chore some months. It helped that Carter's parents lived only a couple of hours away and spent time each month with Andrew. Carter couldn't raise the boy alone—not when Andrew struggled to express the depths of his grief, leading to emotional meltdowns. Andrew needed more support than Carter knew how to give.

The light from the hallway spilled in just enough for Carter to reassure himself that all was well. Andrew's hair spilled over his pillow like raw sienna paint, and his mouth hung open in easy sleep.

Carter eased forward and brushed a bit of the boy's blond hair back, sending up a quick, silent plea for wisdom for himself and protection for his young charge.

He slipped from the room and headed to the kitchen.

He carefully walked around his small home, which had adequate space for the two of them. Andrew's room consumed what could have been the office. Next to it was a small bathroom and then the open floor plan of a living area that flowed into the kitchen and dining area. Carter's workspace, with a docking station and files organized in a single drawer, filled a nook between the small kitchen and dining room— something the home's designers had probably imagined for writing grocery lists and paying bills. The screened porch provided more living space much of the year but right now wasn't used.

His gaze traveled to the door to the basement. It looked like the door was cracked, but he knew he'd closed it before he headed to bed.

That's strange.

Then he noted that the light over his workspace was off. He always left the light on at night in case Andrew got up to wander.

Carter frowned and moved toward the door. He didn't like the feeling that skittered up his back. Had someone invaded his home? He wanted to turn back and check on Andrew or grab his phone from where it charged next to his bed. But either of those felt like a risk if someone was in the shadows.

Stairs edged from the kitchen down to a finished but largely unused space. He and Andrew didn't need it. Other than making sure the door to the outside stayed locked, it was an area Carter usually ignored. But now he couldn't. He started down the stairs.

The third stair from the bottom creaked beneath his weight and he froze. Should he move forward or race back up the stairs?

His pulse pounded in his ears. *Breathe.*

Then he slid around the corner, flipping on the light as he moved. That's when he felt the cold air come across the space from the outside door that stood open to the world. He sagged and then quickly straightened and shuttled around the room. No one was in it or the one next to it. He closed the door, locked it, and put a chair under the doorknob—not sure it would really keep anyone out but at a loss about what else to do before hurrying back upstairs.

Once he assured himself that Andrew still slept safely in his bed, Carter sank along the wall. There'd be no going back to sleep for him, at least not for a while.

Thirty minutes later, Carter stood and tiptoed from Andrew's room. He pulled out the key he kept tucked above the doorframe to the dining room and inserted it into the lock on the drawer of his small workspace. With a twist it opened, and he looked at the envelope. It had rested in the drawer since he came home from the attorney's office several days after Charlotte died. The attorney had seemed as mystified as he about what the envelope contained, but the woman relayed firm instructions to leave it unopened until Andrew turned eighteen . . . or there was a massive emergency.

A nightmare didn't rise to the level of that intervention. Someone invading his home might.

But then he considered again.

Could the door have popped open while Andrew played outside after school? After all, he'd bought the house in part because of the large tree perfect for climbing and the elaborate wooden playset. He often found Andrew with an open book in hand, tucked into the two-story fort at one end of the swing set.

If he really thought there had been an invader, wouldn't he have called the police?

As he stared at the envelope, he didn't know what to do.

Was he overthinking? Being careless? Or too careful? Were there legal ramifications?

Janae's face invaded his thoughts.

She was a lawyer. Maybe she would know what to do. He glanced at his watch and pushed the thought away. It was too early in the morning to burden someone else with his concerns. Especially since she didn't know he was his nephew's guardian. Would she understand if he told her about Andrew? Carter wasn't a typical single dad, but he took his responsibility seriously. Anything that grew between Janae and him had to include Andrew. There wasn't another option.

Whoa. He'd let his thoughts wander into a space that built more from their few interactions than was warranted.

Three short conversations barely created acquaintances, let alone friends.

Yet as he thought about her poised composure slipping into unvarnished honesty, he was intrigued. Could there be more?

Sunlight bathed the rhododendron bushes on either side of the walk to Grandma's front door, and Janae took a moment to soak in the warmth. After the last few days, she needed every bit of hope she could find, even if she found it as the sun kissed her skin.

For a moment she'd let herself imagine it was God reaching down to touch her face.

She needed the reminder he loved her.

Coming home had been miserable. Her job had dried up in two days, and she'd spent fruitless hours yesterday looking for a new one without identifying one solitary lead.

It had been a calculated risk to come home, but she hadn't expected it to be this hard.

"Are you going to stand there staring at the sky all day or come give your old grandma a hug?"

Janae dropped her gaze and then flushed as she spied Grandma standing in the doorway. "I didn't hear you come out."

"Luckily I heard you arrive. Who knows how long you'd have stood there." She opened her arms wide. "I need a hug, and if this door stays open much longer, the cat will escape."

"That cat is glued to your side." Janae hurried up the sidewalk and stairs then gently hugged her.

"What are you doing here? Shouldn't you be off doing something exciting?"

"I gave that up when I came back." She tried to soften the words.

"Why did you do that? Really?"

"I'm not sure anymore. I thought I wanted something different but this is a lot harder"—and more confusing—"than I imagined."

Grandma let her go, then walked inside expecting Janae to follow her. "Then go back."

"I can't."

"There's a story there. One you'll eventually share."

"It's not a pretty one."

"The real-life stories rarely are." Grandma patted her arm. "But those are the ones that matter. Come on. Chocolate chip cookies are on the counter. They're even fresh, and you know everything is better with chocolate."

Janae followed her into and through the house, the faint scent of sugar and butter tingeing the air as they neared the kitchen. "How did you know I'd come over?"

"A birdie told me."

"Mom. What else did she tell you?"

"That you look like someone killed all your dreams. Again. She keeps me filled in on all the happenings." Grandma glanced at the barn clock on the wall, then stepped to the counter where a couple of glasses sat. "So what are you going to do next?"

Janae tried not to wince at the brutal honesty. That question had kept her tossing and turning most of the night. The light of morning hadn't made anything clearer, nor had the time spent walking her parents' acres as she prayed. "I'm not sure. Shadows are making everything murky."

"You only need light for the next step."

"Exactly. And nothing is giving me clarity."

"Maybe rest."

"I need a job. Those school loans won't pay themselves."

"I can cover the next few months. How about you help me clean out the carriage house and then you can live there? It'll give you a bit more independence without adding bills." Janae opened her mouth to respond but stopped when Grandma raised her thin hand. "You can't have many other bills. What you need is time to think and dream."

No need to mention her car loan. "It's too much to let you pay my bills. I'm the one who got into this situation."

"That doesn't mean I can't help my favorite granddaughter out."

"I'm your only granddaughter."

"All the more reason to let me do this. What do I need with the extra sitting in my bank account?"

"Are you sure? You can't really mean you want me to move into the carriage house. Rent-free." A pressure started building in her chest, and she fought to adjust her focus to the gift of having a place to land while she figured out her next steps. She'd promised herself she'd never rely on anyone, but she couldn't handle this alone.

"What else would I mean? It's lonely out here, and I know your mom would feel better if one of you was closer." She grabbed the half gallon of milk from the refrigerator and quickly set it on the counter as if it were too heavy. "Just remember, I don't need a nanny. Besides, I like having you around."

"Thank you."

"You're welcome." Grandma stepped behind her kitchen table, grabbed a plate of cookies, and slid it toward Janae. "Have one. I'll grab the glasses of milk."

Sometimes it was nice to be treated like you were six years old and your only concern was what to wear to school. The cookie practically melted in her mouth, a wonderful blend of gooeyness and all that she loved of her childhood. "While I have time on my hands, how can I help you?"

"Other than cleaning out the carriage house?" Grandma waved her hands. "Don't worry about me."

"I'm not worried, but I'm here. I'd love to spend time with you, and helping is a great way to do that."

"You could just be with me." Grandma looked from the glasses to the milk. "But I will let you pour the milk."

Janae quickly complied, but she couldn't quite push away the shadow she'd felt all day that had lengthened when Grandma admitted she might need help. As Janae scanned the room, she spied ways she could help inside. "Maybe I could help in here too."

Grandma waved a hand as if batting the idea away. "Oh, I don't know. It sounds like a lot of work, and one better suited to the new year."

"Why then?"

"It'll allow me to start my New Year's resolutions with easy wins. We can sort through the carriage house, though. It's such a mess. You think the rent will be free. I might need to hire a service to help."

"And let strangers paw through your things?"

"I'm not sure there's more than junk out there, sweetie."

Janae grimaced at the thought of the building one could hardly walk through. "Then it's *a lot* of junk, and we should send it to the dump without searching through it."

"We might miss some treasures if we did that. After all, someone with less than me might be blessed by my junk."

"I guess it's possible."

"It is." Her grandma took a bite of a cookie, and a slip of melted chocolate drizzled down her lips.

Janae took a bite of her own, then carefully wiped her lips with a napkin. "How about starting with something simple like a room in here? We can consider it a warm-up."

"That will be for later. Besides, it's not so bad in here."

Other than the clear storage containers shoved against the wall and stacked under the kitchen table, but Janae bit down on that thought. If it didn't bother Grandma, then it shouldn't bother her. Despite the fact she was an attorney, she actually didn't enjoy conflict, and that would erupt if she challenged Grandma.

"Rather than worry about me maybe you should look for work in the city?"

"Richmond?"

"No." Grandma picked up the plate of cookies and moved it to the table, and Janae followed with the glasses of milk. "DC."

"I don't want to work for another big-city firm." Even if one would hire her. "I could have stayed in Philadelphia for that." She bought a moment to think while sipping her milk. "I want to actually help people, and that's not really what those big places do. They tend to work for corporate clients on massive litigation. I went days without seeing the sun."

"There's value to learning what you don't want."

"But what *do* I want? Can I find it here?" She had to, or she had moved in vain. Then she reached out and touched Grandma's hand. *No, not in vain.*

"You need to trust the One who has ordered your days." Grandma squeezed her hand. "I am glad you're back for however long you stay."

"Thanks, Grandma. And thanks for the offer. Staying in the carriage house is appealing." It would give her some independence but let her be close too.

Grandma waggled her eyebrows and a hint of mischief sparkled in her eyes. "I'm getting the better end of this bargain, I assure you."

"Then I'm glad to accept." And Janae would give herself a bit of grace to uncover her new why.

For today it would be enough to spend time here with Grandma and then go home. She would worry about her future another day.

Chapter 7

"RISE AND SHINE, SWEETHEART."

Janae groaned the next morning at her mother's intrusion and threw an arm over her eyes. "It's too early. Don't you have students who need you to improve their lives?"

"Sure do, but it's fall break, so I can help you and your grandma with some decluttering. But you only have my help for a few days."

Janae heard the soft swoosh as her mom walked across the laminate floor and then felt the gentle shake of her shoulder. What got her to sit up was the rich aroma of a good cup of coffee that came with the movement. "It feels like I haven't accomplished anything this week."

"True, but you'll figure it out. That firm is not where you should invest your time."

"Why does everyone tell me that now?"

"Because you didn't ask before." Mom sat on the edge of the bed. "I love your independence, but it means you often create a more difficult path than needed."

"I think there's a compliment buried in there somewhere." Janae accepted the mug and held it under her nose. The scent alone would wake her up, but then she took a sip and sighed as the rich flavor danced along her taste buds. "I've missed your coffee."

"You know it. Dad spoils me with the best beans and that amazing machine."

"How is he? I haven't seen him much since I got back."

"It's the busy season." Mom shook her head. "Who am I kidding? It's always busy, but he has two mares that are in the middle of being impregnated. It's a little late, but if all goes well, he'll have some amazing foals, and you know how he gets embroiled in that work. Bloodlines and more."

Even though his commitment to his horses had meant he missed many of her gymnastics competitions, he'd always made a point to attend state. Too bad her performance always suffered on those days—maybe because she pressured herself to do better than her best when he watched from the stands. "I'd hoped to spend more time with both of you before I move to Grandma's."

Mom quirked her brow. "What made you decide to move over there?"

"I hadn't considered it before she offered it in exchange for helping clean the carriage house. I think she's lonely, and I know you're concerned about her living alone." Janae bit her lower lip as she considered her options. "Between that and being closer to town, it seemed like the right choice."

Mom studied her, then nodded. "Makes sense. I'm also savvy enough to know most adult children don't dream of living at home. The carriage house will be a nice option for you, and I will have peace of mind knowing someone is close at hand if Mom needs help." She patted Janae's shoulder. "You have fifteen minutes to get ready while I make your favorite omelet."

Forty minutes later they turned onto the long drive that led to Grandma's house, tucked near a pond and surrounded by trees. Her place sat an hour outside DC, a hidden oasis with history embedded in its acres, unlike her parents' modern horse farm.

Grandma must have been watching for them, because she opened the door as they parked. "There's my girls." She opened her arms and waited for them to exit the car and scramble up the path to stand next to her.

Janae soaked in the warmth of her grandma's love and tried to ignore how frail the woman felt through her layers. The fact she still lived in the two-story home alone was a miracle. "It's good to see you, Grandma."

"It's only been a day, Janae. Come on in. I've got a coffee cake ready and coffee warming."

Once they were seated at the table with both the crumbly cinnamon goodness and strong, black coffee, Mom quickly focused them on the work. "Where should we start, Mom?"

Grandma tapped the table. "With the tubs under here that you two have politely ignored. Let's see how long that takes."

"Not the carriage house?" Now that she'd decided to move in, Janae wanted to get started. She looked at her mug but couldn't force down more than a sip. She'd have to bring some sort of creamer out next time.

"Let's begin with something we can finish." Grandma shook her head. "I've let too much accumulate out there, and it's daunting."

They pulled out tub after tub, and it was astounding how much Grandma had crammed into each. Eight were stacked underneath the table, each stuffed like a time capsule containing photos and clippings from throughout her life.

"I've spent days and weeks going through documents for discovery, but I don't know how to start with all of this." Janae sagged onto one of the kitchen chairs.

"We start one box at a time, just like you do with cases." Mom pulled out another tub. "Mom, what's in this one?"

"It should be labeled on the side." Grandma pointed to an index card taped to the container. The next three hours passed with them working their way through four of the tubs, sorting photos into groups based on who was in them. "Once organized, I'll give them to those people. No need to wait until I'm gone, especially since y'all won't know who many of these people are."

"Oh, Grandma." Janae stood and twisted back and forth, trying to ease the tightness in her muscles. "Let's take a break. All this leaning over the table is making me stiff."

"All right." Mom glanced at her phone and gave a small gasp. "There was a break-in at Ashley and Ashby last night. Poor Mr. Ashley was still working. He was taken to the hospital in Fairfax."

Janae hadn't met the man in her two days of work, but she couldn't imagine a break-in. "I wonder what someone wanted."

"It doesn't have to be anything much these days." Grandma shook her head. "I'll be praying for him. Didn't his wife go to school with you, Lisa?"

"Yes. I'll have to check in with her. See if she needs anything."

As their conversation turned to where to work next, Janae couldn't shake the question of why anyone would break into the law firm. She hadn't seen anything valuable in her time there.

"Janae, have you been listening?" Mom's voice brought her back to the moment.

"What?"

Grandma smiled. "I was just saying we can move to the storage room in the carriage house. If we start with big items, I bet we can load your mom's fancy SUV with things to take to a flea market."

"A thrift store, Mom." Janae's mother shuddered. "We don't want to sort and price everything."

"Or sit in the cold." Janae shivered at the thought. She might die of boredom because she knew Mom would take her for company.

"Y'all are no fun." Grandma grabbed her heavy jacket from the hook by the front door. "Lisa, grab water from the fridge. We'll get Janae the exercise she wants in no time."

The small two-story carriage house sat about a hundred feet to the side of the main house with a stone path connecting the two buildings. The top was filled with windows and light, the lower level built into the hill more like a cozy cave. "When was this used for horses, Grandma?"

"Not in my lifetime. I remember my dad turning it into an office." Grandma headed down the small hill to the ground level. "Your grandpa added the tiny bathroom when we moved in. It was a bit of a honeymoon cottage for us. We had some privacy, only taking meals at the house.

Then Mama and Daddy moved into town when they decided the stairs were too much, and we moved into the main house." A soft rounding of her shoulders hinted at the good memories that must be filling her mind. "I think they really wanted to give us a house of our own."

Janae tried to imagine living in the small space. Ivy covered outside planks that were painted a beige gray with window casings in a soft butter beige. A glossy black door and shutters matched the tin roof. It was probably peaceful when rain tapped a staccato beat. She'd always thought it would make a great guesthouse. Tiny, storybook perfection for someone to rest and recover in the shelter of the trees and peace of the rolling acres.

Grandma paused at the front door. "Maybe we should start up top where there's light."

"Mom, we can start here and work our way up."

"You say that now." Grandma tugged open the door. "But do you see all the rubbish I have in here? We could probably back a dumpster up the lane and fill it. I always said I wouldn't be one of those hoarders, but here I am. A lifetime of stuff I couldn't part with is shoved in here." She stood in the doorway, hands balled on her slim hips, legs braced as if everything would flood out in an avalanche.

"It can't be that bad, Grandma."

"Oh yes it can." Mom's voice held an edge of hysteria as she edged around Grandma. "Well, no time like the present to get started." That was such a Mom statement—one Janae had heard repeatedly.

As Janae followed her mom into the space, she realized there might not even be room for the three of them to work at the same time. "Oh my."

"Yep." Mom sighed as she pulled a rubber band from her pocket and pulled back her shoulder-length hair. "There's only one way to tackle this."

"One box or pile at a time." Janae took in the stacks of boxes piled along one wall. Against another was a hodgepodge of broken and overlooked furniture. "Should we start with the bigger items? We can load the SUV and make some space to sort everything else."

Grandma stepped around Janae and grabbed a blanket off the first stack of chairs. As she pulled it free, dust erupted and they all sneezed. "There will be a lot more of that."

Janae worked up a sweat lugging items to the SUV and fitting pieces of long-forgotten tables and chairs into its back. They could probably open a booth at an antique store with the items if they wanted. When she pulled out a small side table with spindly legs and a round wooden top, she fell in love. "Grandma, can I keep this one?"

"Sure, dear. That was my grandmother's writing table. The house was tiny, so she couldn't have a full-fledged desk. Instead, she'd pull a chair up to that." Grandma used the edge of her sweatshirt to wipe the dust off the top. "She was always writing letters to someone about something."

Janae carefully set it to the side and then carted a couple of lamps to the vehicle. When she returned, she dusted her hands on her jeans. "It's as full as I can make it."

"All right." Janae's mother looked around the space. "Here, Mom, sit in this chair and we can start going through these boxes." She tugged a couple of boxes in front of Grandma, but Grandma didn't open them. "You okay? Do we need to take a break? We've accomplished a lot today."

Grandma blinked and then shook her head. "I do think I'm done for today." Her glance kept returning to the stack of boxes and a suitcase piled on top, visible now that the first boxes had been moved. "I'm not ready to look through those."

"Why not?" Janae couldn't stand seeing the sadness in her grandmother's watery eyes.

"Those hold your grandpa's things. Mostly from the war and the years after." She pushed to her feet. "I'm going to the house." She shuffled from the room as if she couldn't get away fast enough.

"What's that about?"

Mom shook her head, a pucker marring her forehead. "I don't know, but I'd better check on her."

As Mom left, Janae wondered what could be in the boxes that would upset Grandma. Discovering the answer would have to wait for another day because she wouldn't open them without Grandma present, no matter how much she wanted to see her grandfather's things from the war.

After dropping all the items at the local thrift store, Janae and her mom wound their way up to the farm. Once they parked by the barn, Janae paused to take in the view. "If you don't need me, I'm going to take a walk."

"Sure. I noticed you haven't visited the horses yet. Take a minute to reacquaint yourself with them. We've got a couple new ones boarding. You'll find them in the paddocks. Just watch out for the stallion. He's territorial and might not remember you."

"He will, but I won't press my luck." Janae had hoped all the physical labor would help steady her mind, but anxious thoughts still pinged inside her head. She needed to figure out what was next, and she was more likely to do that if she spent some time alone in nature. If she went inside the house, she'd lose herself in some activity that wouldn't bring the same clarity as a walk.

Because the house and surrounding buildings perched on the top of a hill, the wind whipped around her. This wasn't truly part of the Blue Ridge, but it hinted at the larger hills and small mountains that sat visible to the west. She stood still for a moment, letting the sun warm her face as she took a few deep breaths, and then performed a slow spin. While other houses were detectable, they were roughly a quarter mile away on either side. This was as close to isolation as one could get with sixteen acres. If she walked around the edge of their property, her Fitbit told her she could get close to seven-tenths of a mile.

Right now she didn't want precision.

She wanted peace and a vision for what she was supposed to do next.

Moving home should have been the right decision. She'd prayed about it, even before her big mistake that should remain unnamed. Felt a peace about returning. Yet nothing from finding a job to keeping it had gone as planned. Ashley and Ashby hadn't been the easy answer for work. She should feel upset about that. But she didn't. Instead, she was unsettled.

She wanted a five-year plan, and right now, she didn't have a five-day plan.

As she walked along the packed dirt path worn by years of feet approaching the paddocks this way, she watched for the horses.

She loved these huge animals. They were intimidating and made her feel small and powerless. Yet when she climbed on the back of one, she found a freedom through borrowing their strength.

That's really what she longed for now.

Freedom.

Someone to rely on for strength.

To live a life with meaning and purpose. She hadn't found it buried in discovery.

Maybe she could find it here, but it felt like another backward step.

Father, what do you want for my life?

She didn't hear an immediate answer, but she kept her mind quiet as she walked closer to the fence. She'd learned that God might not be an audible voice telling her to go this way or that, but when she invited him to have input in her life, he had a way of directing her steps. She believed he'd nudged her home, but now she'd have to be patient to see what that meant. It didn't mean life wouldn't be complicated or filled with twists, but if he walked with her, she would be all right.

Her thoughts drifted back to her time at Grandma's. The woman was amazing, but Janae hadn't realized how slowly her grandmother was moving until they worked together in the carriage house. Not too many years ago, she would have lifted the boxes on her own. Now she told others what to do. Janae's heart tightened at the reality her grandmother was old and acting her age. While still independent, Grandma wouldn't be able to live in her home alone much longer. But how long wasn't clear.

What would happen to her when she needed to move? Would she give up?

The idea weighed on Janae as she approached the fence and climbed onto the lower rung. From that vantage point she could see four mares clustered at the other side of the paddock. They were beautiful, regal, tails high in the air.

One took off running, and Janae watched with willfulness. What would that feel like?

She wanted to be free like that mare.

Chasing the wind.

Loving the life she'd been given.

Lord, let me find that here.

Chapter 8

Friday, October 28

As afternoon rounded the corner toward evening, Carter was ready to pack up for the day and launch into the weekend.

His hours at the museum could be erratic with gallery shows and events into the night, so he'd gladly take advantage of the chance to head home a few minutes early. He hadn't shaken a deep disquiet about the open basement door the other night and wanted to get home and confirm all was well. While he wanted to believe Andrew had inadvertently left the door open, he couldn't sink into that idea.

But if someone had broken in, who had—and why?

He packed the last couple of files he'd need into his messenger bag so he could work from home and then left his office. He paused as he reached the receptionist's desk. "I'm going to finish up at home."

"Not yet. There's a man waiting to see you. Says it's important." Ariel smacked her gum and then nodded toward the lobby.

Carter glanced at his watch and sighed. It was four o'clock, so reasonable to expect he'd still take a spontaneous meeting. "Did he give you a name?"

"Something boring." She checked a sticky note in front of her. "Jarod Shaw. He's older than you and pretty bland."

"That's an interesting observation."

"What can I say? I'm an interesting person." The phone rang and she sighed. "Guess I'd better answer that."

Carter made a note to have a conversation with her about what she wanted to learn while she was at the museum. There had to be a way to crack through her shell of ennui. He needed to see what this man wanted and still get home before five. That would be a win.

"Where is he?"

Ariel grimaced and pointed toward the chairs clustered around an end table with a small sculpture and pamphlets from current exhibits. A man stood near the door, but another wearing a dark suit sat on a chair reading something on his phone.

Carter looked at Ariel. "Which one?"

"There's only one." She glanced up and pointed at the seated man.

"Thanks." Carter adjusted the strap of his bag and straightened. He glanced back toward the door, but the man was gone. Maybe it had only been a shadow after all. He gave a slight shake of his head, pasted an open expression on his face, and headed toward the chairs. "I'm Dr. Montgomery. You wanted to meet?"

The man stood. "Jarod Shaw." He gave a pointed look to the bag. "Looks like I'm catching you heading out. I only need a few minutes of your time. We can make a longer appointment later if needed."

"All right. Are we waiting for anyone?"

"I'm sorry?"

"I thought I saw someone with you." Carter glanced around and then shook his head. "I must be mistaken. The small conference room is open, so we can step in there."

The man followed him into the room that held a small round table with three chairs around it. An Expressionist print added a splash of color, but the room was fairly bare. Carter took a moment to examine Mr. Shaw. He was tall with the build of a distance runner or biker. His hands were clean, which indicated he wasn't an artist or someone who worked with his hands. His dark hair was brushed to the side, and his skin carried the light tan of someone who enjoyed being outside without copious amounts of sunscreen.

"I'll keep this quick." Shaw sat on one of the chairs and placed his hands on the table, fingers laced. "I represent Mrs. Seeger, a woman who is prepared to file a claim against the museum for the Paula Modersohn-Becker painting that is part of the German Expressionist exhibit." He glanced at his notes. "As well as Botticelli's *Idealised Portrait of a Woman*. I believe it's in gallery four."

"I'm sorry. Who are you?" Carter felt a tightening at the back of his neck and wished someone else was in the meeting with him to hear the claims even as he tried to fathom what the demands meant to the museum.

"Jarod Shaw, attorney-at-law. Mrs. Seeger told me you had a conversation at the exhibit opening."

Carter swallowed as the image of the elderly woman and their brief conversation in front of the painting stepped to the front of his memory. "Maybe. I spoke with many people that night."

"She would have been the one who couldn't leave the Modersohn-Becker."

"What kind of claim?"

"Restitution." The man paused as if letting the word hit in full effect. "It was stolen from her family in 1938 Vienna, and she is asserting her claim as an heir to have it returned."

"It's not ours. We have it on loan."

"But the Botticelli is part of your collection. Both belong to my client's family."

"You understand I can't simply take your word for it."

"I would expect nothing less. Speak with your attorney, but understand other museums have been required to return paintings they held on loan." He pulled out his phone and clicked a few buttons. "Prior to filing a formal suit, my client would like to pursue a peaceful settlement. She is elderly and doesn't want to waste time on a court battle." His steely gaze collided with Carter's. "Don't mistake that as a lack of will on her part. She'd simply prefer avoiding the cost and energy drain of a lawsuit."

"I need to speak with the board."

"I'm sure you do." The man held up his phone. "I have times available to meet, if you'd like to schedule now."

Carter swallowed as he wondered how this had all spiraled.

"I also have a draft of the demand letter." Shaw pulled an envelope from his inside coat pocket and slid it across the table. "Consider this a courtesy heads-up. There is a time frame that will need to be followed. My client isn't guaranteed an abundance of days on this planet."

The envelope sat on the table between them, a threat that couldn't be ignored even as it still felt very vague.

"I'll need to review this and make some calls."

"Understood." The man waved his phone. "However, I'd like to schedule our meeting. I know how these things work. I walk out that door without an appointment and never hear from you. An exchange of missed calls, and four months from now I'll have to file a complaint, kicking off the litigation. Then you'll file every extension known to man, gambling on my client's age." Shaw leaned forward. "That's not how I work. While I'd like to get paid, you can call this a passion project for me. I want to help this woman reclaim her family property. So let's set a date and keep this moving." He shrugged. "If we're wrong, you'll know that much faster."

Carter couldn't argue with Shaw's logic, as the board didn't have a reason to move fast unless forced. This man wasn't to be messed with, especially since purpose straightened his spine and ignited a fire in his eyes. "I'll read this and contact the board."

"Don't misunderstand. We need to meet next week, or Mrs. Seeger has instructed me to file. You don't have weeks."

"I hear you."

"I'd suggest a time of ten in the morning, Monday."

Today was already Friday. That didn't allow much time for Carter to connect with key people. "That's unreasonable since this is already Friday afternoon. I'll need more time." He took a breath, considering how to best help the man understand. "I've been in my role for four months. That might sound like sufficient time, but this is the first incident like this I've experienced. I'm not trying to delay but to make sure I know what I need before a meeting so it's productive. I don't want to waste your client's time."

The man's lips twitched. "But wasting mine is fine. I think I like you." He considered a minute, demonstrating a deliberative style that could make him very good for a negotiation like he'd requested. "All right, I'll let you go. But I'll look for your call by Monday morning to get something scheduled. My card is with the letter."

"I won't be able to call by Monday—maybe Wednesday if all goes brilliantly."

"Wednesday it is."

The man took his leave, and Carter remained at the table. He slit the envelope carefully.

Dear Dr. Montgomery and Board of the Elliott Museum,

This serves as a demand letter. The Elliott Museum has in its possession two paintings that belong to the Jan Seeger family. The family was forced to flee Vienna in 1938, leaving all behind including an elaborate art collection of the family's patriarch, Jan. Those items disappeared into the Nazi machine, and it has only this month come to the attention of the family's remaining heirs that you have in your possession two such paintings, *Five Children* by Paula Modersohn-Becker and *Idealised Portrait of a Woman* by Botticelli.

This is the pre-lawsuit demand of the heir to have the paintings returned to her family.

The below link will take you to the complete record of provenance that has been compiled for each painting.

You have until November 30 to respond or a lawsuit will be filed. Time is of the essence.

He reread the letter. While Carter didn't doubt the man's intent, he couldn't anticipate how the board would respond. There hadn't been time to test the waters with the personalities who governed the museum. Was he headed straight for a storm?

The visit to the horses had calmed Janae a bit, but after a shower she remained unsettled, her mind flitting and never quieting. She hated not knowing what the right next step was. She always had a plan with options A through G carefully designed, and now she couldn't articulate option B.

Getting away from everything that reminded her of how far she'd regressed might help, so she climbed in her car and headed to Kedgewick. A stroll around town might give her some vision for what was next. She knew the city wasn't it, but she needed to take steps toward independent work in the small downtown if she stayed in Kedgewick. Her stomach growled as she hit a stoplight, so Janae altered her plan to include dinner—a panini and latte—at the Lucky Bean. She could eat them there while reading a book, and then return to her parents'. If it was still light, maybe she could ride one of the horses. Sometimes Dad babied the horses more than he ever babied her. She loved watching him croon to the animals, and he'd be delighted to get her on a horse. She'd always been more confident on a balance beam than a horse.

She parked the car in the street and walked into the Lucky Bean to find the barista cleaning the espresso maker. "We close in fifteen minutes."

She glanced at her watch. Almost 5:00 p.m. "Can I still place an order?"

"As long as it's for an iced or brewed coffee. This machine is a bear to clean." The barista set down her rag and stepped behind the cash register. "What can I get you?"

Janae scanned the board and settled on a sandwich from the listed options. "An Italian panini and dark roast."

"Sorry, the panini machine is cleaned for the night."

"How about a bowl of soup? Do you still have tomato?"

The barista shook her head. "That's closed up too."

Janae tried to cover a laugh. "Why don't you tell me what you have, and I'll let you know if it sounds good."

The barista looked over her shoulder then under the counter. "How about a stale muffin and a cup of plain coffee."

"Sounds like you should give me the muffin."

"Can't do that." The woman spread her hands wide. "But if you want a good sandwich, our sister shop at the Elliott is open for another hour. It's a late-night closing for them today. Happens a couple times a month on Friday nights."

Six was late night? Janae stifled a laugh. "Then I'll walk that way. Thanks."

"Do you want a coffee to-go?"

"No thanks." Janae strolled out the door and the couple of blocks to the Elliott. The hair on the back of her neck prickled, but when she glanced back, she didn't notice anyone watching her. College students were out and about even this early on a Friday night, walking arm in arm down the sidewalk between the restaurants and pubs. It almost made Janae nostalgic for her college days. Those had been fun, but she had enough days in a classroom behind her. Even the thought of a master's made her want to break out in hives.

She shook off the feeling someone was behind her and continued toward the museum.

The bite in the air let her know it wouldn't be fall forever. Someone had already strung white lights around the downtown, connecting the light posts and lacing back and forth across the street, giving it a magical feel.

This was one reason why she had come back.

To remember the good about the place she grew up.

Her teenage years had been filled with hours at the gym and the stress of competitions, but if she focused on the good, she knew that sport had molded her into the woman she was. She'd learned so much grit and discipline through the hours of repeated effort to gain each skill. Dedication she'd need as she charted the next chapter of her life.

She reached the steps of the Elliott and realized that in addition to a drink and food, she might also find inspiration.

Entering the building, she took a deep breath and soaked in the atmosphere. The paintings that lined the walls and the sculptures interspersed along the halls were demonstrations of the creative genius and dedication of the artists. They labored in obscurity with no promise anyone would value their work. As an attorney, she wouldn't create something as lasting and permanent, but maybe her efforts would make a life-changing impact on her clients. She wouldn't be a Renoir, a Pissarro, or a Warhol, but she could find her niche and thrive. That felt like a goal she could tackle. As a commitment to making Kedgewick her home, she bought an annual pass, and then headed up the stairs to the cafe.

Only a few people were in front of her, and as she turned with her mug after ordering, she almost ran smack into a stylish man dressed in a three-piece suit. The handkerchief was a little wilted, the only testament that it was the end of a long day, but he stepped back quickly with a small smile.

"Janae." Carter Montgomery looked down at her, and she found herself momentarily caught in his orbit.

A movement behind him caught her attention, and she spotted a man watching Carter intently, then he nodded at her and turned around. Janae refocused on Carter and noticed tight lines around his eyes. "Everything okay?"

"No." He sighed, and it sounded heavy and weighted by cares. "Most of it is irrelevant here, but I do need to head out. Before I leave, are you ready to take on a client, because I've just received a demand letter and need to figure out what to do."

"Ma'am, your sandwich." The young man at the bar waggled a plate with a sandwich and chips.

"Let me get that for you." Carter grabbed it with a slight frown at the server. "Where were you sitting?"

"I hadn't picked a table yet."

"How about this one here?" He led the way to a table that snuggled into the ornate iron railing. "From here you can watch people coming and going below as well as on this floor. It's my favorite place to people watch."

"Perfect." But not for people watching. She needed to shake the niggling feeling of eyes on her, and maybe seeing everyone would allow her to do that. Maybe a coffee wasn't the best idea if she was already jittery. His fingers brushed her arm, and she froze, the moment electric and startling. She swallowed, forcing the incident behind her. She didn't know him and couldn't afford a distraction right now. But as she watched him step away, she wondered if she could make the space. She glanced at the empty chair at the table. "Sure you can't join me for a minute?"

"I wish I could, but I'm on my way home." He looked uncomfortable, like he wanted to say more. Or maybe he remembered her turning down his invitation. "About helping me out . . ."

"I need the weekend to think." She wrapped her fingers around the mug, willing the heat to seep inside her. "I'd really like to work with you on this, but I haven't found another firm." She shrugged and met his gaze. "I don't know how long it will take."

"I understand." He rubbed the back of his neck and then stepped away. "The museum probably has a preferred attorney anyway. I'll look into that too."

Her stomach tightened at the thought that someone else would work with him. "Do you want me to read the letter?"

"Let's see what happens early next week." He walked away, and she pushed her sandwich away, intense disappointment weighing her in place.

Chapter 9

JANAE HAD SPENT MUCH OF the weekend hunched over a computer sending out job inquiries. The only thing that made it survivable was the constantly replaced pint of Cherry Garcia ice cream next to her mousepad. When her eyes threatened to permanently cross Saturday, she drove back to Grandma's for several hours of work. Sunday after church she rinsed and repeated.

No matter how carefully Janae probed while working alongside Grandma, the older woman did not mention what had upset her Friday. Maybe it had been the sight of Grandpa's things, but she had refused to even acknowledge there was an issue, pretending to forget anything had happened. As a compromise, Janae had tucked that stack of boxes and suitcase to the side and focused on the other piles. They would eventually return to it, but for now, they made progress that edged her closer to moving in . . . eventually.

By Monday morning her body was letting her know she hadn't worked this hard in a long time. And her body wouldn't get a break in the foreseeable future unless one of Grandma's piles collapsed on top of her. When Janae's phone dinged, she was relieved to step outside the carriage house long enough to see who had texted.

Want to grab an early dinner?
Girls' night?

The message from Margeaux made her smile.

It might be nice to take a break and spend time away from family. She loved her mom and dad, but the family togetherness could overwhelm her after so many years on her own. A meal with some old teammates sounded like a good alternative.

Sure. When and where?

Chloe really wants to go to a
new place. It's a tea shoppe
(yes, spelled that way).

Name?

High Tea on Main or something
like that.

That's quite the on-brand
name.

Know it. 5:30?

Perfect.

See you there.

Grandma walked up to her. "Everything okay?"

"Friends want to meet for dinner."

"That's good." She linked arms with Janae. "It's important to have friends. They make life richer."

"They do, and I'd forgotten how important they are." That was one area of Janae's life that had been underdeveloped in Philly. Her friends had largely been her work colleagues. They didn't know her, not at any kind of deep level. Now that she had dinner scheduled with people she'd trained and cried with, she could feel a difference.

High Tea on Main sat at the corner of Main and Third Streets, just a few blocks from the Elliott. The brick-front building was sandwiched between a lawyer's office and an accounting firm. She could imagine the folks who worked at each were hungry all the time from the wonderful aromas wafting from the building.

When she stepped inside, the space was light and bright, the color of lemons paired with an Italian sky. A case by the front door was lined with exquisite cakes that were tall and elegantly decorated in sparkling icing. Sunny tablecloths covered the four-top tables, and each held a small vase with a single flower—a daisy on some tables and a carnation on others. Her shoes clicked against the honeyed-wood flooring.

Chloe waved from a spot in the corner. When Janae reached her after weaving through the tables, Chloe stood and gave her a quick hug. They had barely settled onto the seats when Margeaux arrived in a swirl of scarf and skirt.

"Sorry I'm late."

"I just got here too." Janae stood for another quick hug. "Chloe was here early like always."

Margeaux nodded. "Some things never change. It's so good to be back together."

Janae tried to ignore the fact that one of their original group wasn't here. It didn't feel right without Libby, but at some point, she had to pretend it was okay. Maybe then it wouldn't hurt as much . . . still.

Margeaux unwrapped her scarf and then leaned forward on the table. "So Chloe said things are rough."

"Let's just say the job I thought I'd have, I don't." Janae tried to shrug it off, but when she looked down, she saw she'd shredded the paper napkin. "I don't think I'm disappointed, just confused about what's next."

"I am sorry." Chloe stuck a straw in her water and then added a slice of lemon. "What will you do?"

"I don't know. I have this lovely, expensive degree I need to use and a sweet grandmother who's offered to pay my student loans for a few months."

Margeaux took a sip of her water. "That's a blessing."

"It is. All I have to pay from savings is my car and gas. You know Mom and Dad won't let me help with groceries at least for a few weeks." She rubbed her forehead. While all this should make her feel good, in reality, it stressed her out. "I don't want to live in my parents' basement, and my grandmother's carriage house will take a while to get ready."

Chloe wrinkled her nose. "At least you have an option. Some of us are trapped. I really should have gone to college when y'all did. This two-classes-at-a-time thing has dragged on long enough."

"Maybe you have another choice." Margeaux's brow furrowed the way it did when she focused on a problem—whether it was how to add another twist in the air at gymnastics or tackle a more down-to-earth challenge. "My house is small, but I could make room."

Chloe shook her head. "Small is a bit of an understatement. It's got a great yard, but you'd feel cramped over time."

"Do you need a roommate?" Janae hadn't considered moving in with someone, but that might work. It would let her retain some normalcy.

"Not really." Margeaux swirled a finger along the top edge of her glass. "I bought the house for a steal."

"And it's closer to Hamilton than here." Chloe held up her hands when Margeaux shot her a look. "It's a great place but wouldn't work as a long-term solution. I couldn't bear moving out only to have to move in again when funds run short."

The waitress came to their table with a three-tier stand loaded with petite sandwiches and desserts. Another server carried a tray laden with three small teapots. Janae favored English Breakfast, while Margeaux preferred a rooibos, and Chloe took a jasmine tea. The flavors represented the differences between them—a complementary yet different bouquet. As teens they'd created their own high tea after seeing photos of one. Now, they could sit and enjoy as someone else did the work.

After the servers left, the next moments passed as they filled plates with the delicious treats. Janae left the salmon sandwiches for the others but took two of the cucumber sandwiches, because Margeaux wouldn't waste her time on them. At least she hadn't when they were in college.

Gymnastics and the loss of a friend bound the three together. Without that, they would have passed in the halls of Kedgewick High but never become lifelong friends. Margeaux and Chloe knew the pain that Janae kept hidden from everyone else, just like she knew theirs. Margeaux had grown up with the privilege of two parents who adored her and sacrificed for her. Chloe grew up in the instability that only a coach had stabilized, until even that evaporated. Without the family support Janae had taken for granted, Chloe floundered upon graduation, taking classes at the local community college when she could find a ride.

Janae's future had extended like a clear path ever forward. Until it didn't.

"Still with us?" Margeaux's voice pulled Janae from her thoughts.

"Sorry about that. Guess I have a lot on my mind." Janae lifted the lid on her teapot and pulled out the bags.

"Maybe talking will help."

"It's a nice idea, but y'all have enough on your plates." She met Margeaux's gaze. "How many students do you have this semester?"

"Five classes' worth."

"Exactly." Then she turned to Chloe. "And how's your mom doing?"

"Hanging by a thread."

"I know." She reached for each of them and squeezed their nearest hand. "That's why I don't want to add my burdens to yours."

"But that's what friends do." Margeaux didn't let Janae slip her hand free. "We hold on . . . and we help share the burden. We know you well enough to know you're stressed even if we don't know all the details."

Janae considered her friends, the way they didn't let go of her hands, and nodded. If she couldn't let them in, she'd live isolated and alone. "The job I had didn't last two days."

"Fools." Margeaux shook her head and let go of Janae's hand as she leaned back and crossed her arms. "That old firm doesn't understand who they had."

"Bunch of good ole boys if you ask me." Chloe harrumphed and got a wicked gleam. "I think you should do something that will make them regret their stupid decision."

"They had cheap labor to clean out a storage room." Janae sighed and felt a tickle in her nose from the dust she'd inhaled. "I ran the math, and I couldn't have kept up with my loans on what they said they'd pay me, if I ever see a check. But even that is better than nothing, which is exactly what I'm making now."

"You at least have a grandma who can help." Chloe's words reminded Janae how blessed she was.

"You're right, but I don't want to rely on that. Even with Grandma's generous offer, I only have a few months to figure out what's next." She glanced around the tearoom. "I love Kedgewick, and I didn't move home to turn around and leave. But what opportunities are here?"

"Create your own." Margeaux's short sentence landed heavy.

"Create my own?"

"So a law firm isn't here that fits the bill. Start one."

"It's not that easy."

"Maybe not, but it's doable." Chloe stared into the distance as if she could see the future Margeaux imagined. Too bad Janae couldn't. "Did you know I've taken all the classes to be a paralegal?" Her earnest gaze collided with Janae's. "I could help, and this would be the new start we both need."

"Good." Margeaux pulled out her phone and started tapping on it. "So you have an employee. Now you need a storefront."

"Wait a minute." Tension coiled inside Janae as her friends took off with planning her life, even as she realized this would let her help Carter. "I don't have any clients. I can't pay anyone anything." Her bank account was not that robust even with support from her family. She turned to Chloe. "I'm sure you'd be great, but you can't work for nothing."

"But if we can make this work, I won't have to work two dead-end jobs. Maybe I can save enough to go to law school too."

"Is that really what you want?" Janae tried to laugh, but it came out as a squeak. "It hasn't exactly worked out great for me." Part of her wanted to tell Margeaux and Chloe how badly it had gone, but she couldn't. Not now. She needed them to believe in her.

"No, it did. You just decided you didn't want the life you'd created in Philly, and you took steps to do something else. That's the kind of courage I want to find." A shadow dimmed Chloe's face before she shook her head. "I've spent my life hiding, but I don't want to live that way."

If they only understood. But she couldn't let them in—yet. "You were fearless on the beam."

"But I've lived afraid everywhere else."

"I can't pretend I have a pile of savings stored up for this." Those words were so important to air. The list of things she'd need to open a firm would fill a page. "I'd need malpractice insurance, computers, printers."

"A Virginia license." Leave it to Margeaux to focus on the critical detail.

"Have it, it's just not active." Thank God the Philly firm had paid that hundred and twenty-five dollars a year for her. "Then there's the location. I'm not sure Kedgewick is the best place."

"Sure it is. It needs exactly what you would offer. Just think of the buffoons who decided they didn't need you after all. And we're close enough to bigger towns that you can work in multiple places."

"What do you think our town needs? I don't even know."

Chloe grinned. "All the kinds of law you loved. Corporate advising with a side of employment. Maybe a will or two for good measure."

"Add in that tax law you loved. No one around here fills that bill, which means people have to go to DC and pay big-city prices." Margeaux continued to tap away on her phone. "They often go without help rather than pay for what they can't afford, or use the price as the excuse to ignore what really shouldn't be brushed under the rug. Just last week one of the professors in my area told me about the nightmare his sister experienced when her husband left and took the business with him. She helped create it, and they couldn't get a good valuation. So he literally stole it."

Janae straightened. "That shouldn't happen. You only need to know the right people to call."

"And you do." Chloe grinned. "This is why it's perfect. You might not have loved your time in the big city, but you made important connections that will help the people right here in Kedgewick."

Thursday, November 3

The force of their enthusiasm carried Janae through the next two days, which was helpful because Carter had struggled to get direction from the museum's board president. He'd asked Janae to help him push back the meeting with Shaw, but she wasn't ready to yet. With help from her friends she'd found an inexpensive little storefront, and the landlord told her she could have the apartment above for double the rent. Maybe she'd consider that in the future but not yet. Then her parents gave her a small loan that allowed her to get a computer and printer-scanner combo for Chloe. Both got her closer to being ready to help clients, but she wasn't all the way there.

Margeaux then found her a student who would intern for her in exchange for exposure to the law. That meant Chloe was the only one Janae would need to pay, at least at the start. Once she had a bookkeeper and an insurance agent, she'd be in business. The thought had her heart racing in the middle of the night, but it also kept her energized and focused during the day.

How could she find clients? The kind who'd pay a retainer?

That challenge needed to be unlocked quickly, because she couldn't waste all the work and her friends' and parents' investments in her new dream.

Where to start?

Other than scheduling a meeting with Carter, the best suggestion ended up coming from Dad. "Join me at the business breakfast. Many of the small-business owners attend, and I can introduce you around. Remind everyone my brilliant daughter is back in town and has hung her shingle out."

When she'd walked into Flo's with him Thursday morning, she deflated when she spotted Mark Ashby. The man glad-handed everyone like he planned to run for Congress. Maybe that would work to get him out of the legal scene and gain her a few of his clients. She knew she could serve them better than he did with his good-old-boy practices from the last century.

"This way, sweetheart. I want to introduce you to Mayor Allison Lawson."

Janae followed her father through a maze of people that he paused to greet with a kind word. In his late fifties now, the man had been her bedrock throughout her life. He always worked hard for his accounting clients. Accounting paid the bills and balanced the activity of working with his beloved mammals. He had a slight paunch and his hair had started to silver at the temples, giving him a distinguished air of sorts.

As they neared a woman who stood in a pantsuit, gray hair brushed into a twist at the nape of her neck, he stopped. "Mayor Lawson, I'd like to introduce you to my daughter, Janae Simmons."

The woman turned with a smile that tilted and slid from her face. "Janae."

Janae experienced that moment of knowing she should remember someone, but not. "Mayor."

"I see you've grown into a beautiful woman."

"I suppose." She glanced at her father and saw a look of bewilderment that had to match her own. "I'm sorry, but have we met before? Kedgewick isn't too big, but I have lived other places for the last ten years."

The mayor looked through her to her dad. "Gerald, she's charming." Then she turned back to Janae. "My daughter was a year ahead of you in school. She competed on the same gymnastics team for several years." She gave a small nod to someone who passed behind Janae. "I remarried a couple years after Libby's death."

Janae flushed hot and then cold as the knowledge of who this woman was sank through her. "I'm sorry. Of course, I can't believe I didn't recognize you. There were so many girls on the team, but Libby was amazing."

"Yes, she was. And she adored your mother. Your mother always was the loudest woman at the meets." She chuckled, but it sounded forced. "Can you believe she'd ask if your mom attended if she didn't hear her yells of encouragement?"

"I'd imagine she asked because she knew you'd be there, and she had your support." Janae could remember so many meets and her friends saying things like that. If the gym had a gym mom, Janae's had filled the role for a while. She'd done so intentionally for Chloe and a couple of other girls whose moms couldn't attend many of the meets. "We were a family."

"Until you weren't."

Janae stepped back as she absorbed the punch of those three short words. "I've asked myself so many times if there was anything I could have done."

"Of course there was. You were her team sister."

"Now, Mayor." Dad took a step between them, but the woman didn't stop.

"You should have known what she was thinking." Mayor Lawson stood rigid, but her hands trembled at her sides. "No one was closer."

Janae wanted to push back but with each word she remembered more.

She wanted to argue that the words weren't true. But she'd felt the same thing, so many times.

No one was closer.

She should have known.

She should have done something.

And she'd chosen the wrong thing.

Just like in Philadelphia.

Chapter 10

IF SHE NEVER SAW ANOTHER cleaning product and microfiber cloth, Janae imagined she would celebrate with a roundoff, back handspring, twisting double on the floor. Another day spent cleaning and organizing the new office felt different when it meant preparing the space for her firm. Slowly the lobby came together with each bucket of filthy water she dumped as she waited for Chloe to arrive after her shift at the bookstore. Margeaux would add her labor over the weekend.

Janae enjoyed the solitude as she turned on a playlist on her phone and increased the volume on her speaker so the music could fill the space as she worked. She lost herself in the beat of the music as she danced around the space to some T Swift. Then she heard a muffled clapping and looked up, cheeks heating as she realized she'd attracted an audience at some point. With a little bow, she sank to the floor. Then someone tapped on the door, and she groaned.

Still, she pushed to her feet and walked to the door. When she opened it, Carter stood there, two coffees in hand. "Hello."

"You looked like you needed something to drink."

"You saw that?" His grin grew as a funky song popped up on her playlist, and she couldn't help a shoulder shrug or two. "Bet you're looking for another attorney now."

He shook his head and held up one of the coffees. "If anything, I'm more committed to waiting, but I do need advice on what to do with the demand letter."

She took the cup and inhaled deeply as she noted the dark circles under his eyes. "The board give you any direction?"

"None have met with me yet, but a meeting's scheduled for Monday." He took a sip and winced. "Too hot."

"Do you have the letter with you?"

"No. Can you give me general advice without seeing it?"

"Maybe." She probably shouldn't, not until she had her insurance in place, but that would be handled shortly. At least she'd activated her license. Amazing what processes a check could speed up. She glanced around, liking what the removed layer of grime had revealed of the hardwood floor in the entrance. She could imagine a Persian rug topped with a table and surrounded by a couple of comfortable armchairs for clients to wait in. The desk Chloe and the student would use would be surrounded by a front system that went to the ground, protecting rather than exposing the receptionist to all who walked by the large windows. But now the space was still empty except for her cleaning supplies. "I'd offer you a chair, but . . ."

"You aren't exactly open yet."

"Next week. Maybe."

"The floor is fine." Carter eased to the floor and laid one leg out with an elbow propped on the other knee.

Janae looked at him a moment, then slid down opposite him. She pulled her phone out and lowered the volume on the tunes as Carrie Underwood belted a song about being an invincible champion.

"This your amp playlist?"

"You could call it that, I guess." She grinned at the rap sequence. "The letter?"

"Basically, Mrs. Seeger believes the museum is in possession of two paintings that belong to her family."

"Mrs. Seeger?"

"She's an older woman who attended the exhibit opening, and we had a short conversation then."

"I remember seeing her at the opening." Janae frowned as something tickled her memory. "Who did you say her attorney was?"

"Jarod Shaw."

"That's interesting, because I saw her file at Ashley and Ashby."

"Will that be a problem?"

"Shouldn't be." She didn't think, but how could she be sure she wouldn't stumble into an issue? This was exactly why she hadn't wanted to create her own firm. There were elements of the law she didn't know. She couldn't. "What's the demand?"

"Turn the paintings over or she will sue."

"Have they provided any proof that the paintings actually belong to Mrs. Seeger's family?"

"Not yet."

"Then I would ask for that."

"He wants a meeting."

"Make proof a condition of the meeting. That will buy you time."

"To do what?"

"Conduct your own investigation." She took the lid off her drink and blew across the top. It was black, but it had been a thoughtful gesture to bring it. She took a tentative sip and then reattached the lid. "You need to move off the defensive if you can. One way to do that is to determine the paintings' ownership."

He considered her a moment and then nodded. "Makes sense."

"What's your goal for the board meeting?"

"Get direction for how to handle this."

"It's better to go in with a clear ask. Determine who the museum works with and whether they can handle this. If not, gain approval to hire another firm for this matter." She didn't look at him, afraid he'd see how much she needed the business. She'd placed an ad to run the next week in the *Loudoun Times Mirror*, and anticipation warred with nerves at the thought of whether the community would welcome her foray into legal services. From what she could see, the small town needed a new firm, and she'd give it her all. Either she'd run out of money and head to an office in DC, or she'd be a success. She knew which one she wanted, but time would tell. Landing the museum as an early client could be a game-changer for her. "I would like a chance for the work if you need outside counsel."

He nodded. "Sounds like I have some work to do over the weekend."

"Nothing you can't handle. Remember the board wouldn't have hired you if they didn't believe that."

Something she couldn't quite catch flitted across his face. "I hope so." He pushed to his feet, then offered her his hand. After he pulled her up, they were so close she could see the brown flecks threaded through his blue eyes. "Thanks for the advice."

She held up her cup. "Thanks for the caffeine."

"You're welcome." Then he gave the slow and dangerous smile that could curl around her. "I'll see myself out."

She watched him leave, then carried the cup to the small kitchen at the other end of the office.

The next hour passed slowly, her thoughts returning to Carter and his legal work. She needed the ads she had placed to bring in clients. Really she just needed that first client. Maybe she could pair with some local social work agencies to provide low-cost services while she built her reputation and base. Chloe and Margeaux might have some ideas for her along those lines.

It was an idea worth pursuing.

She glanced around, loving the exposed brick wall and the stark white walls everywhere else. There was still work to do to make it a professional space that also checked the homey box.

If she was on this path, she would do it her way.

Not like the firm she'd worked for.

This one would have a personal touch.

Her cell phone rang, and Janae glanced at her watch, expecting to see a spam call. Instead, it showed *unknown*, and curiosity got the better of her. She tugged the phone from her back pocket.

After Carter left Janae's storefront, he didn't try to cover the warmth she inspired. The moment he'd spotted her dancing through the window, she'd mesmerized him. Maybe it was the lingering effect of not sleeping well all week, but he'd hurried to pick up drinks from Java Jane's. A spontaneous gesture, it gave him a reason to see her joy continued.

His sister Charlotte had always been the flighty artist, while he'd focused on the history and business sides of art. Now he was glad he'd let spontaneity carry him inside.

Janae had given him a bit of a road map forward. And her simple directions had alerted him to how much he'd frozen.

None of her advice had been rocket science.

He could take simple steps forward as he prepared the museum for Mrs. Seeger's possible claims. He rubbed against the throb that hadn't stopped all day. Was this a case of being a fool or prepared for whatever came?

If the board had met this week, he might not feel as stuck. But Janae was right. Yes, the board could share important history with him, but he should present a plan. At least as much as he could prepare on his limited experience at the Elliott.

Someone bumped into him, jarring him from his thoughts as he juggled his cup. He looked up. "Hey."

The man didn't stop, and Carter turned to catch a glance. Dark jeans and jacket, a baseball cap covering his head. Carter dropped the half-empty cup into a trash can and considered following the guy, but to what end?

Nothing had happened at his house this week, and he still had no evidence that anyone had broken in, so he had to get over looking for trouble everywhere. There wasn't evidence that any of Charlotte's troubles had followed him here.

A block later he climbed the steps of the Elliott and entered through the heavy front door that served as a solid guard. He wished he comprehended the real risk, if any, the museum faced. Then he'd feel more confident approaching the board Monday. Right now he needed to earn their respect more than he needed their guidance.

If only Stanley Dukes wasn't the chair of the board.

If Carter had known, he wouldn't have accepted the job. Not after everything that had happened with Charlotte. The police said she'd been killed in a shoot-out between opposing crime groups or something like that. And Stanley was friends with the gallery owner in Indianapolis who had been there. In fact, Stanley had taken him to Indy to meet with the owner. Then things had gone wrong, and Stanley had disappeared, only to show up after Carter's interviews had concluded. None of it had ever felt right to Carter.

It all made his heart and mind hurt. And every time he looked at Stanley, Carter wondered how the man had been involved with the events in Indy that killed Carter's sister.

Carter shook free from the thoughts and instead forced himself to note the number of people wandering around the gift shop as he walked past, and how many carried one of the orchids from the new display. Then he turned down the small hallway that led to the offices.

Ariel looked up from her desk with a puckered face. "Stanley is in your office."

"What?" Carter ran his hands down his front. "He didn't have an appointment."

"No. But he's been in there twenty minutes. Insisted he wouldn't wait out here. Said it was too crowded." She rolled her eyes, and he didn't bother saying anything. The space was empty.

"All right. Any indication why he's here?"

"Said he needed to touch base before Monday."

"That's what phones are for."

"Don't let him hear you say that. He likes to throw his presence around." She shivered dramatically but didn't say more. Instead, Ariel pointed toward his door, which was starting to open.

Something hard rose in Carter. He didn't like the idea that anyone would push their way into his office when he wasn't there. It smacked of disrespect and had his back stiffening. He'd worked with Stanley in an earlier postdoctoral position. In fact, he'd always blamed Stanley in part for the fact he was fired from that position. The man had insisted

Carter purchase a painting for the collection, then disappeared on vacation with all the records when the painting's origins were questioned. Carter should never have trusted someone else to properly check the provenance. He wouldn't make that mistake twice.

It bothered him that Stanley had taken him to Indianapolis on that trip two years earlier. That had been the beginning of the end of his employment, yet Stanley had risen to ever greater heights. And now he had to work with the man again. But it didn't mean he had to trust him.

How could he trust a man who was attached at any level to one of the people involved with Charlotte's death?

None of this gave Stanley permission to act like he owned Carter.

If anything, it made Carter more determined to prove he'd earned the job and not received it because of some past connection.

Even more, he wanted to know why Stanley hadn't objected to hiring Carter during the interview process.

He still wasn't completely clear how an art gallery owner from Atlanta with storefronts in Raleigh and Virginia Beach had worked his way onto the board of the Elliott and then wiggled his way to board chair. Stanley came into view as Carter neared his office.

"Where have you been?"

"A meeting." Carter couldn't mask his irritation as he crossed his arms. "Why are you in my office?"

"We need to talk." The man had styled his full head of silver hair, sported a ready smile that bordered on smarmy, and dressed like he'd just returned from his personal tailor in Milan. Stanley had made his money in early tech stocks in the '80s and now invested in art he sold through his galleries—had for twenty-five years. The result was a man who earned tax deductions through donating works to museums. But their first encounters had left Carter uncomfortable, and the trip to Indianapolis and subsequent fallout had left him unwilling to work with the guy. Until he found he had no choice.

"I've tried to reach you all week. Check your voicemail. I must have left ten messages."

Stanley waved a hand in the air as if batting the words away. "Doesn't matter."

Carter pushed past him and moved to the seat behind his desk. He frowned as he noted the leather was warm rather than cold. "Why were you sitting here? At my desk?"

"You've got a big problem."

"Really?" Carter arched a brow and waited, curious where Stanley planned to take this.

"Jarod Shaw called. Told me you've ignored him."

"Only because you've ignored me and left me no choice but to call a full board meeting."

"If you needed immediate input, you should ask."

Sure. Like he hadn't done that in each voicemail. "What's your solution?"

"You're the director."

"Who's been here four months, and you're the chair of the board."

"That doesn't mean anything."

"It should." Stanley should know the history. Had a commitment to protecting the museum and its assets. "This exhibit was the last effort of the prior director. I'm merely the caretaker." Carter sighed. "It's a good exhibit, but I didn't create it. I don't know the art and the history intimately, so I don't know how to answer Mrs. Seeger." He crossed one leg over the other and tried to relax behind the protection of his desk. "Shaw visited a few days ago."

"Last week."

Carter nodded. "That's why I've been trying"—multiple times a day—"to reach you. I need to know what the board knows about the paintings."

Stanley didn't meet his gaze but walked to the bookshelf and ran a finger along the edge as if checking for dust. "You should tell the cleaners to do a better job."

"I'll be sure to do that after I handle emergencies like a potential lawsuit over ownership of our art. What do you know about the paintings?"

"Which ones?"

Why was the man being obtuse? "The Paula Modersohn-Becker and Botticelli."

"The Modersohn-Becker is on loan."

"Yep." A quick look at the card next to the painting revealed that nugget.

"Well, I'm sure you'll handle it just fine." And Stanley spun on his heel and left, leaving Carter staring after him.

"What was that all about?" And why had he ignored the Botticelli? Carter felt the disquiet of the visit rippling through him. There was a reason the man had spent twenty minutes in his office, but a thorough search didn't reveal it.

Instead, even as his search of his computer and desk didn't confirm Stanley had disturbed anything, he couldn't shake the unsettled feeling Stanley hid something from Carter. What was it?

Chapter 11

SATURDAY MORNING, JANAE ARRIVED AT the office with coffees and bagels as the sun was rising. She needed to get a jump start before Chloe and Margeaux appeared so she could make the best use of their time. She'd barely set the drinks down on the counter that had been installed the prior afternoon when she saw Carter walk by with a young boy. She knocked on the glass and waved, but he didn't hear her and kept moving.

Ah well. She turned back to the mess. While she and Chloe had made progress last night, there was still a lot to do to have the lobby and conference room ready for any clients to drop in starting on Monday.

Yesterday's call still bothered her.

A man's voice insisting she would pay. Then hanging up.

She shuddered and made sure the front door was locked.

There was nothing more she could do since she had no number to trace and no recording to take to the police. A few words and that was all.

Could it be someone from Philly who was upset and wanted her looking over her shoulder? If so, they'd been successful.

Janae refocused on the now. She couldn't do anything about the call, but she could get ready for her future. Her office would need work, but if the conference room stood ready, she wouldn't need to take anyone to her office. She could even work from the conference room for now.

A couple of minutes later, Chloe used her key to breeze in with a gallon of water and bag of clementines. "Good morning, boss."

"No need to call me that." In fact, the thought made her skin itch. What if she failed and it impacted Chloe?

"Don't worry. You won't falter."

"Philadelphia..."

"Was there. Now you're back home." Chloe walked to the counter and set the bag of fruit next to the bagels. "I knew you wouldn't stay there forever. You're not a city gal."

"I wanted to be."

"Sure. We all wanted to be anywhere but here. Especially after..."

"I'm sorry—"

"I can't work for you if you're going to apologize throughout every conversation." Chloe shoved her hands in the pockets of her joggers. "None of us escaped without scars. None of us." She held up her hand as if to stop the words building up in Janae. "You have to let it go and fight back. That's what I'm doing."

"What do you mean fight back?"

"I'm not ready to talk about details yet." A fragility shuttered Chloe's face, and Janae nodded.

She'd let the subject drop for now. Instead, she pointed to the bag of bagels. "There's a white chocolate cream cheese in there."

"My favorite."

"Yep, I plan to work you hard in exchange for the bagels and coffee."

"It'll cost more than that during the week."

"I'm sure it will." Janae slathered butter on her asiago cheese bagel and then moved toward the furniture that had been delivered with the counter. It wouldn't take long to slide it into place, making the lobby look finished. "I've wanted to ask... why did you tell me to run from Ashley and Ashby when I ran into you at Chapters and Sips?"

"I said that?"

"Emphatically."

"I don't remember." Chloe flipped through the bag as if digging for her cream cheese was the most important task in front of her.

"Something concerned you about me working there."

"Insight. I knew it wouldn't work. Really." But Chloe refused to meet her gaze. "Remember how awful their boys were in high school? I figured the dads wouldn't be better. Really. That's it."

"All right." Janae dropped it but knew there had to be something there. Chloe was usually direct.

"Am I late?" Margeaux's question entered before she fully walked through the door. "Traffic." She waved a hand as if that explained everything.

"There's so much between here and Hamilton." Janae rolled her eyes.

"There is when a couple deer decide to take a leisurely stroll along the highway and then cross in front of my car." Margeaux shuddered and then waved it away. "You know I was hypervigilant after that happened."

"Have you ever actually hit a deer?"

"After reading that story in *Reader's Digest* about a deer getting stuck with his hoof through the windshield, I have no interest in getting close to the creatures. Add in *Bambi*, and I would be crushed." Margeaux rubbed her hands along her cashmere sweater–covered arms.

Chloe snorted. "Sure you're ready to work dressed like that?"

"I've got a T-shirt in my bag." Margeaux patted the leather satchel she carried over her shoulder. "Did you notice a man loitering out front when y'all came inside?"

Janae strode to the front window and stared out the plate glass. "No, everything was quiet when I arrived."

Chloe shook her head. "I didn't notice anything."

"He must have been waiting for someone at the shop." Margeaux lifted her bag. "I'll just be a minute."

Soon the three of them had settled the two chairs and table into a semblance of a seating arrangement. Margeaux brought in a tall floor lamp and an area rug that made the space homier. "Now all you need are a couple of plants for Chloe to kill."

Janae tapped her chin as if considering. "Maybe I'll try fake plants."

Chloe rolled her eyes. "Let's work on your office. I don't think you've touched it yet."

"I wanted the public spaces set first."

"That's noble, but you need a location to lock client files." Chloe pushed open the door and wrinkled her nose as she walked to the window. "Need to air it out too."

"I'll grab the broom and duster." Margeaux scuttled back to the lobby while Janae surveyed the room.

A fresh coat of the pale gray paint waiting in her trunk would make a difference, and the room was moderately sized, so it wouldn't take too long to accomplish. But first they'd scrub it. They'd finished wiping the walls and floorboards when her phone buzzed. Janae pulled it out and slipped into the hallway. "Hello?"

"This is Carter. Do you happen to have any time this afternoon to meet at the museum?"

She glanced down at her dirty clothes and wiped the sweat from her forehead. "I'm in town but have been working at the firm."

"Should have considered you'd be occupied. Sorry to bother you."

"Wait." Her reaction surprised her as much as it seemed to surprise him.
"Yes?"

"Can you give me half an hour?" She didn't have time to run home, but maybe Margeaux had something she could borrow in that satchel of hers.

"Sure. I'm free until four. Thanks."

"See you soon." Janae turned around to see Margeaux and Chloe crowding the doorway. "I don't suppose either of you has an outfit I can borrow?"

Carter walked Andrew to the art class a few museum docents offered. While he was still learning everything that interested his nephew, the boy enjoyed creating, a testament to an artistic mother who had always worked on several paintings at a time as a young adult. He'd expected her garage studio to showcase more chaotic genius than it had in his one visit before her death, but that visit allowed him to picture the two working at matching easels. When he and Andrew reached the community room on the lower level, he ruffled the boy's blond hair. "Ready to see what this week's project is?"

"Sure." The boy shrugged slim shoulders and didn't look overly enthused, but Dottie had assured Carter he quickly became engrossed in the activities.

"Do you want me to hang out with you?"

"I don't need a babysitter, Uncle Carter."

"Understood. How about I come back in a couple of hours?"

"And if I'm done before that, you'll be in your office since you love work." The imp grinned at him, and Carter gently nudged him toward Dottie and the table covered with canvases.

Carter cupped his hands around his mouth and stage-whispered, "Love you, man."

Andrew gave a little wave with his hand but didn't turn back around.

Carter mimed to Dottie a phone to his ear. She nodded and placed a hand on Andrew's shoulder as she led him toward a boy about his age.

He'd barely reached his office when his phone buzzed.

"I'm here, but not sure where to meet you."

He grimaced. "Sorry about that. Head down the hall with a sign marked Office and I'll meet you at the door."

A minute later he was leading Janae past the empty reception desk to his office. "Saturdays are pretty quiet around here, which is why I wanted to meet. Stanley Dukes was waiting here when I got back yesterday."

"Oh?"

"In my office and he spent at least some time behind my desk." He still remembered finding his chair warm. "I don't know why he did that, but it makes me edgy."

"Maybe he needed a pen."

Carter pointed at the museum-emblazoned container of pens on the corner of his desk.

Her eyes widened as her mouth formed an O. "Okay, so that wasn't it."

"That container was there when I inherited the office. Ariel told me he refused to wait in the lobby like everyone else, but I didn't discover anything missing. Then when I got back here, he accused me of ignoring Shaw before he left."

"Something has him spooked."

"Maybe." That hadn't occurred to him, but it didn't really help. "I asked what he and the board knew about the two paintings, but he didn't really answer." Could Stanley be covering something up? But what? Surely the museum wouldn't knowingly take on a problematic painting. "Want to take a walk?"

"Sure, but why?"

"Let's visit the paintings." It wouldn't be a complete inspection, since he couldn't lift the paintings from the wall—not while the museum had guests. "Maybe we'll notice something in the visual inspection that will give us an avenue to search."

"We?" She wrinkled her nose, and it made her look young and care-free. "I'm not part of this yet."

"But you will be, and I need your perspective now."

"All right. Lead the way."

As they walked, he explained his initial thoughts. "It'll take some time to dig into the provenance and authenticate the paintings."

"Provenance?"

"It's the way we trace ownership in the art world. Many museums post the known history of the paintings in their collections on their websites. It makes the searching easier, but the Elliott is behind the times a bit. I'd planned to make updating that one of my first initiatives." He shrugged, feeling overwhelmed by the sheer magnitude of the task.

He led her down another hall and up a set of stairs.

"Did you know there's a system of tunnels under the museum?" His question felt disconnected from their conversation.

"No." That wasn't something she would have explored as a child, though it sounded intriguing. "What's down there?"

"Everything. Literally treasure next to trash. When someone gifts the museum their estate, it all gets brought to the museum and dumped in the tunnels." He rubbed the back of his neck and met her gaze. "It's a horrible mess, yet I'm certain there are valuable items worthy of display down there. Imagine the treasure hunt to find those items. Everything hodgepodged together. Somehow we sift through to find the good stuff and then identify its history."

"Sounds daunting."

"Yeah. That's why I haven't started yet." He sighed and slowed for a woman with two elementary-aged kids. "I mention that to give you an idea of the scale of what we're working with when it comes to knowing what's in the collection as well as each piece's history. It could take semesters of interns to make a dent in the process, and I need a plan first. I don't know a thing about either painting other than what's posted next to each in the gallery."

"I don't remember seeing the Botticelli before. My love of art didn't really arrive until college, though." She lightly tapped her Apple pencil against the tablet she'd brought with her. "So at this point, you need a plan for understanding the paintings."

"Maybe." Something unidentifiable flashed across his face, and then he stopped. "We're here."

The painting was stunning. An image of a young woman clad in an elegant white dress, seated with her body turned to look off the canvas to the right. Everything about the figure glowed, from the contours of her skin to the lines in her hair and gold woven through her dress. She was intimidating in her utter perfection. "What am I looking for?"

"Anything that might indicate who has owned the painting."

"You expect to see that on the front?"

Carter sighed. "Not really, but I can't take it off the wall right now. I'll get that process in motion. Until then a visual inspection of the frame and canvas might tell us something helpful."

After a few minutes he edged closer until she wondered if his nose would touch the paint.

The guard hustled over, hand on his taser, approaching fast. "Step away from the painting. Sir, do it now."

Carter seemed deaf to his words, so Janae touched his shoulder and he startled.

"Carter, the guard is trying to get your attention."

"Oh." He blinked a couple of times and turned to the man. "Yes, Jimmy?"

"Dr. Montgomery?" The poor man pulled to a stop, cheeks paling, and then looked from the painting to Carter. "Sir, you can't get that close to the paintings. Not here." There was an element of *you should know better* in his tone.

"You're right. Thanks for being so vigilant." Carter clapped the man on the shoulder then hurried past him. "Follow me, Janae."

Soon they stood in the neighboring room in front of the faceless children. This time he stayed several feet back and instead watched her take in the painting.

"The paintings are so different." Her words were soft yet bounced off the floor and around them.

"They are. Renaissance and the beginning of Realism. An old master and a woman who died before her genius could be fully recognized."

"Both represent different aspects and interpretations of what it means to be a woman."

"Yes. The way they've been seen and the way they've pushed the envelope on what they could do. The ideal and the rougher reality."

She nodded. "So why this one?"

"What do you mean?"

"Why did the museum get this painting on loan? Someone went to a lot of effort to arrange the loan from . . ." She leaned closer to the small placard adjacent to the painting. "The Landesmuseum. Where is that?"

"It's a government museum in Hanover, Germany."

"It would take months of work to arrange that, I would imagine." She met his gaze. "Why?"

"An excellent question." He rubbed a hand over his hair, causing the brown strands to point in all directions. "I don't know."

"Then start there."

"Do you work on retainer?"

"Yes." No need to tell him how much retainers could be the life-blood of a nascent firm like hers. "A monthly fee would keep me on call, whereas a retainer is only depleted when you need work." It could sit there for months, but if Mrs. Seeger was intent on following through with her claims, then the month could become busy.

"And you can balance the work when it comes in?"

"Absolutely." No need to share it was more likely an *if*. Though she needed it to be a *when*.

He looked past her, as if studying the five faceless children in the Ger-man painting behind her. "The real question, then, is can you do the work?"

"Yes." There was nothing a little time and research couldn't teach her. "Much of the law is learning on the job."

"Not exactly words to breed confidence."

"It's true, though. Even if I'd handled a dozen cases related to pro-tecting a museum from false claims . . ."

"We don't know it's false."

"True, but we don't know it isn't. Either way, the process is the same. We gather our information, prepare enough to be ready, without over-doing it. And then see what happens."

"It sounds flexible."

"It is. You don't want me doing work now, because you'd pay me to guess, and then pay me again when we have more information than the generic demand. My bank account would love you if I researched and planned now, but I don't like wasting your money."

He considered her, and then a slow grin grew on his face. "I like your approach."

"At the same time, if you start paying now, I can research how museums who've been sued in the past approached those cases. Maybe then I can find a way to take the offensive."

"Definitely like the sound of that, but I'll know more after Monday's board meeting."

"Knowing how to leverage a settlement can save time and money in the long run."

"I like your approach, Janae Simmons, attorney-at-law."

Janae tried to ignore the way she warmed at his approval. She was a professional woman and needed to focus on the legal question, not the client, no matter how much he attracted her attention. "I can put something in writing and send it to you. Then you can work with the board to determine how to proceed. If the museum already has an attorney on retainer, I wouldn't want to interfere with that relationship."

"All right." He stretched out his hand.

As they shook, a current raced up her arm and she prayed she kept the wonder off her face. She was a woman who knew how to make hard arguments and work long hours, and could not get distracted by the man in front of her.

"Thanks for making time." He grinned at her. "Especially before you're officially open for business."

"You're welcome. I can email the engagement letter to you early in the week. Anything you don't like or want to amend, let me know."

As she walked with Carter to the front of the museum, Janae considered her confounding response to him. Maybe the best-case scenario would have his hands tied by the board telling him the museum had a preexisting legal relationship with another attorney.

Then she could go back to fretting about her firm rather than wondering when she'd see Carter Montgomery next.

Chapter 12

THE LAST RAYS OF SUNLIGHT slanted through the wide windows in the museum's top-floor boardroom. Standing at the window, Carter could see the edges of Monroe College spreading out beyond the museum as he considered all he needed to have happen in this meeting.

He needed a unified response so he could address Shaw's demands while time remained to respond rather than react. He'd left more messages for Stanley after his conversation with Janae, but the man hadn't deigned to return any. So Carter had felt limited in what he could do even as time slipped by. While he waited, he started provenance research for the Modersohn-Becker, but since the museum didn't own it, there was only so much he could do that wouldn't arouse suspicion. The Botticelli records weren't easy to find either, even though the museum owned that one. He had to handle the situation with great care, because he didn't want the Elliott facing unwanted media attention and scandals other museums had endured related to ownership questions.

In an effort to sweeten the board's attention, he'd asked Ariel to expend effort with food and an array of drinks. She'd done a nice job arranging a charcuterie board and sparkling water options for the board members to munch on as everyone assembled. As Carter circulated and spoke with each, he felt like he'd dropped into a social hour rather than a board meeting—overdressed and the kid no one really wanted at the party.

Stanley strolled in early but still ignored Carter, picking up a conversation with another board member. Carter squared his shoulders and moved from the window to intersect the chairman.

"Stanley." He tried to hide his aversion to the man but struggled, which risked angering the man. He needed this job and didn't want to uproot Andrew when his nephew had already endured two major disruptions. Carter had to make this opportunity work, but he didn't know how when Stanley refused to communicate. "I left more messages this weekend."

"I was busy." He shrugged as if that explained everything, then strode off to glad-hand someone else.

Carter forced his attention to the members around him. He'd prepared, but as he spoke with Bill Yates, the owner of a local bank, he sensed it might not be enough. Short, intense, and oddly brilliant, Bill knew more about the museum and its collection than Carter could hope to know even with months of late nights and intense homework. The man's mind was a steel trap, and he'd stayed intimately involved with the museum for years. He wasn't the only one.

Barbara Carrera had served on the board for fifteen years. The woman had a small gallery named after her, thanks to her family's generous donation. The owner of a spa and salon by day, she'd made her name with the pampered wives of millionaires around the greater DC area. She'd invited Carter to try her spa's services, but that would be a disaster of unwarranted proportions. He'd sent Ariel instead, a gift that brought his assistant to tears.

At the edge of the group stood a woman he'd met at the exhibit opening. She fit the least with the others. A few years younger than him, Margeaux Robbins served on the faculty at Monroe and had joined the board only the prior month. There was a solidness to her that he couldn't quite define. An attorney, she didn't actively practice but maybe she'd have insight on how to approach the dilemma regarding the Elliott's painting. He headed her direction, and she visibly relaxed as he approached.

"Settling in?"

"I no longer get lost moving through the galleries, though I sense it will take years for anyone to acknowledge I'm a local." The months since he'd started had barely given him a chance to get his desk organized when he considered all he needed and wanted to accomplish. The back-office shop had been in disarray, and there had been an utter lack of vision for future exhibits. It made his gut tighten to think of all the work he had to do to build the reputation of the museum while also enhancing its offerings.

She rolled her lips tightly together as if trying to avoid a smile. "You might not want to say that too loudly around your bosses." She leaned toward him. "I'm on your side, but some of them are old school."

"I'm not sure what you mean."

"I'm not either. This is the first board I've served on, and I'm newer than you. However, they talk a lot about how things were done before. One or two missed which century we're in." She shrugged. "We'll pull them into our time."

"Any words of wisdom?"

She shook her head. "I'm too new to point out the land mines. Remember, you wouldn't be here if the majority didn't think you could handle the museum well." She lowered her voice. "The museum needs new ideas and vision. You'll be great."

As she excused herself and moved to join another board member, Carter considered her words, but embracing a three-piece suit and somber tie wouldn't make the board happy.

Stanley clapped his hands. "Let's gather at the table, y'all." His southern accent was so affected Carter grit his teeth against the artificial sweetness. It was obvious Stanley liked to think he had a special way with people. But the reality was, he had a standoffish snobbery that pushed people away. Eventually, they fell in line to avoid his flashes of wrath.

Before everyone was seated, the silver-haired man stood to his full Napoleonesque height and straightened the bottom of his suit jacket. "We have a challenge in front of us. I received a document from an attorney in Washington. He has a client who claims we have two paintings that belong to her family." He turned the full weight of his attention to the end of the table where Carter sat. "What can you tell us about this claim?"

Carter stayed in his seat as he organized his thoughts. Stanley hadn't given him the courtesy of a heads-up that this would drive the agenda, so this felt like an attack. "I met a woman at the gallery opening who told me she believes a painting is hers. Then a man who claims to be her attorney showed up a week later. He claims two paintings—the Botticelli and the Modersohn-Becker—belong to her. I've started provenance research but haven't located the records for the museum's Botticelli."

"What about the other painting?" Stanley stared at him from the head of the table.

"I want to be careful how I handle that one since it's on loan." He paused to glance around the table. "As you know, I didn't arrange the current exhibit. I need insight you may have on how this loan was arranged and why that painting was selected. Those details will be helpful."

Bill Yates jotted a note. "What are the legal ramifications?"

"To really know, I need to consult an attorney. The situation is complicated because the Landesmuseum will have to answer the questions of provenance and ownership for the Modersohn-Becker painting."

"Robert wouldn't have arranged a loan for a painting that didn't have a clean title." The man who spoke was one Carter hadn't met yet. He'd been quiet, watching the conversation rather than participating during Carter's board interview and first board meeting.

"Would he know?" Carter wasn't sure he would, even with taking all the steps of due diligence.

Stanley glossed over Carter's statement as he frowned at the board member. "Charlie, we don't know enough." He refocused on Carter. "I want you to work with the university's attorney to figure this out. We cannot afford bad publicity."

Margeaux leaned forward and delicately cleared her throat. "Have we had prior claims?"

Stanley's frown deepened. "There's usually someone making noise."

She pressed on. "But have we returned any other works?"

"Not on my watch."

She cocked her head and studied him. "Why not? If the provenance is muddy?"

"Because that is the status of art." Stanley peered down his nose at Margeaux. "We do the best we can and then acknowledge that there are unknowns. Always will be. To think differently is naive."

"So we keep the art? All of it?"

"Yes."

She settled back and interlaced her fingers. "That's a potentially dangerous position."

Carter watched the interaction, grateful she was willing to ask the hard questions. He was glad to have an ally as he navigated this mess.

Bill Yates looked at Margeaux with a smug look. "You're new and have a lot to learn. The law and teaching are very different from running a museum."

"As is working with a bank." Margeaux looked around the table, pausing at each person. "We are each on the board because of a skill or resources we bring. This is an important challenge for the museum, and we must get this right." She held up a hand to forestall Bill's objection and shifted her focus to Carter. "I'm not finished. What do you need from us or others to assess the painting's past? And do we need a process for future claims?"

The questions were the right ones to ask, but he hadn't worked at the museum long enough to have a good answer. That wouldn't satisfy the men and women spread around the massive table.

Stanley didn't seem to appreciate Carter's deliberation. "Well?"

"There's institutional knowledge I need to understand how the museum acquired its collection. Were any of you involved in the purchases or loans? What's our process?"

"Of which item?" Barbara swept her hands wide as if encompassing the entire building. "There are thousands here."

"Eventually we will need to consider the collection as a whole, because depending on how this goes, more disputes will arise." He blew out a breath as he tried to think how to explain the precipice before them. "If there's a problem with Botticelli's *Idealised Portrait of a Woman*, then there could be problems with other art in our collection. Chances are if the museum didn't exercise due diligence in that acquisition, similar challenges exist with other works."

"And?" Charlie leaned forward.

"That sounds expensive." Bill Yates frowned as he crossed his arms. "This is a nonprofit affiliated with the college, not the Getty."

"And I'm working on a plan to bring in interns to do some of the research. You're missing the larger issue. I cannot defend the museum against Mrs. Seeger's claim without information."

Stanley turned to Bill. "Didn't she try to hire an attorney before?"

"Not that I'm aware of. Anyone know?" Bill looked around the table and the others shook their heads.

"Whether she made a claim before could be critically important, but I don't know the law. That's why I need to hire an attorney to provide guidance on how to legally protect the museum." Carter's back straightened as he sensed passive resistance from the board. Only Margeaux gave him a small, encouraging nod. "If y'all won't help me, I need to get someone who can."

"Sounds like you need to use those online databases we pay for." Stanley waved a hand, but his stare looked lethal.

"I have, but it's not clear where it's been. Listen, the Botticelli was in a German museum, then there's a gap in its history and I haven't located our records." He stumbled to a stop, the hard looks worn by several board members confirming he hadn't won any friends. "I want permission to hire an attorney to represent the museum in the negotiation process and any lawsuits." How could he help them understand the gravity of the allegations? "Our response to this woman can impact our reputation for years."

Bill bolted to his feet, face red. "You don't have authority to hire attorneys."

"Then what do you recommend? This impacts the long-term reputation of the museum."

"The university already has an attorney." Barbara straightened and waved a hand dismissively.

Margeaux cocked her head as she watched Barbara. "Barbara, your son isn't right for this type of case."

"You only think that because you don't actually practice, Margeaux." Barbara smirked, and the atmosphere in the room seemed to shift. "You know what they say about teachers."

"What's that?"

"Those who can, do. Those who can't, teach."

Margeaux blinked and her skin blanched. "I don't know what to say."

Carter leaned forward, angry at the nastiness in Barbara's words. "You don't need to say anything. If there isn't collegiality and respect, we'll need to change how we meet." He looked around the table, noting who had a tightened jaw and who wouldn't meet his gaze. "There are too many places where people aren't respected, but this won't be one of them. I've read your bios and searched your companies' websites. Each of you is here for a reason. But this won't be a functional team without the freedom to disagree while still respecting each other."

"Young man, you have overstepped." Stanley's cheeks reddened and his eyes blazed.

"No, I'm doing exactly what the board hired me to do. I'm the director of the museum, so it's my responsibility to set the tone if you won't. Sir." He hoped the last word didn't sound as sarcastic as it felt. He could be angry about how they were treating someone else and still demonstrate respect. He'd have to find a way to do that if he wanted to shift the dysfunction he'd just witnessed.

"Thank you." Margeaux's words were soft, but she sounded composed. "You're right that I haven't practiced actively since moving into teaching, but I am still engaged in the law. That knowledge is why I'm here. Having someone ready to focus on this issue if it blows up is a sound strategy." She cleared her throat and pushed to her feet. "If you'll excuse me, I have a class to prepare for. My students appreciate my expertise." She exited with her head held high.

Carter sensed his only ally had left, and his stomach knotted as he studied the remaining board members. "And I'll hire someone to focus on the legal issues and make sure the museum is protected, because that is my job." And then he followed her from the room.

Chapter 13

"IT WAS TERRIBLE." MARGEAUX GROANED from where she sat on the floor at Janae's parents' home.

The chalk-painted and distressed ivory console table sagged with comfort food. Margeaux had brought her homemade macaroons and honey-lavender syrup for the hot tea or coffee. Chloe had brought a seven-layer taco dip that Janae could eat by the spoonful. Surely it was healthy with avocados and cheese. Janae's meager contribution sat next to the other offerings. The bowl of mandarin oranges should make her feel good since it was unqualifiedly good for you except for the fact the fruit had sat on her counter for a week. That's why she'd added a bag of wings from her mom's freezer.

"Surely not as bad as you think." Chloe folded her lithe body into a pretzel and then reached for three of the boneless wings. Somehow she'd manage to keep her white shirt pristine. "The other board members aren't that special."

"Tell that to Barbara Carrera. And to think I was going to get us an afternoon at her spa over winter break." Margeaux grimaced but then scooped a huge spoonful of dip onto the china plate. At least Janae could provide real dishes.

Janae's stomach churned as she thought about what Margeaux had relayed. "So no one supported the idea of me serving as an attorney for the museum."

"It didn't come up before I left."

Chloe stopped eating, a dab of barbecue sauce on her chin. "Why does it matter?"

"I wanted to take the case and do a great job to start building name recognition." She collapsed against the couch. "It's hard to start a firm, y'all. Chloe, know anyone who needs an attorney? I want to start paying you sometime this century."

"Let me start first."

"As soon as I have a client. I hoped the museum would lead the way." Janae sighed, letting herself think for just a moment what it would be like to work with the very handsome Dr. Montgomery.

"You just got a dreamy look on your face." Margeaux grinned at her.

"I did not." Janae felt heat climb her cheeks as she turned her back on Margeaux and returned her attention to Chloe. "Regardless, I don't know when I can pay you."

"Doesn't matter because I have a plan. I'll start at ten hours a week. Two part-time days. Then as your business grows, you'll get more of my time." She shrugged. "Remember, we were gymnasts. We love hard and challenging."

"True, that." Margeaux smiled. "I'll never forget your first twisting double on the floor, Janae."

"I think my back still remembers it." Janae ran a tortilla chip through the guac layer. "Why'd we do that to ourselves?"

"Because flying is the best." Chloe grinned. "Pounding down the runway to the vault. Blasting off the springboard. That is still the best fun."

"But no flips off the board."

"Sometimes." Chloe ducked her chin until her bangs hid her eyes. "I've agreed to start coaching a couple nights a week at the club."

Janae let her mouth drop open. "Really? You said you'd never go back."

"I want to be there and make sure today's girls are okay."

"That's noble." Margeaux studied her as if looking for the truth in Chloe's soul. "There's nothing we can do about the past."

"But maybe there is. Isn't that what you and Janae are potentially doing with this painting? Why not try to fix our past at the same time?"

Janae wanted to run from the idea, but as the conversation turned to the next movie each wanted to see, the question wouldn't leave her.

Was it possible to fix the darkest moment from her past?

She wanted to, because Janae longed to walk into a future that wasn't tainted by the past—that instead allowed her to thrive and consider what was possible. She'd built a wall around her heart after Libby died and Janae learned Chloe had also been abused by the coach. No one had believed Chloe or Libby when they'd asked for help, and it had been a dark, terrible time. That bred a lack of trust that resulted in her severe independence, which had led to the wrong filing of the motion to dismiss. In most cases, it wouldn't have been such a big issue. But the client had lost millions. Millions the firm's malpractice insurance had to pay.

And she'd lost her reputation. Something she couldn't recover.

So why was she ready to risk everything again?

She hadn't found her voice to ask questions after Libby died. Maybe she could have protected Chloe if she had. And she hadn't stood up for herself or her client after her costly mistake in Philadelphia. Maybe she wouldn't have had to run home if she had.

Why did she think anything would be different if she tried to speak for the museum?

Tuesday, November 8

The night had passed in a restless blur of tossing and turning, his dreams filled with shadowy figures stealing art from the museum's walls, Carter always three steps behind. And then he spotted Janae Simmons standing on the side looking like she wanted to help him but couldn't. He didn't want to explore why she'd made her way into his dreams. When he woke again, he threw back his comforter and slipped from the bed.

As he brewed a cup of coffee, he couldn't shake the conviction that waiting for the board to recognize its vulnerability would be too late. By the time it reached a consensus and formulated a response, a lawsuit could be filed with headlines following.

There had to be a correct response, one that satisfied the museum's legal and ethical obligations.

But to find that, he needed a plan he could present to the board. First, he'd hire Janae to guide the conversations with Shaw and Mrs. Seeger. At the same time, he'd dig into the due diligence that the museum had followed before purchasing the Botticelli while also tracking down information on the Modersohn-Becker.

Then the board would respond to Mrs. Seeger, but from an informed position.

It started with respectfully listening to Mrs. Seeger while determining whether she had a claim. If she didn't, then the museum could explain while acknowledging her.

He trusted Janae because she'd willingly admitted she didn't know this area of law but could tackle the research with a proactive approach. She was hungry for work, and that mattered. He'd school himself to ignore the sparks of attraction when he saw her.

Now wasn't the time to pursue any relationship. Andrew needed his attention. Add the museum, and Carter had to stay focused on the important people around him. Decision made, he finished getting ready, then corralled his nephew out the door and into the car.

After dropping Andrew at school, Carter stopped at Java Jane's to grab a to-go cup of caffeine. A couple of people stood in front of him, so he scanned the menu board while he waited.

"Montgomery."

Carter tried not to stiffen at the single word from Stanley. He shifted back toward the man. "Stanley. How are you this morning?"

"Better as soon as I have some coffee." The man studied him, then glanced around as if to see how close anyone was. "I've noticed a certain tension flowing from you. You have to trust me, Carter, or this relationship won't work. I have the best interests of the museum at heart."

"Unfortunately, sir, that's impossible. You violated trust in every interaction we had at the end of my time at the Burress." That museum had amassed an incredible collection of Expressionist art and had been the perfect place for Carter to conduct his postdoctoral research. At least it had been until Stanley insisted that a painting that was likely forged be heralded as the centerpiece of an exhibit Carter had organized.

Carter had started an investigation when he promptly found himself fired. Without a reference it had been hard to find a new position. He might not prove it, but he knew Stanley had been behind every door that shut in his face. The why remained a mystery.

And then to open this door at the Elliott and find Stanley on the other side.

Carter didn't like it, but he needed the job and knew he could do good work. He would build a program he could be proud of . . . so long as Stanley got out of the way and let him do his job.

In the year since his fellowship had abruptly ended and Charlotte had died, Carter had done a lot of soul searching and thinking hard about the kind of man he wanted to be. And he'd slowly begun the process of rebuilding his reputation.

What role had Stanley played in his sister's life? Carter knew Stanley had been involved . . . especially when he'd dragged Carter along to buy art and Charlotte had been there. Then she'd died and Stanley hadn't been surprised.

"Then we've reached an impasse." Stanley's posture stayed relaxed, yet a muscle in his jaw popped.

"Maybe. The board hired me, and I will do the job well."

"You see, that's where you're mistaken. I *am* the board." Stanley grinned, but there was menace behind it. "The others aren't as committed as me. Thus, they do what I say. It's the power of the chair."

Carter wanted to lash out but decided to bide his time. The man didn't need to know Margeaux was a friendly face on the board. They shuffled forward with the line of caffeine addicts, and Carter accidentally jostled a person ahead of him.

The woman turned. "Carter, good to see you."

He felt his morning improve with her quick words. "Janae, if you have a second, I'd like to introduce you to Stanley Dukes, the museum's board chair." He shifted slightly to Stanley. "This is Janae Simmons, the attorney I'm hiring for the Seeger paintings matter."

"It's a pleasure to meet you." Janae shifted her purse and extended her hand, but Stanley raked her with his gaze without taking her hand.

"What exactly is your experience that qualifies you to work on this?"

Her chin tipped up and her shoulders straightened. "Top of my class at George Mason and five years in Philadelphia with a top litigation firm. I'm smart, and I can find an answer to any legal problem you throw my direction."

"You're inexperienced." He sniffed and turned to Carter. "She cannot be the museum's attorney." Then he stepped back. "I'll get something at the diner. Good day."

Carter knew his mouth hung open, but he couldn't believe the man had been that intentionally rude. "I don't know what to say."

"Don't worry." She smiled, but it didn't reach her shadowed eyes. "I'd better get to work since I'll need another client. See you later." She turned and exited without a drink.

When Carter reached the museum fifteen minutes later, he still fumed. Stanley had been insufferably rude. He paused by Ariel's desk, and his assistant slipped her headphones from her ears but didn't turn her attention from the monitor. "What?"

He tilted his head as he noted her red rimmed eyes. "Everything okay?"

She swallowed, mashing her bright red lips together, then shook her head. "My mom called a bit ago to tell me Grandma died." She blinked quickly a couple of times but raised her hand. "Don't. She lived a good life and I'll always be grateful for the time with her."

"If you need to go home, be with your family . . ."

"No, I'll do that when we know more." She pulled her shoulders back and handed an envelope to him. "I don't know when this got delivered. Must have been when I stepped away."

"All right." He hesitated to grab it. What if it was from that attorney? Did it count as service of process if no one received it? "Let me know if you need anything."

Ariel nodded and then pulled her headphones back up.

Carter tapped the envelope against his thigh and then headed to his office. After he sank into his chair, he opened it, scanning the enclosed document. Then he reread the demand letter, a close repeat of the first he had received. He set it on the desk and stared at the phone. There were a few facts in the letter, but too few to be helpful. What would Janae say if he called now? She knew Stanley Dukes wasn't in favor . . . the man couldn't have been more blunt. Yet he'd sensed she didn't have a client yet. That might work to his advantage as she could give the museum her full focus. Was that what he needed?

Yes, she didn't have specific experience on this question, but how many attorneys did? She did have passion and commitment, which created the intangible that could make all the difference as they navigated this splotched landscape. It felt like the stripes of bold paints on a Rothko canvas or one of van Gogh's crazed self-portraits, brilliance with a blend of insanity.

Sometimes the best things happened when one took that kind of risk.

The board might not agree, but his allegiance belonged to the museum and those who had invested their art and antiquities to its care. If he had to find another job after doing the right thing for those patrons, then he would.

Sometimes you had to do the right thing even if it ended up not being the best for you personally.

He blew out a prayer, then picked up the phone.

God might fight for him, but that didn't mean Carter should stand on the sidelines and wait. Sometimes God's instruction was to wait, but often his orders included an element of action. Carter might not fully understand the legal system and all its deadlines, but waiting could be disastrous.

Chapter 14

THE REPURPOSED ROUND TABLE FROM Monroe's Surplus Shop stood halfway in the hall with the other half twisted into the small conference room when her cell pulsed in her pocket. She couldn't take it, but then it sounded again and Dad set his end of the table down.

"Take that while I figure out the geometry puzzle we've got here."

"You sure?"

"Far as I can see, we're stuck. Maybe I'll remove the legs." He took off his baseball hat and scratched his head. "Working with horses and numbers is easier than this."

"I appreciate you, Dad." She slipped down the hall to her office, pulling her phone from her back pocket. She slid her finger along the screen to take the call. "Hello?"

"Janae?"

She flinched as she realized how unprofessionally she'd answered. "Yes, this is Janae Simmons."

"Carter, with a question for you."

His voice soothed her nerves and she leaned against the wall. "How can I help? Or did you miss the snub from Mr. Dukes? I'm sure you're not supposed to talk to me."

A loud sigh echoed down the line. "Please hear me out."

Well, that was ominous. "Okay."

"Will you agree to be the museum's attorney regarding the dispute about ownership of the two paintings we discussed?"

"As your board chair so publicly told me, I don't have the experience."

"Neither do I." He paused, and she could almost hear his regret at saying that out loud.

"Better to admit it, right?" She could offer him that. Then she considered how to respond. "I will work harder than anyone else."

"I know. That's why I need you. I want to do this the right way, and that doesn't automatically mean giving the paintings back. Art has a checkered past even without all that happened during World War II. The Nazis and Russians did a number on the European collections. But it wasn't the last time or the first."

There was something engaging about listening to Carter talk about his passion. "You know so much about the history."

"In generalities, and the demand letter doesn't fill in missing details. This situation is complicated by the fact we own one painting and the other is on loan. We have a collection filled with items that I don't know how the museum acquired. I have to figure that out, while you buy us time to determine what the right thing is."

"I must have full access to you and the other staff." She thought of the cases she'd been part of that hadn't gone well. Most times it involved a client who didn't provide critical information and access as needed. "I can't do this with the board and staff against me." Not when she was in the earliest stages of building a reputation.

"Not a problem."

"Dr. Montgomery, it's not negotiable."

"I'll make it happen. And call me Carter." He paused. "We're going to spend a lot of time together."

"Yes."

She rubbed her forehead. He sounded certain, but she knew someone who could give her the real story about the board. And somehow she'd have to keep her crazy attraction to him in check. She'd have to focus on the case. And her law practice. Establishing her place in Kedgewick. Each of those had to take precedence or she'd never make her place here.

That was what she wanted.

What she needed.

Not whatever flashed between them.

Not when the chair of the board emphatically did not want her on the case.

"Carter."

"Yes?"

Did he sense the tension too?

"When can you meet?"

"I have two meetings early afternoon I can't move."

"Grab a couple drinks from Java Jane's. Latte for me. I'll be here and you'll be my priority when you arrive."

"See you around three."

After she hung up, Janae dialed Margeaux's number, chewing on her thumbnail while she waited for her friend to pick up. When it went to voicemail, she left a message asking for information. Then she walked past her dad, toward the front where Chloe worked on organizing the desk. It had been the right decision to put the best desk where everyone would see it. "We have the museum."

Chloe whooped and held up a hand for a high five. "I knew it."

"It should feel good."

"Why doesn't it?"

"Stanley Dukes."

"Oh?"

At Chloe's one word response, Janae nodded. "I bumped into him and Carter at Java Jane's. They didn't realize I was there and argued about the case. Then Mr. Dukes forbade Carter from hiring me."

"And he did anyway?" Chloe's eyebrows climbed to her bangs.

"Yes."

"He has guts."

"Yes." Janae rolled her shoulders. "I need an engagement letter, which means I need a billable rate."

"Already got you covered." Chloe pulled an envelope from her backpack. "I prepared it last night."

Janae took the envelope and scanned the letter. "This is great. You really believed the museum would come through. Thank you."

"Of course they would." Chloe beamed at her. "Now you've got the hardest client. The first."

Janae wanted to celebrate, but reality wouldn't let her. "Now we have to win an impossible case about a subject I know nothing about. And land a dozen more clients."

"And then the next one hundred. No problem. Nothing's impossible when you have our skills."

Janae kneaded her lower back to loosen the tension accumulating there. "I love your enthusiasm. We might pull this off."

"Of course we will. And then the world will be your oyster, whatever that means. And I'll go to law school with a small tuition stipend from my generous boss." She waggled her eyebrows, and Janae laughed at her energy.

"If I can afford it, you know I will." Frankly, it would be the least she could do after the tangible ways Chloe helped her chase this new dream. "It'll be your turn to pursue your future. But first we have a lot of work to do."

"Don't worry, I've got a few ideas. This is going to work." Chloe's grin was radiant.

"Janae, ready to finish moving this table?"

At Dad's words, Chloe grinned. "Better help him first. I'll get the file created."

Not necessarily the most valuable use of Chloe's time, but a good start as Janae figured out next steps while helping Dad. After all, she did need the conference room ready before Dr. Montgomery—no, Carter—arrived. That gave her a few hours to get set up, do some research, and get cleaned up for her only and most important client.

Carter slogged through his meetings, but the lawsuit and his questions about whether he'd taken the right stand in hiring Janae lingered.

What magic had she wrought on him to keep pushing to the front of his mind when usually he'd forget a woman as soon as a conversation ended? He didn't have time to let himself sink into the possibilities of a relationship when he had a museum to run and a nephew to guide.

He needed to focus. This was why he'd hired Janae.

She could help him piece together the full story in a way that the truth or the best guess at it could be identified. The scans of the demand letter and what he'd found on the paintings had finished printing, so he scooped them into a folder and then slid that into his bag. After a quick stop at Java Jane's, he continued to her office.

The narrow storefront opened to a small lobby area with a cheerful woman sitting behind a desk. "May I help you?"

"I have an appointment with Janae Simmons."

"Dr. Montgomery, I presume?" She seemed to find delight in everything.

"You are?"

"Chloe Ainsworth." She stood and he noticed her black blazer and white shirt topped slashed jeans.

"Artsy."

"Hmm?" She stopped and arched her eyebrows in a challenge. "Follow me."

Prints of landscapes leaned against the wall, something that hadn't been there the last time he'd walked in. They must mark the spots someone should hang them along the exposed-brick wall. The first doorway on the left revealed a round table that would have been a beast to fit through the door. The scent of lemon cleaner hung in the air and the wood surface glowed as if freshly polished.

Carter turned to Chloe. "Settling in?"

"You have no idea." She seemed to realize what she said. "Don't worry. You're our main client right now so the museum will get most of Janae's time and attention. That means good things will happen."

"I'm aware the museum is the only client." Wonders had been worked since Friday, but had he made the right choice? It didn't matter that the other attorneys in town didn't strike him as the right choice, because there were Richmond and DC attorneys in easy proximity. He didn't have to be here, but he wanted to be. The question remained if he was here for the right reasons.

"We're grateful. Feel free to take a seat." Chloe noticed his cup. "I hope that's a latte. Janae likes them plain and hot."

"That's what she ordered." He grimaced at the thought of the black coffees he'd brought before.

"Good deal. Well, have a good meeting." She closed the door, and he was alone.

Nothing hung on the walls to remind him he'd been brilliant to hire a summa cum laude graduate of George Mason Law School who'd then spent several years working for a top firm on the East Coast. He'd read her bio online, knew the outlines of her experience. That had assured him he'd made a smart gamble. He needed to trust his instincts.

The door opened and Janae walked in. She stood wrapped in a dress of some sort that mimicked the color of lavender in the most vibrant sunset. The way it foiled her blonde hair arrested his attention, and she carried herself with the air of a petite warrior. The direct assessment in her hazel eyes emphasized the noble set to her face that would have fascinated many of the artists whose work lined his museum's walls. He couldn't tear his gaze from her.

She raised an eyebrow at him as she took a seat at one of two chairs at the table. "Sorry to disappoint. I can put back on the jeans and sweatshirt I was cleaning in if you prefer." Her eyes sparkled with a tease.

"All good. Thanks for making time so quickly. I know you have a lot to do."

"Yes, but figuring out what you need is my priority."

He cleared his throat and took the other chair, only to realize that with just the two of them in the room, he had nowhere to focus but her. Then he pulled his bag off his shoulder and set it on the table, tugging out the file a moment later. "Here's the initial information the museum has on the painting we own. It's cursory at best."

"Do you have the demand letter?"

"Guess I should have led with that."

"Show me." He slipped out a second file as she held out her hand and waggled her fingers for it. She took it from him and speed-read it, then looked up, her intelligent hazel eyes assessing him. "Have you checked the link?"

"Yes. I couldn't get it to work."

"Did you call Shaw to ask for the corrected link?"

"No."

"Why?"

He ran his fingers through his hair, not caring if it made the ends stand up like he'd survived a hurricane. This had the potential to be more dangerous than that. "Because I'm in denial. This assignment should launch my career and lead to bigger museums." He didn't add the *if I want* postscript that ran through his mind. "However, this is not what I want to form the foundation for my tenure here. This could devastate the collection if it calls the history of our art into question." He stood and paced a moment before plopping back down. "I also wasn't sure contacting him was the smart choice."

"Seems like a leap from this short missive to all that."

"Once there's a single question, it can throw everything into chaos."

And that could mean the end of his career before it fully launched.

She returned to the file and flipped through the pages like an Impressionist, speed and precision in her movements as her finger slid down the page. "What does the letter mean to you?"

"The heir claims the painting should have been restituted to her family prior to it being sold to us. However, she also claims that we should have known of the questioned history and not purchased it."

"What does your documentation show?"

"It's what it doesn't show that is troubling."

"Oh?"

"There's a twenty-year period that is blank. Anything could have happened."

"So what do you need to know to fill that gap?"

"Probably a trip to the place the gap started, but the board won't pay for that."

"What about insurance?"

"Most museums are woefully underinsured. There's simply too much art and too many unknowns on valuation."

"Okay, so work your network and find someone local who can dig through the archives."

"It'd be more fun to go myself." He tried to smile, but his face didn't cooperate.

"Sure, but since that's not an option, let's focus on next best. While you find someone to do that investigation, I'll contact Mr. Shaw, set up a meeting. Then you and I will dig into the research."

"This is why you were perfect to hire." Carter grinned at her. "I already feel better having concrete steps."

"None of it was hard. I'll need something too."

"Oh?"

"A retainer." She looked around the bare room. "Fast."

"I can have it here tomorrow."

"Good. Let's hope you can find a local resource as quickly." She glanced at the letter again. "Because we're on a tight timetable."

Chapter 15

JANAE HUDDLED IN FRONT OF her laptop trying to read through pages of old records. Quiet music piped into her earbuds while thin sunlight filtered through her office window. Getting a docking station and large monitor were moving up her priority list for the sake of her eyesight and posture. So many details required screen time, and her eyes felt dry from all the squinting.

Her phone rang and she clicked to accept the call. "Simmons Law Practice."

"Where is it?" The male voice was agitated and one she couldn't place.

"I'm sorry. Who is this?"

"Mark Ashby."

Why was the man calling her? "I don't know what you mean."

"You took a box when you left."

"Mr. Ashby, I only took what your receptionist gave me. It was a box with the few things I brought to the office." In those couple of misguided days of believing she could make a living working for him.

"That idiot receptionist sent you with the wrong box." His volume rose with each word, and Janae pulled the phone from her ear.

"What do you want me to do?"

"Bring it back now." The man sounded slightly unhinged, and she could imagine spittle flying from his mouth as he spoke.

"I don't have the box here." It might be in her trunk, but she wasn't going to check when he acted so unreasonably.

"Janae, this is life and death."

She rolled her eyes even though he couldn't see. "If there's anything in there, I'll bring it to you tomorrow."

"That'll be too late."

"Good-bye, Mark." The man was completely unrealistic. After the way he had treated her, there was no reason for her to drop everything to see if somehow she had something he thought she did.

Before her music restarted, her phone rang again.

She clicked to take the call and before she could say anything, he spoke. "Janae, I need those files."

"I don't know what you're talking about."

"Look, can you bring them by first thing in the morning? I have a meeting at eight where I need them."

She wanted to deny him, but instead sighed. "Fine. If I find I have these files, I'll bring them first thing. Good-bye, Mark."

"Wait. Come around to the back door. Angie won't be in yet."

So that was the receptionist's name. "Good-bye, Mark."

Thursday, November 10

The next morning she was still miffed as she walked up to the Ashley and Ashby front door. As she pulled on the locked door, she remembered Mark's words to come around to the back, so she reversed course and headed to the rear of the building. A white pickup was headed away from her down the alley, but other than that, all was quiet.

When she reached the door, she found it ajar.

She frowned but opened it. The hall was dark, but light seeped from beneath a door down the hallway about where she'd expect Mark's office to be. "Mark, I've got your files."

She'd been surprised to grab the box and find folders at the bottom. Someone had scrawled "Seeger" across the tab of one, and she realized the receptionist must have grabbed the closest box when throwing Janae's items into it, not realizing four files had fallen to the bottom. Janae had resisted reading the files, since she now represented the museum, but it had taken everything in her not to do so since it wasn't her fault she had them. She could make a straight-faced argument she hadn't done anything wrong, but it didn't feel ethical to read them when they could be attorney work product. So she'd slipped them unread into the bag she'd slung over her shoulder.

"Mark, I'm here." Her flats were quiet on the carpet as she moved toward the light. "Are you here? The back door was open, so I came on in."

No one answered even as she neared the door etched in light. She frowned, the hair on the back of her arms standing at attention as goose bumps pebbled her skin.

"Mark?"

Silence.

That was all that greeted her.

She reached for the phone in the outside pocket of her bag.

Glanced over her shoulder.

Looked up the hall.

Then took a deep breath.

Pushed open the door.

"Mark?"

Inhaled as her eyes focused in the bright light.

She hurried toward the desk where he slouched and then froze.

Should she touch him? She had to if she wanted to confirm whether he was dead or needed medical assistance. Her fingers trembled as she reached for his neck and felt for a pulse.

With her other hand she tugged out her phone and dialed 911. After the operator answered, her voice wavered. "I need an ambulance at

Ashley and Ashby. Use the back door. It's Mark Ashby. He isn't breathing and I can't find a pulse."

Then she collapsed in a chair as she waited for the paramedics. What had she stumbled into?

Chapter 16

I need an attorney. I think.

Janae's hands trembled as she wrote the text to Margeaux. In fact, it felt like her body had abandoned her in a swoosh of jitters and light-headedness.

Should she leave Mark?

Should she stay with him?

Should she sit?

Should she stand?

She didn't want to touch anything or contaminate the scene, but she didn't want to do the wrong thing either. Law school hadn't taught her how to handle a potential crime scene.

Then she heard noise in the hallway and hurried toward the door. "In here."

The paramedics raced in and a minute later a police officer arrived. He looked at her with a weird expression but hurried to Mark.

I definitely need an attorney.

Maybe.

A moment later Margeaux responded.

What?!?!?

> Mark Ashby asked me to come
> by this morning. He's dead.

What?!?!?

> Exactly.

Janae collapsed in the chair.

> I don't know what happened,
> but the police just arrived.

Don't say anything. I'm on my
way.

> Thank you.

> Come to the back door.

Janae slid her phone in her pocket and watched in mute shock as the paramedics pulled Mark to the floor, searched for a pulse, and did other things she couldn't see. Then she heard the whine of the defibrillator and watched his body respond to the electric jolt.

The police officer looked younger than she was with smooth cheeks that looked like they'd never needed shaving. He watched the paramedics a minute, then approached her. "Ma'am, can you tell me what happened?"

"I don't know." She paused, trying to collect her thoughts and buy time. She didn't want to say much before Margeaux arrived. She might not practice, but Janae's friend was better than Janae handling this on her own.

"I'm here." Margeaux swept through the door, twisting her hair into a clip as she sailed into the room. She pulled to an abrupt stop as the paramedics eased a cloth over Mark's face. "Oh my."

The officer looked at the paramedics. "Y'all calling the coroner?"

"On it."

He turned back to them. "Let's head to the hallway."

"You sure we should do that?" Margeaux widened her eyes at him. "What if this is a crime scene?"

"I'm sorry, but who are you and why are you here?"

"Margeaux Robbins, professor at Monroe College, attorney-at-law, and her friend." Margeaux gave him a look edged with steel. "I've watched enough *NCIS* to know we shouldn't move without knowing if this is a murder scene."

"Fine." The officer crossed his arms and studied her. "Don't move." He called someone, probably the police station, and then turned back to them. "We're to walk directly outside into the alley since that's where you both entered."

"Did we?" Margeaux arched a brow. "Or did you just make an assumption?"

He stared at Margeaux, then pulled out a notepad and shifted toward Janae. "Where did you enter the building?"

Janae frowned at Margeaux. Maybe texting her for help hadn't been the best idea. "The back door. Going to the alley is a great idea. Thank you." Janae gladly followed him out of the room. She was concerned that any evidence could have been destroyed by the paramedics' efforts to save Mark. "What if it was natural causes?"

"Then we'll learn that." The officer held the back door and then waited for them to stand in the alley. "Why were you here?"

"Mark asked me to meet him here to give him something before an eight o'clock meeting he had." Janae glanced at her watch. "It's eight thirty, and that appointment didn't show."

"The ambulance probably scared them away."

"Maybe." Janae met Margeaux's gaze, and her friend subtly shook her head. Janae shouldn't volunteer anything. Fine. Margeaux would provide an extra set of ears to make sure Janae didn't inadvertently say anything that got her in trouble.

The officer looked up from making a couple of notes in his phone. "Why did he want to meet?"

"I'm not entirely sure." The files felt heavy in her bag, but she didn't want to turn them over to the police—not without looking at them to see if they were connected to his death. Was there something in them that would shed light on why he wanted to meet? Or had it really been about getting a few thin client files back? "I was employed here for a couple of days at the end of October, before Mark decided it wouldn't work. We hadn't talked since, so his call surprised me." Margeaux's eyes widened, so Janae pressed her lips together.

"Really? No idea?"

"No." She met his gaze even as her stomach clenched. Could he see through her bag to the files? She needed a minute to review them. Why hadn't she done that last night when she found the files? Had she let her sense of ethics get the best of her? No, but now she wondered if the files were why he'd been killed. Margeaux's comment about a possible crime scene had gotten to her. There was no reason to think that, but she wanted to know what was in them before handing them over.

He took down her information. "That's all I need for now, but the chief might have other questions when he's back on duty."

"All right."

As she and Margeaux walked away, Janae felt the officer's gaze on her. Margeaux hooked her arm through Janae's and steered her from the alley toward the Lucky Bean. Janae resisted. "Not there. Let's go to my office."

"You're fortunate I was already on campus this morning. If I'd been driving from Hamilton, I'd only be arriving now."

Janae nodded, pausing long enough to swipe her office keys from the bag. Once they were inside, she hurried through the lobby to her office, turned on the light, and then tugged the files from her bag.

Margeaux came to stand next to her. "What are those?"

"The files Mark asked for."

Margeaux pivoted to her so fast her elbow knocked Janae to the side. "You lied to Joel Alston?"

"Who?"

"The officer."

"I guess." Janae rubbed her hands up and down her arms. "Mark called last night in a panic, looking for these files."

"You guess? You took them?"

"No. I didn't know I had them. Once I saw them in the box the receptionist packed, I didn't open them because they aren't my files and one of the files could relate to the woman suing the museum. Do you think these could be tied to his death?"

That question lingered as Janae opened the files and took photos of the few sheets in each with her phone. Margeaux watched the whole time, recording the activity.

"What are you recording?"

"I can prove you didn't destroy anything if we have to."

Janae swallowed at the reality Margeaux's words communicated. "Here's hoping we won't need it." She'd just finished when her cell rang and she looked at her friend. "It says it's the police."

"Then you'd better take it."

Janae nodded, but her stomach clenched and sweat slicked her hands. "Hello?"

"Janae Simmons?"

"Yes."

"This is Chief Dusty Sanderson. My officer tells me you found Mark Ashby this morning."

"I did."

"Can you come down and file your report officially?" His voice was cordial even as his words were a question spoken as a statement.

Tension knotted her neck. "I could come now."

"I'd appreciate it."

She hung up and then met Margeaux's gaze. "I don't suppose you want to come with me?"

"Of course. And you know you're taking that file."

"Yes." The first thing Janae did when Chief Sanderson walked her into a small conference room was hand him the four files. "Mark asked me to bring these files to him this morning. When he called last night, I didn't know I had them."

The chief had the lean frame of a man who enjoyed running and settled into one of the metal folding chairs as he considered the files she held. "Go ahead and have a seat." He glanced at Margeaux. "You too." After they were both seated, he turned his focus back to the files. "Why do you think he wanted them?"

"I don't know. I haven't read them yet."

"Any reason?"

"There's a woman threatening to sue a client. Her last name is Seeger, the name written on one of the files. I don't know that it's the same person, but I was being extra cautious. All the files are property of another firm, and I didn't want to do anything improper. It's an attorney thing."

He just studied her, gaze seeming to pierce through her, and she fought not to squirm. "All right."

"All right?"

"Yep. Right now it looks like Mark had a heart attack. An autopsy will be performed since he died alone, but that doesn't mean anything happened out of the ordinary. We're all born. And we all die."

Margeaux leaned forward. "That's a bit callous, Chief."

"You know me, Margeaux. All flowers and sunshine."

She shook her head and laughed. "Don't worry, Janae, you'll like Chief Sanderson as you get to know him. He's got a dry wit."

Janae stared at her friend, then slowly turned her attention back to the chief. "Would you like the files?"

"Nah, drop them off for Ashley on your way back." He leaned forward. "There have been some strange happenings around that law firm with the break-in and now Mark's death. Be warned. If the autopsy shows it wasn't natural causes, we'll be in touch."

Janae swallowed and nodded. "I understand."

As soon as they were away from the police station, she gulped big breaths and then handed the folders to Margeaux. "Can you drop these off?"

"Sure. Where are you going?"

"I've got to try to get some research done before tomorrow's meeting with Shaw and the museum." And shake off the heaviness of finding Mark. She might not have liked the man, but she hadn't wished him dead.

Chapter 17

THURSDAY PASSED IN A BLUR of endless research that led down alleys and black holes. Janae and Carter met late afternoon, and frustration rolled off him. He wanted to find the perfect answer and solution. Instead, the search for answers clearly wasn't going to be easy. She tried to remind him litigation was a marathon, but he wanted to avoid a lawsuit as quickly as possible. Period.

But she couldn't shake the distraction of Mark's death and wondering whether it was straightforward.

Had he died of natural causes even if it felt too early?

Or had someone helped him along?

She had no reason to think he hadn't died of natural causes but . . . she was so unsettled.

Now Carter stood in Janae's office, nervous energy thrumming from him. In a little less than an hour, they would be meeting with Mrs. Seeger and her attorney.

He straightened his jacket, repeatedly fastening and unfastening the top button. Janae leaned forward and then stopped. "This is only the initial meeting, Carter. If it doesn't go well, no problem." She tried to make her voice soothing, but he grimaced. "Tell me more about provenance."

"What?"

"I need to more fully understand it." If nothing else, it would get him talking about something comfortable to him.

"Okay." He stilled as he blinked rapidly. She could almost see his mind organizing an answer. "The question of provenance has bedeviled the art world for centuries but came into real focus after World War II with the looting that occurred at the direction of the Nazis." He paused, and his fingers straightened his tie. "How can I explain this in a way that isn't too technical?" He snapped his fingers. "It's how you show good title to the painting."

"That's a nice legal term, but why doesn't good title exist already?"

"The history of art can deviate based on the larger historical context. Wars muddy what happened to a piece. At times, the art community focused heavily on whether art was properly bought and sold. At other times, that question took a back seat to other priorities. Thanks to cases like *Austria v. Altmann*, but even more the movie about the case, people expect art to be handled a certain way if the Nazis stole or confiscated it."

"And how do you do that?"

"Find the true history. And that's the challenge. Each piece traverses a unique journey to a museum or private collector's walls. Even with a thorough search, many have points in that progression that remain hidden despite our best efforts."

"So we'll look for documents?"

"And third-party historical records. Owners don't maintain perfect paperwork across generations."

"That would be critical to determining ownership."

"Absolutely. The greatest challenge is finding the truth when holes exist. With Mrs. Seeger claiming rights to two paintings, we'll be busy." He straightened and pushed his hands into his slacks pockets. "It's not that I'm worried."

She arched an eyebrow, and his frown deepened.

"All right. I am. It's complicated and I don't know answers yet."

"It's understandable if you are. The law is my space, not yours." She snagged her iPad from her desk and nodded toward the door. "They're here now. Remember, we can set the tone. You need to stride into the room with humble confidence. We'll listen to what they have to say, but not assume they're right and the museum wrong."

"It feels antagonistic."

"But it doesn't need to. Trust me, the best thing we can do is walk in there without an agenda or fear. We all want the same thing: each painting with its rightful owners."

"With different interpretations of who that is."

She nodded at the fair point. "Possibly, but we don't know what they do. And they don't understand what you know. Today is about identifying common ground." Sometimes that could be found—and she hoped today it could—but it was impossible to guess ahead of the meeting.

His chin tipped down as he studied the carpet, and she hoped he didn't notice the stain that was partially covered with the area rug. After a moment he nodded and looked up. "We'll take your approach. The board gave me no negotiating room."

"Until we talk, we won't know if there's anything to bargain."

"Understood." His intense gaze collided with hers. "What do you need me to do?"

"Keep an open mind and posture. If you start to shut down, they will react. If instead you take notes and seem willing to talk, they will likely remain open as well." She shrugged as she swiped up on the tablet to check the battery on the pencil. "People respond to what we convey without saying a word. Remember your first reaction to the heir?"

"A demure yet steely woman. Calm yet focused."

"We can work with that. It's anger that is harder to diffuse. Ready?"

"As I'll ever be."

"Then let's go meet them." Janae led the way from her office, trying not to give the kaleidoscope of butterflies soaring through her stomach sway over how she handled the next moments. She firmly believed everything she'd told Carter, but she didn't know this attorney and hadn't interacted with the heir. She needed to keep her eyes on her client and not let her feelings about the woman's story cloud her ability to represent the museum effectively.

She knocked on the conference door and then opened it. "Hello." She reached across the table to where a man surged to his feet. "I'm Janae Simmons, and this is my client's representative, Dr. Carter Montgomery."

"I'm Jarod Shaw, and my client Clara Seeger." The man reminded her of a middle-aged Jimmy Stewart, all aw-shucks and down-home with a southern drawl. "Thanks for making time to meet."

"Of course. We're more than willing to hear what your client has to say." She stopped short of promising anything. It was way too early to start down that road. The woman had much to prove before she established any sort of ownership interest in anything the museum owned or held on loan. She reached toward the woman, but Mrs. Seeger merely nodded her head as if she'd taken lessons from Queen Elizabeth II. Janae kept her smile in place and then gestured to the chairs. "Let's settle in."

Carter and Jarod waited until she took a seat, then sank onto chairs across from each other.

Carter shifted but she gave him a quick look and he stilled, lightly clutching his hands on top of the table.

"Jarod, you asked for this meeting, and we're ready to hear what you have to say." She typed in the password for the tablet and then readied her pen for taking notes. "First, can you send us the link from the demand letter again? Neither of us has gotten it to work."

"Sure." Jarod set a battered briefcase on the edge of the table, then pulled a couple of files from it. He slid one across the table to Carter and another toward Janae. "I took the liberty of preparing some materials for you."

Carter didn't want to reach for the file but knew that would be rude and probably convey the opposite of what Janae wanted. What documents would fill that bland folder? He didn't want to consider the board's response if Carter walked into the next meeting with proof the Botticelli didn't belong to the museum or that the Paula Modersohn-Becker, though on loan, didn't belong to the German museum either. The whole situation felt like he'd been set up to fail before he accepted the job, but he couldn't sense a way to extricate himself from the mess. Or prove what he was beginning to fear.

Had there been a conspiracy to cover something up?

And he'd been hired to take the fall?

Opening that folder could commit him to deeper layers of confusion and tension with the museum's board. Stanley Dukes had determined to battle him on every front, making meetings like this even more difficult. He should work with the board to rectify any errors of the past. And frankly it was a big unknown as to whether the museum should do anything. He needed allies. Maybe Bill Yates and Margeaux Robbins would be in his court, but he couldn't be sure. However, he needed to increase his search for at least one board member who was an ally and advocate. Both roles were critical.

Did it matter that the Elliott didn't own the Paula Modersohn-Becker painting of the five children? Would it impact the process that the painting was loaned, as often occurred when museums composed exhibits?

The director who had worked so carefully to create the incredible display of Expressionist development had likely not considered the fact the painting might have a colored past, yet he probably should have. At the same time, the Landesmuseum in Hanover was a German museum that contained German art. Not all art in Europe had been harmed in World War II. As with many things, too broad a brushstroke shouldn't be used, glossing over details.

One shouldn't assume all German-held art was tainted by the horrible acts during World War II.

Neither should one assume it was not.

He rubbed his forehead, then caught the action and clasped his hands again. Janae glanced at him, then back at the pair.

Carter refocused on the two across the table.

Jarod Shaw still had a hand on each folder and slid them a bit farther across the table. "If you look at the first page, you'll note it's a German document."

Janae opened the folder in front of her and frowned. "While it looks like it might be official because of the seal, I don't read German." She looked up from the document.

"I didn't gather you would." He tapped the top of Carter's still unopened file. "You'll find a translation underneath the first document." His smile was tight and did not reach his eyes. "My client is intent on making this process as quick and easy as possible. She does not presume to have years ahead of her and wants to ensure this matter is resolved while she can enjoy the art's return."

Mrs. Seeger placed a hand on her attorney's arm. "It is not as dire as all that." Her words held the faint hint of the accent that he had noted when they first talked at the exhibit opening. The woman focused on Carter, her rheumy blue eyes looking through him. "It is a necessary goal to reclaim what was taken." She sighed. "So much has been lost to time and the war. What feels like generations ago to you was a terrible part of my childhood and shadowed my life. I want to honor my grandparents before I join them."

Janae lightly cleared her throat. "That's an understandable desire, ma'am."

"Clara." The woman's voice softened with her interjection.

"Yes, ma'am. But we need more than your desire to determine whether ownership can trace to your family." Janae made a note on her tablet, then looked up, firm yet kind. "If the painting is your family's, the courts can help return it. But you need to understand the Elliott Museum doesn't own both paintings. One is on loan from another museum. That impacts what we can do."

"I saw the note when I viewed the painting." Her eyes narrowed slightly. "And that is why we must act now. I cannot travel to Germany. I cannot fight in the courts of that country. But I read. A lot." She smiled and it revealed steel. "I know that when the painting is here, in my adopted country, now I can try to right the past. It is . . ." She looked at her attorney. "What was the phrase you used?"

"*In rem* jurisdiction."

"Yes, that."

Janae's shoulder tightened and her spine straightened even more, causing Carter to freeze. Was that bad?

"Maybe, but there is also the matter of the amount of time that has passed. The war ended more than seventy years ago." Janae clasped her hands on top of the tablet, the pencil extending from her fingers. "Even if it did belong to your family before the war, there were many mechanisms to reclaim it long before now."

"And that is why we are here." Shaw edged the folder even closer, so that Carter couldn't avoid it. "When you review this, you will see that this is not a frivolous claim, but instead one that this museum must deal with. In fact, I suggest you call the Landesmuseum. You will each have some decisions to make. Or we'll sue."

Carter glanced at Mrs. Seeger. "Is that what you want?"

"I do not want conflict. However, my family and I have waited too long for the return of our property. I am the last of my line, with a nephew and niece." She glanced down and swallowed as she collected herself. "I do not have time to dillydally."

The Jimmy Stewart look-alike sneered in a way that felt downright smarmy. "Like I said, there's one real chance to make this a situation that doesn't become splashed all over the newspapers like the Altmann case. But that's up to you."

"Is that a threat?" Janae frowned and leaned forward on the table.

"Take it as you will, but we won't simply disappear." He turned to his client. "She and her family have waited too long to have the paintings restituted. And do not mistake me. We want both."

144

Chapter 18

SHAW'S FIRM WORDS ECHOED IN Carter's mind, a dirge that wouldn't go away even after the man had escorted his client from Janae's office. Carter had waited for Janae to return, turning the words over in his mind.

She sank onto the chair Mrs. Seeger had abandoned and sighed.

"That bad?"

"I'm not sure." She turned to him with a concerned expression. "What stood out to you?"

"She wants both pieces. There's not much room for negotiating that I heard."

"Me either. So what's the next step from your perspective?"

He tapped the file. "I need to dig through this, talk to someone in Germany, and update the board."

"While you do that, I'll dig through more cases. I've found a good book for background, but each case is different, because the facts are unique." She grinned up at him. "This is why I'll always have a job. The answer to every legal question is 'It depends.' You focus on the facts, and then I'll build the case." She glanced at her watch. "I'd better get started since the demand letter only gives until the end of the month."

"Anything we can do to get more time?"

"We can try a tolling agreement, but if I were Jarod, I wouldn't give it without some indication we were seriously considering the problem as they've presented it. Enough that they think we're open to a settlement." She glanced at the list she'd created. "We've got a lot to do to investigate her claims."

After he returned to the museum, Carter scheduled a late-afternoon meeting with Bill Yates and then spent an hour trying to find someone to connect him to the curators at Landesmuseum while Ariel searched for the paperwork on the loan.

Finally Ariel hurried in. "I found the file. I think this is who Robert worked with."

The prior director, Robert Stevens, had a filing system. He had to, but it wasn't clear to anyone Carter had talked to. He took the file and flipped to the front page, disappointment sagging his shoulders as he saw a name and number he'd already dialed. "I've tried this number, but it's a dead end. I've also tried Robert, but he hasn't responded either." In fact, at this rate, he was beginning to believe his message disappeared into some sort of purgatory.

"Robert always spent a week about this time in the wilds of Michigan. Said it was to clear his head. I bet he doesn't have cell service if that's where he is. I can call his wife if that helps."

"That would. Thanks." Carter took the file and scanned it for any other names and possible connections at the Landesmuseum. Finally, he found one and dialed the number. After a series of decision trees, he reached a mailbox for Dr. Suzy Werblow. "Please call me as soon as you can related to a potential claim against the painting you've loaned us." He left the number and followed up the call with a quick email. Maybe that would be a better way to get the communication started.

One glance at his clock had Carter hurrying from his office. He stopped at Ariel's desk. "I'm meeting Bill Yates at the cafe. If Dr. Werblow from Germany calls back, do whatever it takes to get my attention."

"Got it." She scribbled a note. "Good luck."

"Thanks." He strode through the glass door and down a short hallway to the main lobby. An exposed stairwell took him to the second floor with its small cafe and scattered bistro tables with chairs. Often a couple of the tables had patrons enjoying a break or members meeting for coffee and conversation. It was an area where the museum could expand its efforts to include a broader menu of sandwiches and other snacks. Maybe a high tea on occasion, like other museums he'd seen.

When he reached the area, Bill was already seated at a table. Unlike his usual three-piece suit, the man wore khakis and a polo as if he'd finished a round of golf. A tiny espresso cup rested on the table in front of him.

Carter waved at the barista, and the young man, a college student who worked part time for the museum, nodded and started brewing a cup. After joining Bill at the table, it only took five minutes for Carter to update the man. "So that's how the meeting went."

Carter watched as red climbed Bill's neck.

"That's it? What did you do?" The man sputtered a moment. "We aren't turning over either painting."

"Maybe not, but we should investigate."

"What's there to investigate? The prior director created an exhibit. He found a piece of art that someone misplaced in basement storage and displayed it. Then as part of that display of German Expressionist art, he negotiated the loan of a piece of art from a museum in Hanover. It wasn't a cheap loan either." The man growled. "Don't people understand the idea of a loan is that you aren't buying the piece?"

Carter opened his mouth, then decided against trying to insert some truth into the man's rant. He didn't know of a real loan that didn't charge something, and the loaning museum or collector had the right to make sure their work wasn't harmed and was well insured while at another location. Somehow he knew that wouldn't matter to Bill.

"What? Have something to say? Spit it out."

"The key isn't what we think. It's what the heir wants. If we approach her with consideration, we may diffuse the situation. If we instead bluster about it not being our problem, she will make it ours."

"How? How on earth could one old woman do that?"

"For the loaned piece, she files a lawsuit saying that as the custodian of the painting, it's our problem. Maybe she seeks an injunction that will prohibit us from sending it back when the loan ends." He sighed. "Then she can sue for restitution of the one in our collection. There are probably a dozen ways she could keep us tied in knots."

"She's old."

"And that matters?"

"We wait her out."

How had this man been appointed to the board? "That's not in the best interest of the museum or the art."

"The art is an object that is owned by a museum in Germany. If she wants it so badly, she can sue them. I still say we wait her out on the one in our collection." Bill clenched his jaw, then huffed out his breath. "Look, I'm not trying to be difficult. My job is to protect the museum's interests. It's also your job. If we can't get loans from collections and museums, our ability to hold fresh exhibits disappears. It's that simple."

"It's not that simple to her or the law." He should have requested Janae come to this meeting. Thinking he could explain the devil-in-the-details nature of a lawsuit in a way that Bill would listen to and understand had been foolhardy. His passion was the art. Not the legal nuances. "Look, I know you think I'm not focused on the museum, but a lawsuit that drags on for years won't serve us well. It will suck up financial resources and staff time and land in the press. We will spend every board meeting for as long as it's happening talking about the litigation, what's going wrong, what might go right, and what the media will say or do to harm the long-term reputation of the museum. It will be a distraction and nuisance. If you can get the board to give me the authority to negotiate with Mrs. Seeger, we could find a solution. Often people just want to be heard. Stonewalling and ignoring her will only make things worse."

"No."

The silence stretched as Carter waited for an indication the man would reconsider. "No?"

"Absolutely not." He rubbed a hand over his face. "Look, there's no way Stanley will agree. I'm shielding you from his wrath."

"I don't need your protection."

"You really do. There are things at stake you don't understand."

"Then explain them." He bit out the words, knowing his frustration leaked through.

"No."

"Then I'll track down the prior director, because someone has to work with me before this explodes."

"Don't be ridiculous or overly dramatic." Bill took a sip of his coffee. "Trust me. This is for the best."

As he walked away, Carter realized the problem.

He didn't trust Stanley's yes-man.

After Janae closed the door to her office, she took time to write her notes on the meeting with Mrs. Seeger and her attorney while it remained fresh in her mind. Then she worked through some emails that had come in before heading to the reception area. Chloe stood as she reached the desk.

"So? How did it go?"

"I'm not sure. Shaw gave me a folder with documents I'll review. But we'll need background legal research. He's staying coy on the specifics of his claim other than the Germans stole the art and the museum has to fix it." Janae picked up one of the sticky-note pads from Chloe's desk and jotted a couple thoughts. "In addition to the painting the museum owns, he's focused on the idea the Elliott is the bailee for the loaned painting. That's creating an urgency to move while the painting is still here."

Chloe's shoulders scrunched up toward her ears, and she frowned. "What does that mean? Remember I didn't go to law school."

"Not yet." Janae considered her friend. "Bailee is a fancy legal term for someone who holds another's property in trust. Think about when someone stores their belongings in a storage unit. The owner of the storage company doesn't own the items deposited in a specific unit. They're owned by the person who bought the goods. The owner simply stores the goods outside their apartment or home."

"Okay." Chloe drew out the word in a way that reminded Janae what was simple to her didn't necessarily translate that way to someone else.

"Or how about when you take your clothes to a dry cleaner. Who owns the clothes while they're cleaned?"

"I do."

"But you don't possess them while the company cleans them."

Chloe's eyes widened and she straightened. "I understand. So Mr. Shaw is arguing the museum is holding the painting for someone else. So it's got the responsibilities of a . . . bailee."

"Exactly. Nothing would challenge that idea. The Elliott doesn't claim it owns that painting." She made a note on the paper. "So that's the first thread I'll explore. But I want you to look into the statute of limitations."

"Under what theory?"

That was the question. There were many directions Shaw could take. "Let's look at laches and bailee status." She tapped her pen against the paper before pulling off the top note and handing it to Chloe. "I'll know more after I examine what he gave us."

Chloe took the slip and gave it a cursory read. "You know it will be one-sided."

"Yes, which is why we're going to spend tomorrow at the museum to see what it has on the history of the painting. We need to know that before we dig deeper in the legal options."

Chloe slipped behind her desk and settled in her chair. "I'll start with Google."

"And this is a good time to use one of the legal search engines. It's all about finding the right case." Once she found that, the rest would begin to unravel. It would still take effort, but the way forward would make sense. "I'll be in my office."

Chloe barely nodded as her fingers started flying across her keyboard.

What she didn't have in a law degree, she made up for as a logical and critical thinker.

Janae entered the conference room, quickly sliding all the chairs back up to the table and wiping it down before collecting the file. A minute later, she sat behind her desk and started with the first document. She frowned as she struggled to read what was printed on the photocopied page. After a minute she picked up her phone and dialed Carter. When he answered, she launched into her questions. "Have you had a chance to read the file?"

"Not yet."

"Do you have it near you?"

There was a pause, and then he answered. "Got it now."

"Can you look at the first couple of documents?"

Another pause then a whistle. "This looks like German." A pause. "That's right. Shaw said it was in German."

"You don't happen to be fluent?"

"Nope. Took French in college. Hasn't done a lot for me and doesn't help here."

Janae flipped through the papers in the file. "I don't see a translation, though I thought he mentioned one. Do you happen to have it?"

"No, and I don't know that I'd trust his."

"True, but it would give us a starting point while we got our own." She rubbed her forehead. "This was supposed to help or at least give us some clarity. I'll call him and ask for his translation while we work on our own."

"Do you think Monroe has a German professor?"

"I don't know, but I know someone who does. You know her too."

"I do?"

"Margeaux Robbins. She's on your board and teaches at Monroe." Janae wished she'd had the thought first. "If there's not a professor, there might be an exchange student who can at least help us get a basic understanding of what we're looking at. Anything would be better than the nothing I'm getting right now."

"Do you want me to reach out to her?"

"No, I can do that. We've been friends for years." She wrote a note on the folder, and then chewed on the end of the pen as she considered what he could focus on. "How's your hunt going? Maybe give me everything on the history of the painting and its painter. Does it have value?"

"It's a Botticelli."

"And?"

"He was an Italian master, but no it doesn't have value on the level of the one included in the auction of Paul Allen's estate collection."

"What do you mean?"

"That collection sold for more than a billion dollars."

"I can't fathom that many zeroes."

Carter snorted. "That makes two of us. But I'll have to do some digging on Paula Modersohn-Becker. She's not someone I'm very familiar with."

"Me either, but I like the look."

"She fits nicely with some of the other women artists from her time." There was a murmur of voices. "I'd better go."

"Before you do, have you updated Bill Yates yet?"

"Yes. He wasn't thrilled or cooperative. He thinks I need to be protected from Stanley." He sighed and she heard a rustle like his phone rubbed against his face. "We'll have to be creative and not look for help from him."

"He's not the only board member."

"But he is influential and has the institutional knowledge I'm missing. I've got to run."

After the call ended, Janae gave herself a couple of minutes to consider what Carter had shared before she jotted a quick email to Margeaux asking for a German speaker at the college. Maybe there wasn't one, but she'd bet Margeaux would find a way.

Why would Bill be unwilling to help protect the museum against a lawsuit?

She didn't know enough yet to probe, but she made a note to dig deeper, then picked up the stack of paper and decided to try again. She didn't need to understand every word to get the gist of the message. Then she'd try the new link and see if between the two she had enough to anticipate potential problems for the museum. If not, she'd find someone in DC who could help.

Chapter 19

Sunday, November 13

JANAE ROLLED UP HER SLEEVES and rubbed her arm across her forehead. She would think that by early November in the top floor of the carriage house, she'd be too cold to get much work done, but the way her mother directed her to move items about in ever-changing piles, she was hot enough to spontaneously combust. They'd made progress, but she hadn't planned to spend another night out here until the call from Grandma asking for more help had her making the drive with Mom as the sky turned colors with the setting sun.

Frankly, after getting her downtown office ready, she was over cleaning. Another week on the horse farm wouldn't be terrible. But if Grandma needed her, she'd show up and work.

"I hoped we'd reached the end." Janae studied the piles all around the walls. Suitcases lined the far back wall with boxes stacked all around. It represented the detritus of a lifetime pushed everywhere there was a gap. "Guess not."

"We're closer than we used to be." Mom's cheeks had turned red as she dragged another suitcase from under one of the windows. "This room will make a wonderful escape for you after we clear it." She gave the case another tug. "Too bad I can't just roll this to the light. Mom thought suitcases made good storage, but this one's heavy." She paused and took a deep breath. "Do you wonder why your grandma's so focused on cleaning this space now?"

"She's ready for a roommate."

"Maybe." There was hesitation in the word. Mom placed her hands on her hips and surveyed the space, blinking hard the whole time as if that could hide her emotion. "I think we've made a dent."

Janae mimicked her mom's akimbo stance. "A very small one."

"Minuscule."

"Tiny." She pointed at the next item because it was move forward or admit defeat. "So what's in this one?"

"I don't know." Mom moved the suitcase to the lone open space in the room. "Let's find out."

The unzipping sound was loud in the silence. Each time they opened a new box or suitcase, Janae wondered what treasure they'd uncover. One carton might have photographs. The next box held baby clothes. And the one after that, books collected on travels. It was a cacophony of items from a life lived to the full. But each held a mystery that needed Grandma's interpretation or it would remain unsolved.

Mom frowned as she opened the lid. "What's this?"

"The question of the night." Janae leaned closer. "Is that a uniform?"

"Army maybe." Mom carefully lifted it from the case and set it to the side. "My dad served in the Army during World War II. Did he ever tell you about that time?"

"I vaguely remember a story or two. Unfortunately, I wasn't really interested before he died."

"That doesn't surprise me. He was a quiet man. A big teddy bear if you didn't give up on him. It took persistence to get him to hug me."

An old canteen and then some papers came out. At the bottom of the suitcase, a tissue-paper-wrapped item rested.

Janae wanted to rip the paper back but waited for Mom to move. "What do you think that is?"

"I don't know." Something in Mom's voice indicated hesitation to continue.

"I can open it."

"No, that's all right." Mom reached into the suitcase and carefully unfolded the tissue paper from the item.

When she'd removed the last piece, they both stared in the suitcase.

Janae reached forward, then pulled her arms back. "Is that what I think it is?"

"A painting? Out here?" Mom looked around. "This is a terrible place to store an oil painting."

Janae pulled out the small, plain frame and tilted the painting to better see the brushstrokes in the light. She squinted as she tried to make out the scrawled name in the left-hand corner. "Can you read that?"

Mom leaned closer, then shook her head. "We'll have to try the main house where the light is better. Maybe Grandma can fill us in on what this is."

"Good idea." Janae studied it more closely.

They headed outside and then up the steps to the wide porch lining the front of the house.

Janae stood cradling the piece in her arms. It was not quite twelve inches wide and on the small side, but her arms felt the heaviness of a much larger weight.

Grandma met them at the front door, a cardigan wrapped around her frame. "What do you have there?"

"I'm not sure." Janae carried it to the kitchen table where the overhead light gave her a better look at it. She sucked in a breath. "Mom? Grandma, does that say *Brvegel*?" She stumbled over the pronunciation of the odd word.

Grandma laughed, a sound that was rich and flowed from her. "Girl, I love you, but I don't know what that means."

Mom stepped closer and looked at the corner. "Bruegel? This could be old enough the *v* would represent a *u*."

Janae's heart stopped, then lurched into rhythm again. "Wasn't there a famous painter with that name? It's tickling at the back of my mind."

"I don't know." Mom's face scrunched as she studied the small painting of dogs in a window. "What is this?"

Janae felt a sheen of sweat at her temples. "This could be valuable."

Why had Grandpa tucked it under his old military uniform in a suitcase in storage? "I think we need help."

"I think you're right." Mom shook her head. "Who do we ask?"

"You girls are overthinking. It's a cute painting. Odd but cute." Grandma shook her head, her grin spreading as she studied it. "The idea that it's more than a silly painting of dogs is ridiculous. Your dad wouldn't store something valuable in that catchall."

Janae couldn't shake the tingle at the back of her neck that indicated this was something more than they were seeing. She couldn't say why, other than overanalyzing the situation thanks to her meetings with Carter and Mrs. Seeger, but she needed to scrape below the surface. "Looks like we have a mystery." Janae stepped back and studied the painting with a bit of distance. "Grandma, are you sure you've never seen this?"

"Absolutely. I would remember something that silly, but . . ." She shrugged and then gestured at it. "I don't know. Why would it be in a suitcase? Most of the stuff out there is just that. Stuff. Things I should have given away years ago, but never made the time to."

That made sense. "How do we find out more about it?"

Mom frowned and shook her head. "I work with kids. I'm a speech therapist, not an art appraiser."

"Maybe a museum curator could help."

"No need to bother someone like that. Arnold wouldn't store a valuable painting out there. Mice or some other vermin could have found and nibbled on it." Grandma practically swooned. "We lived simple lives."

Janae wondered what Carter Montgomery would make of this mystery. "Let me take it to the Elliott's director. He can help us identify what this is, and he might enjoy the distraction."

Monday, November 14

The first floor of the museum filled with a couple of busloads of middle school kids, and the noise level in the cavernous rooms exploded as their footsteps and laughter reverberated off the stone floor. This group was bused in from Purcellville, their seventh-grade art teachers exposing them to what art looked like in real life. While many had probably explored the halls of the National Gallery of Art an hour away, others would have never wandered the halls of a museum. The visit to the Elliott formed their first exposure to the wonders of seeing the actual paint strokes or chisel marks.

Carter wanted to sink into the moment and form an idea of how the museum could expand its community offerings. Instead, the call he'd taken earlier continued to circulate through his mind. Jarod Shaw had promised the deadline in the demand letter wouldn't move.

All well and good except for the need to conduct his own searches. Relying on the information provided by the opposing attorney wouldn't be adequate since it would contain a bias leaning toward the heirs. But an independent and thorough search would take time he didn't have.

He forced himself to focus on the here and now.

A few of the kids had slowed their steps and paused in front of different works, while others swirled around the edges of the room at a speed that suggested they didn't really see anything. Still, they were here and that created the opportunity for discovery.

Several adults circulated among the kids, likely the parent volunteers.

Doris McGready, one of the docents, stepped next to him and ran fingers through her short gray hair as she eyed the students. "Wish I had their energy."

Carter watched for stragglers in the group. "It would be nice. I've heard you get the school groups wrapped around your fingers quickly."

"Those microphones and receivers you got us help immensely. It's nice to not yell to be heard." She straightened the edge of her navy blazer and grinned, turning her into a charming, older elf. "Let's see if we can't teach those young minds something fun."

The next hour passed as Carter walked between Doris's group and the other. Both women did an admirable job getting and keeping the middle schoolers' attention as they wandered through different wings of the museum on the highlight tour.

Then the students were let loose to try their hand at drawing a copy of their favorite art piece. Carter couldn't wait to see which one each child picked. It would give valuable insight into the items they should emphasize in the future with this demographic. Keeping art relevant and interesting, particularly the eclectic mix that one found in the various exhibits, formed a key part of his job.

Art told stories.

It had always done so, but the docents translated the foreign language into one others could appreciate. They tackled the key challenge of making each piece's story interesting and understandable centuries or millennia after the artist gifted his or her talent to the world.

A young girl with heavy color around her eyes studied him from her seat.

"Can I help you?"

Her intensity didn't waver as she considered him. "Why are you here?"

"I run the museum."

"You spend your days here with old stuff?"

"Yep."

"And you like that?" One eyebrow arched as if she questioned his sanity.

"I do." He took a step closer but made sure she had ample space around her. "What caught your interest today?"

She shrugged but partially leaned over her notebook as if to conceal her work. "Not much."

"You'd help me if you gave me your perspective."

"How?"

"I need to know what you like and what you'd come back to see."

"That's easy."

"Oh?"

"The little sculpture of the dancer."

"The one by Degas?" It was one of the clear treasures in the collection. Small, but a valued gift from a patron.

"Think so."

"Why that one?"

"She looks so alive. How'd he do that?"

"That is the question behind art. We know what we like when we see it. But how did one artist make that piece of metal come to life, when another could do the same thing and it wouldn't feel animated?"

"Exactly. She could stand up and start dancing in the room and I'd join her."

Carter grinned at the image. "That's what drew me to working in a museum. I love art because there's something special that happens when we interact with it."

"Sure." She looked down at her drawing and then frowned. "It's not right."

"May I?" He gestured to the edge of the bench near her. When she nodded, he sat on the edge, and then glanced over her shoulder. "You have a good start. Maybe draw around the spaces where nothing is. I had an art tutor once who told me that was the key to good art. Focus on what isn't there, on the voids. That technique helps us see what *is* really there." A man moved—someone who had caught his attention a couple of times. The man stayed on the periphery but always where Carter could see him. However, he never interacted with the students. "Good luck with your drawing."

"Thanks."

Carter stood and edged toward the man. A simple conversation would confirm he was overthinking the man's quiet alertness. As Carter stepped across the room, the man met his gaze, and his eyes widened before he turned away. Then the man stepped into an alcove and disappeared.

Carter picked up his pace, dodging a group of giggling girls and between a gaggle of boys who watched the girls. When he reached the alcove, it was empty. He hurried past, but the adjoining room was empty as well.

Was it the same man he'd seen a couple of other times?

Or was Carter just paranoid?

He turned, examining his memory. First his sister, the strange envelope she'd left behind. Then all the questions about the paintings and Stanley's strange reaction to the threat of lawsuit. No, his mind was alerting him to something.

Ariel appeared in the entrance to the gallery and waved him over.

Carter joined her in the doorway. Her bohemian outfit of flowing skirt and colorful T-shirt had reds and greens today, a reflection of the drawing she'd posted in the small kitchenette of a drooping Christmas tree with tired red ribbons decking its boughs.

"There's an important call for you."

"Take a message, Ariel." He still wanted to search for the man, make sure he was gone.

"No, this one's too important."

"That sounds mysterious."

"You have no idea." At this statement her eyes widened, as if that should tell him something.

"All right." Probably better to go along with her so he could get back to talking with the classes' chaperones and kids. As they walked toward the administrative suite, he tried to pull more information from his assistant.

"I can't tell you much. If I do it might become real, and that would be weird. And bad. And a mess."

Ariel hustled back toward the office like someone chased her.

Carter touched her arm and she startled to a stop with a squeak. "Ariel, what's wrong?"

"There's a man in the office waiting for you. He wanted me to call you, but I didn't feel safe with him." She shuddered. "I work in a museum. A museum." She raised her hands. "We handle art, not drugs. So why is someone who looks like they could be a drug lord in the office asking to see you?"

"What?"

"Exactly!" She turned away and started back toward the office. "It doesn't make any sense. And I know I'm probably showing my bias all over the place, but I couldn't stay alone with him, so I pretended you didn't pick up your phone."

Carter touched her shoulder and she startled again. "Why don't you go to the cafe and get one of those expensive waters you like so much? I'll handle the mystery man and text you when he's left."

"Would you do that?" Her posture collapsed and she wobbled. "Thank you." Before he could respond, she changed direction and charged for the stairs. "I'm putting it on your tab."

"Fine." He took a moment to rub his hands over his face, trying to decipher what she'd said and what it meant. With his intuition pinging and her fears exploding, he was more than a little concerned that he was walking into something potentially dangerous. But what was he supposed to do? The only way to know was to move forward. He'd grab one of the security guards, but like many museums the security at the Elliott consisted of retired police officers and volunteers. He didn't want to unnecessarily escalate a situation.

When he reached the glass door to the office, he looked through it before pulling it open. A man stood on the other side studying one of the lesser works the museum owned that hung on the wall. The man was dressed in black, and Carter squinted. He looked like the man he had tried to follow from the Virginia gallery.

He opened the door and marched in with a firm step. "I heard you were looking for me."

The man pivoted, his dark eyes intense. "I see your lovely assistant did not return."

"Taking a break."

"I think she does that a lot."

Carter gave a noncommittal shrug. "How can I help you?"

"I'm looking for your sister." The man's attention lanced through him as the words caused Carter's mind to freeze.

"You're a year too late. You can find her in a graveyard."

"You are a fool if you believe that." The corner of the man's lips curled in a snarl, and Carter noted the hint of an accent. "Charlotte is not dead."

"Tell that to her mourning son."

"Little boys do as they are told."

Carter slipped his hands into his pockets wishing he had his cell phone. He needed to call the police. Get this nut out of here. "You need to leave."

"No."

"Yes." Carter forced eye contact even as he wanted to retreat.

"See, Dr. Montgomery, your sister has something very important to us. Tell her we will take something important to her if she does not cooperate. And if that doesn't work, then we can take something important to you." The man shrugged. He flipped a card to the floor. "We will be in touch." The man sauntered from the office, leaving Carter sucking in air and staring at a card empty of everything but ten digits.

Chapter 20

THE DOG PAINTING STOOD ON the corner of the credenza in Janae's office, a light shining on it. It filled a canvas slightly smaller than a sheet of paper, made somewhat larger by the small frame, simple and unadorned. She tapped her thumb against her teeth, the other arm wrapped around her stomach as she considered the painting. "What were you doing with this, Grandpa?"

He hadn't always been the most talkative man, but this seemed big to keep hidden.

There was no other word for putting a possible Bruegel in a suitcase in a room no one would search. She'd conducted online hunts in pockets of time, and each seemed to confirm this might be an actual Bruegel. It didn't make sense.

She picked up her phone and dialed Grandma. When her grandmother answered, she launched into her questions. "What did Grandpa do after the war?"

"Well, hello to you too, young lady."

"Sorry. I'm staring at the painting we found and trying to understand how Grandpa had it."

"I wouldn't read too much into it, dear. You act like this painter was important."

"He is." No need to explain to Grandma how much his paintings could sell for. The numbers would send the women into a heart attack. "What was Grandpa's job?"

"He sold insurance for a time. Then got tired of that and switched to several other jobs. He moved a lot but always landed on his feet. By the time we met he'd finally outrun whatever demons chased him after the war. It always surprised me because he said he hadn't seen much in the way of combat, but the war still marked him."

"Did you have enough money?"

"Always. He was a good provider and a hard worker. It felt like he was outrunning something. I was never sure exactly what." There was a wistfulness to her tone. "He stumbled into teaching, you know. It was never his plan, but it became his calling. Those kids loved him, and the boys needed his tough love. He helped set many a James Dean wannabe back on track."

"Sounds like an amazing influence."

"He really was." Grandma sighed. "Is there anything else you needed? I'm tired."

"No. Thanks, Grandma."

The conversation hadn't highlighted how Grandpa collected the piece Janae stared at. It didn't explain why he'd owned it and tucked it in a hidden place. And it certainly didn't stop her imagination from running to nefarious reasons for hiding it other than he'd grown bored with it or forgotten it. There was a whimsy to the painting that reminded her of some little items in his study. He hadn't often let her in there, but she'd helped Grandma with cleaning out the old books after he died. Then she'd gotten busy on another case and when she returned home next, the room served as Grandma's sewing room.

The paint had a crackled character to it that made her think it was old. Very old. A stone window framed the painting of two lapdogs tied to the same stake. It was small—about nine by ten inches—yet the detail was exquisite. Janae felt she could reach out and pet the dogs. The smallest was black with a tuft of white on one ear. The other looked like a bichon frise with its fluffy white hair.

A tap at her office door startled her, and she hurried away from the credenza.

Chloe watched her quizzically. "Wanted to let you know I'm leaving."

"Thanks."

"You all right?"

"Yeah." Janae sighed. "Just a long day." She didn't want to burden Chloe with just how long.

"Margeaux told me."

"Told you what?"

"About you finding Mark Ashby. That's not the kind of thing you keep from a friend."

Janae swallowed, feeling the truth of the words to her core. "I didn't want to burden you."

"Then I guess we aren't really friends, because friends share burdens."

"You're right. I'm sorry."

Chloe studied her a minute, then nodded as if seeing what she needed to. "Thank you." Then she smiled. "Don't stay too late. Remember you came back here to get away from fifteen-hour days."

"Thanks, Gym Mom. See you in the morning."

"Tomorrow I have to work my paying job." Chloe rolled her eyes, softening the impact of her words. Then she straightened the edges of her cardigan that hung over skinny jeans and a clean white T-shirt. She looked cuddly and mildly professional in a casual way. "Don't forget to lock up behind me."

"Yes, ma'am." Janae tried to keep the tone light, but Chloe watched her another moment before nodding and heading toward the front door. Janae followed and made a show of locking up because otherwise her friend wouldn't leave.

As soon as Chloe got in her car, Janae unlocked the door for Carter and went back to her office. She slumped in her office chair and studied the small painting from that vantage point. "Where did you get this, Grandpa? And why did you hide it?"

Or had he forgotten it?

The answer to that question wouldn't tell her how he got it.

Grandpa had treated her like a princess. He always told her how special she was—the only child of his only child—and that she could do anything. His savings had paid for half her tuition in undergrad, and then he'd believed in her enough to continue that through law school. He'd invested in her, and that had made the difference when she'd wanted to give up during calculus and then torts.

But this painting? It didn't fit with the man she'd known.

He was more likely to have *Dogs Playing Poker* on his wall than art like this. The dogs were the same, but this one looked like a master. Could it be a really good copy? Maybe. Was it a Bruegel? She wasn't sure, but it belonged on the wall of a fine home, not wrapped carelessly in a suitcase hidden in storage.

"Hello?" Carter's voice carried from the reception area. She'd sunk too deeply into her thoughts and must have missed the bell.

"Back here." She stayed in the chair, too drained to pretend to know how to handle the coming conversation. Did she dare to bring him into her secret? What kind of power would that give him over her?

Carter stepped in, his pants pressed perfectly, even though it was the end of what had to be a long day for him. His gray cashmere sweater topped a white button-down poking out from the neck. His light hair was tousled as if he'd run his fingers through it a few minutes ago, creating a casual air that she liked. A lot. A slight smile creased his mouth, and she found herself responding.

"Hi, Carter."

"Janae." He glanced around her office, and she'd bet he noticed every detail, but he somehow skimmed past the painting. "What's the grand mystery?"

She pointed at her credenza. "What do you make of the painting?"

"Painting?"

"*Dogs tied together in a window.* At least that's what I'm calling it."

He approached the desk, hands shoved in his pockets as if to keep from reaching for it, and he took a minute to study it. "Where did you find this?"

"Not yet. What's your initial impression?"

"I'm not an expert in all art."

"Of course not." She pressed against her heart where it had started pounding. "I just want your thoughts. From your years in museums and studying."

"Can I pick it up?"

She nodded.

He wished he'd brought gloves. Something to protect the art from his oily fingers.

The piece was striking in its simplicity and beauty, much like the woman standing next to him. Yet, while she was a new beauty, this one felt like he'd seen it or something like it before. The question was where. Lapdogs weren't an uncommon theme in the old masters, but usually they functioned as props to identify the wealth of the people in the painting. This piece focused on the dogs and had them chained as if in a zoo, yet they weren't. The setting wasn't clear, but it wasn't a typical portrait or landscape.

"Tell me how you found this."

He continued to study the painting and tried not to cringe as she told of finding it when helping her mom and grandma at her grandparents' home. The sadness in her voice as she said her grandpa's name caught his attention. "You miss him."

She swallowed hard and blinked a few times. "My family is small. Just my parents, grandparents, and me. Helping Grandma clean everything reminds me of how much I miss Grandpa. He was my biggest cheerleader."

"I'm sorry." The words seemed small, but they were honest because he understood the experience of saying good-bye to people who made up your world.

"Thank you." She cleared her throat. "Do you think this is valuable?"

"I'm not sure, but it has the look of the Flemish painters, maybe from the 1500s. I'd need to do some research."

"Would you be willing?" She pointed at the name in the left-hand corner. "Did you see the name?"

"I did." But he didn't want to tell her what that name might mean, not yet. "We have some tools at the museum that can help us examine the pigments and brushwork. The animals are unique." He let his gaze rove the small painting. "It's charming in its own way." And could be valuable beyond what she imagined.

She had her thumbnail between her teeth as if to keep from coming undone. "My grandpa was more of a velvet-dogs-on-the-wall guy. He never understood my appreciation for art when I took a college class."

"He had good taste in this one. Have you found others?"

"Paintings?" She paled as if the thought hadn't occurred to her. "No."

"Hmm. Then he wasn't a collector."

"If he was, he didn't know how to protect them."

"Yes, there's some cracilature, but that could be based on age alone. Let me take it to the museum as a piece I'm consulting on."

"If you can keep my grandpa out of it, that would be nice." She looked worried rather than excited.

"What are you concerned about?"

"I don't know. But it feels very odd and unlike my grandpa." She kept looking at the painting, brow furrowed and shoulders hunched. "He was a quiet man but respected around town. I'm counting on his reputation to help me launch my firm. Small towns can be so funny."

"Maybe he picked it up on a trip and forgot about it or changed his mind about hanging it."

"That's the thing. Grandpa didn't like traveling. He served at the end of World War II and spent a couple years in Germany. He said that was all the time away from home he needed." She wrapped her arms around her middle as if trying to protect herself.

"Do you have a time frame for when he got it?"

She pulled herself from whatever thoughts had captured her attention. "Not really. Grandma's not saying much."

He considered the painting, pointing at the block letters at the bottom. "Bruegel. There were several successful Bruegels, but I'd start with Pieter Bruegel the Elder and work my way forward."

"I can do that." She finally turned her attention to him. "It's not normal for a family like ours to have a Pieter Bruegel the Elder painting in a suitcase."

"No."

"How on earth could one of his paintings be hidden in my grandparents' carriage house?"

"I don't know, but there are a lot of intermediate steps to determine if this is a Bruegel or just a clever copy. That wouldn't be extraordinary."

"The last name on the canvas helps, right?"

He could feel the teacher taking over even as he knew he needed to wrap up and get home to Andrew. He wasn't the same person who could talk about all of art's mysteries for hours as he used to. He had larger responsibilities in the shape of a nine-year-old nephew. "Pieter the Elder was the patriarch of a family of accomplished painters, but it could be his because of similar paintings that have been attributed to him involving other animals. I'd want to compare this to those other paintings." He rubbed his chin. "We'll also need to do more detailed analysis of the canvas and pigments to be certain the age matches when he painted."

"How do I do that?"

"I can recommend a firm in DC. There are many you could use, but this one is close and should do a good job for you." He pulled up some information on his phone and jotted it on a piece of paper he then slid across the desk. "Call them for an appointment. Then look for a catalogue raisonné. It will be a book that contains all his paintings and prints. If there isn't one, then it's a harder search for paintings attributed to him." Had this formed a part of a larger painting, or could it have served as a test for another painting? "I can take it to do some initial tests while you wait for an appointment."

While he'd leave the bulk of the research to her, Carter knew he'd do a bit of research himself. It was fun to imagine what could be this painting's story.

He turned to her, to see if she had any more questions, but froze as he caught her studying him. What did she see?

***

There was something infinitely charming about a man who was this educated and easy with others yet melted into a bit of uncertainty around her. There was electricity in the air between them, and she didn't know what to do with it. She swallowed and tried to remember what he'd said, then glanced down and picked up the paper.

"Where should I store this for now? Doesn't seem right to take it back to the carriage house and here isn't the safest place in town."

"Does anyone know you have it?"

"Just Mom and Grandma."

"Then it should be okay here. If you're not comfortable with that, I can always take it on loan to the museum and slide it into our safe." He studied it with that curious cock to his head. "It might be nothing more than a charming copy, but if it's real . . . well, it should be somewhere protected."

"Yes. It's that what-if that will keep me from sleeping." She pulled out her phone. "Let me take a couple photos of the painting, and then I can follow you to the museum."

He watched as she snapped several images with her phone. "Don't forget to photograph the back."

"Oh?"

"Yes. There are often identifying marks that can reveal parts of the story."

"What should I look for?"

"Things like stickers and marks that indicate where the painting has been. If it's been consigned for sale, the auction house will put a stamp on it. Some private owners have stamps as well. I like to be prepared with photos of anything we might need in the future."

"I can appreciate that."

"My first step at the museum will be a series of photos and then sim-ple testing."

"That sounds dangerous." She put her phone in her pocket and picked up the painting, placing it in a tissue-paper-lined box. There was some-thing about the tied dogs that made her smile. "Like it could harm the painting."

"I won't hurt it." He gravely accepted the box she handed him. "Thanks for trusting me with it."

She nodded, and her throat suddenly closed. It took a moment to get her voice back. "Help me find the truth?"

"Absolutely."

It was a single word, but she believed him.

She followed him to the museum in her car, the roads relatively empty as if the town had rolled up the rug and gone to bed early. He waited for her to park and then led her to a side door she'd never noticed.

"This will take us straight into the administrative wing." He held the door for her, then hurried to the security panel inside the entryway and entered a code of some sort. She intentionally turned aside, waiting for him to lead the way.

"Wow."

"Underwhelming?"

"I don't know. I guess I expected something like *Wonder Woman 1984*."

"Even if that was real, that was set at the Smithsonian. We don't have the budget for all those bells and whistles, but we do have a few at our disposal."

"What should I do next?" Part of Janae wanted to yank back the ques-tion and pretend she hadn't asked it. The other part knew she had to find an answer, but she wasn't sure she liked the way Carter watched her. "What?"

"What if you hate the answer you find?" He led the way down the hall and into his office.

"Don't you think my mind is already spinning in a dozen what-ifs, none of them good?"

"Contact Haney & Sons. They can give you an opinion on what you have."

"That feels risky."

"Searching for the truth usually is. The painting will be ready whenever you need it. We're merely holding it for you."

"Acting as my bailee."

"Exactly." He grinned at her. "See, I am learning something from you."

She looked from the box holding the painting to him. "What would you do?"

He didn't answer immediately. "I'm not sure. You're right that this could launch a process that's uncomfortable, but I would. The truth matters more than how we feel."

She rubbed her face and then raised her eyebrows. "Ah, ethics."

"It matters." He reached into a drawer in his desk and then started filling out a paper.

"I know."

"I think you even study it at law school." Carter extended the paper to her.

"A sort of ethics." She took the paper. "Thank you."

"You're welcome." He restacked his items and stood. "You don't have to do anything today. The painting is protected in the Elliott's safe. It was hidden for years and doesn't have to come into the light right away." He placed everything in his messenger bag but didn't leave. "Don't let some sense of guilt or obligation force you into a rushed decision. It will take time to figure out that painting's history."

"Thank you."

"You'll make the right decision." A ding sounded, and he pulled out his phone. "Sorry, but I need to respond quickly."

"No problem, I'll wait here." As he stepped away, she didn't follow him. Instead, she opened the box and stared at the painting. She wanted to get this right but didn't want to ruin a good man's reputation with careless speed. Grandpa had always been her rock, and she felt shaken by how the discovery and the questions it generated shook her. What else was hidden?

Carter returned to grab the painting, a frown marring his forehead. "Everything okay?"

"No. Yes, I have to get home." He didn't meet her gaze as he spoke, so she decided to let him off the hook.

She replaced the lid on the box and stepped back. "I appreciate your help. We can put that in the safe and connect later."

He nodded, though he seemed far away.

As she watched him carefully place the painting in a small safe in his office and then walked beside him back outside, she wondered what had happened to pull him so far away from her. Had the text been an easy excuse to end the night early? For the life of her she couldn't figure out why.

Chapter 21

DURING THE SHORT DRIVE TO his home on the edge of Kedgewick, Carter couldn't shake the feeling he'd had the opportunity to take things deeper with Janae. Could she be the best thing that had happened to him for a while? Maybe, but the timing couldn't be worse. When his security system had alerted, he'd known he had to call it a night. Andrew was in the middle of a meltdown, and though his nephew didn't have those often anymore, when they happened, he turned into someone the teenage sitter couldn't handle.

This shadow part of his life he hid from most people he knew. Not on purpose, necessarily.

He'd been so surprised by Charlotte's return after eight years of silence. He and his parents had accepted she might be dead, when she'd called and asked for help. Charlotte's last frantic calls made him wonder what she had become involved in. She'd begged their parents to come and take Andrew immediately, insisting that he needed to disappear because her ex-boyfriend had reappeared after being absent for eight years. In the middle of that, Stanley had dragged Carter to Indianapolis on an art buying spree, and he'd found himself somewhere he'd never been invited on his own—his sister's studio.

It had been surreal. And left his head spinning.

She'd insisted she was okay, but he hadn't been convinced.

Next thing Carter knew, they were planning a funeral, and he was guardian of his nephew, determined to protect Andrew from whatever Charlotte had feared.

The what or who remained a mystery. So Carter was very careful. Maybe to an extreme.

But when he didn't know if the danger was real or imagined, or where it came from, he didn't know what else to do.

Moving into the area months earlier meant most people didn't know him. They didn't realize he came with a nephew who depended on him, and that was a double-edged sword. It gave Andrew a layer of protection, but it also meant no one cut Carter slack when he had to attend to the most important person in his life even when inconvenient.

Carter had to find a way to develop a life independent of Andrew while still making his nephew a key priority. It could happen if he applied creativity to the scenario now that he'd found a woman who intrigued him.

After parking in the bungalow's driveway, he hurried through the back door into the kitchen. "Lindsay? Andrew?"

"In the living room." Lindsay's voice didn't sound strained, and Carter couldn't hear any evidence of an ongoing crisis.

When he stepped into the room, he knew why. Andrew lay across the couch, head on a pillow, while Lindsay brushed his hair off his forehead in a rhythmic, repeating motion.

"Is he asleep?"

"No. My mom told me to try this the next time he panicked. Drew picked a movie, and we took a bit of a break, didn't we?" Andrew didn't twitch, and she kept up the circling motion. "*Monsters University* for the win."

"I'm glad." He sank onto the recliner that sat kitty-corner to the couch and the large-screen TV. "You can head home."

The teenager eased away from Andrew and then stood, her jeans torn in that way Carter didn't understand, but the oversized sweatshirt looked like she'd painted the design.

"Did you create that?"

She glanced down at her shirt, color rising in her cheeks. "Yes."

"It's nice." The details in the white hydrangeas against the purple cloth were impressive.

"Thank you. It was an art project." She walked toward the door then paused. "Sure you don't need me anymore tonight?"

Andrew shifted as if waiting for the answer, the first sign of independent life Carter had noticed. "We're good, aren't we, Andrew?"

Andrew nodded, and she met Carter's gaze with a wise look.

"Sounds good. See you later, Drew." Lindsay was the only one who called the nine-year-old that, but he seemed to like it from her.

Right about the time Carter wanted to remind him about politeness, Andrew stirred and then pushed to a sitting position. "Bye, Lindsay."

After the door closed behind the nanny, Carter stood. "Hungry?"

Andrew shrugged. "I guess." He trailed Carter into the kitchen and sat at the small table. "Can we have corn dogs?"

Carter's stomach rebelled at the idea, but he could always make something else for himself. "What? Not up for a steak tonight?"

"Nope."

"All right, let's get a corn dog going for you." It might not win him Dad of the Year awards, but Andrew's animated conversation let him know that Uncle of the Day was in his future.

Wednesday, November 16

The next day started with a call almost as soon as Janae reached the office. Since she was the only one there, Janae quickly started taking notes. Eleanor Larsen's voice barely reached Janae through the phone, but enough to learn she might have a new client.

"My brother died and I need help."

"With his estate?" Janae hadn't done any estate work in Philly, but it should be simple to learn. After all, Joseph Larsen had been larger than life and she well remembered his class. A high school geometry teacher for fifty years, he had every person in town between her grandma and Janae in his classes. Then he'd retired and invested the next years in mentoring young people. The man had made an impact on most of Kedgewick and the surrounding communities.

"Yes." The woman's voice took on a more forceful edge. "His will left everything to his beloved goldendoodle, Mr. Whiskers."

Janae blinked. "His dog?"

"Yes. I don't think that's right or what he really wanted."

"I see." She thought a moment. "Do you have a copy of his will?"

"Yes."

"Did he have an attorney?"

"That nasty Mark Ashby."

Jane fought not to flinch at the man's name.

"It's sad about his death, but who would let my brother leave everything to a dog? I could see one of the charities he worked with, but a dog?" A note of indignation filled her voice.

"Can I ask who recommended me to you?"

"Your grandma. Faye and I have been friends since we both joined a Bible study twenty years ago." She sighed. "Your grandma insisted I call you when I told her about this fiasco yesterday."

"Can you come by this morning?"

"I'm in town now."

"Great. I'll have the coffee ready when you arrive."

Ten minutes later, Janae scanned the simple will while the older woman sat at the conference table with a mug of black coffee. The *You've got this* message on the mug made Janae smile each time she looked across the table—it was so incongruous in the woman's hands. But she'd take the message that she could figure this out. One thing about the law was that you could research your way to any answer if you were stubborn enough.

A scan of the will showed a straightforward directive. "My quick research since your call revealed that trusts for the care of pets are liberally construed in their favor." She kept scanning and then reread a paragraph. "How much do you think your brother had accumulated?"

"His estate should be around a million dollars. He was frugal and his home has increased in value like everyone else's around here."

"And you aren't the trustee."

"No. The attorney wrote himself in."

Janae kept scanning and found the language, then she turned on her tablet and scanned the code again. "I think we have a couple ways to challenge the trust. First, we can challenge that Mark made himself the trustee, and then we can challenge that the scope of the trust is too much for one dog. There's a provision for limiting the amount kept in trust when it exceeds what will be needed to provide for the dog."

"So you can get it cancelled?"

"We can try, but I think the better path is to have you appointed as trustee while at the same time stating a much smaller trust than one million dollars will more than adequately care for the dog." She scanned the will. "What's the dog's name again?"

"Mr. Whiskers."

Oh my. "How long did your brother have the animal?"

"About five years. He's a nice dog, but I'm so confused about how everything transpired."

"Did your brother marry or have children?" Janae couldn't remember him talking about his family, but it had been at least twelve years since she'd had his class.

"No. So if the trust is overturned or made smaller, what happens to the rest?"

"Under Virginia's code, it would go to you and any other surviving siblings so long as you don't have surviving parents."

She shook her head with a wry twist to her lips. "Oh no. They've been gone for years." She considered the copy of the will she'd kept. "I don't need the money, though a bit would be nice. I just think it should go to a charity he believed in. There were many that he invested his time and talent in since retirement."

"If the court agrees that the trust is excessive, then you will have the opportunity to make those decisions on your brother's behalf."

Eleanor blinked rapidly and then swiped under her eyes. "Thank you."

After they discussed the fee, Janae walked her to the door. "I'll get started on this today and be in touch by the end of the week."

After her second client left, Janae locked the door so she could focus on researching the best approach and determine whether the will had already been filed with the probate court. Once she determined that hadn't happened, she drafted a request for administration of the will, laying out the details as Eleanor had explained them.

She wasn't sure who to serve. Probably Mr. Ashley since Mark had died, but she crafted the argument in such a way that the firm would have no choice but to go on the defensive and convince the court the dog should inherit roughly a million dollars that the firm would administer, likely with a hefty fee that would line the trustee's pockets.

Mr. Larsen might have grown eccentric, but he had been a good man, and there was a way to make sure Mr. Whiskers was well cared for while also making sure everything Mr. Larsen had worked hard to accumulate was used appropriately now.

Her professors had never warned her the life of an attorney was filled with such unglamorous cases. But this one would help pay for the ones that everyone dreamed about. The ones that could change and expand the law. The ones she had dreamed about taking when in law school. And she also needed to recognize that to Eleanor, this was important.

Reviewing the trust made her wonder what the police had learned about Mark's death.

Had it been natural causes? She hoped so, because she knew she'd never forget finding him in his office like that.

She clicked through entry after entry in the legal database she'd opened. She was surprised how many cases involved pets being cared for through trusts like the one Mark had written for Mr. Whiskers. People did the craziest things for their four-legged furry friends.

A pounding at the front door jolted her from the riveting, rabbit trail–infused research. "Coming." She muttered the word under her breath, well aware the person couldn't hear her but also annoyed they would attack her door like that. Hopefully the person would leave the plate glass windows alone. She didn't want to invest the cost to replace those.

The disruption finally stopped as she made her way down the short hallway to the front of the office.

A man cloaked in a heavy coat with a hat pulled low over his ears and forehead stood at the door. Nothing seemed familiar about him, and Janae hesitated before she reached the door. Should she let him in or was she being paranoid?

Kedgewick was smaller-town Virginia, away from the heart of the nation's capital, and in a place where many knew their neighbors. But it was cold and early enough there weren't many walking around the small downtown.

The man spotted her, and she knew she couldn't retreat to her office now. She finished the walk to the door. "How can I help you?"

He cupped a hand to his ear and frowned. He mouthed the word *what*.

She sighed and raised her voice. "How can I help?"

He mimed opening the door. She unlocked the door, and before she could ease it open, he pushed in.

"Hey!"

He shoved her to the side and started down the hallway.

"What do you think you're doing?" Janae hurried to the reception desk and grabbed the phone. "I'm going to call the police."

"Where is she?"

"Who?" The man ignored her as he pushed open the door to the conference room, grunted, and then stormed to the next door.

"Stop it." Her fingers shook as she tried to dial 911. She finally heard the dispatcher but kept her attention focused on the man. "Who are you looking for?"

"Chloe." He growled the word before following it with a less flattering one.

Janae froze. What could this mass of angry human want with her friend? "She's not here." As the man pivoted and started lumbering to her, she froze. "The police are on the way." She held up the phone. "The dispatcher is on with me now." At least she hoped the person hadn't given up on her when she didn't respond.

The man growled, and Janae wished she had her cell phone so she could snap his picture as he stormed from the lobby, letting in cold air as he slammed outside. Once sure he was gone, Janae hurried to her office to grab her cell while keeping the office handheld with her. She needed to warn Chloe some man hunted her while Janae waited for the police. Was he connected to the other men she'd seen, or was she being paranoid? The others hadn't forced their way into her office and searched for her friend. It scared her to think someone like that could hurt Chloe.

"Janae? Why are you calling?" Chloe didn't sound glad to hear from her, and that was only going to get worse.

"A man came to the office. He was angry, Chloe, and looking for you."

Silence settled between them. "Who was he?"

"I don't know, but he was older. Maybe midfifties, and he wanted you. Stormed through the office trying to find you."

"Did you tell the police?"

"They're on the way. What's going on?"

"Probably just an old boyfriend." Chloe tried to laugh and that made Janae boil.

"We'll get a restraining order, but I don't think he's an ex." Surely he was too old.

Her friend sighed, and Janae could imagine her expanding her petite frame to fill the space wherever she was. "Let me worry about it."

"You know who this was?"

"Maybe. I don't know, I wasn't there."

"I know that." It was Janae's turn to gather her thoughts and collect the fear. "He scared me but left when he realized you weren't here."

"Okay."

"Okay? That's all you have to say?" Janae couldn't squelch the way her voice rose.

"I was talking with the director of Almost Home about taking referrals. Maybe he got the word before we got our first referral."

"Almost Home?"

"A domestic violence center that needs attorneys willing to take referrals."

"Oh. Good idea."

"Thanks. Each woman will come with unique factors and challenges. You won't be bored, but we haven't had a referral. Yet."

"Could be, but he wanted you." The man had been incredibly clear on that point.

"I'm the main point of contact. You'll meet with the clients when we're ready for a hearing. I'll talk them through the process. It's a different level of involvement. Easier to scale and will let you get me to full time faster since my rate is lower than yours."

Janae knew the truth of Chloe's statement. Chloe would amplify her work by handling many client interactions and allowing Janae to focus on the true legal aspects of the work. Her friend would make an amazing attorney if she could find the will to believe in herself in that way. "You'll be careful?"

"There's nothing to worry about."

"You'd tell me if there was?"

"Absolutely."

But there was something in the way that Chloe said the single word that left an uneasy feeling in the pit of Janae's stomach. A rap at the door brought Janae's attention back to the front of the office. "The police arrived."

"File the report. I'll see you tomorrow." Chloe ended the call before Janae could say anything more.

Janae pasted on her professional smile and let the police in. It wasn't easy to report the crime of intimidation without anything to go on other than any images captured on the camera that was tucked behind the front desk.

That would have to be enough, because something was definitely going on.

Chapter 22

THURSDAY MORNING WHEN CHLOE ARRIVED at the firm, Janae hurried to her friend and gave her a quick visual inspection.

Chloe watched with a frown. "What are you doing?"

"Making sure you're okay."

"Why wouldn't I be?"

"The man? Remember the one I called you about?" Janae planted her fists on her hips and stared Chloe down. "That scared me to death. Are you sure you don't know who he was?"

Chloe stashed her mini backpack in the desk's bottom drawer and then stood. "This"—she made a sweeping motion with her arms—"isn't going to work. I survived ten years without you watching over me. I will continue to do so." Something softened in her face. "I appreciate your concern, but I'll let you know if there's anything to be concerned about."

"Trust me, yesterday there was."

"But he's not here now and I am. I'll be fine." She pulled a piece of paper from her jacket pocket. "Here's contact information for one of Margeaux's international students. She thought Anneliese could help with the translation you needed."

Janae took the note. "Thanks. I'll reach out to her today since I don't trust online programs."

"Nor should you." Chloe rolled her eyes. "That won't get you the flavor you need. Margeaux assured me Anneliese is really good."

"Thanks." Janae looked up from the note. "Are you sure you're okay?"

Chloe nodded, but her smile didn't reach her eyes. Janae slipped an arm around her for a quick hug, then headed to her office. She couldn't force Chloe to confide in her, but she could try to reassure her she wasn't alone.

Today that would have to be enough, because she hadn't convinced Libby of the same. The mayor might not believe her, but she had tried to reach out to her friend. The older girl had just pushed her concerns aside. Maybe that was why Libby's suicide still ricocheted through Janae—she was haunted by the sense she could have done more.

She couldn't live through that despair again. The knowledge she could have pushed harder to make sure they were all heard. There was always something that could be done to make a difference.

Janae sank onto her seat, and then before the memories sucked her back in time, she called Carter and gave him Anneliese's information.

"Thanks. Have you called the appraiser I gave you?" His voice sounded curious, but she felt the poke.

"No. I'll do it now."

"Do you need the number?"

"Nope." She pulled the slip of paper with the information from the corner of her desk. "Got it right here." In fact, her gaze had strayed to the piece of paper with his scrawl first thing that morning. "You're sure this is the right firm?"

"Best one I know. We used them at my last job."

"All right. I'll call them."

"Good luck."

"Thanks. Any luck with your research?"

"None, but I haven't had a ton of time to dig in. It almost feels like a conspiracy to keep me busy."

"Well, you call Anneliese, and I'll call the appraiser."

"Deal."

After she hung up, Janae studied the paper. *What's the right thing to do with the painting, God?*

She didn't want to learn her grandfather had been involved in something criminal. In fact, it felt like a betrayal of the man she knew to think that way. But she couldn't think of another reason he'd have that painting. Yet there had to be one.

That question wouldn't leave her alone.

She missed having colleagues to bounce ideas around with. Chloe could get to that point but was still very new to the law, and Margeaux taught. She had barely practiced a year before moving into adjunct teaching. While she was a good attorney, her passion was the classroom. Maybe she could brainstorm, but not when she was in the middle of classes.

So Janae would rely on experts in the various fields. She could do that and needed to in order to get this right. Although she didn't feel like there was a clear response to her prayer, maybe that was because she already knew what she had to do. Slowly she reached for her phone, as if waiting for it to turn into a snake and bite her.

After dialing the appraiser, she set up an appointment for Monday afternoon, then sat back. She'd collect the painting from Carter on the way.

Friday, November 18

The week had passed in a blaze of frustration as Carter left messages in Germany and dug through boxes, choking on dust as he searched for answers. It was easy to believe tracing ownership would require a simple database search, but that relied on people and institutions uploading documents. If the Elliott stood as a representative model, then work remained to modernize records.

On Friday morning, a glance at his calendar set the tone. The day would be cloudy with a chance of millions if he handled an appointment right. The museum's board had made it clear that raising funds fast factored in as one condition of success. Too bad his graduate program in art curation hadn't included fund development in its curriculum. The idea of asking someone for money made his palms slick and heart race.

He'd learn how to do it, but right now he'd rather stroll through a room with Jackson Pollock, teaching high schoolers how to fling paint against a wall.

The good news was, he had another appointment after that. This one with a journalist who wanted to interview him about the exhibit on important female Expressionist artists. He'd spent time last night refreshing his knowledge on the women whose art filled the gallery. It was an impressive list that included the Finnish artist Helene Schjerfbeck, Paula Modersohn-Becker from the German school, and Janet Sobel, the Ukrainian-American artist who had inspired Jackson Pollock's style. There were more, and he hoped the interviewer really was interested in the women and their contributions. He'd be sure to walk her by the Georgia O'Keeffe watercolors, too, since she'd been another transformative artist.

He'd been delighted to see that the first exhibit under his watch would focus on the Expressionist art that he'd written his dissertation on. Now he needed to identify his stamp to put on the museum's future programs. Fortunately he didn't have to do it alone, because the art program at Monroe College could provide a steady stream of students, interns, and professors.

But this job would allow him to focus on his passions only if he managed to keep the lights on, which meant talking to people about investing in the arts.

He looked at his calendar again, his shoulders hunched as he ran his fingers roughly through his hair. His self-education started today. He'd met lots of people through the gallery opening and a few smaller events, but one-on-ones felt forced and intimidating. Guess he'd be himself and ask questions. That would take the focus off himself and help him do what mattered.

The walk from the museum to the Lucky Bean didn't take long, especially when the cold kept him moving. He loved Kedgewick's classic downtown filled with brick storefronts, big plate glass windows, and the occasional wood building. Professional offices were interspersed with restaurants, boutiques, and art shops—the kind that beckoned him to walk through and appreciate the local talent. A country radio station filled a slot next to a brewery, which sat next to a therapist's office. A Pilates studio stood across the street from an old-fashioned soda fountain and candy store. His favorite had to be the bookstore that held game nights and book clubs each week. The amount of traffic that walked through the doors impressed him each time he stopped to look for his next read, and Andrew enjoyed browsing the offerings in the children's section, though the LEGO sets often captured his attention more than the books did. The coworking space next to the bookstore was the créme de la créme. It filled a former gas station and garage with a vibe that breathed industrial creativity and made him wish he didn't have an office so he could take advantage of the espresso maker. This was the kind of picturesque town he'd read about but never lived in, and he found it the perfect blend of charming and welcoming.

The Lucky Bean had a blessedly short line. The dark wood floor was countered by soft ecru walls. A rugged coffee bar of dark wood and imperfect beams provided a barrier between customers and baristas, but the air buzzed with the hiss of the machine and chatter of customers placing their orders. Carter reviewed the menu board before settling on a Dr. Strangelove coffee, hoping the blend of orange, clove, and cinnamon–infused simple syrup didn't taste as odd as the name.

There was a single empty table tucked in a corner by the window, and he carried his mug to it. While he waited, he pulled out his phone and added items to his never-ending to-do list. One day he might get it under control, but this wasn't that season. The first period in any job felt chaotic and overwhelming, and this transition left him feeling like Edvard Munch's *The Scream*.

A dapper man dressed in an out-of-season seersucker suit topped with a heavy coat and hat strolled in, a cane hooked over his arm. The man had a belly to counter his stature and wore a jovial grin. The moment he spotted Carter, he made a beeline for him. "I believe you are my meeting, young man."

Carter hid the inner sigh at the address. "Carter Montgomery. You must be Archibald?"

"At your service." The man gave a small bow, then pointed at the mug. "I see you've already imbibed."

"Coffee."

Archibald inhaled appreciatively. "A Dr. Strangelove I believe. It's a magical blend of aromas, but too sweet for my taste. I'm off to get a cortado. Be back in a moment."

In a few minutes the man returned with the small double espresso cut with milk and sank onto the chair. "This is the best coffee shop in the region, don't you think?"

"I've liked it so far."

The man arched a brow. "So far?"

"Only my second time."

"You are new after all." Archibald took a small sip and closed his eyes. "I can almost imagine I'm in Spain." He opened his eyes, and his expression fell momentarily. "Too bad. Still Virginia in the winter." He set the cup down and studied Carter. "How can I help you?"

"Today's just to learn more about you, sir."

"No sirring required or desired. That's my father after all, God rest his soul." He leaned back and studied Carter as if he could read his heart and mind in a glance. "No one wants to meet with me without an agenda that involves dollar signs. When your assistant reached out, I knew your motives."

The man's abrupt, all-knowing tone set Carter on edge. "Honestly, I'd like to ask you for money, but I don't know what we need or what your interests are. Instead, I hoped to learn from you."

"About me, you mean."

Carter shrugged. "Maybe. But only because I want to find the connection between your passions and the museum."

"If they don't?"

"Exist? Then I'll enjoy a strangely named beverage and walk back to the museum."

The man froze. "You walked?"

"It's not that far, and the sun's shining today." Carter shrugged as he picked up his mug. "Thought I should take advantage of both."

Then Archibald did something completely unexpected. He laughed. "We'll get along brilliantly."

Over the next hour the man provided Carter with an overview of the town and its place in Virginia's history from colonial times to today.

"This area alternately was overrun by or cleared of the Union Army during the Civil War. Leesburg and the surrounding environs changed hands repeatedly. You should explore the local battlefields. It wasn't uncommon when I was young to find items from the war. A bit of digging and you could unearth something." He frowned and crossed his arms over his belly. "Now the developers are scooping up everything and leveling it for communities. You should get involved in the preservation efforts before all our history is bulldozed."

"I'm always willing to listen, but the museum will keep me spinning for a while."

"And while you use that as an excuse, we'll lose another hundred acres of land to development." Something buzzed and Archibald looked at his wrist, then lurched to his feet. "Sorry, but I've got to run. There's a planning meeting for a reenactment. We'll have to do this again." Then the man disappeared through the door, leaving Carter scratching his head.

Had he learned anything valuable? He wasn't sure, but he had gotten a sense of the man's passions, and those ran deep.

By Friday afternoon, Janae was beyond exhausted.

She was physically tired from getting the office finished but was relieved it was ready to welcome anyone who walked through the doors. She'd also made progress at Grandma's, the never-ending project, but she wanted to finish so she didn't live at her parents' for the rest of her life. She had to acknowledge she was also mentally tired. She had welcomed falling into Eleanor's matter regarding Mr. Larsen's trust for Mr. Whiskers, yet she couldn't forget the mystery of her grandfather's painting.

She'd tried a few of the searches that Carter had suggested for the painting, but nothing.

There had to be a way to track down its history, but the painting was as much a mystery today as it was when she found it.

She was trained in logic.

She'd eventually track down the information.

But she couldn't answer the fundamental questions.

Why on earth did Grandpa have this painting? Why store it in a suitcase? And what was she supposed to do with it?

They could squeeze it onto Grandma's walls among the samplers, oil paintings, and framed kindergarten art accumulated across a lifetime. She pulled up the image on her phone. It had a story she needed to uncover. She could use the information Jarod Shaw had provided on the paintings he was contesting to model her search, but she was in over her head and knew it.

Law school had prepared her for many aspects of law, but it had not made her an art historian.

Tracking the history of a painting felt like doing a family genealogy, only with layers of complexity. There were basics she didn't know. Simple things like the title of the painting. It was cute with the two dogs, but she didn't know what to enter into any of the art-specific search engines she'd found online. Honestly, she couldn't be certain she knew who the artist was. The Bruegel in the corner might not mean anything, because she'd come to realize that it could signify a couple of different artists or have been made in a studio but not by that artist.

The complexity left her mind spinning like climbing the stairs in Escher's *Relativity*.

Add in the man who had come after Chloe and finding Mark Ashby's body, and Janae couldn't figure out all the pieces of what was happening in her simple hometown.

She grabbed her laptop and slipped it into her bag. She'd order a pizza and take it home to eat, and then try working again from her parents' home. If all else failed, Janae could slip out to the old schoolhouse that her mom had turned into a studio and see if she could focus there.

Twenty minutes later she parked in front of Margherita's, an Italian eatery that sat on the corner of Founders and Third Streets, a couple of blocks from her office. Another brick building in the charming downtown area, it was sandwiched between a boutique and florist.

When she stepped inside, the yeasty scent of fresh bread and tangy spice of tomatoes and garlic filled her senses. Red-and-white-checked oilcloth covered the tables, with napkin dispenser, salt and pepper, and parmesan cheese nestled on top. The terra-cotta-colored floor tile warmed the room as she approached the rustic wood counter and gave the high school kid manning the register her name.

"We'll have your order in about five minutes."

"Thanks." She accepted her Dr Pepper and went to sit on the padded bench against one of the walls while she waited. She scanned the booths and tables, half of which had people enjoying sandwiches and pizza. Most were unfamiliar to her, but then her gaze landed on a booth in the corner with a man and a young boy.

She frowned as she studied the man. Could that be Carter?

Maybe she could ask his advice on next steps. Then she could focus her efforts over the weekend.

She stood and walked toward them, her joy growing as she recognized his voice. He was talking with the boy about school.

The boy looked up at her, his tousled hair a little long around his ears, and a frown tightening his mouth as he noticed her. "Who are you?"

"Hello, I'm Janae." She held out her hand, which the boy looked at before shaking. Then she turned to Carter. "It's good to see you." Her words died as she realized he didn't seem excited to see her standing at his booth.

There was a guardedness in his expression as he watched her. "Hello, Janae."

"Who is this fine young man?" She forced her smile not to slide from her face as she gestured to the boy.

"This is Andrew." He didn't say anything more but shifted on the seat, the vinyl squeaking with his movement.

She arched an eyebrow as the silence stretched in an awkward taffy pull before she nodded. "Okay. Well, nice to meet you, Andrew. I'd better get my food." Then she spun on her heel and left, forcing herself not to sprint away.

"Who is she, Uncle Carter?" The small voice shook behind her.

"Just a person I know."

The words shouldn't hurt, because they were true, but as she collected her order and walked out, she reminded herself Carter was a client and could be nothing more.

That shouldn't hurt, but it did.

Chapter 23

FRIDAY HAD ENDED WITH A couple of referrals from Almost Home, giving Janae the sense that she might make a swing of this law firm. The pressure to succeed didn't disappear, but now she could take a breath and gather sips of oxygen. Next, she could get on some lists for court-appointed work, but she specialized in civil law, so she didn't anticipate taking on criminal clients unless necessary. Still, it felt good to gain even little bits of traction.

Next week she'd create a website to provide another way people could discover her firm. It would all come together.

Last night had been so weird at Margherita's, and she spent Saturday morning reviewing the awkward scene. She couldn't let it bother her that Carter wanted to draw a fence around his personal life. He was a client. She needed to write that in capital letters across her mind. For all she knew she'd invaded some intense conversation between the two. Maybe he was a big-brother-type mentor to the boy, even if he'd called him Uncle Carter. She simply had to ignore the sparks that had seemed to flare to life any time she was around Dr. Montgomery and instead focus on the business relationship they had.

He clearly didn't consider there to be anything more between them, but she didn't want him to overlook her.

She was used to men in the work context thinking she was a pixie who needed protecting, but she wore a power suit to cover the Tinker Bell. People were wrong to think she hadn't been the strongest character in *Peter Pan*. And they were wrong to underestimate Janae.

But she leveraged that underestimation into her hidden superpower. While she wouldn't mind being Black Widow or her sister Yelena Belova, she'd settle for being the hero for her clients when they needed her to be.

She didn't need Carter to help her clients . . . except he was her only long-term client.

She groaned and closed her eyes.

She'd follow his lead and try to avoid extra interactions with him. Yet her heart didn't want to follow her head. She kept thinking about their time together, looking for a solution to their mysteries. She'd never spent so much time thinking about art, nor had she enjoyed it so much. Carter was the reason why.

Trying to figure out the right approach while sitting at her desk wasn't working, so instead of opening her laptop and working on fruitless research, she spent Saturday at her grandma's working on the carriage house. Together, they'd made significant progress, and as the area cleared, her vision developed for what a lovely living space she could make it. A vision that left her eager to move.

Janae took another black trash bag filled with junk outside. It was a good thing Mom had driven the pickup, because Janae and Mom had almost filled the bed with bags and boxes they'd drop at the dump on the return to the farm.

She paused to take in the peace of the wind rustling the tops of the trees that surrounded the historic home and buildings. She'd begun to imagine what the inside of the carriage house would look like with a fresh coat of paint and her furniture.

Yes, she was excited about the idea.

She clicked through some images on her phone and then sent a couple of texts. Fifteen minutes later her crazy idea looked like a workable plan.

The upper room of the carriage house had been their focus today. She returned there and grabbed a bottle of water from the cooler. "How much more time do you think this will take?"

Mom stopped and rubbed an arm across her forehead, leaving a smear of dirt in its wake. "The two of us working together? A few days."

"Do you think we could do it by Thanksgiving?" Janae imagined moving in by the holiday weekend as she pulled up the image on her phone. "I can use evenings this week to finish this room. It's amazing what a fresh coat of paint can do. You and Dad can even help if you're willing." She grinned as she saw it in her mind's eye. "With all the windows, this room will be my office and living space. Then the downstairs room can become my bedroom since it's connected to the small bathroom."

"We'll have to help, or you'll never get through the rest of the junk in there." Her mom gazed out the window.

"I can also use the time to try to learn more about the painting we found. Grandma might know something she's forgotten, or I'll find something lying in all this stuff." Janae sighed. "Monday I'm taking it to an appraiser Carter recommended."

"Carter?"

"Dr. Montgomery." Her cheeks warmed as she met her mom's curious stare. "The museum director."

"Ah." Mom rubbed her forehead as her gaze swept the room. "Well, we'd better keep working. It's not ready for you yet, but we can get it there with hard work. And I would like to know more about that painting."

"Me too." Because it didn't line up with anything Janae knew about her grandfather.

And that fact left a niggle of concern eating at the edges of her mind.

Andrew looked around the bookstore with a dramatic sigh. "This is so much fun."

"You love coming to Chapters and Sips."

"Sure, when I have something I want to read or money to spend." The nine-year-old rolled his eyes in a stage-worthy performance. "Today I don't, and this is dumb."

Carter shoved his hands in his pockets as he considered his nephew. "What would you rather do?"

"Go to the museum."

Carter dipped his chin toward Andrew and then stooped next to him. "Really?"

"Yes. I want to finish a sketch I started." He mirrored Carter as he shoved his hands in his jacket pockets and shrugged as if he didn't really care, but Carter could sense the intense longing. "But if it feels too much like work..."

"No, I think it's a good idea. Let me purchase this book and then we can leave."

Delight brightened the boy's face. "Great. But can I get hot chocolate here?"

"We could get it at the museum."

The boy's face scrunched as if the idea was offensive. "They ruin hot chocolate."

"How can it be ruined?"

"Using powder. I've watched them open and dump it into water. Use real milk like they do here and it's so much better. Then there's the whipped cream and drizzle of chocolate on top." The boy licked his lips as if in anticipation of his first sip. "It's soooooooo good."

"Maybe you can help the baristas experiment with good hot chocolate."

"Could I get paid?"

"In hot chocolate."

The boy sighed but the smile didn't leave his eyes. "If it helps you improve what you sell, then I suppose I can."

Thirty minutes later they were in the Elliott, and Andrew led Carter to the new exhibit. He promptly sat in front of an O'Keeffe from her time at the University of Virginia. "I want to copy this one."

"Not *copy*, because forgery is illegal. Instead, you're making an interpretation of her work."

The boy frowned and then shrugged. "Whatever."

He settled on one of the padded benches in front of the painting and pulled supplies from his drawstring backpack. Once Carter could tell Andrew was absorbed in his work, he strolled past several paintings and stopped in front of the *Five Children* painting by Paula Modersohn-Becker—one of the two creating chaos in his world.

The placard next to the *Fünf Kinder an einem Hang, rechts Elsbeth* denoted it was on loan from the Landesmuseum in Hanover, Germany. Two of the five faces appeared blank of features, with the other three having rudimentary eyes dotted on them. The style placed the work in the crossroads between Impressionism with its quick brushstrokes and Expressionism with its allusions to what was with a dose of artist's interpretation. The result was a pleasing pastoral scene with birds flying in a flock while a couple of adults worked in the background, up the slope from the children.

"What's your story?"

The painting didn't respond. That would be too simple, and the reality was the provenance research was detailed and painstaking. It also was unlikely he could complete it by the end of the month to stave off a lawsuit unless Janae created a legal theory that resolved the dispute.

Someone stepped next to him, and he ignored the intrusion. It was a public museum after all, and anyone could pay to appreciate the art.

A moment later the person spoke. "It's lovely, isn't it?"

Carter stiffened as he recognized the voice. "Should you be speaking to me, or isn't there some sort of rule that prohibits an attorney from talking to the opposing party once a case has started?"

"I can certainly address my comments to Ms. Simmons. However, no lawsuit has been filed . . . yet." The *yet* hung in the air for a moment before Shaw continued. "My client and her family have suffered enough. Make this simple and give her the painting."

"There are two problems with that. The first is a big one. The Elliott doesn't own this painting. I can't decide what happens to a work we don't control."

"I will get it."

"Maybe, but it won't be because I caved without doing my work."

Shaw shrugged. "You do own the Botticelli."

Carter glanced over his shoulder to make sure Andrew still worked on his drawing. He fought a grin at the way his nephew's tongue had slipped between his teeth as he concentrated. Charlotte used to do the same thing. "I can't do anything about either until I finish our research into the provenance. That takes time."

"Ask your attorney about tolling the statute of limitations."

"What is that?"

"She can explain, but give it serious consideration."

"Okay." He glanced again at Andrew.

"Then I'll leave you to it. Let Ms. Simmons know the offer to toll is open until Monday at 5:00 p.m."

"But today's Saturday."

"Like I said, my client doesn't have an abundance of time." He turned to walk away. "Tell Janae I'll look for a call Monday."

Chapter 24

Saturday, November 19

JANAE HADN'T WANTED TO MEET on the weekend, especially after the weirdness Friday night at Margherita's, but knew she needed Carter's recommendation as she hunted for more clients. She'd create boundaries when she had the luxury of paying clients, but when he'd called saying Jarod Shaw had just spoken with him, she couldn't put him off until Monday. So she found herself driving to the museum in the clothes she'd worn while cleaning the carriage house.

If she'd wanted him to find her attractive, this wasn't the way, but it didn't matter.

She hurried across the first floor of the Elliott, up the stairs and then to the cafe where Carter had asked to meet. When she reached the bar, most of the tables were full, and the young boy from the Italian restaurant sat at one. His blond head was bent over a notepad as he wrote on the paper. She scanned the open space for Carter, warmth slipping through her when she spotted him standing at the end where the baristas set finished drinks. An intent frown marked his face as he studied something on his phone.

It was only as she placed her order that he looked up. "This one's on the house, Pepper."

The high school–aged girl entered something in the computer. "Happy Saturday."

"Thank you." Janae slid down the bar to stand next to Carter. "Hello."

The way he wouldn't meet her gaze told Janae there was more going on than what he'd suggested on the phone. That had been something about a quick deadline from Shaw, which made her a bit frustrated because the attorney should have contacted her, but without an active lawsuit his direct contact with the museum might be technically okay, if bad form.

"Carter?"

He started and there was a distant look in his eyes. "Hi."

She frowned as she watched him. "Look, I don't know why you wanted to meet today, but it's the weekend, and I'd like to address whatever you need and return to my life."

"Fair enough." But nothing followed the short sentence.

She fought back irritation. Maybe he felt bad about last night too? Nothing had been wrong. Just awkward. Maybe it was best to address this head-on. "Carter, what's going on? If this is about last night, don't let that bother you."

"What do you mean?"

"Being rude when I came over to say hi and meet the boy who's sitting at that table."

"His name is Andrew Montgomery."

She stilled. "Your son?"

"My nephew." He scrubbed a hand over his face. "It's a complicated story, but he lives with me. Has for about a year."

"Oh." Words abandoned her, which was unusual.

"That's why I didn't mention it." He sighed, and it seemed to come from his toes. "Today I can't get into that because we have forty-eight hours to decide if we want to enter a tolling agreement. Whatever that is."

Janae cocked her head as she refocused from the boy to the reason Carter had called her. "A tolling agreement."

"On the statute of limitations. But we have to agree to settlement talks."

"That might be a possibility." Janae ran through the options. "A tolling agreement means we agree to waive the statute of limitations on the plaintiff filing a lawsuit for a set period of time. It lets everything slow down, because the plaintiff, Mrs. Seeger in this case, isn't pressured to file before she's ready. Otherwise, if she misses her statutory deadline, she can't sue. By agreeing to toll the statute of limitations, we agree that she can sue later if talks break down."

"That makes some sense. The only problem is we have to let him know by Monday at five if we agree to the tolling agreement."

"Shaw must think there's a problem with the statute of limitations." Janae considered what she knew, but it wasn't enough. "Let's look at the demand letter again."

He held up his phone. "That's what I was reviewing when you walked up." He handed it to her. "I don't see anything."

"You shouldn't, but does any of your research change anything?"

"That assumes I've found something, and I haven't." He ran his fingers through his hair until it stood on end. "I haven't made enough progress."

"I know what we're doing the rest of the weekend." She glanced at Andrew. "Is there anywhere he can go so we can focus?"

"He can stay in my office with us."

Pepper walked over. "Or he can stay with me and we can work on the hot chocolate like he wanted." She glanced around the bar area. "We aren't overrun, so this is a good time to experiment on the best way to improve our recipe." She wrinkled her nose as she held up a powder-filled envelope. "He isn't wrong that this is nasty. At least compared to what other places serve."

Carter hesitated in a way that didn't make sense, but then he sagged. "Just make sure he stays where you can see him. Call me if he gets bored, and I'll come get him."

"Sure thing." A minute later Pepper and Andrew had their heads together looking at online recipes as Janae followed Carter from the area.

When they reached his office, she handed his phone back. "Can you print that?"

"Sure."

Once she had a paper copy, she scanned it again. Something about the information in the letter caused more turmoil for Carter than she'd expect, but she wasn't seeing it. "The key to understand with a tolling agreement is that it lifts some of the pressure of time but doesn't end that pressure. We can give ourselves a couple more weeks or a month but still keep pressure on them to file the lawsuit by the end of the year if that's important."

"How does that help us?"

"It gives you time to find the information on the Botticelli while connecting with the German museum. Have you been able to do either yet?"

"No. It's fruitless."

"Then giving Shaw a few more weeks also gives us time to figure out what we need to know. It's a benefit. At the same time, if we force them to file the lawsuit at the end of this month, Mrs. Seeger has to decide how committed she is. Maybe she doesn't have the stomach for that level of conflict and won't file. That's the risk of tolling."

"She seems committed." Carter groaned as he dropped into his chair. "What would you do?"

"Settlement is usually a good option, but you can't settle based on what you know now. You need time, and a tolling agreement buys that. Remember, a demand doesn't mean Mrs. Seeger is right. If their information is wrong, then it goes away. If not, then we decide what the next steps are."

Carter pushed his chair away from the desk and looked out the small window. "If Mrs. Seeger is right about the Botticelli, other items in our collection could also have provenance questions. It could create a domino effect of one painting toppling into the next until all are lost."

"Dramatic much?" She thought she'd kept the thought in, but based on his expression, it had slipped out. "Sorry, but you've hired me to worry and make this as painless as possible. Trust me to do my job."

"I don't know if you can do it."

The honest words hit home. "Then I guess you get to find out." She set the letter down and stepped toward the door, then looked back. "It's what you pay me for."

His phone rang as she left his office, so Carter didn't follow her as she returned to the administrative hub. "Ariel, what's the best way to get back to the galleries?"

"Take that hall and at the third door go up the stairs."

"Thank you." The hallway was austere, bare of even bad replicas of art the museum held. It felt cold and industrial rather than warm and welcoming. Good thing she didn't need to linger here but instead wanted a minute with the paintings in question. Maybe she could clear her head and gain a plan by standing in front of what mattered.

She wound her way to the gallery with the Botticelli. It filled a space almost two feet by eighteen inches, longer on the vertical. A woman's profile was painted, her hair an auburn shade arranged in an elaborate hairstyle. Her white gown had a similar level of intricate detail. She was young and beautiful, idealized like the name on the placard suggested.

Where did this painting belong, if not here on display?

Centered on a wall with plenty of space for people to soak in the beauty of the woman, the painting created a contrast of what could be with what was. It didn't really matter if she was a noblewoman or a hardworking housewife stealing a moment, the painting let Janae know the woman had an education—likely rare for the time the artist had created it stroke by stroke.

Janae didn't know how much time passed as she stood in front of the painting before she felt a presence next to her. "Call over?"

"Yes. Sorry about that." Carter's voice drew her attention, but she resolutely stayed fixed on the painting, not sure if he apologized for the call or his harsh words. "I love this luminous Botticelli."

She decided to let his words go. Something bothered him, but she couldn't demand to know what. "Why do you describe it that way?"

"The sense of light and shadow gives it a saturation of color that is unique."

Janae rifled through her mind for a matching descriptor and came up short. "It's nice."

"Nice?" He sputtered a moment before laughing. "It is nice."

His laugh warmed her. "What can you tell me about its history?"

"Not enough. It's been hard to learn more than is here." He tapped the white rectangle containing basic information about the painting. "Did you know this is my first real job?" He shoved both hands in his pockets, creating a look that he stood buffeted by winds. "I finished my post-doc and had to fight to find it. It's supposed to lead to a bigger one at a more prestigious museum."

Janae slowly pivoted, taking in the space in the gallery. "I think this one is charming."

"It is. I just don't imagine a future living here permanently."

"How long then?"

"Five years is about right."

She bit her lower lip to prevent herself from telling him that was barely long enough to become part of the southern community.

"What?"

"Don't limit yourself."

His eyebrows rose at her words. "How is that limiting?"

"You might find something unexpected and charming here. Big cities aren't everything. There's a special beauty to smaller communities. The kind where you can't go anyplace without being recognized by at least one person." She glanced down as she walked across the highly polished wood floor. Maybe she'd overstepped, saying too much in her rediscovered passion for her town and curiosity about this man. "What do you want from life?"

He did her the favor of not immediately answering as he trailed her across the room, arms hanging loosely at his sides, taking time to consider. She appreciated that, even as the silence stretched between them like a long line painted to give a canvas a horizon. She paused in front of another painting, this one a part of a triptych altarpiece with an abundance of gold leaf.

"I want to make my mark." He grinned in a boyish way that let her see the young man lurking beneath the serious exterior. "Art museums stand at a curious juxtaposition of recognizing the beauty of what's been created over our collective history while also recognizing we've done our job imperfectly. There are voices that need to be heard and gaps to fill. I want to contribute in a way that doesn't throw out the beauty and history in the effort to expand the narrative to include richer layers."

"Wow."

He looked up at her from under the mop of hair that fell over his forehead. "Too much?"

"Not at all. In fact, it's beautifully said. How will you do it?"

"I don't know yet." He tucked his hands in his pants back pockets and took a few steps back toward the Botticelli. "Maybe she is the beginning of walking that mission."

"Maybe." Janae followed him and cocked her head as she took in the woman and her surroundings. "It's fascinating that she's at leisure in a sense, yet not overly wealthy."

"I think that's why so many like this painting. She reminds visitors of themselves but idealized into who they want to be."

"Sort of like Instagram."

He snorted. "I like my version of the story better."

"I do too." Their shoulders brushed, and Janae took a half step away as the jolt of electricity ran up her arm. What was it about this man that tugged her closer even as his words pushed her away? "I've discovered I'm a small-town Virginia girl."

He turned and studied her, a slight quirk to his lips communicating something like amusement. "And?"

"I tried the big-city experience after law school. I hated it but liked my job. I appreciate the access to museums and culture, but I don't need to live there and deal with traffic, overcrowding, and overbearing expectations. I like elbow room and the ability to walk without fear or concern. I like people to know who I am even when they sometimes get involved in my business. There's something nice about being known." And hiding in plain sight. People assumed they knew her today because they knew her in the past.

"That does sound nice."

"All I'm saying is, give Kedgewick a chance. The nation's capital is only an hour away, and thanks to the commuter trains, you don't have to deal with the traffic on 66. The city also comes to us when people need to escape."

"Challenge accepted, so long as you help me discover the joys of this particular small town."

As she met his gaze, she knew she was in trouble. Despite her need to create distance, everything in her wanted to lean closer and see what might be possible.

Chapter 25

FIRST THING MONDAY MORNING, JANAE headed to the museum. Before she could head to the appraiser in the city, she needed to collect her grandfather's painting.

Am I doing the right thing?

Could this company give her the answers she sought?

Or would this open a chain to additional questions?

The fundamental conundrum hadn't changed. Why did Grandpa have this painting?

This was the core frustration that stayed inside her. Why did he have it, and why had he hidden it? There was a story, but he wasn't here to tell it.

She pulled into a street parking slot in front of the Elliott and hurried up the steps. When she tried the door, it was locked, so she called Carter. "I'm here."

"Can you come around to the side door?"

"Sure." A minute later she'd made her way to the side, and Carter let her in.

He stepped toward her, almost like he wanted to hug her, then stepped back, a bit of color creeping up his neck. "Hey. I was about ready to pull it out."

"Great." She took a deep breath to ease her heart rate. "If I get on the road quickly, I won't be late for the appointment."

"I went to school with one of the owners and trust him. The company has been in his family for generations, but he's a recent addition thanks to getting his PhD."

"All right." She followed Carter back to his office and then watched as he removed a painting and entered a code in his safe. "What do you want to do about Shaw's demand letter?"

Carter pulled on a pair of white gloves. "Can you call and feel him out?"

"Sure. I can do that today."

He opened the safe, carefully easing the small painting and its box free. "Let me know if you need anything."

"I should be good, thanks." She took the box and slid it in her bag. "I'll keep you posted."

He walked her back to the door, and Janae returned to her car and headed east to the city. She kept glancing in her rearview mirror, aware that she had a painting in her bag that could be very valuable. She would feel better when she knew if it was a copy or an original.

While leaving Kedgewick, she used her Bluetooth to place a call to Shaw's office, leaving a message that asked him to return her call. Then she settled in for the drive, enjoying the rolling hills that morphed into major highways spooling ever closer to the capital.

Haney & Sons sat tucked on one of those roads that ran parallel to the main area of Old Town Alexandria, across the Potomac from Washington, DC. She parked her car in one of the public garages and then walked the couple of blocks in a zigzag until she reached Haney & Sons Restoration and Conservation. The painting seemed to weigh down the bag far beyond its small size as she walked. The firm worked with the Smithsonian and other museums, so hopefully the restorer she had an appointment with could give her insight.

From the street the company looked like a small storefront, brick with large windows shaded by forest-green awnings. No sound greeted her as she walked through the door, and the front reception area stood empty.

"Hello?" She wandered toward the hallway behind the reception desk as she shifted the bag on her shoulder. It wasn't exactly acceptable to wander in an office, but she was ready to hand the painting to someone and watch them work their magic.

No one lingered beyond the desk. She sighed and pulled her phone from her coat pocket. As she looked for the contact in her calls, someone bumped into her from behind.

"Sorry, ma'am, but you aren't supposed to be back here without an authorized employee." The young man was probably a couple of years older than she with the officious air of someone self-important.

"Good, because I'm looking for someone who can help." She gave him one of her superior, don't-treat-me-like-I'm-an-idiot smirks. She held up her phone. "I have an appointment."

He gave her a tight grimace, one that did nothing to hide his annoyance. "Then it's a good thing I'm here." He took a seat at the computer and clicked a series of keys. "You are?"

"Janae Simmons. I have a ten o'clock with one of your curators."

"You must mean one of our restorers."

"Someone who can help me with a painting." She patted her bag. "I brought it as requested."

He frowned and clicked more keys. "Who is your appointment with?"

She resisted the urge to roll her eyes as she slid her fingers along the screen and then squinted at the calendar app. "The email confirmation states Victoria Grayson."

"That explains it." He gave her his full attention for the first time. "She's no longer here."

Janae frowned at him. "As of when? This appointment was created last week."

"That was an error on the part of whoever helped you."

For someone who worked a reception area, this man was getting on her nerves with his self-important style. "Then who can I see?"

"What school and era of painting do you have?"

"That's why I'm here." She looked toward the door. "A friend recommended this firm as a place filled with experts who could help me determine what I have."

He sniffed. "We are not *Antiques Roadshow.*"

"I certainly hope not, because I have something more valuable than anything you'll find on that show." He arched one eyebrow, and she decided that was more than enough snobbery to endure. "I think I'll take my questions somewhere else." She turned and headed back to the door.

The man sighed loudly. "If you show me what you have, I can assess whether we can help you."

"Thank you, but no. I don't need some receptionist talking down to me." She got enough of that in court. She wouldn't put up with it here when she was the prospective client.

The man sniffed. "I'm the director of this location. Everyone else is out today at training." He waved his fingers in a show-me motion.

Janae studied him a moment, still not sure she trusted him, then decided she didn't want to drive back without trying. What did she have to lose? She unzipped the bag and tugged the box free.

She set it on the desk's raised platform and lifted the lid free.

The man studied it before reaching into a drawer and pulling on a pair of white gloves. "May I?"

Janae nodded and then waited as he picked it up and carefully flipped the frame over and then back to the front. "The wood and the canvas are oxidized, indicating some age." He looked up at her. "Where did you say you found this?"

"My grandparents' home."

"Ah." He seemed to think that meant something, a hidden value that eluded her.

"Ah what?"

"On occasion a piece like this will be discovered when going through people's estates." He set the painting down and then gestured to the bag. "Do you have more?"

"No." There was something in the man's about-face that made her uncomfortable. "I think you've seen enough. You have my number. Feel free to call when someone can give my painting some time and attention."

She reached for the painting, but he snatched it up before she could. "What are you doing?"

"I'll keep this and analyze it, as was agreed."

"No. I'll call the police."

"As will I." He gave her a cold stare. "And I'll be the one they believe. You're clearly trying to pawn off a stolen painting."

When Carter's phone buzzed, he was eyeball deep in research and had opened another drawer in the third file cabinet of the day. The good news about touching each and every file was he had developed a good idea of what the museum had and was forming an idea of how to manage it once he had an army of interns and volunteers to help digitize the mess. It was incredible to think that images of all the paper could be contained on one hard drive, but he'd bet they could do it. Then the paper originals would be organized and stored in a way to protect them.

The phone stopped buzzing and then started again.

He pulled it from his back pocket and noted it was Janae. "Hello?"

"This bozo you sent me to is accusing me of stealing the painting."

"What?"

"I'm supposed to have an appointment at Haney & Sons, only the person it was with doesn't work here, and everyone's gone except for one person who is going to call the police if you don't convince him I'm not pulling an *Ocean's Eleven* on the art world."

"You're at Haney & Sons?"

"Yes." There was so much frustration in that one word.

"Put the man on the phone."

There was a rustling, and he could hear her angst as she said, "Here. Talk to Carter."

"Who?"

"Dr. Montgomery."

Then a male voice he recognized came on. "Carter, what are you mixed up in this time?"

"Nothing."

"I highly doubt that." The man sighed. "Do you know this Janae Simmons?"

"I'm the one who told her to go to you. Ethan, I think it's real."

"A quick inspection has me concurring."

Carter groaned at the legal language. "Spare me the fancy British words."

There was a sharp inhale of breath. "Did she find a Bruegel?"

"I think so."

Ethan Haney blew out a breath. "She's a skittish one."

"Can be. Trust me though, she's the real deal trying to figure out what she has."

"That's a good thing, considering everything we went through last year. That said, without more, it could be attributed to the school or workshop."

"Still valuable."

"And you're telling me she found it?"

Carter nodded and then started flipping through the files again. "Yes. The key question is, how did the painting end up in a stone house built in the '40s?"

"1940s?" Ethan didn't sound very impressed. "That's quite young, Carter."

"No, 1740s."

"Ah, so a moneyed family. That makes more sense."

"I don't think so." Carter stopped to pull a file out. Nope, not that one. "I don't get the sense that there's a lot of family wealth until her father started buying horses." Even then he wasn't sure there was actual wealth in the family.

"Then what's the story?"

"You're asking the wrong person." Carter sighed and stopped to rub the back of his neck. "Look, I can't tell you the story, but I can tell you that Janae and her family are good people. They wouldn't be involved in anything nefarious."

"Now who's using the big words." There was silence for a minute before Ethan spoke again. "Be careful. There's something here. And your career can't handle another scandal."

"Then don't ask me about the potential heir who claims the Botticelli the Elliott owns should be restituted to her because it was stolen during the war."

"Wow."

"Yeah." Carter cleared his throat. "Look, give Janae the best, most accurate assessment you can. She's not sure what she has but wants to do the right thing."

"Glad she does."

"Me too." Carter sneezed as more dust flew in his face. "Call if you need anything." After the call ended, he turned back to the files. He sneezed and felt another one building. That was enough dust for a bit. He marked where he had stopped and closed the storage room behind him.

While he knew holes were routine, he didn't like the difficulty of finding the Botticelli's history. It wouldn't be a simple process to go through the painter's catalogue raisonné, but it was a necessary step. Carter pulled it up on his computer and started clicking through the images.

How would he know he'd done enough research?

That was never an easy question to answer, so he got to work and prayed that eventually he'd make the right connections. He also prayed they'd be clear enough to provide good direction on how to proceed.

Chapter 26

CARTER HURRIED FROM THE ADMINISTRATIVE wing to his car. After-school care would close in ten minutes, and the director had threatened to remove Andrew from the program if Carter didn't start arriving on time. To quote, the staff couldn't afford to keep waiting to see if Carter remembered he had a child waiting for a ride. It had made him see burnt-sienna red when the woman said that in Andrew's hearing. Her careless words had struck home, making the boy's eyes widen and his posture slump.

Carter tried to stay a mile or two over the speed limit, but his foot kept pressing down on the gas, the urgency to arrive boring through him like weevils through a wood-paneled painting.

Maybe it hadn't been fair moving his nephew here with him, but he'd needed a job desperately as the pandemic cleared, and this had been the only museum to give him a chance. The fact it sat on the edge of the campus of a well-known liberal arts college made it better positioned than the small community museums he'd prepared the next round of applications for. Being closer to his parents helped, but they still lived over an hour away.

Pulling into the center's parking lot, he spotted Andrew staring out the window, but his nephew quickly turned away when Carter stepped from his classic Camaro. It wasn't exactly the vehicle for a responsible adult, but the summer after his junior year of college he'd restored it with his dad.

Now he needed to work on restoring his nephew. Helping him find a place in the new community that didn't yet feel like home was a start. One way was picking up Andrew before he was the last child again.

Carter opened the door with an apologetic bob of his head.

"Thank you for joining us, Dr. Montgomery."

He glanced at his watch. "Right on time." He held up his wrist so the woman could read its display. "See."

"Very last second." The words were short, but he saw a softness at the corner of Sherry Ames's eyes. The director looked about the age of his mom, and he exhaled at the understanding he found there. "Please keep trying." She lowered her voice. "Andrew is doing well here, but I am running short on staff who can stay."

"Even for the extra penalty?" It was a steep ten dollars per extra ten minutes.

"Even then."

"Understood."

"Put the watch to work and add a few alarms. Some parents start them an hour before they need to leave. Others twenty minutes before they arrive. Whatever works for you, it's worth trying."

Andrew walked over, and Carter roughed the blond mop. "Hey, bud."

"Hi." The boy looked up at him with puppy dog eyes. "Can we get fries on the way home?"

"You and your fries."

"We could get chicken nuggets instead."

"Oh no you don't. We are not driving over to Leesburg for nuggets."

"Eat more chicken."

Carter laughed, then looked for Andrew's coat and bag. "Grab your coat, buddy."

"All right." The boy scampered off.

Carter looked at Sherry. "I'll add some alarms to my watch tonight. Thanks for your patience. I am trying."

"I know you are." She moved to the wall to turn off the lights. "Keep rolling back your arrival."

"Yes, ma'am."

Upon returning from DC, Janae had kept the painting with her. Ethan had told her a thorough identification would take time, but the initial look suggested she did indeed have a painting by Pieter Bruegel the Elder or his workshop. She could have left the painting, but despite Carter's assurances, she wasn't sure she trusted Ethan.

She stared at it as she called Shaw again and left another message. After hanging up she rubbed her eyes, which felt blurry after spending the afternoon hunched in front of her computer screen. After hours searching online, she didn't feel any closer to tracking down the provenance of any of the paintings. However, she did have a starting place for the legal research for the museum. In *Republic of Austria v. Altmann*, the Supreme Court had addressed the issue of whether a foreign country could be required to return art that had been allegedly stolen by the Nazis during World War II to the heir of the family it had been taken from. While the case wasn't a direct match, it did involve a foreign government brought to the US courts. That mirrored the scenario with the Modersohn-Becker painting on loan from the state museum collection in Germany.

She'd also found a website for searching for Nazi-era provenance, coordinated by the American Alliance of Museums. The problem remained that she didn't know enough about the specific paintings in question to know how to search for the Modersohn-Becker's or Botticelli's history. She really needed Carter to conduct this part of the research or for him to guide her through the process. Washington, DC, with its world-class museums, was little more than an hour away by train, but she wanted to use her local expert rather than take a morning to zip into the city.

She wasn't surprised when her phone rang at 4:55, literally the last moment.

"You ready to enter a tolling agreement?" Jarod's voice held the right note of curiosity without pushing.

"Giving us the weekend wasn't enough time." There was so much she didn't know.

"The research you're scrambling to do takes time. You can't do it in four weeks unless someone updated the catalogue raisonné for each artist recently."

"I'm guessing that didn't happen."

"Not that I've found."

She thought a minute. "If your client has been without the paintings for seventy years, why the rush now?"

"She's getting old."

"I understand that, but there's more. Her age hasn't changed." It had to be the statute of limitations. "When did you say she became aware of where the paintings were?"

"I didn't."

Ah. Light dawned for Janae. "That's why you have to push. If I don't agree to this pause, then you'll blow by the statute of limitations."

It was his turn to be quiet. "Don't get too hasty."

"I'm not, but I'm also not going to be pressured into a decision. Tell me your date, or it's an automatic no." She glanced at the demand letter. "It's not November thirtieth."

"It's in the file."

"According to you, we don't have time for games or delays." She hardened her voice. "If I give you this valuable concession, you have to give me something in exchange. Talk to your client and get back to me by the end of the week."

She hung up and sagged. Had she made the right decision? She could understand Shaw's desire to keep the case moving, but she couldn't allow him to bully them into a decision that might hurt her client. She sent Carter a quick email, letting him know about the conversation, then returned to her research.

Maybe something she learned related to the museum's art could also help with the painting she and Mom had discovered. She wanted to believe nothing was wrong, but one didn't hide art in a suitcase—especially if the artist was world renowned.

Maybe her grandparents simply hadn't understood what they had. It was possible.

After all, people sold valuable paintings in yard sales or donated them to thrift stores often enough to create the legend of finding an original copy of the Declaration of Independence in a ten-dollar framed piece behind glass and canvas.

Anything was possible.

But was it practical and probable?

She was trained in critical thinking and problem-solving. She'd invested her education in making decisions for others with her eyes wide open. It would be wise to apply those skills to her grandparents. There was a story to the painting. She just had to dig deep enough to uncover it.

She rubbed her eyes and then pulled out her phone. A minute later her mom answered. "Do you know if Grandma has anything from Grandpa's time during the war?"

"Well, hello to you too." Mom chuckled lightly. "I had a wonderful day with my kids and hope yours has been good. Should we hold supper for you?"

"Mom."

She heard a throat clearing. "Why the sudden interest in your grandparents?"

"I'm curious about the painting and wondered if Grandpa wrote about it."

"Why not call Grandma?"

"I'm not sure how to frame it so she doesn't start to worry."

"I guarantee she's already curious."

"Sure, but there's a difference between a mystery and something that could be illegal."

"That's a leap." There was silence before Mom continued. "You have some explaining to do. Let's meet at Grandma's. I'll bring dinner."

Janae agreed and an hour later followed her mom up the path to Grandma's front door.

"Do you think Grandma has anything?"

"Let's ask." Mom rapped on the door, then opened it. "We're here, Mom."

"Come on in why don't you." Grandma stepped from the kitchen with a big smile. "My two favorite ladies. I'm glad to see you, but not sure why you're here." She gave Janae a small hug. "Need anything for the carriage house?"

"No, ma'am."

Mom took over. "I brought dinner and it's getting cold." When a fried chicken dinner with all the fixings had been pulled from the large basket and they were all seated, she got down to business. "Mom, Janae has questions about you and Dad."

"Oh?" Grandma looked at Janae expectantly. "Ask away."

"Did Grandpa tell you much about his time in the war?"

"You don't know much of our story, do you?" Grandma passed the basket of biscuits.

"I thought I did." But something in Grandma's expression had her rethinking that assumption as Janae filled her plate.

"He seemed glad I didn't know him then." Her brow wrinkled as she put a chicken breast on her plate. "He didn't like talking about that time, and I never saw letters or anything from then. I think that's why I was so surprised to see that suitcase of things. He barely mentioned coming home for the last time at the end of the art tour."

"What tour?" The clank of silverware against plates provided background music as they talked.

"The US government brought paintings over from Germany after the war for a tour. Grandpa was assigned to the tour as some sort of protective detail. Always said it felt like a waste of time to spend his days watching paintings hang on walls." Grandma stood and walked to the built-in bookcase surrounding the fireplace Grandpa had built for their fortieth anniversary. "There's a book about the tour somewhere on here."

"Oh?" Janae didn't know how Grandma would find it on the crowded shelves.

"Yes, your mom went to an art museum in Cincinnati for an exhibit related to that tour, and I bought the book instead. One of the pictures included Grandpa."

Mom shook her head. "I've always thought that was a bit of a stretch." She stood and moved next to Grandma, running her finger along the spines on the shelves. "Here it is." She handed the book to Grandma and then the two returned to the table.

"How did I not know this part of your story, Grandma?"

"You were busy with college and law school, and then Grandpa died your first year out. You didn't have the time or energy to be curious about an old man's experience in the war."

"I should have." She felt the loss of the opportunity to ask important questions and learn.

"You can live with regrets, or you can be grateful for the opportunities you had. Grandpa wasn't always an easy man to live with or understand. But he loved us in his own gruff way." Grandma's gaze shifted to somewhere in the distance as if she examined memories only she could see. "We built a good life." Then she extended the book. "I don't know if this book will help, but it contains interesting articles."

Janae accepted the book, taking in the blue cloth cover adorned with a black-and-white photo. "About what?"

"All things art. The typical article on what the Nazis did with art, but more on the journey of art here and how to understand provenance." Grandma patted the cover. "Who knows? Maybe you'll find something that helps your case."

"Do you think there will be anything about the painting we found?"

"I can't imagine there would be." She shrugged.

Janae set the book next to her plate, then considered the small rooms. There was nothing about the way Grandma had decorated the house that indicated her grandparents cared about art and other items other than the classic antiques that fit the style of the home. Grandma had favored clean white walls and trim, with pops of color coming from the furniture or throw pillows. Grandpa had forever removed the "confounded" props from the couch or his favorite chair, only to have Grandma come along and rearrange them. She claimed the extra support helped her survive the couches sized for Grandpa's lanky frame rather than her petite one.

Their good-natured bantering had occasionally gotten loud, especially as Grandpa's hearing worsened, but Janae knew their love ran deep even if it wasn't expressed in flowery words and soft phrases.

That love was the stubborn kind that lasted a lifetime. Love hurt sometimes, but not having it hurt even more. Her life was filled with work, with friends filling the cracks. She hadn't wanted or looked for a man.

But then Dr. Carter Montgomery entered her world.

He was steady. Stable. Saw her. And cared for his nephew. The package made her heart melt a bit, even though she wanted to say the timing was all wrong. Her life was too messy and chaotic at the moment to risk more, and it seemed like Carter was hesitant as well.

And now her thoughts traveled along trails she had considered overgrown from neglect.

"Where'd you go?"

Her mom's voice pulled Janae back to the moment. "Thinking about someone I met."

Mom's eyes sparked with interest and she leaned closer. "Who?"

"No one I want to talk about." At least not yet. Janae patted the book and headed to the door. "I'll put this in my car so I don't forget it."

"Don't disappear." Mom stood and cleared her plate, placing it in the sink. "We can get an hour invested in here and get the shelves cleaned off and books boxed up."

"Sounds great, Mom." But no matter how Mom chattered or Grandma handed her books to donate, Janae couldn't shake Carter from her thoughts—a reality she didn't want to examine too closely.

Chapter 27

THE DRIVE TO THE OFFICE normally passed in a few minutes while Carter listened to a podcast from either the *Washington Post* or the *Wall Street Journal*. However, on Tuesday morning, after he dropped Andrew at school, he noticed a white pickup following him. He'd seen it earlier but assumed it was another parent dropping off a child.

The fact it continued to match him turn for turn? Unsettling at best.

He turned away from the museum and northwest toward Purcellville. He wasn't sure why, other than wanting to confirm that he wasn't crazy.

As soon as he was on Highway 611, the pickup sped up and rode the bumper of his '70 Camaro. He grimaced and edged his speed up further to create distance, but the pickup kept coming.

Carter turned the wheel at the last moment, sliding the sports car into the parking lot of a factory on the outskirts of town. He hadn't counted on the pickup taking the next cut in, so he quickly hurried down a couple of rows of cars before slipping into a vacant spot sandwiched between two large pickups outfitted for hunting. He inched down in the seat, knowing that wouldn't do anything to make his bumblebee Camaro less noticeable, but he felt trapped. The question was how long to wait before he could be sure the white pickup had left if it had followed him.

He stopped the thought.

No, the truck *had* followed him.

The moment it pulled into the parking lot, there was no other plausible explanation.

After ten minutes, his pulse had slowed, and he carefully eased from the slot.

He looped through Purcellville and back south to Kedgewick, never seeing a white pickup. He wished he'd caught a license plate or anything that would be helpful to the police, but what was the point of calling them? What could they do with his information that he'd been followed—maybe—by a truck?

Why would anyone follow him?

The question bothered him until he arrived at the Elliott.

Silence dominated the administrative wing, and he glanced at his watch with a frown. Where was Ariel?

He headed toward the kitchenette. "Ariel?"

The hall echoed his word back at him, the sound eerie.

A moan rose as he neared the small space, and he moved faster. A form was sprawled on the ground at the base of the refrigerator, and he hurried to her side. Ariel's long hair covered her face, blood oozing from a gash on the back of her head. He brushed back her hair so he could see her face. "Hang in there."

She moaned again, and he scrambled to pull his phone from his jacket pocket and dial 911. Then he waited next to her for the ambulance to arrive. Ariel didn't fully regain consciousness, but he was grateful for every moan and shift that suggested she was with him.

When the paramedics rushed in and a police officer followed them, his relief was like the release of air from a balloon.

The officer approached him. "I'm Officer Joel Alston."

"Is she going to be okay?"

"The paramedics could tell you. What happened?"

"Not much to tell." Carter explained the little he knew.

"Anyone who would want to hurt her?"

"I hope she slipped and hit her head."

"Here?" The officer glanced around. "Probably not. Is anything missing?"

Carter swallowed hard. "I have no idea. I only made it this far."

"Then let's do a walk around. Be careful not to touch surfaces until we know what's going on."

"All right." Carter wasn't sure how that would help, if they were walking all over, but he wanted to make sure nothing had been disturbed. "It could take a while to assess every area."

"Let's focus on this wing right now."

Carter moved across the hall to his office. What he saw froze him in place. It looked like someone had taken every piece of paper in the office and upended it. Even the books from his shelves were tossed around.

"I take it this isn't normal."

So the officer had the gift of understatement. "No."

"What was the person looking for?"

Carter shook his head. "I have no idea." He went to his desk and tried to remember what files had been on top but gave up. The storm of paper made it impossible to recall.

After Officer Alston asked a few more questions, he walked with Carter into the museum, where they took a quick tour of the galleries. All looked well until he reached the place where the Botticelli hung. The frame looked like someone had hacked at it but given up. Had Ariel somehow interrupted a robbery? She did tend to sing in the mornings.

"We'll need to close the museum while we collect some evidence." Officer Alston pulled out his phone.

"Whatever you need." Carter stood in a daze as the officer stepped away to make the call.

Fast steps startled him, and he spun to find Stanley bolting toward him.

"Why didn't you call? Tell me there was an issue?" The man skidded to a stop when his gaze landed on the painting, chest heaving as if he'd run a great distance. "What happened?"

"I don't know." Carter stared at the work, heartsick at the destruction. "Looks like someone tried to steal it but gave up. I'll get a call in to our insurance company, once I confirm Ariel is okay."

Stanley shook his head. "I'll call the insurance."

"No need. That's part of my job."

"You have bigger issues, like where the security was. I'll make the call. What happened to Ariel?"

"Paramedics just took her to the hospital." He loosened his tie, feeling like his lungs froze. "Someone—probably whoever did this—attacked her." He pulled out his phone and scrolled for the security firm. "I've got work to do. If you could let the board know what happened, I'd appreciate it. Someone will have to talk to the media, and I'll need help with that. We'll also have to close this gallery while the police work." His mind whirled as he walked away from Stanley.

Then he pivoted to take a few photos of the damage. Stanley stood close to the painting, almost nose to nose with the woman, both hands around the frame. "Stanley?"

The man startled. "I'll call the board." Then he spun on his heel and exited the gallery at a clip.

Carter stared after him, then returned to his phone and started making calls. He'd call the police back while leaving the board and insurance to Stanley.

When Janae stopped at Java Jane's for a midmorning coffee, rumors swirled that something had happened at the Elliott, but when Carter didn't answer his phone, she sent him a text. If he needed help, he knew how to reach her. She considered walking to the museum but didn't want to overstep and insert herself into a situation that didn't need her.

Early that afternoon, her phone rang, and without looking at the caller ID, Janae picked up her trilling cell and accepted the call. "Hello?"

"Honey, I need you to come to Grandma's."

Janae pulled the phone from her ear and checked the time on it. "Now? It's only 1:30."

"I am well aware. Come here, please. Now." There was no honey in that tone.

"Wait, Mom, why aren't you at school?"

"Teacher in-service day, and I'm not a teacher."

"Is Grandma okay?"

"She's fine."

Mom's short answers had Janae quickly pulling up her calendar to confirm she had no appointments until 4:00. "I can come for a bit."

"See you soon." Mom hung up before Janae could respond.

What could Mom have found that required Janae to drop everything and drive to Grandma's this instant? Whatever it was, Mom's insistence amped Janae's concern.

When she pulled her hybrid into the driveway, Mom watched from the porch. Huh. That wasn't typical. Janae grabbed her bag, and before she reached the cardinal-red front door, Mom had it opened, hugging her oversized cardigan tight around her.

"Thank you for coming."

"Sure." Janae noted a tightness around her mom's eyes as well as a whiteness to her skin. "What's wrong?"

"I don't know, but Grandma found something." Mom stepped back and then closed the door after Janae entered the small foyer. "I probably wouldn't have thought anything of it, but we found that painting in the suitcase, and I don't know. It feels . . . off." She pivoted and led the way to the kitchen.

The exposed stone walls and timbered ceiling usually made the space feel cozy, weak fall light filtering in from the single window. The wall of honeyed-wood cabinets created the galley feel of the kitchen that blended into the table and the large fireplace at the end of the room. Most days she relaxed into the space that held so many memories of meals and cookie decorating at the large table. Now her gaze froze on a small painting, about the size of a sheet of paper, that held the image of an old man staring straight at the viewer. The painting had the dark look of a Dutch master, with the stark background broken up by the man's face and white cuffs and collar.

Janae's heart skipped as her hand covered her mouth as she studied it. "Grandpa, what is going on?"

"Why did you say 'Grandpa'?"

"If we found the first painting in his things, then I'm guessing this was too."

Mom shook her head, worry lines creasing her forehead. "Grandma found this on a top shelf in the basement."

Grandma huffed into the room. "I can speak for myself, Lisa."

"I know you can, Mom."

"This house doesn't have a single closet thanks to when it was built, so there's hidey-holes everywhere in the furniture. You know I'm too small to reach the top shelves in the basement, but I decided for some unknown reason today was a good day to sort through a couple. Guess I was inspired by all our work in the carriage house and then on the built-ins up here. Hasn't been done since Grandpa died." She swallowed hard and blinked a few times. "That's what I found." She gestured to the painting.

"Okay." Janae studied it but didn't reach for it. She felt oddly frozen in place, as if taking a single step could alter the future in ways she couldn't anticipate, and she was the queen of what-ifs.

"Okay? That's the best you've got?" Grandma sounded put out.

"Where exactly did you find it?"

"Shoved between some of Grandpa's old work clothes in a box. I guess it was kind of like his books on the top shelf in the other room. If I left the books he loved to collect, they comforted me like he might walk back in the room to grab one at any time."

"And that applies to his work clothes?" Janae shuddered at the thought of what they must have smelled like. "I hope the painting doesn't smell like his clothes."

"He had it in a big Ziploc, only fancier."

At least he'd taken some steps to protect it.

228

"Why would Dad have something like that? And there of all places? On a shelf above your head?" Mom shook her head, arms crossed protectively in front of her.

"He was hiding it." Janae knew it with certainty, but not why.

"What a thing to say." Grandma's eyes sparked. "I bet he got it as a gift for me and then died before he could give it."

Mom nodded and kept looking at the painting as if waiting for the man to speak. "There's something special about this one, and I think I know what."

"Oh?" Something tickled at Janae's mind, but she couldn't quiet it enough to figure out what.

"It looks like a Rembrandt."

Chapter 28

JANAE PULLED OUT HER PHONE and stepped closer to the table. "I'm going to take a few photos, and then I'd like to take this to my friend at the Elliott like the other painting. Carter should know whether Mom's right."

Grandma rubbed her hands up and down her cardigan sleeves. "It can't be a Rembrandt. I've heard of him."

Janae wanted to scream that everyone had, but part of her clung to the probability this was merely a good copy. People bought those all the time. The problem was that she didn't know anyone who had a copied Rembrandt.

Rembrandt!

She pressed a hand against her stomach as it clenched against the thought.

Mom remained pale and swayed a bit. "Taking it to the Elliott is an excellent idea. I can't imagine keeping it here until we know more. If it's real, it's priceless." She swallowed hard, then pushed from the sink she'd collapsed against. "I'll have a list of last-minute things for you to pick up at the store. I don't want to wait until tomorrow. Too close to Thanksgiving, and we'll be stuck with canned green beans." She wrinkled her nose and made a face at Grandma.

Some of the tension broke as Grandma chuckled. "There are worse things in the world than classic green bean casserole, Lisa."

"Not when we can have fresh green beans with almonds and olive oil."

Janae tuned out their banter, which had a note of forced cheerfulness, as she edged her phone around the painting to take photos. Then she used her blouse as a glove of sorts as she eased the painting over to get the back side like Carter had showed her. "Do you have a box I can put it in, Grandma?"

"Sure, honey." Grandma came back a minute later with a white gift box. "Will this work?"

Janae slid the frame inside and then put the top on. "Perfect." She blew out a breath. "I'm going to take this in now." She gave her grandma a quick hug. "Is it okay if I start bringing some things over this week? With Thanksgiving, I thought it would be a good time to move."

"Sure. I'm not going anywhere."

"Thanks."

Mom crossed her arms protectively over her stomach. "Be careful."

"Always am."

"I know, but I don't mean watch out for deer this time."

Janae nodded. "This feels big."

"It does. Tell Carter I want to meet him soon. Thank him for his help with these paintings."

"I will." The drive passed quickly, yet she felt the burden of traveling with the painting. She considered stopping for coffee but quickly abandoned the idea. She wasn't sure her stomach could handle the caffeine, and she knew she couldn't leave the painting in her car even for a minute. What if that was the one time someone decided to break in? She'd be sick.

Instead, she pulled into the visitor lot at the Elliott and hurried up the stairs to the entrance, but the door was locked. A note flapped in the breeze, held in place by two pieces of tape, alerting visitors to the fact the museum was closed for the day.

A news van pulled up while she considered what to do. The passenger door opened, and a woman with perfect hair and bright lips popped out. "Are you with the museum?"

Janae stepped back. There was no way she wanted anything to do with the media, not with what she carried. "No."

"Sure?"

"Just visiting." Janae turned and started walking away.

What a terrible, never-ending, awful day. Officer Alston hadn't been thrilled to come back and seemed to think the second trip was Carter's fault. And a team had been at the museum for hours. The whole time Carter expected to hear from the insurance company but hadn't, which baffled him. Surely they would have reached out to get more information after Stanley contacted them. Damage like this would usually have an adjuster out quickly. It could launch an audit and more, which sounded like a nightmare but might be necessary. He had an injured employee, a trashed office, and a damaged painting.

None of that should have happened.

Margeaux Robbins had called to make sure he was okay and to see where Ariel was, but the other board members hadn't reached out. Carter had handled the details alone, leaving him no choice but to close the museum.

He had to get security figured out, then clean things up and get the painting secured.

His phone rang and he almost ignored it, but picked up when he didn't recognize the number. Maybe this was finally the insurance company.

"Carter, this is Archibald. What do you need?"

"What do you mean?"

"I've heard there was a mess at the museum this morning, and now you've got the media outside your doors. What do you need?"

"Other than the media to leave us alone?"

"Yes, because I don't think anyone can work that miracle."

"I'm not sure." Carter sighed and pressed his fingers at the bridge of his nose as he closed his eyes.

"Quite all right. Let me know if anything comes up that I can help with. You're not alone, young man."

"Thank you." After the call ended, Carter sat at his desk a moment. Media at the door? Maybe leaving was his best option. No, he had to figure out what happened with the security. Someone broke in to the museum. At least a break-in felt preferable to the idea it wasn't.

While the museum didn't have overnight on-site security, it did have cameras and alarms. He couldn't imagine the cost of adding overnight security, but maybe that was next. Had the museum flirted with danger by not having it?

Tension pounded at his temples.

This morning said it had.

He placed a call to the security company and explained what had happened. The owner promised to send someone over with the footage. "Can you scan it first to see what you can find? I don't need to watch all of it myself to prove there's a problem if there is. I just need to know what you see."

"On it. Are you ready to consider nighttime security?"

"I wanted to request a proposal."

"I can send the one we put together six months ago. It wasn't cheap, but considering your collection, it seemed reasonable."

"Would you mind resending the proposal? I haven't seen it. Can you give me a ballpark of the charge?"

The man quoted a price that wasn't as high as Carter would have anticipated. "Why didn't the museum move forward?"

"I don't know. Stanley refused, and the other director quit. He was concerned something like today would happen. Even if I had someone actively watching your feeds at the time of the attack, it would take too long for us to arrive to stop harm. Our office is in Leesburg."

"That's at least fifteen minutes."

"If we were breaking every speed limit. And in that time a smash-and-grab has happened, and the thieves disappeared."

"Email me the proposal. I think we have proof it's necessary now."

After the call ended, Carter stood and walked to the office entryway. Why would Stanley say no to security—especially when the director said it was necessary?

Irreplaceable items filled museums, which were habitually under-insured and understaffed, but this bordered on negligence. He'd ask for clarification and press into the why.

A light knock on the door pulled his head up. Janae stood there, blonde hair blowing in the breeze, carrying a small box. She shivered, and he headed to the door to open it.

"Janae?"

"Hi, Carter. Hurry." She pushed past him. "Close the door before the media come around the side."

"I think they've given up." But he pulled the door tight because he knew she was right, and he didn't have it in him to dodge the press. "Why are you here?"

"Is it okay that I came? I can leave because I hear it's been crazy." But she seemed rooted in place.

"That's an understatement." He noted the box she clutched. "What do you have?"

She swallowed.

Carter followed the movement and then pulled his attention from her slim neck back to her eyes.

"I don't know what to say because everything sounds crazy." She flitted past him and sank onto one of the chairs.

"Try me."

She set the box on the end table and edged it toward him. "My mom and Grandma found this today."

"Another painting?"

She nodded.

"You think this one is special?"

"You will too." She rolled her lower lip between her teeth then tapped the box. "Please."

He glanced from her to the box and back again. "You're serious."

"I wouldn't be here the day of a break-in if I wasn't."

He opened the box and then let out a whistle. "I see what you mean."

"Is it?"

"Is it what?"

"A Rembrandt?"

He tugged the box closer. "I'm surprised you're back with another treasure."

"Do you think it is one?"

"A real Rembrandt?"

She nodded as if afraid to voice the words.

"He's considered the greatest artist of the Dutch golden era. He was born forty years after Bruegel died. Here's the thing that makes him different. Rembrandt's style is easily recognizable and often copied. Because he was a prolific artist, more than three hundred paintings, three hundred fifty etchings, and hundreds of drawings survived him. However, he was also a gifted teacher, often with multiple pupils— which means many more items could be attributed to his school than to him." Carter tapped the edge of the box. "This might be a Rembrandt. Or it could be a copy or painted by a pupil. It'll take time to unwind."

"What should I do?" Janae looked lost and overwhelmed.

"Why are you worried? It's likely a really good copy, but not anything to worry about."

"Where do I take it to find out?"

"Normally I'd say Haney & Sons."

"No." There was a firm set to her chin.

"I'll need time."

"Can I leave it here in the interim? I can't imagine taking this back to Grandma's."

"Not a problem." Carter watched her. "What's bothering you? Most people would be thrilled by the idea their grandpa left them a potential fortune in art."

"What if Grandpa did something wrong to acquire them? He was a good man, but he wasn't perfect. There are pre-Grandma parts of his life we don't know about." She sighed heavily and didn't meet his gaze.

"That doesn't mean he did anything nefarious."

"But it doesn't mean he didn't." Wells of sadness filled her eyes as she studied the painting. "He's my hero, and lots of people around here loved him. What if that stops? He didn't have money. Not like this." She waved at the paintings.

"He's not alive. It won't impact him anymore."

"But it would devastate my grandma." She blew out a breath. "And what if it harms my ability to launch the firm well?" She slumped in the chair. "That sounds so selfish."

"Yet practical."

"Yes."

Carter put the lid back on the box, knowing he'd take the painting out as soon as he could to protect it. "Don't borrow trouble from tomorrow until you know what happened. That'll be early enough to worry."

She stood with a small smile. "Thanks for letting me take so much of your time on a hard day. We can put the painting in your safe, and I'll get to last-minute Thanksgiving shopping for my mom."

A few minutes later Janae was gone, and Carter grabbed a mug of hot tea, then settled at his computer and logged into his email. He needed to take a few minutes to make sure nothing else was burning around the museum while he dealt with the break-in. As soon as the latest mail downloaded, relief flooded him when he spotted an email with attachment from Suzy Werblow, the curator at the Landesmuseum. Maybe this contained the information he and Janae needed to plan a strategy related to the Modersohn-Becker piece.

There was both an ethical and a legal angle to these situations. He was glad Janae focused on the legal, but he needed to make sure he charted a path for the museum that he could support following across the museum's collection. This situation emphasized the need to develop a strategy that he could apply consistently in the future.

He downloaded and printed the attachment. There was something about holding a paper copy of the documents that made it easier to follow. He double-checked the time stamp on the email and saw she had sent it in the last half hour. Then he called Suzy, hoping she was in. When she picked up, he got straight to the point. "Sorry this is so late, but I just got your email and attachment. Danke."

"Of course. You might call me a night bird." Her accent touched the English in a way that felt like heavy cream. "Do you understand what I sent?"

"I will. What is most important, from your perspective?"

"Paula Modersohn-Becker is an artist recognized around the world for both her art and her letters. She died young at thirty-one, so at the time of the war, she'd been gone for thirty years. I have not found anything in our collection that indicates this painting was taken from anyone. It was conveyed in a will to the museum."

"When was that?"

"As the documents show, it happened in 2021. We incorporated it into an exhibit that year."

"Anything before then?"

"The typical. It was in Vienna for a period. Then in a gallery during the war before going into a private collection around 1947. The history from that point until it was donated to us is unclear. Like many works, while it is in a private collection it can be bought and sold before reappearing. This is not unusual."

"True, but would any of that history be accessible to heirs who aren't in the art world?"

"That's the question, correct?"

He knew the truth of her words. Privately held art could pass hands with the larger world unaware. That complicated determining the right course of action with that painting.

Such private sales meant Mrs. Seeger could have stayed in the dark about its location until it resurfaced in 2023.

"What will you do next?"

There was a pause before her response. "What do you mean?"

"Based on what you've told me, your museum can't refute a claim that Mrs. Seeger is within three years of the painting's whereabouts becoming publicly available."

"That may be, but you and your museum owe us a duty of care regarding *Fünf Kinder an einem Hang*."

"What did you call it?"

"*Fünf Kinder an einem Hang*."

"You left off words, right?"

"Of course. It is too long to state the whole each time."

"Could there be more than one painting in question?"

He could almost hear her shrug. "Anything is possible. It is art."

"Can I ask you to keep digging while we work from here?"

"Yes, but I wonder if we should end the loan."

"That is your right but might cause this situation to escalate."

Her silence was the only answer.

"Please continue digging into the painting's provenance. This isn't the only piece the heirs are asserting rights to."

"Ah, you have one at risk as well." She snorted. "The picture is clearer now."

"Yes, each of our museums stands to lose something. You know it's not simply the paintings to which Mrs. Seeger is raising a claim of ownership."

"Frau Seeger could open the door to many challenges."

"Which is why how we handle this situation matters."

There was silence for a moment as if she were considering her response. "I will let you know what else we find."

"Danke."

"I suggest you not rely on us alone, Dr. Montgomery, if as much is at risk as you suggest."

With those words ringing in his mind, the call ended—his concern heightened rather than settled.

Chapter 29

ANDREW WAS ACTING OUT IN rare form by the time Carter got supper on the table. A simple meal of mac and cheese with ham—something Andrew usually loved—but he didn't want to touch it.

"Come on, Andrew. It's time to eat."

"I want my mom and not more mac and cheese. You can't cook and she can!"

Carter froze. It had been weeks since Andrew had made a statement like that. In fact, Carter had begun to believe Andrew had accepted that his mom wouldn't return. Maybe living closer to a grave he could take the boy to would help. But he'd had to move for work, and that had disrupted Andrew's world yet again. Becoming the surrogate parent for a scared and grieving eight-year-old who barely knew him hadn't been easy. The first months had stretched Carter to the breaking point as he tried to figure out what Andrew needed. He'd taken the job in part to relocate closer to his parents and Andrew's grandparents, but it didn't mean the boy had adapted.

"I'm sorry, Drew. I want her too, but we can't always have the things we want most."

"You can't call me Drew." His nephew looked away from him, but not before Carter caught his chin quivering. "Only Mommy and Lindsay call me that."

"Come here."

Andrew shook his head, blond hair falling into his eyes, his narrow frame stiffening.

"Buddy, it's okay to miss your mom." In fact, it was healthy and good. "I know she didn't want to leave you, but I promise I'll always be here."

"That's what she said." The whispered words landed heavily on Carter.

"Your mom loved you deeply. You were the most important thing to her." Charlotte had been a passionate, all-in person who loved with abandon and fiercely protected those in her circle.

Eight years of his sister's life were a mystery. He had been neck-deep in his PhD at the time, but he'd return the doctorate if it meant he had his sister. That quick visit weeks before her death hadn't been enough.

"I thought I saw her today."

Carter froze at Andrew's words. "Who?"

"Mom." The boy rubbed a hand over his eyes. "I couldn't have, right?"

"No. There's no way you did." Was there? His mind flashed back to the man who had flicked the card with only ten digits on it to the floor of his office. The man who had alluded to Charlotte having something that had belonged to him. Could he have been behind the break-in?

No, that didn't make sense.

Or did it?

He pulled his thoughts back to Andrew. "I'm sorry, bud, I wish it was her."

Not possible, though. No, he'd learned the hard way to look at life the way it was, not the way he wanted it to be. He'd allowed himself to believe anything was possible during his post-doc, and he wouldn't make that mistake again.

Carter's mom told Andrew stories about Charlotte, kept her alive to him, but it wasn't the same as having his mom with him.

Maybe it was time to ask a few questions of his own, even if the answers hurt.

Thanksgiving

Her vibrating phone woke Janae up Thanksgiving morning, and she had to take a minute to remember where she was. Then the aroma of turkey baking flavored the air, and she realized she was back in her room at her parents' house rather than in the cave of the carriage house. She'd moved so many boxes, she could start sleeping there in the next day or two, but right now she groped along the top of her side table for her phone. "Hello?" She cleared her throat and tried again after swiping to take the call. "Hello?"

"Janae?" Was that Carter? Why was he calling her?

She scrambled to a seated position and pushed hair from her face. "Carter? Happy Thanksgiving."

"You too. Just wanted to let you know Ariel will be okay. She'll be out with a concussion for the next week, but the doctors expect her to make a full recovery."

"That's great news." She wiped at her eyes as she tried to wake up. "What else do you need?"

"Uncle Carter . . ." She grinned at the exasperated voice in the background. "Don't we have a turkey? It's not Thanksgiving without turkey."

"Andrew, we'll talk when I'm off the phone." He sighed. "Sorry about that."

"No problem. Do y'all have plans for today?"

"I got distracted with putting everything at the museum back in order and didn't get a turkey."

"It's understandable. Not a great week."

"Yeah, but Andrew doesn't understand all that. Uncle Carter for the win."

"Why don't y'all come here? Mom always makes more than enough food, and I bet your nephew would enjoy meeting the horses." What was she doing? Inviting him over for Thanksgiving was playing with fire. Her parents and grandmother would definitely notice. And that would mean questions. Lots of questions. Questions she didn't want to answer.

He hesitated. "Don't you need to ask?"

She could take the easy way out, but that wasn't her style. "Nope. I promise there will be plenty of food, including turkey. My grandma will be here and probably a few more people that Mom invited. Football will be on in the background, and we'll play some games. If Andrew's comfortable with it, I could talk Dad into putting him on a horse."

"I don't know if I'm comfortable with it, but all right. What can we bring?"

"If you pass an open store, a small bouquet for Mom would be the thing. I'll text you the address." She clicked a few buttons. "Did it come through?"

"Got it. We'll be there in an hour." He paused. "Thank you."

Her heart melted a bit at the softness in his words.

As soon as she was off the call, Janae hurried through getting ready, pretending to ignore the extra moments she spent on her makeup. Once she was in the green sweater dress with her hair in a messy updo, she hurried down to alert her mom.

"Of course it's fine that you invited a couple people." Mom scanned her, then a small smile toyed at her mouth. "Is this Carter someone special? You've mentioned him a lot."

"No, Mom. We're working together, that's all." She frowned, hoping her mom couldn't see the way her thoughts wandered to what could be. "I'm not sure why he called this morning, but inviting them to join us seemed the right thing to do."

"Absolutely. Just remember the rule. No work. We're going to enjoy today."

"I'll remember that." She settled in to help her mom with the meal prep, making a salad while Mom whipped up the mashed potatoes and slid them into the oven to stay warm. Janae slipped the apron over her head when the doorbell rang. "I'll get it."

Her mom nodded, her attention not straying from the pie crust lattice magic she was creating on top of an apple pie.

Janae wiped her sweaty palms along the sides of her dress before opening the door with a small wave. She touched the back of her hair, checking it hadn't fallen out, as she stepped back. "Come on in." She nodded to the blond boy who stood next to Carter. "You might not remember meeting me, Andrew. I'm Janae."

"Yes, we met." Carter elbowed him, and the boy pasted on a smile that didn't quite meet his dark blue eyes. "Thanks for inviting us over." He leaned closer. "Can you believe he forgot to get a turkey?" He rolled his eyes, then marched in. "Do you really have horses?"

"We do. Maybe after we eat, we can walk to the stables." She glanced at his khakis. "We'll make sure you don't get cold."

"I won't." He shoved his hands in his pockets and cocked his chin a notch with the assurance a young boy brings to life.

"Good. No getting sick after spending a day with us."

Carter stood behind Andrew, a hand on the boy's shoulder. "We'll be glad to do whatever works best."

Mom strode down the hall, her black slacks carrying a telltale dusting of white where the apron had failed to protect her. After introductions were made and Carter gave her a bouquet filled with yellow and orange roses, Mom leaned close to Janae and used a stage whisper. "I like this one."

"Mom." Janae mimicked Andrew with the dramatic eye roll. Then she grinned at the boy. "You see why I'm moving out."

"It's about time." Grandma walked in with a grin and extended a hand. "Welcome to the family Thanksgiving, young men. Andrew, why don't you come with me. I need help sorting this puzzle I thought was a good idea to start."

Mom followed them, leaving Carter next to Janae in the entryway. "Welcome to the family."

"You weren't kidding." Carter shoved his hands in his pockets as his gaze caressed her, causing heat to shoot up her neck. "I'm kind of glad my parents are on the last day of a cruise after all."

"That sounds fun."

He took a step closer to her. "I'm grateful to be right here. Thanks again for the invitation."

"You're welcome." She stepped back as her dad stomped in the front door.

"I see we've got company." He stuck out his hand to Carter. "I'm Gerald Simmons. Glad you could join us."

"Carter Montgomery, and my nephew Andrew is with . . ."

"Grandma. Andrew's helping with the puzzle, though he might like to visit your horses later."

"Always ready to show off the mares." Her dad grinned as he continued through to the kitchen where he gave Mom a big kiss on the cheek. "Smells good."

"Anything smells better than the horses."

"Not to me."

The meal was a blur of conversation and amazing food. Andrew tried everything and kept reaching for more. Janae leaned toward Carter. "Does he have a hollow leg?"

"I didn't think so."

"The cooking's better here." Andrew grinned from his place across the table, a smear of raspberry jam on his cheek. "Besides, I need to fuel up if I'm going to ride the horses."

After the meal, Dad led the way, Andrew tripping along at his heels asking excited questions.

Carter stayed back with Janae, his gaze sweeping the horizon. "This is peaceful."

"It is."

"So why move?" He held his hands wide. "This is a great setup."

"It is, but Grandma is closer to town, and staying here feels a little too much like I'm in college and home for a summer."

"It's nice to have a place to land, though." He gave her a sideways glance.

She climbed up onto the bottom rung of the wooden fence. "You're right, I just imagined I'd be somewhere very different by this point in my life."

"Different isn't necessarily bad." He leaned against the fence next to her. "My life definitely looks different than I imagined, but I wouldn't change it." He swallowed hard. "Actually, I'd make one change. I'd have Charlotte back."

Silence fell between them, and she tried to focus on the horses standing under a tree across the field, but she felt his attention. She turned to him. "Why did you call? This morning?"

"I don't remember anymore. Probably something about the museum that doesn't really matter on a holiday." He pushed out a laugh. "Andrew's right. I forgot today was a holiday. Who does that?"

"Someone who's had a rough couple of weeks."

Carter pushed away from the fence and glanced around. "Where's Andrew?"

"Dad's probably got him about ready to come out on Coconut."

"That's a horse or a candy bar?"

She snorted. "Definitely a horse, but a gentle one. She's great with new riders."

Carter seemed to relax and came back to the fence. "Would you like to grab dinner some time?"

Janae turned to stare at him. "Carter?"

He leaned a shoulder into the fence as he studied her. "I'd like to have dinner and get to know you better if you're willing."

She felt heat warring with confusion rise in her chest. Then she hopped down from the fence and put several feet between them as she remembered it was impossible. "You are my client." She emphasized each word.

"No. The museum is your client. I just work for it." A shadow flitted across his face but then cleared. "That doesn't mean we can't explore this . . ." He gestured between them.

"I don't date clients."

"Then it's a good thing I'm not a client." Carter took a step toward her, and she couldn't move, didn't want to move. "Because this is something I'd like to test." He leaned down and kissed her cheek, his lips the lightest brush.

A shiver crawled across her shoulders as he met her gaze with intensity.

"Uncle Carter, look at me." Andrew's voice jerked Carter away from her and he pivoted to watch his nephew.

All Janae could do was watch Carter, one hand protecting the spot on her cheek where he'd kissed her.

Chapter 30

SNOW FELL THE NEXT MONDAY morning as Carter prepared a school lunch for Andrew. The boy didn't appreciate the finer features of school cuisine and instead insisted on a lunch of salami, pepper jack cheese, and salty treats. An occasional Rice Krispies treat made him happy, but Andrew appreciated having the same thing every day in a routine that would have destroyed Carter's taste buds.

Carter inserted an ice pack and then zipped up the lunch box. Handing it to Andrew, he waited until his nephew accepted it. "Anything exciting happening at school today?"

"Nope."

"Any projects?"

The boy shook his blond head.

"Sports?

Another shake.

"PE?"

"Nope."

"Hmm. Sounds exciting."

"Nope."

"Will you learn anything?"

The boy shrugged, but a mischievous grin tipped his mouth up. "Not if I can help it."

"Ah."

"Can I walk to school today?"

"Walk?" Carter pointed toward the kitchen window. "It's flurrying."

"We didn't get snow where we lived."

"Really? Indianapolis never had snow?"

"Not often enough."

"Hmm." He hadn't enticed Andrew to say much about where he'd lived with his mom, and a counselor had warned him not to ask too much but instead let the child volunteer information. The whys didn't make a lot of sense to him, but his parents had reinforced the need to let Andrew talk when ready. It'd gotten to the point that Carter didn't poke or prod but instead pretended life hadn't existed for either of them before Andrew was turned over to Carter's care.

The challenge was creating conversation when one didn't know what to ask. Slowly though, Andrew was coming to him and volunteering more information.

"How about Froyo tonight after dinner?"

His nephew brightened, his grin growing even broader. "Pink Walrus?"

"I think we can do that."

"Shake?" Andrew thrust out his hand and watched him expectantly.

"Sure." He shook, then pulled Andrew close for a hug turned tickle. It felt good to watch the boy laugh with abandon. There hadn't been enough moments like this, and Carter determined to create more.

The mood carried him to the museum, where he found a double cappuccino waiting at his desk along with one of the curators. Todd Fremont was the closest person the museum had to someone who could oversee the restoration process on the damaged painting. Carter wasn't convinced he could actually conduct a complete restoration, but as he accepted the drink with thanks, he wondered what the fifty-year-old man had on his mind.

"Thanks for the caffeine." He took a sip and savored the nutty roast.

"You're going to need it."

"Why?"

"I arrived to a message from our insurance provider."

"Oh?"

"They're sending someone to assess the validity of our security."

"It's about time. The break-in was last Tuesday. I planned to follow up if I didn't hear from them today." Carter leaned back and took another fortifying sip. "When did they last conduct one?"

"About three years ago." Todd twirled the end of his dark mustache as he stared at the ceiling. "At the time, the director took the matter under advisement but didn't act on the recommendations. Partly because Stanley refused. You'd think a gallery owner would understand the importance of insurance."

"Were they advisory opinions or directives from the company?"

"Look for yourself." Todd pulled a thin sheaf of papers from a file Carter hadn't noticed.

Carter accepted the stapled document and started scanning. "Give me the CliffsNotes version."

"We need more cameras to cover blind spots, a better array of sensors, or more than one overnight guard."

Carter held up a hand. "We had an on-site night guard?"

"We did then, and the board decided we didn't need one anymore." Todd sighed. "Off-site monitoring isn't ideal, and last week proved that." He shook his head and continued ticking items off his fingers. "We needed more training and tools for the daytime security. Overall, we are an underdefended site that could easily be robbed. And this is without them taking much notice of how we store the items that aren't displayed in the galleries."

"Why would that matter?"

"Some museums have had untold numbers of items walk out from under their noses because they were hiring former felons to work unsupervised in the storage areas. Most don't have any idea what is actually in their collections, and we fall squarely in that category."

"I'd noticed the jumble in the basement tunnels."

"It happens when families donate entire estates of art to us. Did you hear how the family of Cora Kelly Ward donated all her unsold art to the Hilliard in Louisiana? There were 1,100 items, and the museum sold works of art from an artist we have hanging on our walls for a couple dollars a square foot. That was 2012, not a generation ago. The staff were too overwhelmed by the volume to do anything more with it. The entire collection sold for around eleven thousand dollars, and now one of the large paintings might sell for that."

Carter hadn't heard that particular story but didn't doubt its veracity. "That's a worst nightmare for me."

"And that's why we have too much in the basement."

"We'll make clearing that out in the right way a priority next year."

"That would be a start." Todd pushed to his feet. "We'll need a plan."

Carter rubbed the back of his neck as he flipped to the next page. "From your perspective, what is the number one thing we have to do?"

"Hire night security."

Carter nodded. Still, that might not be enough. This problem went deeper than he'd anticipated.

Monday morning Janae waited in line at the Lucky Bean for her morning infusion of caffeine. At some point she should buy an espresso machine so she could quit spending five dollars every morning, but there was something comforting about the familiarity of the buzz of background conversations and the spicy aroma of good coffee roasted fresh in the back rooms of the shop.

She was distracted, off her game as her thoughts kept drifting to the time with Carter and Andrew on Thanksgiving, which inevitably meant her thoughts returned to his kiss. She wondered what he would have done if she'd shifted the slightest bit, changing the trajectory of the kiss. Maybe it was a good thing she hadn't been able to move, because she couldn't imagine how much that kiss would impact her if it hadn't been on her cheek.

"Janae!"

A warm voice had her searching the space for someone she knew. Janae spotted a friend of her mother's sitting in the corner, a large mug that looked more like a bowl resting on the table in front of her. "Mrs. Apple, how are you?"

"It's Dottie now that you're all grown up."

"Yes, ma'am."

"Have you talked to your mom lately? She hasn't returned my call from last week."

"We've been working at my grandmother's."

"I'm sure that's a process. My parents waited to get rid of anything until it was too late. The number of margarine bowls they'd acquired stunned me. They were lovely people but had lived in that home too long." She shook her head, but a small smile touched her lips. "It's why I tell my husband we have to pretend we're moving every four or five years. I refuse to do that to my kids."

"I can imagine that was a lot."

"It was, but that's how that generation was. They worked hard but lived as if the Depression had never ended."

Janae nodded. "Grandma wants to get through it all, but it takes time to weed through memories and deal with everything. I'm proud of what we've accomplished."

"I'm sure you are."

Janae glanced at her watch. "I need to grab my latte and get to the office, but I'll be sure to let Mom know you say hi when I see her."

"No need. I'm sure I'll see her at Bible study."

"Of course. Have a nice day." Janae turned to the drink counter and picked up her cup, glad she wouldn't have to wait longer. She didn't have the emotional energy to deal with people right now. The mention of her grandmother had resurrected the questions she'd barely put aside long enough to get some sleep. Instead, her dreams had been papered with soldier-styled silhouettes who stuck to the shadows, spiriting away small, medium, and large frames.

The meaning didn't elude her. She remained preoccupied about how her grandfather had come to be in possession of the paintings. The book Grandma had sent home with her didn't help.

Could Grandpa have stolen them? Or had he as a young GI Joe purchased them legally? She imagined people were desperate in the desolation after the war and would have sold family treasures to survive.

She hurried the last few feet to her firm and unlocked the front door with a forceful twist of the key.

There was always a way to find answers. The challenge was finding the first thread. She pulled up her computer files with the photos she'd taken of the front and back of the paintings at the museum. Carter had urged her to do that to capture the information on where each might have been stored or consigned. It didn't matter how she blew up the images, she had no idea what the stamps and marks meant. The back of each was a maze of scratches and scrawls. The front, paint and a frame.

After a minute she admitted defeat and pushed back from her computer and monitor. She didn't have the training to know what to do. Carter was so busy with his own problems, she didn't want to ask for time-consuming favors. Surely with the Smithsonian an hour away she could find someone who could help. Anyone would know more than she did.

But how to know who to ask?

If the paintings were stolen, would she get in trouble by asking for help identifying it?

Ethan at Haney & Sons had immediately assumed she'd stolen the Bruegel.

Would someone at a museum make the same assumption?

That chilled her urge to get help. It felt like unlocking a Pandora's box of questions and decisions she couldn't anticipate. What would it do to Grandma if Janae's worst fears were accurate?

She rubbed her forehead as she tried to decide the right approach.

Hiding from the truth wasn't an option.

But if it harmed her grandma, it might not be worth the cost.

Does it really hurt to wait?

Then she thought of her interaction with Clara Seeger. The woman was a few years older than Grandma, and she remained haunted by all that had been taken from her family during the war. What if Grandpa had done something similar by picking up a painting? Her stomach roiled at the thought. She couldn't imagine him participating in something that broke the law. Surely war didn't change the rules of engagement to allow for taking others' personal property. But as she did a quick online search, she was struck by the way the Russian army had absorbed cultural treasures as a form of restitution during the brutal days along the Eastern Front.

Her grandfather was gone, so she couldn't ask him. And every attorney knew the only good question to ask was the one you already knew the answer to. Not letting someone ask you a question you couldn't answer effectively could serve as its corollary. She certainly didn't have that kind of knowledge right now.

Chloe rapped on the door and entered. "A prospective client is on the way."

"What type of case?"

"Not sure yet. The woman wouldn't give much detail beyond her name, even though I told her it might be a waste of her time." Her friend shuddered. "What if she's an accused murderer?"

"I'm pretty certain no one would direct her to me." Janae rubbed her eyes and examined her friend. "Are you ready to apply to law school yet? You know I believe in you."

Chloe's shoulders hunched, and she wrapped her arms around her middle as if protecting herself from attack. "I don't know if that's what I want anymore."

"Of the three of us, you were the one most likely to argue and win." Janae decided to ease up and pray the idea took root. "I'll write a letter of recommendation whenever you're ready. All you have to do is ask."

"Don't wait with expectation." Chloe turned back to the door. "Her name is Agatha Lansbury. She should be here in twenty minutes."

"Lansbury?"

"I know. Be careful."

"She must mean Angela, a nom de plume." Janae turned to social media and did a quick search on a couple of sites to see if anyone nearby had that name. Nothing came up, confirming her suspicion it wasn't the woman's actual name.

That didn't make her excited to meet the mystery woman, but she'd try to reserve judgment and not assume the woman was borrowing the famous actress's name with a slight twist. Time dragged by as Janae tried to focus on anything but her circling questions about the paintings. Between the two at the museum and the two from her grandparents, she felt surrounded by art with questionable histories. Or was that a euphemistic way of hiding her real fear? Did the paintings have checkered pasts that included theft?

Chapter 31

A KNOCK ON HER DOOR brought Janae's head up with a jerk. Chloe stood there with a petite woman behind her.

"Janae, this is our Agatha Lansbury." Chloe's eyes were wide, but she had a polite smile in place. "She came from Almost Home and has some questions for you. You might remember her as Arianna Hough from high school."

Janae stood, relieved to have a bit of a break. "I do. It's good to see you, though I'm sorry it's in these circumstances."

"Thank you."

"Why don't you have a seat and tell me how I can help?"

Arianna met her gaze squarely. "I need someone to go to court with me on Wednesday. My friend works at the shelter and suggested you."

"What type of hearing?" Janae took a moment to observe the woman. Her dark chestnut hair was pulled back in a low ponytail with a paisley scarf tied around it. Her lavender sweater matched her eyes, and she had a quiet attractiveness that would catch attention.

"It's a bit crazy, but my neighbor has sued me for defamation." Arianna went on to explain how her neighbor had stalked her and then sued her after Arianna got a preliminary restraining order. When Arianna had arrived in court to turn the preliminary into a more permanent order that would last up to two years, the other woman had served her with the lawsuit. "The hearing on that is Wednesday, and I want it all to go away." Her eyes turned glassy, and she swallowed hard. "I need this to end."

Janae's heart went out to the woman. "I think I can help. Did you bring the paperwork with you?"

Twenty minutes later, she walked Arianna to the front door with a promise to meet her at court on Wednesday. Now she had just a few minutes to get ready for her next appointment with Carter. When Chloe showed him in, Janae was set up in the conference room, with a memo that outlined her ideas. His reaction would tell her a lot about how they should proceed.

She forced herself to remember he was the client and not the man who had teased a kiss onto her cheek. She couldn't afford to dream about what a real kiss would be like.

Carter studied her from his seat at the table. She felt the warmth of his attention surround her, as did a silence that wasn't uncomfortable. Finally, he looked at the folder she'd set at his seat. "What's this?"

"My strategy."

He arched a brow. "The high-level view?"

"We have two choices. We can wait to see Shaw's plan or take the initiative."

"Let me guess. You prefer action."

"I do, but only because it allows us to stop responding and start leading." She settled back, certain she had the right approach. "One of the vagaries of the law is that it can be difficult to get ahead of a case you don't control. It's not impossible, just challenging. So far, we've had to respond to Shaw because his client has the information. It's possible to change that."

"Take a trip to Hanover."

"Much as I'd love a quick trip to Germany, I'm not fluent in German. Have you hired someone to explore the archives in Berlin and at the Landesmuseum?"

"The head curator there is emailing everything they have by to-morrow."

"That's great and should give us key information to build our strat-egy around."

"What's next?"

"How technical do you want me to get with the legal piece of this puzzle?"

"As technical as necessary."

"The information from Hanover will help on that painting, but I'm not as concerned about that one because it's on loan."

"Do we owe the Landesmuseum anything because of the loan?"

"Not that I can tell because you have the painting as bailee. Shaw will have to go after the Landesmuseum. There's really nothing we can do about the one on loan." She mentally ran back through the research. There had been a case or two where the US museum was asked to turn over the painting, but she didn't think that would happen successfully here. There were too many variables to be certain. Her look strayed to him. He was rubbing his face as he studied the file. Then he looked up, and their gazes locked. She wanted to reach across the table and kiss him for real. Assure him they'd be a good team. Maybe then she could focus. This was exactly why she didn't consider dating clients. She couldn't afford the distraction.

"That's a serious look."

"Hmm?" She blinked a couple of times and refocused on Carter.

He gestured to her. "You weren't here a minute ago."

She refused to meet his gaze. "Deciding how to keep this under-standable."

He rolled his eyes. "I might not have gone to law school, but I'll keep up."

"All right." She pulled her legal pad from the stack and sketched a couple of circles. "So let's focus on the painting in the Elliott's collec-tion. My research indicates museums have taken a variety of approaches in prior cases. Some settled with the heirs prior to a lawsuit being filed.

Others waited and responded to the lawsuits after they were filed. Still others hurried to file lawsuits that had claims ranging from laches to quiet title."

"Wait a minute. What do you mean by laches?"

"Basically, that the heirs waited too long to file, and that placed the museums at a disadvantage. At the moment I like the idea of using both laches and quiet title. The key will be demonstrating when the heirs became aware of the current locations of the paintings."

"If we can find the most up-to-date catalogue raisonné, we might learn a lot of that. And if not, we can hire someone to create it for our two paintings. When properly compiled and documented, each artwork has a clear list of who has owned it from the artist to the current owner." He leaned forward on the table, his excitement evident. "A good one will include details like purchase price, who sold it, if an intermediary was used, and more."

"And if it isn't a good one?"

"Then there will be holes. That's where looking at past correspondence and other documentation can help."

"How long does it take to create one?"

"Months if you're lucky. The compilers are like art history detectives." He leaned back and crossed his arms as if protecting himself from a hard truth. "The challenge is, I've looked through the ones I could find, and I haven't clearly found our paintings. Just ones that are similar. These seem to fall in holes that could take a year or more to try to fill."

"We don't have that kind of time, so I think we push them on the defensive. We can argue that the heirs have their rights barred by laches."

"How?"

"Make the heirs show they haven't missed a statute of limitations related to the paintings. The key to laches is explaining that a passage of time combined with a change in condition would make it inequitable to enforce a claim against the Elliott. The question revolves around what information is available that reinforces the claim." She filled in one of the circles on the paper with a three. "Since the statute of limitations for a claim like this is three years, we need to demonstrate that Mrs. Seeger and any other heirs should have come forward within an earlier three-year time period."

Carter grimaced. "No problem."

"I need you to give me a clear picture of the history of the painting since, roughly, 1930 to when the museum acquired it."

"Why that window?"

"Because it's before the Nazis took power in Austria. One of the main grounds for these types of claims is that even if the Nazis didn't force the sale, their persecution of Jews led to others doing the same, creating an environment that led to systemic persecution." And that called all sales or dispersals of art and other goods during the window before and after the war into question.

"Which circles us back to the catalogue raisonné for the Botticelli."

"And means your priority is finishing the search of the museum's records as well as hiring someone to do a search in Germany and Austria. You have to close the window on any gaps related to who owned that painting."

"Suzy Werblow might know someone who can help with that."

"Who?"

"The curator at the Landesmuseum. The records she's emailing may contain everything we need."

"Perfect. The key is she needs to understand the importance and time sensitivity of this."

"I think she gets it." Carter sighed and it turned into a yawn. "I need some caffeine before I absorb more."

"Follow me." She led him to the postcard-sized kitchen. After refilling the Nespresso with water, she showed him where the pods were and pulled out half-and-half from the dorm-sized fridge.

As he waited for his drink to brew, Carter watched her. "So focus on the provenance since 1930?"

"That seems to be the key to each of the legal theories. Our best defense is showing that the heirs knew where the paintings were and had ample opportunity to claim them." She handed him his mug and then started a shot for her latte. "There's some room for interpretation, but the Monuments Men turned over art to countries following World War II, and there was a process to file a claim at that time."

"What if the family was more focused on survival?"

"Then that's their burden to prove, not ours. With the Botticelli, a quiet title action is another unique approach, because it asks the court to determine whether the museum properly acquired the painting as a good faith purchaser. This simply requires that the museum had no actual or constructive knowledge that the painting carried a tainted history—in this case, that it had been bought, sold, or stolen due to its owners being persecuted because they were Jewish." She swirled frothed milk into her mug. "Shall we go back?"

They carried their finished coffees back to the conference room.

With both back in their seats, Janae told Carter how she'd file the lawsuit in the local federal district court since Mrs. Seeger resided in Arizona, but the museum and the painting were in Virginia. That satisfied the requirement of parties from different states. The dollar amount wasn't hard to reach since the last fair-market purchase of a similar Botticelli had been more than ninety-two million dollars.

However, the *Five Children* painting was more complicated, because it was on loan from the Landesmuseum rather than owned by the Elliott. "Some heirs file *in rem* jurisdiction lawsuits, but I'm unconvinced we can get ahead of anything Shaw has planned for that painting."

Carter looked up from the notebook where he'd taken notes. "Those are the legal issues."

"Most of them."

"We haven't talked about the ethical issues."

To Carter the ethics were more complicated than the legal issues. Janae didn't look like she agreed as she frowned at him.

"The ethical ones?"

"Yes, what's the right thing to do? Museums owe an ethical duty of due diligence in the stewardship of our collections. We're supposed to verify the ownership of the items in our control and verify the attribution. With these two paintings, the attribution isn't questioned. Then we have to decide whether to support or resist a claim for restitution." He knew she already knew more than he could hope to learn about the legal issues. She'd become an expert in the couple of weeks she'd been hired, but he had the deeper understanding of the stewardship issues inherent with museums.

"I suppose."

"But if you're right that the legal issues are moot, then the remaining issue is what do we do? What's the right response?"

"First you need to verify Mrs. Seeger's claims."

He sighed as the weight of responsibility settled on him. "Whatever we do will set a precedent. I've got to get a handle on our collection and make sure the prior directors and curators have completed due diligence on the provenance prior to purchasing works." He blew out a breath at the scope of what would be required to confirm the history of each piece.

"The ethical issues you've outlined are board-level decisions. I can give advice but not direction. However, if you get to the point of deciding whether to settle or file, you have several options that I saw in the cases. One, you can return the object in dispute."

"Probably not something the board will support."

"Two, you can repurchase at an appropriate price from the prewar owner's heirs. Three, you can let the heirs purchase it from you."

"If it's been on display here, both of those could be hard sells."

"Four, you could consider a joint sale to a third party and split the proceeds. Or five, you could give a formal acknowledgment of new information leading to a rediscovered provenance." Janae looked up from her notes. "That's the best I have for you right now."

"That's a lot to think about. The ethical issues run much deeper and will be more challenging to navigate with the board. What do you recommend I take to it?"

"Set up a meeting, and I can outline the legal options we discussed. I'm leaning toward a combined laches and quiet title suit. Between the two, the judge should decide who gets the Botticelli."

"Then I'd better get to work." He stood and collected the papers and his notes into a pile. "We've been doing a lot of work, and my mom is here with Andrew tonight. Want to join me for dinner?"

Janae stood and studied him a moment, wishing everything inside her didn't scream yes. But there wasn't a single no where he was concerned. "I think we can do that. But only if you agree to one thing."

"What's that?"

"Help me figure out what is the right thing to do with my grandma's paintings." Her cell rang before Carter could answer. She frowned at it and then looked at him. "Sorry, it's listing as the police department." She blanched, and he reached out to catch her if she fainted. "Hello?"

He waited for her to say something, but she only got whiter and then hung up.

Her eyes were big as she looked up at him. "The police chief wants me to come in to talk about Mark Ashby."

"Did he say why?"

"The man was poisoned."

Chapter 32

JANAE CHEWED ON HER THUMBNAIL as she waited for Margeaux to sprint up the sidewalk outside the police station.

Margeaux wore a red beret that combined with her navy dress and brown boots to give her a jaunty air that didn't match the concern in her eyes. She pulled Janae into a hug. "What did he say?"

"Nothing other than someone poisoned Mark." Janae didn't let herself melt into Margeaux. Instead, she straightened and turned toward the door. "Let's get this over with."

"Just a minute." Margeaux didn't let go as Janae tried to move on. "Is there anything I need to know? Anything at all?"

The intensity in her friend's gaze paused Janae. "No. I really don't know what happened."

"Do you have the files Mark wanted?"

"I gave them to you to give to Mr. Ashley on the day Mark died."

Margeaux frowned. "Then I must have taken them there. And you never read them?"

"No." She sighed. "Maybe I should."

"It might give us an idea of who wanted to kill him."

"It didn't seem as important as figuring out how to stop the lawsuits."

Or figuring out her grandma's paintings. Janae rubbed her forehead as she sensed pressure building. "I never thought art could be this dangerous."

"I don't know that it's the art."

"It is if the Seeger files caused the murder."

The door opened and Officer Alston stuck his head outside. "You two coming inside? Or do you want us to conduct the interview out here?"

"Inside is great." Margeaux swept in with a regal bearing. "No need to be churlish, Joel."

Janae marveled at the way her friend ignored the flash of anger that tightened the officer's jaw. "Where would you like us to go?"

"The interview room is this way." He let the door close behind them and sauntered down a hallway. At an open door, he paused and waited for them to precede him. "I'll let the chief know you're here."

Janae sank onto a chair, her knees weak. "They don't think I had anything to do with his death, right?"

"Sure. Just like everyone believed us when we complained about that doctor." Margeaux's words had a bitter edge as she plopped next to Janae. "It'll be fine. Chief Sanderson is a good man. There isn't much crime here, so I'm sure this is just a precaution."

"But poison." Janae didn't want to imagine anyone thought her capable of murder, but it was there. She'd found the man's body and hadn't mourned his death. The door opened and she couldn't stop a small squeak.

The police chief walked in with a subtle limp and settled into a chair opposite Janae and Margeaux. "Welcome back, ladies."

"What happened to you, Chief?" Margeaux leaned forward and watched him.

"Pulled a muscle running in the Turkey Trot." He focused on Janae. "You still have those files from the other day?"

"No sir. Margeaux dropped them off for me like you asked."

"Read them?"

"No."

He settled back and watched her. "Why not? Not even curious?"

"Of course, but it didn't feel right."

"Didn't take pictures with your phone?" She grimaced as he nailed her, and he leaned forward. "Thought so. Look at those?"

"Not yet."

He pulled a card from his pocket and handed it to her. "Send them here. I'll work on getting the actual files too." Then he settled back against the chair. "Tell me more about the morning you arrived at the law firm."

"There's nothing much to tell. No one was there."

"No vehicles in the parking lot?"

"No."

"Alley?"

"No." Then she paused, a memory tugging at the corners of her mind. "There was a pickup pulling out of the alley."

"Color?"

"White."

"Make?"

"No idea. And no idea on year either."

"All right. See anything else?"

"No." She wished there was something she could say. Something that would make him look far from her, but there wasn't anything. "I saw him and called 911 as quickly as I could. Then I waited until your officer and the paramedics arrived."

"And no idea who could want to kill him?"

Janae swallowed. Hard. The words were so stark and harsh. "No."

Margeaux seemed to decide it had gone long enough. "Anything else, Chief?"

He considered them both a minute. "Not right now."

"Great. You know where to find Janae if anything else comes up." She stood and put a hand on Janae's arm. "Come on, Janae. I know you have a hearing to prepare for."

Janae followed her out but turned and saw Chief Sanderson standing in the doorway, watching her. It was only when she was standing back outside that Janae could breathe.

Janae had seemed distant since Carter picked her up at the law firm. She'd asked not to talk about the police, and he understood that desire. So he tried not to watch as she shivered and tugged her scarf tighter. But as she strolled next to him, he knew they needed this. They'd both worked hard and needed the chance to relax and forget everything for a bit. Their arms brushed occasionally as they walked side by side along the sidewalk, and he liked the closeness it implied.

"Where are we going?" She'd let the silence linger about a minute longer than he expected.

Carter shrugged his shoulders and kept his hands firmly in his pockets. "I'm not sure."

"Really?"

"I thought we could walk until we found a place with food that sounded good."

"The no plans method?"

"Yep." He stopped in front of a store window surrounded with twinkle lights. "I guess I should go Christmas shopping soon."

"It would be a good idea to avoid repeating the whole forgetting-a-major-holiday thing."

"I didn't really forget Thanksgiving. That was Andrew being dramatic. Even if I had, Christmas is a little more in my face." He paused and waved an arm around him. "Look at all the lights."

"We do like our Christmas around here." She started walking and he gladly followed.

"Why?"

"I don't really know. We don't play up a fox hunt like other nearby towns. Maybe we want a unique identity. We're not DC, but we're also distinct from Leesburg and other towns."

"Doesn't Monroe College help with that fresh identity?"

"Most of the time, but if you don't work for or attend Monroe, it's not as impactful as you might imagine." She paused in front of a Chinese restaurant. "Do you want to try this one?"

Carter glanced at the menu taped to the front window. "What's not to love about copious amounts of rice and MSG?"

"We don't have to eat here."

But he opened the door and ushered her through. Soon they sat at a small table, knees touching underneath its surface, and he tried to think of witty things to say that kept her laughing as they ate until he couldn't find space for a fortune cookie.

"See? This was better than spinning our wheels another night." He took a sip of lukewarm green tea and sat back, a feeling of contentment settling over him.

"I have to admit you're right." She looked over his shoulder, seeing something in the distance, then she refocused on him. "What's your BHAG?"

"My what?"

"The big, hairy, audacious goal that scares you."

"Wow, you don't ask easy questions."

She leaned forward on the table and propped her head on a hand. "Nope. I don't know what mine is right now, so inspire me."

Carter considered her a moment, reluctant to give a quick answer. After a moment he gave a firm nod. "I want to know what happened to Charlotte. She's my sister, and the reason I have Andrew." He swallowed and looked away, his shoulder rounding a bit. "Andrew hasn't asked many questions, but when he does, I can't answer them." He swallowed again and blinked a few times. "She loved creating art. But something Stanley said . . ."

"Stanley Dukes?"

"Yes. Charlotte was killed when the gallery owner who sold her paintings got into a shoot-out with a member of an Italian crime family, who was also Andrew's father. Stanley hinted that Charlotte forged paintings. None of it makes sense." He rubbed the back of his neck and shifted on the chair. "He's this Goliath with a reputation. I was a lowly post-doc. He suggested Charlotte was the painter and involved with money laundering somehow."

"That's a big accusation." Janae studied him as her thumb moved rhythmically over the top of his hand. "Is there any way to determine whether he was right?"

"He owns a small string of galleries and sat on the board of the museum where I had my post-doc. He successfully blamed me for a forged painting that surfaced at that museum. Claimed Charlotte had painted it, but she had been killed, and I couldn't disprove his claims. He about destroyed my reputation."

"Why?"

"I've never been sure. He didn't like that I asked questions, I guess."

"Then why hire you here?"

"I'm not sure he knew."

"Come on. He had to."

Carter shook his head. "Maybe not. He was in the middle of getting kicked off that other board for abuse of power. If I'd known he was involved at the Elliott in any way, I would have stayed far away. He wasn't listed on the website anywhere, then when I show up for my first day, he's suddenly the chair." He grimaced. "There's something about him, and I'm not sure what it is. He gets others to trust him but abuses that trust. He'll take us all in a direction we shouldn't go, and I'm afraid of what he'll convince the board to do."

"So how do we counter that?"

He pushed his bowl back, stacking the chopsticks across the top. "I'm not sure."

"Why are you worried?" Janae's eyes filled with concern. "Surely you can stop him."

"Not without returning to a museum where I'm persona non grata. He thoroughly destroyed me there. Nobody took my side." It had been the loneliest period of his life, made worse by the loss of Charlotte. "Then my sister died, leaving Andrew behind." He pushed back from the table, slipping his hand free from Janae's, and clasped his hands in front of him.

"I'm so sorry, Carter." She reached out again, and her touch lent more comfort than a thousand words. He looked down and noted how small her hand was compared to his, yet there was such strength in her too. "What can I do to help?"

"Listening is more than I expected."

"Of course." She smiled, but it was tinged with sadness.

"Listening can be a great gift." He rolled his neck and pushed the thoughts away. "Thanks."

"And not listening is a curse."

It sounded like there was a story there, but without an invitation to go deeper. "I can't do anything for Charlotte but take good care of Andrew. He's all she had."

"Then that's your focus." She leaned back. "Kedgewick can be a great place to grow up. And we can make it that for Andrew. There are all kinds of places to get involved."

"We'll explore the mountains this spring."

"You'll love all that the Shenandoah and Blue Ridge Mountains have to offer." She looked at him through lowered lashes. "I could show you a few excellent trails."

"I'd like that." The conversation spiraled from there to their experiences in college and living in other places. It felt like one long exhale, a chance to sink into the moment and build a friendship that might become more.

The night ended before he was ready to leave Janae's company, but she was the one to recognize he should go home to Andrew. And he appreciated her even more for that.

That night, Janae sat in the upstairs carriage room, the lights off, watching the night sky through the windows. There had been something sacred and special about the dinner with Carter. She wanted to deny the way she felt around him, but he saw her in a way no one else had. Maybe because she hadn't let them. She hadn't exactly made time for men.

She'd been driven through college and law school, knowing she had to put her head down and work hard if she wanted the degrees to open the doors she aspired to walk through. She'd been disciplined, and it had paid off. She'd accomplished everything she'd hoped for and found it hollow.

Would that happen again?

Part of her was afraid to dream about the future. Her first dream had left her empty.

Would this one be different?

She thought of Andrew and how he'd lit up during Thanksgiving. That young man deserved the truth about his mother, but she didn't have any more info than Carter. Still, a quick Google search wouldn't hurt. She went downstairs and grabbed her laptop before going back to the small love seat she'd tucked against the wall. She leaned over to find the outlet but had to push a box out of the way to reach it. A book fell from the box, and she scooped it up. It opened, revealing rough hand-writing, and she set it to the side. She could give it to Grandma when she went to the house in the morning.

Maybe she could learn more about Charlotte Montgomery and the scandal Carter had mentioned. A quick search didn't reveal anything that matched what Carter had discussed. She needed to know where Charlotte had lived. She entered the museum that appeared in Carter's bio, but that didn't help either.

She set the laptop aside and reached for her phone. A quick text could start filling in the blanks if he wanted to share.

Then she paused. Maybe she was overreaching.

They were building a friendship, but she sensed he kept his past close. The fact he had started sharing with her was something she didn't want to short-circuit. Not when she wanted to spend more time with him.

She carried the book to the house and grabbed an orange from the kitchen. Grandma must have already gone to bed, because all the lights except the one over the kitchen sink were turned off. She cracked the book again, noted it looked like Grandpa's handwriting, and left it on the kitchen table. She grabbed a piece of scrap paper from the drawer and scrawled a quick note.

Found this in the carriage house. Looks like Grandpa's writing, so I thought you'd want to read it. Love you.

She signed her name and then headed back to the carriage house.

Chapter 33

AFTER A TUESDAY SPENT ON research, Janae felt excited butterflies at the thought of returning to a courtroom. She used to love court and the planned chaos that erupted there. It was her home away from home, at times more so than her parents' horse farm where she'd grown up. Then she'd lost her mind and filed the wrong paperwork, and now she found her stomach in knots as she thought about that morning's hearing. The Loudon County Courthouse was under renovation, one of those never-ending construction projects that made life miserable for everyone. It reminded her of her time as an undergrad at Purdue University, which had been a carousel of construction and change.

She'd left ample time to travel from her office in Kedgewick to Leesburg and the courthouse since it usually took twenty minutes, but as she dashed down Church Street, she'd cut it close.

Her late-night review of the filed documents had confirmed Arianna's story that the case would be straightforward.

She glanced both directions before crossing the street and noted a woman several paces behind her. The woman was stylishly dressed in an all-black ensemble. Then, when Janae passed the window display of a boutique, she paused long enough to look like she examined the latest dresses on display. Instead, she used the large window to spot the woman similarly pause a couple of storefronts down.

Janae frowned and then hustled across the street to the courthouse emblazoned against a bright blue sky. The brick court and government building sprawled across the block with a distinctly colonial feel, trees and grass surrounding what wasn't edged by sidewalk. Once she was inside, anyone following her would have to make the same pass through the metal detectors, so she picked up her pace.

She stood in the security line while attorneys with court IDs bypassed the X-ray machines and headed for the stairs. She needed to get one of those to save time on future court days. While she waited, she kept sneaking a look over her shoulder, tensing as the woman appeared about ten people behind her. Finally she was through the line and bypassed the ornamental main elevator as well as the more modern elevator that could hold six or seven smushed people. Good thing she preferred the stairs any day as she hurried to disappear into the maze of courtrooms.

Janae hustled up the stairs, then stood in the rotunda looking for her client. Today's hearing should be relatively fast and straightforward. Simply ask the judge to dismiss the suit, because the issuing judge believed the facts as presented, or the judge wouldn't have extended the protective order past the preliminary stage.

After she circled the rotunda, she found Arianna, who approached with hesitant movements, chin tucked and shoulders rounded. Her brown hair was pulled in front of her ears in a way that shielded her face from scrutiny. She wore simple dark-wash jeans, a white turtleneck, and a cognac leather jacket with matching heeled booties. The clothes and shoes indicated a woman who knew how to dress to impress in a classic way, yet her current demeanor showed a woman who was cowed by something or someone.

Janae placed a steadying hand on the woman's arm. "Are you okay, Arianna?"

The young woman nodded. "Just nervous about seeing my neighbor."

"Let's sit here." She returned to the bench and waited for Arianna to ease next to her. "As we discussed Monday, this will be simple. It's your chance to ask the judge to dismiss the defamation charge. If she doesn't agree, we'll move forward."

"I thought I was ready, but the moment I walked into the court-house, something changed." Arianna shook her head. "All I want is to be left alone. I'm pretty sure my ex-boyfriend is behind this. He told me he'd make my life miserable if I didn't come back to him, but this is more than I can handle. I don't have the money to pay for more than today."

"Keep your focus on right now. When we know what the judge does, then you can worry about next steps." Janae would keep thinking and working, but Arianna didn't need to consider that far down the road, especially if it made her a nervous witness now. The judge had to believe her. "Let me tell the bailiff we're here. Then we can go into court."

"Can I come with you?" Arianna's breath had started to come in quick gulps.

"It's okay. You're safe here."

"If that was true, I wouldn't be back here. I'd be at work where I be-long, helping people."

"Tell me about your job." Maybe that would distract her long enough to calm and center her.

"I work with children who have learning challenges. I used to go to the schools, but now I work primarily from home."

"Remind me how you were stalked?" If the woman rarely left her house, it might be challenging to prove stalking had occurred.

"Notes left on my door. Calls and texts multiple times a day. Some-times every five minutes for an hour. It was crazy chaos. When I did leave, my neighbor always appeared where I was. Then she was so an-gry after I asked for the emergency protective order that she punched through my front window."

"Do you have photos?" Arianna hadn't mentioned this in their meeting.

"On my phone."

"Let's get this started. You can stand outside the door while I'm in the office."

Arianna waited immediately outside the glass door, and Janae kept an eye on her as she approached the judge's assistant, freezing momentarily when she spotted the woman in black again. What was going on? "Defendant is here for the hearing." She showed the clerk the cause number and then collected Arianna. "We can head on in. The judge will appear in a few minutes."

This general court wasn't for complex disputes. No big cases or juries. Just the judge and the parties, maybe a few witnesses.

Arianna stopped inside the doors. "Which table do we sit at?"

"The one on the left when facing the judge." Janae led the way. "Not all judges care, but it's a good rule of thumb." The plaintiff's table was empty as they sat. Janae barely had time to organize her file and notebook when the judge entered with a swish of her robes.

The bailiff stood. "All rise. The court is now in session."

Arianna and Janae stood, but the judge motioned them down. "Be seated." She looked around the court with a pointed pause on the plaintiff's table. "Is the other party here?"

Janae shook her head. "No, Your Honor."

Judge Plautz frowned as she slid reading glasses on her nose and then she looked at her court reporter. "Have we heard from the plaintiff or her attorney?"

"No, Your Honor."

"We will wait five minutes and then we'll have a continuance."

Janae stood. "If I may."

"Yes."

"We are here because the plaintiff filed an action against my client. We would like to have the arguments on our motion to dismiss. The plaintiff through her attorney had notice of this hearing. Because it also relates to the underlying facts that were grounds for the protective order my client received, it is important to resolve this in a timely matter."

"It would be irregular to proceed without the plaintiff."

"Not if she fails to show after proper service of process. My office filed that a second time as a precaution with the court yesterday." She was so glad Chloe had stayed on top of the details. Her friend was well on her way to becoming an excellent paralegal.

The judge considered for a moment, leaning back in her chair and staring at the ceiling. "Let's see if they arrive. You might call opposing counsel while we wait."

"All right." Janae turned to Arianna. "You can stay here while I make that call." As her client hunched her shoulders and looked down, Janae's stomach fell. "You'll be safe here. I'll stand outside the door and make sure no one enters before me."

Fortunately, there was a small nook between the courtroom's doors and the rotunda, so Janae placed the call there. No one answered at the law firm, so she called Chloe on her cell. "Sorry to bother you at your other job. Any word from opposing counsel? He and his client haven't arrived, and the judge won't wait."

"Nothing here."

"Okay." She rubbed her forehead as she tried to figure out what the endgame was. "They filed the lawsuit and demanded a quick hearing."

"Any reason to think this is a distraction?"

"Every case is for somebody." Janae leaned back against the wall as she looked into the rotunda. "There's no one here, and Arianna looks ready to implode."

"This stalking has done a number on her." Chloe's sigh reached Janae. "She was a different woman in high school. Bubbly. Full of confidence. The quintessential homecoming queen."

"Sometimes life beats us down."

"Not this much."

Janae bit the inside of her mouth to keep from denying that statement. "I'd better get inside the courtroom and see what the judge wants to do."

"All right. I'll text if I hear anything."

"Thanks." When Janae returned to the courtroom, Arianna hadn't moved. Janae retook her seat and leaned toward her client. "Chloe reminded me you were homecoming queen."

"That was a long time ago."

"It was, but let's find some of that confidence again. What this woman has done isn't fair, but you're still the woman who was voted to that role."

"It takes a bit more than a few words to undo the last ten years."

"Then let's dig in and do what it takes." Janae covered her hand where it rested on the table, felt the light tremble. "I don't see the judge, so let me touch base with her in her chambers and see how she wants to move forward."

"Okay."

Janae squeezed Arianna's hand and then stood. "I'll be right back."

When Janae reached the courthouse rotunda, the woman in black waited against the wall.

Enough.

Janae marched up to her, and the woman didn't move.

Instead, she smirked at Janae. "Took you long enough."

"Who are you and why are you following me?"

"I don't matter, but you tell your friend at the museum that we know what he has, and my boss wants it back. If he doesn't cooperate, something will happen to the boy." There was a slight accent to her words, but before Janae could say anything more, the woman pushed from the wall and slipped a card into Janae's blazer pocket. "He can call this number." Then she sashayed around the rotunda and disappeared down the stairs.

Janae pulled out her phone, racing to get the camera app to open, but by the time it was, the woman was already blending into the crowd. The few photos Janae snapped didn't show any specific details that would help her find the woman. She looked around but none of the sheriff's deputies who usually lingered in the area as security were around. Janae hurried to the stairs but didn't see the woman, then she glanced back to the courtroom and saw Arianna's worried face. She headed to the judge's chambers and asked the receptionist to alert the deputies to the woman's threats. A minute later a deputy hurried in, a hand on his gun, but when he realized there was no immediate threat, he relaxed.

"Can't you do something?"

"Do you see her, ma'am?"

"No." Janae tried not to growl her frustration.

"Then all we can do is keep an eye out for your mystery woman."

"Fine." But Janae knew she wouldn't let Arianna leave on her own.

An hour later the judge had postponed the hearing with a firmly worded order, and Arianna had followed Janae to the street, walking with new strength, giving Janae a quick hug before sliding into her car. Janae considered the transformation. She'd never had this type of quick impact when working for large companies.

Then her fingers brushed the card in her pocket and her thoughts traveled to the woman and her veiled threat. What was she going to tell Carter?

Chapter 34

THE SOUND OF STEPS RUNNING down the hall pulled Carter from the conference room where he'd spent the day working. "Janae?" His gaze raked her as he took in her wide eyes and flushed cheeks. "What's wrong?"

She slowed and took a couple of deep breaths. "Nothing."

"This doesn't look like nothing."

She reached into her blazer pocket and pulled out a card. "While I was at court in Leesburg this morning, a woman gave me this. For you."

"What?" He took the card and held it by the edge.

"Exactly."

He glanced down at the card and felt his hand go cold. The name was one he knew. Emilio Piancone. It was a name Charlotte used to talk about all the time and then had stopped, months before her life changed. "This man is part of an Italian crime family." And the numbers matched those on the card that had been given to him. "He's also dead."

"That's bad."

"It gets worse."

Janae frowned and glanced over the card. "I don't recognize the name."

"I think he was Andrew's dad." Carter flipped the card over, noted another scrawl. "Can you read this?"

"Rahul Gershkovich?" She looked at him. "Do you know this name?"

"No."

"Oh." She swallowed and looked up at Carter. "Did Andrew know his dad?"

"No. My understanding is Emilio didn't want anything to do with being a dad nine years ago. Then he showed up right before Charlotte's death." He rubbed his forehead. "There was a man in Indianapolis. Maybe he was Rahul?" He held up the card. "This suggests there's a connection." What was he supposed to do with that?

"What sort of connection?"

"I don't know. He was there, as was Emilio. In fact, that's how Stanley bought a painting." He started to have a bad feeling. The painting . . .

"You look like you've seen a ghost."

"I might have." He shook his head. "Right now I need to protect Andrew. Did you hear the part about Emilio being involved with a crime family?"

Janae walked away in that pacing-thinking way she had. "Then we just have to prepare our best defense."

Carter groaned. "I'm sick of being on the defensive."

Thursday, December 1

When Janae stepped into her office's lobby, Shaw stood there, his briefcase clutched in one hand, studying one of the landscape photos she'd hung on the walls. The particular image was one of the Blue Ridge Mountains laced in fog and shadows, a haunting image that showed one aspect of the terrain outside Kedgewick. She watched him a minute, wondering if he'd heard her approach.

"There's something to learn from the mountains."

What an interesting opening statement. "Oh?"

"They stand firm whether cloaked in mist or basking in the sun. But we get to enjoy their beauty more in the sunlight."

"There's something eerie and gripping about the play of shadows and light." Janae took a step closer and watched him. "Why are you here, Mr. Shaw?"

A small smile touched his lips but didn't move to his eyes. "I had hoped we wouldn't get to this point, but Mrs. Seeger can't wait any longer for the museum to make the right choice, so we're taking you to court."

His words ricocheted through her, confirming that the museum had lost the opportunity to move to the front on the mystery of the Botticelli. "I understand, but you realize that any hope of settlement will evaporate?"

"The museum has shown no interest in talking since that first meeting. That was almost a month ago, and I can't allow the museum to stonewall my client while it banks on her dying."

Janae nodded. "Is this a courtesy? Or do you want mediation?"

"My client wants what is rightfully hers."

Janae sank onto one of the two chairs and waited. A moment later he took the other seat. "Can you give me more time? Through the end of the year?"

"What will that accomplish?"

"As much as and maybe more than filing this lawsuit." She considered him carefully, noting the way he gripped the bag. "I can go to the board, tell them we talked and you are filing January second." She held up a hand as he sputtered. "The courts don't accomplish much between now and the new year. Give me that time to position a settlement."

"Mrs. Seeger isn't willing to wait." His jaw jutted at a stubborn angle.

Janae needed to tread carefully if she wanted to keep the door open. "She has waited seventy years. Giving me four weeks rather than launching what will be an extensive litigation process will save her time. It will also save you the expense of unpaid litigation." She thought back over the work she and Carter had done. "We're having the documents you gave us translated, although if you gave us the translation you have, that would help speed things up."

"I already did."

"We don't have it." He sputtered a moment, but she continued. "We're conducting research here and coordinating with the museum in Germany. That takes a lot of time since the museum records aren't digitized yet. While you don't see much activity, we've been moving. They're slogging through mountains of paperwork. But I need more information and time before we can get the board to understand."

"Can you give me any guarantee to take back to my client?"

"Let's agree to toll the statute of limitations through January fifteenth. That gives us time to try for a resolution."

"And you won't file before I do."

"Does it really matter which of us files first in court?"

"It does for the optics."

So he did want the court of public opinion. That was an important tidbit to tuck away. "I will discuss the museum's options as fully as I can with the board."

"Then give me the courtesy of a heads-up before you move." He gestured in front of him. "Like I did today."

"I will, but we both know today was showmanship. You wanted to apply the pressure I needed to take this to the board."

He didn't deny it as he watched her. "What can I take to my client?"

"The tolling agreement. You can also tell her that Dr. Montgomery continues to take her claims very seriously. He wants to do the right thing and is working hard to compile the information to determine what that is. You know how hard this research is. It can take years, but we are expediting it in recognition of your client's needs." She took a breath, trying to find the words to communicate what she could without overpromising. "I don't control the board and won't promise I can force settlement."

He continued to study her a minute, then nodded. "I'll wait for the tolling agreement."

"Fair enough. I'll make a call and update an earlier draft I wrote."

He leaned his bag on the table and then opened it. "I have work I can do while I wait."

Janae nodded, then hurried to her office. She left the door cracked since the front was empty except for Mr. Shaw. A moment later Carter picked up. "Shaw is ready to file."

"Have you seen it?"

"No, but he's in my office. I've talked him into a delay if we agree to a tolling agreement through January fifteenth."

"Does that harm the museum in any way?"

"Not that I anticipate. Instead, it gives us time to get the board to agree about next steps."

"Have we lost the potential to file first?"

"Yes, he wants the media coverage of filing the complaint." She rubbed her forehead. "Can you schedule the board conversation soon to discuss our options? With the holidays, January fifteenth will be here fast."

"I'll get on the phone now. What else do you need?"

"A signature on the tolling agreement and then the Elliott's research on the Botticelli."

"I still haven't found it."

She could hear the frustration in his voice. "I know, but it's the priority now. We're out of time."

And then she was listening to a dial tone and wondering if she'd lost her client.

The phone rang again and showed Carter's number. She slowly took it. "Yes?"

"Get the tolling agreement over here and I'll sign it. And then I'll find that file." He sighed. "Thank you."

"You're welcome." This time when they hung up, she looked at the phone a minute. Then she shook her head and got back to work.

Friday, December 9

Carter had spent the week doing everything he could to build defenses around Andrew in the pockets of time allowed for by his work. He squeezed in visits to the school and installation of a top-notch security system at home around budget meetings, meetings with the insurance company about museum security, and more meetings with potential donors. Still, he knew there was nothing he could do that would truly make Andrew safe.

Not if someone attached to the mob wanted his nephew.

Friday afternoon, he felt a desperate need to do something that could close a loop. He stood in front of the Botticelli wondering where it had disappeared during the black hole of 1933 to 2021. "Where were you?"

The lady didn't respond as she looked into the distance.

Someone could have added her to a personal collection and then run out of money and been forced to sell her.

She could have been stored in a free port in Switzerland by a legitimate investor.

The painting could even be a copy. Not that this was his preferred choice, but it was possible.

Ariel clicked across the marble, and Carter smiled. It was good to have her back for her first full day since she'd been attacked. While her injuries hadn't been as serious as he'd first feared, he'd missed her sassy approach to the office, though now as he watched her approach, he reassessed.

She came to stand beside him. "It would be nice if you carried your phone with you."

He felt a surge of adrenaline as he patted his pockets for the phone. "Is Andrew okay? Please tell me he is."

"Return the call." She raised his phone and held on an extra second before releasing it. "Carter, as crazy as you've been, I hope he's okay."

"Me too." He unlocked the phone and looked at her. "Who am I calling?"

"The school."

He searched contacts for the number as he started sprinting to his car and hit call. "This is Carter Montgomery. What happened to my nephew, Andrew?"

"Dr. Montgomery." The voice of the assistant principal was calm and collected. "Andrew had an accident on the school grounds. Says he was pushed by a man. The police are here, but he's upset."

"A man? Is he all right?" Carter moved to the gallery's exit and trotted down the stairs.

"He'll likely have a bruise where he fell, but we don't think he broke anything." The assistant principal paused. "If you hadn't warned us to be watchful . . ."

Carter closed his eyes, not wanting to think what could have happened. "I'll come get him right away and take him to urgent care." Then as soon as he was home, he'd call his parents to take Andrew on a vacation to somewhere far away. The echo of Charlotte's desperate call to his parents caused him to shudder.

The drive to the school passed in a blur, and he couldn't take a deep breath until he saw Andrew. Carter hurried through a conversation with the assistant principal.

"The students were out on the playground for recess, and the teacher monitoring noticed Andrew by the fence." The man took off glasses to pinch the bridge of his nose. "She separated some kids, and when she turned back around, Andrew was on the ground crying."

"Did she see what happened?" Carter clenched and unclenched his hands as he watched his nephew sit next to the nurse. The boy looked shell-shocked but largely unharmed. Andrew didn't flinch but had retreated so deeply Carter wasn't sure how he'd come back.

"No, but she's filling out paperwork now and then we'll need you to complete some too." The man sighed. "Andrew was adamant it was a man who pushed him, but now he won't say anything. Maybe you can get him to talk to you."

"I'll try after I know Andrew's okay."

"Sherry's taking good care of him."

Carter bit back a retort as the police officer joined them, the same one who came for the museum's break-in. "Anything you can tell us, Officer Alston?"

"A couple of kids say a man was on the playground." He glanced at his slim notebook. "They really couldn't tell me much more. Other than the man walked away after Andrew started crying."

"A man? That's not any more helpful than what Andrew said." The assistant principal groaned. "That could describe one of the teachers."

"I'll check the video if you can send it over."

"Sure thing."

Carter glanced at Andrew again. "Look, can I take him to urgent care? Make sure he's okay?"

The two men looked at each other, and the officer shrugged. "Shouldn't be a problem. I don't expect to see anything on the video."

"Thanks." At this point Carter didn't really care. He just wanted to get Andrew to urgent care, and then home. Once they were checked in and shown to an examination room by the medical tech, Andrew finally looked at him.

"I want my mom." A single tear slid down his cheek.

"Me, too, bud. I have no idea what I'm doing here." He needed to figure it out. He needed the rule book, the "do and say this, but don't say or do that." He wanted to remind Andrew that whatever training moms and dads got, he had missed by becoming an instant guardian. "Did you know the man?"

"I saw a woman." Andrew rolled into a ball. "She looked like Mom."

"I thought it was a man?"

"No." Andrew curled tighter as he cradled his arm. "I saw my mom, and then a man pushed me. I didn't see who pushed me."

Carter didn't know what to do with that. Charlotte hadn't looked that unique. A cute blonde with a bright personality. But Andrew didn't let it go, and as they walked to the car after getting a splint, Carter wondered who he'd really seen.

Chapter 35

BY MONDAY MORNING, CARTER HAD Andrew safely out of town. As soon as he watched his parents drive away with Andrew in the back seat, he'd felt a burden lift. He fingered the business card and placed a call that went to a generic voicemail.

"This is Carter Montgomery. Someone gave this card to my friend. I have a feeling you know how to find me." He hung up, saved the contact, and then shredded the card.

Now what? He'd thrown down something, but he didn't know what.

In the museum, the basement's air felt dank and heavy with dust as Carter worked through a file cabinet.

The enormous room overflowed with them, lining the walls of the research room and forming a wall down the middle of it too. He made a mental note to get more dehumidifiers installed and have the space deep-cleaned. All this damp dustiness wouldn't preserve any artwork stored in the other rooms. Some had climate-controlled features, but the addition of filters would help limit the harm.

As he had every day for the last two weeks, he worked his way slowly through the files stuffed in the drawers. It was important to be thorough so he didn't miss the one about the Botticelli's purchase, but it was mind-numbing work.

He opened a drawer and froze.

There it was.

His fingers trembled as he pulled out the file and checked the front for the paper-clipped image of the painting. It was a match. Thank God.

He sent a quick text to Janae.

> I found the Botticelli file.

She emphasized his text and then sent back a thumbs-up emoji.

> What does it say?

>> Don't know yet. Headed to
>> office to read.

> Make sure you note which
> cabinet it came from. I'm on
> my way.

A sound caught his attention, and he looked up.

A man stepped from the shadows. He was big with a nose that had a crook like someone had broken it. Carter set the file down and looked for something that he could use for protection if he needed it.

"What, no words?" The man's voice was quiet, cultured.

Carter shrugged. "Don't see much sense. You are?"

"The man your sister stole from. I'm here to reclaim what is mine." He grinned, revealing a small gap between his front teeth, which enhanced his easy bad-boy air that said more than James Dean. "I would like it back."

"I'm not sure what you mean."

"You are a smart man with the big degrees." The man's grin took on a menacing air. "But you guessed wrong. The boy I do not care about any more than his father did. He was just to get your attention." He waved a hand in the air, and two men stepped out of the shadows. "That worked. But what I want is much more valuable than a child."

"Nothing is more valuable to me than that child." As soon as he said it, he realized his mistake.

"We understand each other then." He snapped his fingers, and one of the men showed Carter a phone. A video played of his parents' SUV on the highway, a time stamp clear. "You will do as I say, yes?"

Carter swallowed. "If I can."

"You can, because their lives depend on it. Find the treasure your sister stole from me, and we are good."

"Charlotte didn't have treasures."

The man puffed up and snarled. "You have forty-eight hours." He turned to go, his two goons turning with him.

"You have to tell me something." Carter felt a sense of panic rising at the utter nonsense of the demand.

"She was an artist. She sent something valuable, but it has something that belongs to me. I want it." And they were gone.

Carter picked up the Botticelli file, but when he took a step, he felt his legs wobble. What on earth could he do with the nothing the thug had given him?

He'd barely returned to his office when someone knocked on his door. Ariel stepped inside his office. "You don't look so good, boss man."

"I'll be all right."

She squinted at him and shook her head. "I'll get you some 7UP, but you should know she's back. I think she might be a stalker."

"Who?"

"Your attorney. Janae Simmons."

"Thanks, Ariel." He followed her out, grateful for the excuse to stand. "Hey."

Janae hurried back to his office, her dark pencil skirt doing nothing to hide the swaying of her hips—a movement he could lose himself in if he weren't scared out of his mind for his parents and Andrew. She looked up at him. "Where's the file?"

"On my desk."

She slipped behind his desk and started reading. He put a hand on the page, and she looked up. "What's going on?"

He quickly updated her on what had happened.

"Are you going to call the police?"

"And tell them what?" He slumped into the chair in front of his desk. "That some crazy man barged in here? Threatened my parents and nephew?"

"Do you have any idea what he wants?"

"No. But I wonder if there's something with the Botticelli."

"Why?"

"It was the painting that was damaged in the break-in . . . but I don't see how it ties to the mob."

"Let me scan the file. Maybe something in here will help." After a couple of pages, she paused and looked up at him. "Did you see Botticelli was part of a tour in the US after the war?" Janae scrambled for her bag and pulled out a book. "This is a book my grandma loaned me. That painting was on tour in thirteen cities." She flipped to a page before turning it to him. "Look."

"That's Botticelli's lady."

"My grandpa was one of the soldiers who toured with the paintings." She flipped a few more pages. "Look, there's a Pieter Bruegel the Elder painting that is similar to the one I have, but it's monkeys instead of dogs."

"Why were the paintings here?" He tried to search his memory for any mention of a tour but came up blank.

"It had something to do with the Monuments Men." She frowned and flipped to the front of the book. "No, that's not quite right. The Monuments Men signed a Wiesbaden Manifesto against the tour. The US government said it was 'safekeeping' the art." She made air quotes around the word. "But the war was over, and the Monuments Men didn't think it was right for our government to take a couple hundred paintings and put them on tour for two years. No safekeeping was needed since the war had ended."

"That doesn't tell us what happened to her in between the tour and when she arrived here." It also didn't tie the painting to his sister.

"What if she disappeared on the tour?"

"That's a big leap. And it would have made headlines."

"Okay, so maybe she got sold on tour. Where was she supposed to be?" Janae collapsed against a chair. "There's an answer."

"Maybe the answer is we'll never know for sure."

"But what does this have to do with your sister?"

"I don't know. She didn't have an interest in old masters like Botticelli, that I remember." Carter paused and rubbed the spot on his forehead where his brain warned he was overthinking. "Flip the script."

"What?"

"Pretend you're representing Mrs. Seeger instead of Shaw. What would you do?"

"I'd understand there are factual issues, but that my goal is to force the museum to settle. I'd launch an all-out media campaign and highlight the way Mrs. Seeger's family was victimized and how horrible and obstructionist the Elliott is by not immediately returning it to her."

"Why hasn't he?"

"He isn't me." She grinned at him, and there was a fresh energy flowing from her. Then she frowned. "But seriously, why hasn't he? Most attorneys understand that the court of public opinion can be more important than an actual court." She froze. "Maybe he is and we just don't know it."

Carter shook his head. "I'd get the calls asking for a response."

"Then we have even more reason to stay ahead of his actions." She pushed off the chair and turned to her phone.

"What are you doing?"

"It's time to see what the experts can tell us."

"I am the expert."

"Of course you are." She smirked at him, and he knew one fun way to wipe that from her face. "But we need the restitution expert opinion." She held up the file. "Why isn't there an Art Loss Register certificate in this file?"

"What do you mean?"

"There was for the loaned painting, right?"

Carter slowly nodded, then reached for the file. "Let me look through that."

"You won't find it."

"Maybe not, but I need to see for myself." A minute later he looked up, but there was no file registering the Botticelli as a lost family heirloom. "Well, that's a good next step."

"That's a good next step for me too." She pulled out her phone and started clicking and in moments held it up so he could see the website. "A search is only ninety dollars an item. Filing a request for the Bruegel will give me such peace of mind."

"It's only as good as those who have submitted claims."

"It's a starting point." She clicked a few more times. "See?" She turned her phone back toward him. "If we can find one for the Botticelli, it'll show the Elliott took the steps a reasonable museum would have when purchasing the painting. Due diligence can be one of our biggest defenses. The museum did all it could, all any museum would be expected to do, prior to purchasing the artwork." She bookmarked the page. "And if I order one for the Bruegel, we'll know much more than we do now. I'll finish this tonight from my laptop."

"It's a solid idea." Carter slid the file back to her. "While you keep looking through the paper file, I'll look for a digital copy on the server."

They worked in silence for a while. Carter looked up from the monitor. "Did you see who facilitated the sale of the painting to the Elliott?"

Janae shook her head. "Who?"

"Stanley."

"Is that usual?"

"I'd consider it a conflict of interest. He's profiting from an item he's sold to the museum he sits on the board of." Then he checked the date. "Never mind, he joined the board two years later." He sighed. "This is all interesting, but it's not helping solve that challenge."

"Maybe it is. It's one more piece of the puzzle." Janae went methodically through the file. She'd stop occasionally to make a notation on her tablet, mouthing the words as she wrote. Was she aware she did that? It was an adorable quirk. She caught him watching and smiled. He forced his gaze back to the computer.

Janae tried to ignore the way he watched her. It would be charming if they weren't so pressured by all the challenges piling on them. Her mind spun through the latest. The mobster had pulled her in when he sent his minion to give Janae that business card. She didn't like being used by anyone. Not when it could hurt a nine-year-old and his grandparents.

Neither she nor Carter could afford to be distracted right now. And she was. Every little thing about him drew her from what had to matter. There was a growing awareness of where he was and what he was doing. She found she counted down the hours until she had a valid excuse to be around him. It was ridiculous, but undeniable. It also confirmed she needed to get this matter settled so she could return to her normal life.

She looked up from the file. "Why would this thug tie the Botticelli to your nephew? Out of all the paintings here, why that one? You're sure Charlotte doesn't have a tie to it?"

"As sure as I can be." He rubbed the back of his neck. "But I'm not certain anymore. When I was at her house with Stanley, there was a painting. The one Stanley bought." He ran his hands over the back of his head. "It had the look of a master, and she wasn't happy about the bidding war that erupted. But it couldn't be a Botticelli."

"Why?"

"There's no reason she would have had a painting by a master in her garage. Restoration would have occurred in a place like Haney & Sons or a museum, not a garage in Indianapolis. Another thing, Stanley bought it for forty thousand dollars, but I didn't get a good look before it was packaged for shipping to one of his galleries. What if . . ." He shook his head. "It's too crazy."

"What happened to the Botticelli after the break-in?"

"We removed it from the floor, and I've had it in the museum's large safe while Todd and I figure out what to do. The insurance company hasn't sent the adjuster yet."

"Let's look at it." He stared at her, but Janae stood. "What do you have to lose, Carter?"

"You're right." She expected him to move to the safe behind his desk, but instead he led her to a door she hadn't noticed before that opened to another room. "This contains some of our larger items that are under closer examination." He paused to put on his ever-present gloves, then he entered the room and pulled out a small frame from a row of slots and set it on a metal table in the middle of the small, sterile room. Bright florescent lights illuminated the room. "Don't touch it without gloves, okay?"

"Sure." She leaned close but kept her hands behind her back. The frame was battered and cracked, the gold leaf overlay chipped in places, but what she could see of the canvas looked okay to her untrained eye. "What would you look for first?"

"We've already photographed it, and those are in the file." He considered the frame.

"I wonder why someone went after the frame? What if something was tucked in the frame?"

"That seems like a stretch."

Then Janae shrugged as she considered all that was happening. "So does the idea that someone is following your parents down the interstate."

He didn't argue as he slid his fingers along the frame and carefully manipulated where it was cracked.

She edged to the side to get a clearer view around his shoulder. "Feel anything?"

"No." He moved methodically around the edges, then frowned.

"What did you find?"

"I'm not sure." He picked up the frame and eased it back and forth as if trying to get better light on something.

Janae pulled out her cell and turned on the flashlight. "Will this help?"

"Maybe." He set the painting down and took the phone. "How did I feel that?"

She edged closer. "What?"

He pulled a thin square from the edge of the frame that looked like a mini USB drive of some sort. "Now what?"

"We call the FBI."

He slid the Botticelli back into its slot. "There may be issues with the painting too, but first let's see what's on here." He inserted the drive and clicked a few keys that copied it onto his computer before ejecting it.

There were a dozen files, and as he clicked on each one, Janae noticed they were encrypted spreadsheets. "We aren't going to open these. We should definitely contact experts like the FBI."

"I don't have time. I have to make sure Andrew and my parents are safe." He pulled out his phone and placed a call.

Janae watched a moment, then stepped out of the room back into Carter's office and headed for the hallway. She could call the FBI if he wouldn't. She wasn't certain that was the correct agency, but handling whatever this was felt too big on their own. She hadn't gotten ten feet down the hall when the sound of rushing feet reached her, and she looked up. Ariel was being pushed down the hallway by a large man flanked by two more.

"You found what I wanted." He looked to the shorter man on his left. "Your listening device worked. Now get me the drive."

The man pushed Janae, and she stumbled into the wall. "Hey."

The man ignored her as he continued into Carter's office.

Ariel whimpered, and Janae wished she could spirit the younger woman away. Instead, the man tightened his hold on Ariel's arm and gave her a jerk. "As soon as we have what I want, we'll disappear." His voice carried an accent, one Janae couldn't place other than it wasn't from anywhere she'd lived.

Janae fingered her phone, sliding for the emergency SOS button. She could only pray it worked, because she didn't know how else to alert someone that they needed help. "Why are you here?"

"We aren't. That is the beauty of technology. We will leave and no one will believe we were here." He snapped his fingers. "That's all it takes and we are erased. Never here." He gave another vicious yank on Ariel. "Other than her arm." Ariel wobbled and the man sneered. "You are weak."

Ariel blinked, and it was like the woman transformed as she stomped on the man's foot and he howled. "I'm not weak, you . . ." She sputtered and then turned to flee, but not before he yanked her ponytail, tugging her against his chest hard enough she bounced.

"Do not try anything like that again." The man's ears turned red as he gripped Ariel against him.

Janae glanced along the hall, but there was nothing she could grab to use as a weapon. Even if she could, the man's stocky build and fierce intensity suggested he would make short work of anything she could use. Still she had to try. She couldn't just wait to see what happened or if the call went through and the dispatcher on the other end sent someone to their aid.

She heard a commotion, thuds like bodies pushed into each other, and another man—this one with a ball cap pulled low—hurried from the office, a grin on his face. "Got it. Let's go."

"You're sure it's the right thing?"

"Yes."

"Should we bring them with us?"

"No. We need to get out quickly." The man glanced back at the office. "We must leave now. Rahul wants the files destroyed."

The man holding Ariel grunted and then flung her at Janae before sprinting down the hallway.

Janae tried to grab Ariel but instead collapsed under her weight.

The young woman groaned. "I never should have gotten out of bed."

"You okay?" Janae slowly started disentangling herself from Ariel.

Ariel nodded but, as soon as she started to push up on her hands, sank back to the floor. "I think I'll just stay here."

Janae took her hand and felt for a pulse. It was strong but fast. "Rest sounds good. I'm going to check on Carter." But first she pulled out her phone and put it at her ear. "Hello?"

"Ma'am, do you need the emergency services I've sent to your location?"

"Yes, a woman has been injured and two men are fleeing the Elliott. Should I go after them?" *Please say no.* She wanted to be brave, but not rush headlong into danger. She was an attorney, not a superhero or someone trained to be one like Yelena Belova.

"Absolutely not. Police are on the way. Can you give me a description of the men?"

Janae pulled the phone from her ear as she looked at Ariel. Her mind was a blank. She wanted to spit out a perfect description but every study she'd ever read about how imperfect eyewitness descriptions were flashed through her mind in quick succession. Now she understood.

Where she wanted a perfect description to dictate to the 911 dispatcher, only the barest outlines and shadows formed in her mind's eye.

Carter groaned as he rolled to his side and then his feet.

What had happened?

He shook his head, but quickly stopped the motion as a bolt of sharp pain jolted through his brain.

The last thing he remembered, he'd pulled out his cell phone to call his mom. He'd heard it ringing when another sound pushed into his awareness.

Someone asking him a question.

Something about a flash drive.

Then an explosion in his head.

Now he struggled to regain his equilibrium.

"Carter?" Janae rushed into the room. "Are you okay?" She hurried to his side and collapsed next to him. She reached out as if to touch him, then pulled back. Then her fingers brushed the hair at the nape of his neck by his ear. "You're bleeding."

"I'll be okay." He swallowed. "Where's Ariel?"

"In the hall. She's about as good as you are. Police are on the way. Paramedics too."

"I don't need that."

She raised an eyebrow. "I think you do."

Did she realize her fingers were twisted into his hair? It was the gentlest touch and almost took away the pain that throbbed where he must have been hit. Her eyes softened and she licked her lower lip. He couldn't look away if he'd wanted to, his thoughts continuing in a muddled stream. Her fingers brushed against his skin and he winced, breaking the spell.

She jolted. "I'm so sorry."

"It's okay. Someone will need to let the police and paramedics in."

"I can do that." She started to stand, but paused halfway up. "What were they looking for?"

"The flash drive." He rubbed at his forehead as if that would quell the killer headache. "I'm glad I copied it."

"We need help."

"Yes, but who?" It hurt to think. "I still need to talk to Mom, make sure they're okay."

"Did you see who hit you?"

"No. Did you see anyone?"

"I did, but it doesn't matter." Her jaw clenched and she pushed to her feet. "I didn't get a clear picture. Just have an impression of accents. I should have done better."

Footsteps in the hall had him tensing.

"I'll go check on that. Don't move."

"Don't worry." After she left, he stumbled to his feet and then to the small couch in his office to lie down on it. Maybe then he wouldn't feel so much like everything he'd eaten that day wanted to crawl back up his throat.

The next hours were filled with talking to police from first Kedgewick and then a Loudon County Sheriff's Deputy who came in to provide support. Carter tried to explain why he didn't know much. He showed the officers the files he'd copied onto his hard drive and then asked for help locating his parents and Andrew when repeated calls went unanswered.

He knew there could be a dozen reasons from the battery had died to sitting in a movie theater. But his brain hurt too much to properly process it all. Through it all Janae stayed as close as the police would allow. Occasionally, they explained to different officers what had happened, until Carter felt like a broken record as he repeated the story.

Finally a man in a suit appeared and asked more questions about why Carter needed to confirm his parents and Andrew were safe. When Carter asked who he worked for, the man vaguely said the federal government.

Janae marched into the conversation, completely unintimidated by the man who towered over her petite frame. "We're not answering any more questions, until we understand who you're with." She placed her hands on her hips and stared him down, as Carter held an ice pack a paramedic had handed him to the knot on his skull.

The man stared back, unblinking.

Carter was about to tell Janae it didn't matter, he just wanted to leave, when the man swallowed.

"Ma'am, I can't answer your questions. But I can say that we will do all we can to find Drew."

Carter frowned as he watched the man. "His name is Andrew."

"Yes." He didn't elaborate. Instead, he held out his hand for Carter's phone. "If you give me your phone, we'll add a tracking feature for the next call you place to them."

"You don't need the phone for that."

"It makes it faster." He sighed. "Look, I'm here to help and we can wait to see if the BOLO leads to someone finding the vehicle, but tracing a call is the fastest."

"Let me try one more time."

The man crossed his arms and nodded. "Go ahead."

Carter stood and walked to the window as the call rang and rang. Then there was a click followed a moment later by the glorious sound of his mother's voice. "Hello?"

"Are you all right?"

"Yes. Why?"

"I'll explain, but first can you give me your location? We're going to send someone to you."

"We're in California."

He looked at Janae, but she shrugged. "Why there?"

"You made it sound like we should get far away, so we've been taking Andrew around to the National Parks out here. The weather's been perfect for hiking and exploring."

Carter turned to the agent. "Can you still get someone to them?"

"Sure. I just need a narrowed location."

"Mom, I'm going to put a man on who will get the details."

After he handed off the phone, Janae slipped into his arms, and he felt his muscles relax as the tension leached from him.

Her stomach grumbled, and he looked at his watch. It was nearly seven. No wonder he was hungry too. "Have dinner with me?"

Chapter 36

CARTER'S WORDS ROLLED AROUND HER as she stood in the shelter of his arms. The events of the afternoon had reminded her how short life could be, and she wanted to lean in to what might be possible. The only way to find out was to open herself to the risk of losing her heart to this man.

She wanted to take exactly that risk.

"Are you sure you're up for it?" She reached up to touch the egg on the back of his head and noted the way his eyes tightened.

"I need to eat, as do you, and I don't want to do it alone." His arms snugged her closer, and she felt so protected. "Please. We can meet somewhere and keep it short."

She leaned her head against his chest and listened to the steady beat of his heart, absorbing the way it reflected his steadiness of character. "All right." She let out a slow exhale. "Give me an hour to check on the office and my grandma, and then I can meet you somewhere unless you start feeling different."

"All right."

The agent came back with the phone, and Janae startled and eased from the circle of Carter's arms. She'd forgotten the man hadn't left.

"I have a good team on the way." He glanced at his watch. "They'll arrive in a couple of hours, and your parents promised not to leave before then." He reached into his back pocket and pulled out his wallet, slipping a card from it.

Carter studied it, and his jaw slackened. "You're with the marshals?"

"Yes. My cell number is on the back. You can call if you remember anything or notice anything off, like those men returning." He considered them both. "Don't pretend to be heroes. They're associated with an Italian crime family. We captured several in Indiana."

Carter frowned. "Does this have anything to do with my sister?"

"We won't know until we apprehend them." He turned to Janae. "Have you remembered anything else?"

"No. I'm sorry." She met Carter's gaze and glanced at the computer. The files weren't hers to share with the agent, but maybe they should.

He seemed to sense her hesitancy as he handed her a card. "If that changes, you can call as well."

Carter took a deep breath. "The flash drive they took? I made a copy, and it's on my computer. You could get a copy from the police, but I can give it to you now."

The agent considered him. "That would help. I can give it to one of our analysts and possibly the FBI team working on the case too."

A few minutes later, Carter handed him a new drive with the files. "If they killed my sister, please find them."

"We're doing our best." He held up the drive. "Thank you for this." Then he turned and left the room.

Carter watched him, then grabbed Janae's hand and held it tightly. "Dinner at Margherita's in an hour?"

"Sounds wonderful."

"All right. Be careful."

"I will." She hadn't meant the words flippantly, but Carter placed a hand on her arm, stopping her.

"I mean it."

"I know. And I will be." She reached up and kissed his cheek. "You too." Then she spun and hurried from his office.

When Janae finally got home, she wanted to hug her grandma and assure herself that those she loved were safe. After changing into a navy sweater dress and boots, Janae hurried up the stone path to the main house. She entered through the side door. "Grandma, are you home?"

There wasn't an immediate answer, but she heard a noise like a scrape of a chair in the kitchen, so she headed that direction. It only took a few steps, and she froze at the sight of her grandma bowed over the table, a box of tissues in front of her.

Janae hurried toward her and knelt next to her chair. "Grandma, are you okay?"

The woman sniffled and then shook her head. "Oh, Arnold."

"Are you missing Grandpa?" Janae tried to remember if this had been an important day for them but came up blank. "Grandma, you're scaring me."

"I'm sorry." When Grandma raised her head and looked at her, there was such sorrow etched into the lines of her face.

"What do you need? I was going out to dinner, but I can stay here with you." Janae frowned and scanned the table, looking for a clue. Then her glance landed on the book she had found in the carriage house and left days earlier for Grandma. "Does it have something to do with that?"

"It tells a story. One I can hardly believe." She sighed and edged the book toward Janae. "It's one you need to read."

Janae looked at the book and then at Grandma. "Should I stay with you and read it tonight?"

Grandma shook her head. "No. Read it first, then we can talk about it." Grandma put her hand on top of it as Janae reached for it. "In fact, I'll hang on to it until later tonight." A whisper of her spunk reappeared. "If you take it now, you won't go."

"Will too."

"Nope. I know you too well to believe that." She reached for Janae's hand and gave it a squeeze. "I'm fine. It was just a shock. Nothing we can't handle tomorrow."

"You have to give me something or I'm not leaving."

Grandma jutted her chin out and the flash in her eyes let Janae know the answer before she spoke. "I am in control of this, young lady. Go have a good time, and we will talk tomorrow."

During the quick drive to town, Janae kept glancing into the rearview mirror while trying to figure out what had impacted her grandma so deeply. What had Grandpa written? All through the dinner at Margherita's, she couldn't shake a general feeling of foreboding.

"You okay?" Carter looked at her with concern, his tie tipped slightly off-center.

"I'm good." Then she met his gaze and decided to share her burden with him. "Actually, as I was ready to leave, I headed to the house to let Grandma know. She was more upset than I've seen her in a long time."

"Do you know why?"

"Not really, and she refused to tell me. She didn't want to interfere with our dinner."

Carter sensed the deep love Janae had for her grandmother and how unrealistic it was to think she could walk away and not be impacted by whatever had affected the woman. "Do you need to go back? We can leave now."

"No. She's as stubborn as anyone I know."

"I wondered where you got it."

Janae rolled her eyes, but there was the faintest hint of a crease around them too. "There is that." She sighed. "I'm worried about her, but we'll sort it out in the morning. She won't say anything until she's ready." Her gaze met his, and he felt the connection. "I tried to learn more about your sister."

"You did?" Why would she do that?

"I could tell you miss her, and I want to help you find closure."

"Thank you, but there's nothing to find." Though now that a US marshal had been in town, the possible connection to Charlotte made him want to reconsider her death too.

"That strikes me as odd." She twirled her straw through her iced tea. "Shouldn't there be something? There's not even an obituary."

"She left strict instructions that she didn't want one."

"Why?"

"I guess she didn't want everyone to be able to google her and find her life story."

"Well, she successfully prevented that." Janae tapped a finger against the tablecloth in time to the music playing in the background. "There's a story there."

"Just like there's a story with the marshal."

"And everything that happened today. I still think we need to turn the spreadsheets over to the FBI, but maybe the marshal will share the files."

"I wouldn't know where to start, so I think we have to trust him at least for a while. See what happens." He reached across the table and traced a pattern along her hand. "I hope they find the men soon. I kept looking over my shoulder on the way here."

"Me too." She gave a small shudder. "I don't want to live afraid."

"Me either." He rubbed lightly at the base of his scalp, being careful of the tenderness. "I'm still not certain my parents and nephew are okay, and that's crazy. Even so, I want to focus on the living. I will always miss Charlotte, but Andrew needs my attention." He met her gaze, finding only openness. "I'd like to explore what's possible." He swallowed hard, feeling exposed as he laid his heart out for her. "Between us."

The corners of her lips curved upward. "I'd like that too. After we figure out what's happening with the art you've hired me to protect."

"Can you give me a hint about when that will be resolved?"

"Hopefully by the time the tolling agreement ends."

"I'll be patient, but know I'm ready to see where this goes."

"Me too." Her smile hinted at more to come.

As they walked the downtown area after the meal, Carter reached for her hand, and she slid hers into his. He'd take the encouragement and pray for a fast resolution to the matters with Shaw.

The next morning Janae got up early after a night of restless sleep punctuated by dreams that would startle her awake. Then she'd slide back into a light sleep only to jerk awake again, and she finally gave up and headed up the hill before seven. Grandma waited at the kitchen table, her hand on the journal, a mug of tea in front of her. After Janae poured herself a cup with a splash of creamer, she took a seat across from Grandma. The woman slid the book over the table but kept her hand on its cover until Janae met her gaze.

"I want you to remember the wonderful man your grandpa was. What you're about to read doesn't change what you know of him."

"That sounds ominous."

"Maybe, but I need your promise." Her eyes misted, and she swallowed hard. "He was a good man who loved us well."

"He did."

Grandma removed her hand from the cover and pushed to her feet. "I'm going into town. I don't know for sure when I'll be back." And then she walked out, leaving Janae alone with a small book that felt like it had the power to change everything she knew about a man she'd loved and respected her whole life.

Janae took a deep breath. *Help me discern the truth, Lord.*

Then she pulled the book in front of her and opened it.

It started with a painting.

I walked with my platoon across Belgium into Germany. Somewhere on that long journey we spent a night in an old castle. It probably wasn't considered that by the locals, but to a farm boy from rural Virginia, it was impressive. Abandoned, the front door barely hanging on, and I saw this little painting. There were many squares and rectangles on the entryway wall that showed where others had hung, but this one had been left behind.

Maybe someone didn't think the dogs were worth saving. After all, they were small, barely bigger than my hand with the fingers spread wide. That also made it the perfect size to slide into my pack, not heavy enough to weigh me down and small enough to avoid too much notice.

The G.I. Joes did that you know.

Spoils of war.

Not everyone, mind you, but enough that nobody cared if I took home a small painting with two silly lapdogs rather than a German handgun.

I didn't want another gun. I was already sick of hauling mine around. But my mom, she would like this little picture. And so I took it, mailed it home in a small box. Her reply via the tiny airmail letter let me know how much she appreciated knowing I'd thought of her as I marched across parts of Europe I never wanted to see again.

It wasn't much, but I knew it'd make her smile.

In the wastes of war, that made it worth the effort.

Wiesbaden, Germany.

Not a place I thought I'd spend months at the close of hostilities. Certainly not guarding art and furniture. It seemed like someone's cruel joke.

Thank you for serving honorably in the last days of the fighting. Here's your bronze star and orders to stand guard in a cold, former museum.

And to think I was afraid I wouldn't make it to Europe in time to play a role. Stupid fool.

No one warns you when you're young that you're going to do the wrong thing. Stick your nose where it doesn't belong and invest years in the aftermath.

By now, Esther's married another man, one who came home. Mom sent the word, apology in the tone, as if it was her fault her youngest son ran off to war when his age should have protected him. Nope, that was all me. The hubris of the young. Couldn't dare miss the fun. I wish I could go back and undo my decision. There is nothing fun about war. Death. Destruction. Tearing down of lives and communities. And now I can't leave. It's the ultimate punishment.

So I stand guard around the building at night.

Wonder whose lives are represented in this collection of things. Random. Sporadic. Odd. A mishmash of life's leftovers. The supreme irony is that many won't be able to claim what was theirs.

The turning of a page, and the ending of lives.

These items are records of all that is wrong with the men who led this country and those who let them.

Following 202 paintings from city to city is not how I wanted to invest two years of my life. It's a further pause on making a life for myself. Going to college. Getting a degree. Leaving the farm and the war far behind me.

*Instead, I've gone from city to city for **eighteen months**, more time wasted on art.*

Then I noticed.

There's a mistake in the paperwork.

We aren't as meticulous as the Nazis were. There are only supposed to be 202 paintings. Somehow a 203rd made the trip.

It's not on any inventory. This art that came from German museums. Which museums? I don't know. I hope I never see a Raphael or Rembrandt again. I'm over them. I have learned my first painting is likely a Pieter Bruegel the Elder. There's a painting of monkeys that is a lot like the painting I sent home to Mom. Interesting.

But now there's a 203rd.

The Nazis stole lives and livelihoods. Families and art.

Now I'm going to take this extra painting. The one no one will miss. The one they didn't bother to put on an inventory. While no one will know, I will. I have made the Germans pay a very small piece of the great debt they owe to the world and all those taken too early and violently from this world.

It's been years.

No one looked for the paintings. Maybe people chalked it up to one more casualty of war.

I don't know what to do with the paintings, now that I am old. My legs move slowly, and my mind feels not far behind.

I tried to return the dog painting. But the location of the house? A complete mystery to me. I went back to Belgium once to look, but too much time had passed. It's all a fog of war and walking. Too much rebuilding had occurred. Did I really think it would look the same as it did when I was an eighteen-year-old kid trying to stay alive?

What should I do?

That newfangled internet hasn't helped much.

I've searched what I could find.

Nothing looks like my paintings.

I'm stumped.

So I've put them in a safe place. Maybe someone smarter than me can figure it out. Maybe Janae. She's sharp, and she's got a core that will make her do the right thing, even if it's hard and uncomfortable. I needed more of that when I was a private. And now, well, it'd be embarrassing and would destroy what everyone thinks of me.

Guess I'm a coward after all.

Janae sat back, struggling to digest what she'd read and what it meant.

Chapter 37

JANAE DROVE TO TOWN, QUIVERING with nervous energy as the journal sat beside her. Her grandpa's journal changed everything. She couldn't pretend he was anything but a broken man who had made poor choices that led to terrible decisions that then led to a life of fear and ultimately cowardice.

He'd known the right thing to do but hadn't made himself do it beyond one small attempt.

And now she faced the same crossroads.

What was the right path forward?

There was only one person she could think to go to, but she was afraid of what he would tell her. Did she have the strength to do what her grandfather hadn't done? Could she turn over the paintings?

She didn't have a choice.

Part of her wanted to do it immediately, but she needed guidance to know the right way to do it.

After she parked in the Elliott's lot, she climbed from her car and hurried to the doors.

Closed.

She glanced at her watch.

Forty-five minutes to opening. As she bounced on her toes, she knew

310

she couldn't wait. She pulled out her phone and called Carter. When he finally answered, she forced herself to sound as calm as possible. "Are you at the Elliott?"

"Yes. Why?"

"I have something to show you."

There was a tired pause before he cleared his throat. "It can't wait until opening?"

"No." She barely squeaked the word out.

"Come around to the administrative wing, and I'll let you in."

When she reached the side door, he waited for her. After taking one look at her, he pulled her into a hug, and she let herself relax into it. "Is everything okay?"

She shook her head then shifted to a nod. "It will be."

"Okay." He rubbed her neck, and she sank into the moment. "Can you tell me what's going on? Maybe somewhere we don't have an audience?"

She stepped back and forced her back straight, clutching her bag so tightly her fingers turned white. "Of course."

"Can I take that from you?"

"No, thank you."

He opened the door to a small conference room. "Can I get you something to drink?"

"No." Then she closed her eyes. "Actually, that would be nice. Thank you."

A minute later he was back and cautiously set the glass of water on the table in front of her. "Why don't you start at the beginning. Whatever it is we'll handle together."

She took a sip, and then turned from him to pull the book from the bag. "You should scan the tabbed pages."

"What is this?"

"My grandpa's journal. He didn't write in it much, but what he wrote . . ." Her words trailed off. He waited, but she didn't continue.

He didn't react as he read, until he sat back with a sigh. "Wow."

"Yeah."

"You're sure this is your grandpa's writing?"

"Yes, and more important, Grandma believes he's the author." Her face crumpled, but Janae refused to give in to the desire to weep. She took a deep breath and released it slowly. "What do we do?"

"Is that a rhetorical question, because I'm not sure what to tell you."

"No, Carter. That doesn't work. You can't dump this decision on me, because my grandma is going to trust me to solve this for her. She's eighty-seven. This can't be the thing that breaks her will to live." Janae covered her mouth with her hand but couldn't bite back the sob that hiccuped through her.

Carter's face sobered and he leaned onto the table. "I didn't mean to say this isn't important."

"I know." She took a shuddering breath. "This feels so different from what you're facing. Here you know who the art belonged to. You can figure it out. And if it needs to be returned, you can choose what to do. How am I supposed to tell Grandma what to do when I have no idea who owned the paintings?"

"We can figure it out. Did you finish filing the request with the Art Loss Register?"

"Yes."

"That's a great starting point. The one that was part of the tour might be in the book you showed me."

"Except Grandpa said it wasn't logged anywhere."

"It might not have been logged on the tour, but it had to go through the Wiesbaden Collection Point. There would be some record in its archives."

"You do realize you're speaking Greek to me." Janae rubbed at the tension that had settled between her shoulders and wouldn't release. "I don't know what any of that means."

"Then let's back up a minute. What do you want to do?"

"I want to go back to not having found this and knowing what I know today."

"That's not true. You're a truth seeker. And you fight for what's right. Hiding from this isn't, and you know it."

His words rang like a clarion call in her mind. "Maybe I do. Want to pretend."

"No, that's not the woman I've gotten to know. So we'll do exactly what we've done for the two paintings here. You already started by putting the request in with the Art Loss Register, so we'll move to the Wiesbaden records to see if we can find the owners." He reached across the table and squeezed her hand. "You will make the right decision."

She studied how their fingers laced together, grateful he hadn't pushed her away. "Grandpa was this amazing man." She sniffed against the tears that threatened to surge. "He was gruff on the outside, but to me he was all gooey on the inside. I don't want this to color how other people remember him." She slipped her hand free and swiped under her eyes.

"You can't control what other people think."

"I know that, but I want to." She sat for a minute staring into the distance, then pulled out her tablet and started making a list.

"Don't forget we have the board meeting tomorrow."

She groaned. "How am I supposed to prepare?"

"Nothing has changed." He grinned. "We're probably overprepared. We just need to convey the seriousness of what Shaw will do if we don't act."

"How am I supposed to do that when I don't know what to do with the two paintings my grandpa stole?" Her voice had risen with each word, and she forced herself to breathe. "I'm sorry."

"It's okay. I understand what it's like to have everything you believe about someone threatened. It doesn't change how important he is to you." Carter ran his hands along his pants legs. "There's a lot I'll never know about Charlotte, but she will always be one of the most important people I knew."

"You're right." Janae stood and took a step back. "I need to prepare for the board meeting. I appreciate your perspective." She snatched the journal, spun on her heel, and fled.

Instead of walking toward downtown and her office, she strode onto

campus. The buildings were stately red brick, the uniformity remi-
niscent of a campus like UVA or Purdue. People were out and about
walking around campus, but she didn't see them as she tried to pray
and figure out what to do next. It was easy to have the answers when the
issues were remote, impacting other people. But now that the questions
were directed at her, she was lost.

God, I don't know what to do.

Her grandpa had been a rock. The strong, silent type until the day
he died. She could count on one hand the number of times she had seen
a vibrant smile directed at her, yet she'd always known he loved her.
He'd been nine years older than Grandma and always loved her well, if
stoically.

How could that man have this shadow self that he hid from everyone?

Or was that why he'd had the air of brusqueness?

The questions cycled through her mind as she walked to her favorite
spot on campus, one she hadn't visited since returning to Kedgewick.
There was a small horticultural garden that students maintained, the
flowers and plants changing by the season and sometimes by the month.
A couple of bistro-style tables and wire chairs sat beneath a pergola
in the middle of the garden. It felt like a secret garden whenever she
slipped inside it.

There was a sacredness to it.

Something special that made it a place to exhale and feel her blood
pressure lower.

She sank onto the closest chair and closed her eyes for a minute. She
needed the kind of wisdom that came straight from heaven, because this
was not a situation she could purely logic her way out of. It would be so
much easier if she could.

Instead, she asked God into the process. He could untangle a mess
that she didn't know how to start addressing. Without titles and more
information, this felt like a horrible dead-end where she needed an open
door. Otherwise, reuniting the paintings with the true owners would be
exceedingly hard, a thought her mind returned to throughout the day.

When she made it home that evening, Grandma and Mom waited

on the porch. Grandma clutched Mom's arm, a V pinched between her eyes. She waited for Janae to exit her car before taking a halting step forward. "Are you all right, Janae?"

"You worried us, sweetheart." Mom looked like she wanted to step toward her but hesitated.

Janae followed the stone walkway up to the porch and gave each of the women a hug. "We're going to be okay."

Grandma's smile trembled, but she held it in place. "Let's go inside and get something hot to drink. I'll confess I've been cold all day." She rubbed her arms, then laced one through Janae's as if afraid Janae would bolt for the carriage house.

"I visited the horticultural garden for a bit today."

Mom stilled. "Did you hear from God?"

"Not in an audible way, but he reminded me we will always be okay." Janae entwined her fingers with Mom's manicured ones. "And we will be. God isn't surprised by what we discovered or what Grandpa wrote. We have to trust him to give us the right steps to take."

"That's all we can do in any situation." Grandma walked through the living room to the kitchen, where she moved the teakettle to a burner. "Anything more or less is a waste of our time and effort. I guess I forgot that in the shock of Grandpa's words." She settled mugs on the counter. "But I know one thing—we'll do the right thing. Just because Grandpa couldn't doesn't mean we won't."

It might not be easy, but they would make it through and, if possible, see the paintings home.

Chapter 38

CARTER'S WATCH VIBRATED. TIME TO move. He pushed from his desk and headed for the galleries. A quick walk through to see who was in the halls and watch without hovering helped him understand the scope of what the museum offered the community.

This morning offered a special session for individuals with memory issues along with a caregiver. They would tour a gallery and then work on projects under the direction of specially trained docents. If he remembered correctly, the project would take place in the Native American galleries, so he wandered in that direction, noting where work needed to be done to clean the corners and prepare for visitors.

When he reached one of the galleries, a large square had been created from two folding tables standing together. Chairs lined the edges, each holding an older individual. Together they drew in pencil on a large square of butcher paper. Doris McGready spoke in a soft yet firm voice as she talked about a painting and then invited those gathered at the table to repeat some aspect of the art on the paper in front of them.

Carter watched as the docent guided the participants through some exercises.

He'd heard about how people who struggled with Alzheimer's and other diseases could engage in these interactions with art. It inspired him to watch the connection between the individuals and the docent as she gently guided one hand, then touched another shoulder, and worked her way slowly around the tables. She kept her attention on her students but winked at him as she walked around. He nodded at her, then edged from the room.

After wandering through the other galleries, it was time for the board meeting. He should feel invigorated, especially after he and Janae had plotted out a plan of attack for the presentation to the board members, but he couldn't get there.

The aroma of sandwiches and sweet treats filled the conference room when he arrived. It had worked best for all to meet over lunch, and Carter hadn't fought the idea because that meant he'd actually *get* lunch. Too many days passed with him missing meals as he ran around trying to get caught up on everything.

Stanley Dukes swept into the room a couple of minutes later. "Carter."

"Hello, Mr. Dukes."

"Ready for a productive meeting?"

"Always. What's your top priority for today's meeting?"

"We have to discuss a key supporter who is not happy with the museum's direction."

"Anything you can share now?"

"No, I'll tell it once." He headed to the small buffet of sandwiches and salads and began to fill a plate.

Carter clenched his jaw and refrained from speaking the words cycling through his mind. In an ideal world, he and the board chair would work together to ensure the success of the museum rather than him constantly having to play catch-up and respond in the moment to questions that needed time and preparation. How could he keep a key donor happy if he didn't know there was a problem? It was an intractable problem. And one the man feasting on the buffet fostered.

Margeaux Robbins hurried in, dropping a backpack on a chair before she paused. "Oh. I guess I'm not late."

Stanley made a show of tipping his wrist to show off his oversized gold watch. "You are, but the others are later."

"Blame it on the southern concept of time." Her voice lilted, but Carter caught the tightness around her eyes. So Stanley made her nervous too. What had the man done to hold sway over everyone?

"I'm glad you're here." Carter lowered his voice. "Do you know anything about this donor Stanley wants to talk about?"

She frowned as she twisted the edges of her scarf. "No, today's meeting is to review the budget. I thought we'd get it in advance, but Stanley said it'd be ready for us when we arrived."

"Seems the man is playing fast and loose with both of us. I wonder what he told the others." Carter couldn't prepare for this meeting, but he could assert more control over the agenda before the next meeting. While the chair had the right to ask questions, Carter could set the context with a proposed agenda that he circulated to the board ahead of time. He could also come to them with specific challenges rather than passively waiting.

It was time for him to act like the director of the museum.

She might not be standing in front of the Supreme Court, but this experience had a feeling of that same level of urgency and weight. If Janae couldn't convince the Elliott's board of directors that filing the lawsuit was the way to go, then she would lose her biggest client from a very small pool. She could feel the weight of this argument resting firmly on her shoulders along with the need to pay Chloe for all the time she'd invested in the firm.

She watched Stanley as he bullied Carter. What was he trying to accomplish?

Carter had asked Janae about her grandma, but she'd deflected him. She couldn't get bogged down in her personal matters when she needed to be wholly present for the conversation with the board.

"You've got this." Chloe squeezed her hand and then slipped to the door. "I'll be right out here if you need anything."

"I wish you could stay."

"I know, but hey, you've got Margeaux and Carter as friendly faces. I'd get in the way."

And that was if Stanley Dukes finally got off his high horse and recognized Chloe as a key piece of the legal team. Considering he barely acknowledged Janae had a JD, she wouldn't waste her time trying to change his mind.

Instead, she set her outline in front of her with the tablet to the side, tabs open with her research. Then she blew out a slow breath while she waited for Stanley to turn the meeting over to Carter. When he finally did, it felt like she entered a tunnel where all she could see was the notes in front of her.

"Janae Simmons, the attorney the museum hired, will outline the legal rights and duties the Elliott has with its collection and alleged restitution claims. Janae." Carter gave her an encouraging nod and then sat.

"Hello, everyone. Thank you for making time for an extra meeting." She looked at Margeaux, who flicked her fingers in a small get-moving motion. "We've negotiated a tolling agreement but are under a time crunch if we want to settle or counter Mrs. Seeger's claim related to the Botticelli." She quickly outlined the meetings that had occurred since the exhibit opened. "The Modersohn-Becker piece attracted her attention. Then she noted the Botticelli. Dr. Montgomery is communicating with the Landesmuseum about how it will proceed regarding the loaned painting, but I have suggestions related to your piece."

She quickly set the stage by reviewing a couple of prior cases. "First, we can sue, asking a court to quiet title on the piece."

"What does that mean?" Barbara Carrera leaned forward, brow wrinkled. "I haven't heard that term before."

"It means the parties disagree about who owns an item, and the judge should decide. The other argument we should make is that the heirs took too long to come forward. Because too much time has passed, Mrs. Seeger's lawsuit is barred by laches. The lawsuit should have been filed long before now and is time barred."

Bill Yates made a note and then looked at her. "Is that true?"

"It's unclear but this will force the issue. Finding a clear chain of title hasn't been easy, and it's also uncertain when Mrs. Seeger or other heirs should have known the Elliott had the painting."

"All they had to do was create a Google alert." Tiffany Grace made a typing motion. "It's that simple to stay aware of what's happening."

"If you're tech savvy, that might work if everyone used the same title for a painting." Janae took a deep breath to retain her poise. "Mrs. Seeger is a couple years older than my grandmother. Neither woman is going to do programming for Microsoft. Let's also not get distracted by the bigger issue. All these arguments are designed to push settlement or the dismissal of the case. Would you like me to push mediation or wait for Mr. Shaw to file?"

"Neither is a good option." Bill Yates frowned, his arms crossed over his chest. "Why would we mediate before we know the validity of Mrs. Seeger's claim?"

"Because her attorney has told me he will file. The only reason he hasn't is we agreed to toll the statute of limitations to possibly settle." She held up a hand as various board members started rumbling. "Lawsuits are expensive and suck up time and resources. Settlement can avoid that and tolling gave us extra time to investigate the provenance. We can either stay on the defensive waiting to see what happens. Or we can try to maneuver ahead and steal the momentum while simultaneously continuing our research." She glanced at her notes. "I've spent a couple of days helping Dr. Montgomery and have seen how involved and painstaking the research is. Doing it right will take months, or we can force Mrs. Seeger to prove her claim. Then we'll know exactly what we're dealing with."

Sean Chang turned to Margeaux. "You're an attorney. What do you think?"

Margeaux considered a moment. "It's like so much of the law, the best course depends on what we're trying to accomplish and the facts. What we know for certain is that Mrs. Seeger is not going away."

"How can you say that?" Stanley snorted. "The exhibit opened two months ago."

"Her attorney is in weekly contact."

Janae nodded. "He calls like clockwork. Every Thursday at 4:00 p.m.—and won't leave a message if I'm busy."

"So stay busy on Thursday afternoons."

"My momma didn't raise a coward. I will take his calls as long as I'm in the office and not in a meeting." She looked around the table. "If we choose mediation, then you need to decide if you want to return the painting, offer it for repurchase to Mrs. Seeger—"

Stanley guffawed. "Like the woman could afford that."

She ignored him and continued. "We can also offer to repurchase it at an appropriate price, agree to a joint sale with split proceeds, or—the best option if we can get her to agree—a formal acknowledgment of the provenance being corrected based on new information." She turned to meet the gaze of each of the board members. "Haven't you ever wondered how such a small museum in an out of the way location managed to acquire a Botticelli?"

Color immediately flashed up Stanley's neck and into his face. "You are out of line."

Chapter 39

"No, she's not. We need a decision. And if we want to make this work in our favor, it has to be now." Carter resisted the urge to run his hands through his hair. "Janae and I have worked on this for six weeks, and Mrs. Seeger is not going away. If anything, we're going to spend a lot more time on this before we can resolve it." He studied each person at the table. "If we know the painting's history, then the rest becomes easy." He spread his hands wide. "Despite hours of searching, all I've uncovered is that Stanley was part of the transaction. Any of you know more?"

Sean Chang met his gaze. "I wasn't on the board when it was acquired, but I'm willing to help you search. What about the prior director? Does he know?"

"That's enough. We're not proceeding with any of these courses of action." Stanley's voice echoed with an ultimatum, and board members shifted in their seats.

Bill Yates met Carter's gaze with a quirk of his shoulders. "Stanley, don't be so hasty. What if the best approach is exactly what Ms. Simmons outlined?"

"And how would you know?" The sneer was barely contained.

Margeaux put her hands on the table as if prepared to push to her feet. "And how would you know it isn't?"

"You're too inexperienced to know what to suggest." Stanley's face turned beet red as he fumed. "You are a bunch of fools if you believe giving the painting away solves anything. You'll open the floodgates to people claiming they have a right to other items in our collection."

"Why do you care so much?" Bill leaned back and studied Stanley. "How were you involved in the sale? I don't remember that, and I remember most details about our acquisitions."

"What makes you think I was?"

Bill studied him, with his head cocked to the side, eyes slits. "You were involved. Even though you weren't on the board yet."

Barbara nodded. "That's right. That was our first transaction with you. The old director was thrilled."

"I don't know why you think that."

"Because it's true." Barbara smiled, but it had ice in it. "I'm not just a pretty face."

Stanley's face flushed, but he said nothing.

Carter let the back-and-forth play out, gleaning what he could from it. What was Stanley trying to hide? "Stanley, what are you afraid of?"

"Nothing other than the group of you steering this museum into dangerous waters. I will stand between you and the cliff." He pressed his palms into the table but stopped short of standing. "This museum is under my protection, and I will not fail."

Barbara rolled her eyes. "Don't be melodramatic. After all, that's my role."

A few muffled chuckles followed her words, easing a bit of the tension in the room. Carter realized that was exactly what she'd aimed for. Maybe he'd underestimated her, and she was a smart ally after all.

Janae had stayed out of the fray, a reality that surprised him. She didn't strike him as the retiring type, but she seemed to think the process would work better without her interference. As he looked around the table, noting the body language that was closed off toward Stanley, he thought she might be right. Was it possible he had made the same mistake Stanley was making? Had both underestimated the wisdom and art smarts at the table?

He didn't like the thought that it painted him and Stanley in a similar color. The man was not a role model to emulate.

Stanley looked at his watch. "We've been at this an hour. We'll take a fifteen-minute break. Be back at one o'clock sharp." He stood and strode to the coffee service and selected a mug he doctored with cream.

"You should talk to him." Janae's voice was low as she turned to look at Carter. "You could also let a few board members know about your history with Stanley."

"And have them think I've danced on the wrong side of ethics?"

"No, it would explain why you are so committed to the right thing. Especially when it would be expedient to do something else. You act like a David squared off against Goliath."

"I don't know about that."

"I do. Now go chase down that Goliath. We've got to figure out why he's so adamant against mediation." She frowned as she watched him. "You sure he purchased the Botticelli?"

"It's in the file."

"Do you think he knew the flash drive was there?"

"I don't know. Maybe." Carter squared his shoulders and stood straighter. "I could ask him."

"I'm not sure that will help us."

"He's got to know something about the Botticelli. Something he hasn't told us." Carter tipped his chin up.

"I don't think you need to puff up." There was a hint of laughter in her words.

Little did she know.

Carter strode across the room until he stood next to Stanley.

The man didn't bother to look at him. "Need something? Other than a spine?"

"Just to know why you won't consider the options we laid out."

Stanley turned the full force of his attention on Carter, and Carter had to resist the strong desire to step back and away. "Because you have no idea what will be unleashed when you release the hounds on the museum."

"That doesn't change the fact we have to do the right thing. If that means a season of hard work, then it needs to be done."

"You are just like your sister."

Carter froze. "What do you mean?"

"Such an idealist. Only she was part of creating the art. But you already know that." Stanley bared his teeth in a grin. "What you don't know is that Char created the best forgeries. Until she didn't."

"What do you mean?" There was so much he didn't know about Charlotte's missing eight years, but Stanley's accusations didn't fill that hole in a way that made any sense.

"She knew what she was doing. Had the guts to negotiate for the money." Stanley picked up his mug, then gestured with his free hand for Carter to move back. "Stand down or you won't like what else you learn."

"Is that a threat?"

"What do you think?" The man shoved past Carter.

"You mean the Botticelli isn't real? Is that why you sent someone to destroy the painting? You didn't want anyone to know?"

Stanley hesitated just a second, then continued, but it was enough to tell Carter he needed to keep digging. After the meeting. There was a connection between Stanley and Charlotte's death. And somehow the Botticelli was connected, but that didn't make any sense. It was an old master. There was no reason to think that anything was wrong with the painting.

"Char created the best forgeries." It wasn't the first time Stanley had insinuated that, but the words still reverberated through him, heavy with implication.

"You okay?" Janae's words startled him from whatever fugue he was in.

"Sorry, I didn't hear you."

"We noticed." Margeaux's eyes were filled with concern. "What did he say to you?"

"Something about your sister?"

Carter nodded. "Yes, but he's trying to distract me."

"I'd say he's doing a good job." Janae scanned the assembled group. "You have ten minutes to convince your board that you have a plan that will work legally and ethically."

"While you have my vote, you'll need more." Margeaux straightened. "I can help, but the board needs to see you as the strong leader." She gave him a small push. "You need to give them a sense that if Stanley is Goliath, you're David and can be victorious."

"I need a big enough sword."

"No." Janae shook her head. "You need one small stone and faith."

"Wait, David had five."

"But he only used one."

The image hit him. The young man had walked into battle with five stones and a slingshot. All it had taken was one small stone and a firm faith in the God who had walked with him through earlier battles to take down Goliath. It was only then that he used the giant's own sword to end the battle once and for all. "I see."

"I hope so, because you now have seven minutes to sway people enough to give you a fair hearing." Janae gave him a little push. "Get to work. We'll figure out what he meant about your sister later."

Janae held back, which made sense even though he wanted her next to him, lending him her strength. Bill Yates had already told Carter where he stood, and Margeaux strode to the back of the room where she started a conversation with Barbara. That left Tiffany Grace, Charlie Blackwell, and Sean Chang, but he didn't know them well yet. If the other three would at least give him a fair hearing, then he stood a chance.

The board meeting had ended in a deadlock, with Yates, Blackwell, and Carrera siding with Stanley, who couldn't vote as chair, and Margeaux, Tiffany, and Sean standing firm. That left Carter to find other leverage to make Stanley do the right thing.

Something had niggled at the back of Carter's mind since the board meeting. Why would Stanley know details about Charlotte's work? Yes, his sister had an education in fine arts and was a brilliant painter. Everything they'd found in her cottage after her death suggested she'd worked at an accounting firm during many of the years she'd been gone. Nothing suggested hidden accounts or a secret studio where she created forgeries.

So Carter found himself in front of his computer long after he should have been in bed.

His fingers flew along the keyboard as he did search after search. The Botticelli being added to the Elliott's collection should have caused a stir. It was a small museum to have an old master of that caliber. And there should be notes in the museum's records authenticating it. That would be the bare minimum in due diligence.

But there were no articles.

He turned and studied the painting of a two-year-old Andrew that hung in the living room. Charlotte had painted Andrew in a park studying a butterfly perched on a plant, all chubby legs and intense focus. It was the type of painting that mimicked an Impressionist style. Then he thought back to her exhibits he'd attended. While he'd attended art school with the purpose of working on the preservation and financial side, Charlotte had always gravitated toward actually creating. Her shows had been filled with paintings that imitated other artists from across times and schools.

One time he'd asked her how she did it, and she said she imagined she was the artist. She would study the artist and then slide into his or her skin, in a way. It had allowed her to create pieces that were brilliant copies.

But could she create something good enough to fool a museum?

Or was Stanley getting under his skin by attacking one of the people who mattered most?

It was the kind of thing he'd expect Stanley to do.

He hated the questions cycling through his mind: Was the Botticelli a forgery? Had his sister had a hand in it? He didn't know, but there was one way to find out for sure.

He'd need to go to the museum when no one else was there and do some cursory looking before deciding whether to bring in UV lights and other tools to gauge the age of the paint and canvas.

The next morning, he slipped in and took a portable light to the Botticelli. Nothing showed that wasn't expected. Pigment popped where the painting had been touched up, but considering its age, it wasn't surprising to find spots of newer paint.

In fact, the UV light showed that there were larger portions of older paint, exactly as there should be in a situation like this. There was nothing to indicate that the painting was a recent forgery based on this. Maybe Stanley had simply been unscrupulous in the way he participated in selling it to a museum where he later served as a board member.

He could send it for further analysis in a lab, but nothing raised immediate concerns.

No, he wouldn't find anything this way. Stanley had successfully shifted his focus by suggesting Charlotte had been involved with the painting. Carter had fallen for his trap.

They would simply have to do the right thing because it was the right thing.

When he opened his email, he found a report from the Art Loss Register. When he scanned it, the report showed a claim had been filed for the Botticelli prior to the museum adding it to its collection.

He sat back and considered the best approach. Then he picked up the phone. "Stanley, I just received a report that shows the Seeger heirs filed a claim for the painting prior to the museum purchasing it. I'm forwarding it to you and the rest of the board now."

"Your point?"

"Due diligence didn't happen. This is a courtesy call to let you know I'm scheduling a Zoom meeting and vote." Stanley sputtered, but Carter didn't care. "Once that formality has been cleared, Janae and I will arrange mediation with Mrs. Seeger and her attorney."

"You're wrong. I will make sure you never work at a museum again."

Carter found he didn't care. "You can sputter all you want, but it won't change what I do." The words were right. "Mrs. Seeger should have had the painting years ago, and the fact you didn't do the right thing then doesn't mean we won't now. Look for the link in your inbox."

Now he prayed God would guide his words so truth prevailed.

Chapter 40

MRS. SEEGER WALKED THROUGH THE front door that Jarod Shaw held for her, dressed in a powder-pink sheath, a faux fur coat on top. While petite, there was an air of authority to her that had Janae standing a bit straighter as she welcomed the woman back to the firm and then led the way to the conference room. Carter waited there alone since Dukes had continued to refuse to participate. Janae had forwarded the information she had gleaned on his actions to the marshal, knowing the man might not be interested, but something still felt very off about Dukes's actions related to the painting. However, she couldn't research her way down to the crux of it.

Janae pulled her attention back to the moment and suggested everyone take a seat. As soon as they had, Janae leaned forward. "Mrs. Seeger, thank you for coming today. I hope Mr. Shaw has told you this is a settlement conference. If we can't agree today, then we have mediation scheduled for early January. The museum takes your claims seriously, and Dr. Montgomery and I will do our best to find a satisfactory agreement for all parties. I can't promise anything other than we are committed to this process."

The woman smiled at her, but there was steel in her words. "Those are pretty words, and I hope they are true." She turned to her attorney. "Jarod?"

He gave her an aw-shucks grin and then slid two folders across the table. "We would like to propose what we believe is a reasonable sale. We all know the painting is worth millions at auction, so let's make this a private sale of say, fifty million dollars."

Carter inhaled next to her, but she grabbed his hand and willed him to stay quiet. Instead, she let the number hang in the air. It was a ridiculous starting point, and Shaw knew it. However, it might be his way of looking good for his client, and if that allowed her to negotiate him to a better position, Janae wouldn't get in his way.

Shaw finally looked away, and Janae knew it was time for the real negotiating to begin.

This was her opportunity to talk to Mrs. Seeger. To be respectful yet realistic. To give her a sense of the true possibilities.

"Mrs. Seeger, I am truly saddened by what happened to your family. Dr. Montgomery and I have talked about how we're both sickened by that time in history. We have worked diligently since you arrived at the gallery opening two months ago." She didn't need her notes, as the words flowed from her heart. "Doing our due diligence to identify the ownership path of the *Idealised Portrait of a Woman* hasn't been easy, and we aren't done. There are holes in her history we still hope to fill."

Carter nodded next to her but stayed silent, his body language open and honest.

Janae noticed her heart had started to race, so she paused and exhaled slowly. This was not the time to let emotion take over. "Fifty million might be a starting point, even a valid price, but it's an excessive one. The museum doesn't have those sorts of resources. The Elliott is a regional museum attached to a small liberal arts school. It has been blessed with some incredible donations, but its resources largely come from private donors, with state funding directed to buildings." She glanced at Carter, who had an intense look on his face but nodded for her to continue. "Mrs. Seeger, there are some practical matters we should put on the table as well. We all know that you do not have the security in place to protect the painting from theft. Insuring it is quite expensive as well."

Shaw leaned forward. "On that, we know that the insurance company isn't happy with the systems you have in place. Seems you're not in a better position yourself."

Janae started to respond, but Carter leaned forward and put a hand on her arm. "May I?"

She nodded.

"I've only been here about six months, and the last two have been consumed with continuing to learn the job while also directing a lot of effort to the Botticelli." He glanced down a second, then looked directly at Mrs. Seeger. "Ma'am, this process has identified several places where we can do better, including inspecting the provenance for all our paintings. That will be labor intensive, but I have a plan in place to work with Monroe students to improve our efforts." Then he looked at Shaw. "Part of that is also working with the insurance company to address its concerns. The first conversation is scheduled for immediately after the new year, but I've already taken steps to address the quick fixes." He gave a small shrug. "I won't pretend I can fix everything with a snap of my fingers, but I can promise I am actively working to rectify those oversights and do it in a way that brings permanent change."

Mrs. Seeger watched him closely, as if making some internal weighing of what he said. "You have been respectful always."

"Yes, ma'am, and that will continue." He sighed. "Janae is probably going to kill me for saying this . . ." Her hand tightened around his arm, but he didn't stop. "There's what the law requires, and then there's what is right. I always want to land on the side of what is right. The law is the bare minimum, but I know we can do better. That's why I pushed the board so hard to do this."

"You haven't always focused on what's right." Shaw gave a tight smile, but his eyes bored into Carter. "Mr. Stanley Dukes was very forthcoming with your history."

Carter stiffened and then visibly relaxed. "That man isn't all that he seems, but I can tell you my standards have not changed. Instead, my awareness of how others operate and manipulate has." He refocused on Mrs. Seeger. "Ma'am, you can listen to rumors, or you can trust what you hear from me now. That is your choice." He settled back, and Janae watched the others closely for their reaction.

"Well, that was unscripted, young man, but your attorney does not seem ready to kill you quite yet." Mrs. Seeger tucked a strand of hair behind her ear and set her hands primly in her lap.

"I wish I could help you see how very serious we are." Janae echoed his words. "However, we are constrained by what the museum can afford. Litigation can quickly turn expensive and long. I don't think that's what any of us want."

"I want the truth brought to light."

"We can accomplish that, but it may take a little more time." Janae pulled out a file of her own. "We have a preliminary report from the Art Loss Register, but there are still a couple of holes that may require hiring a researcher in Germany."

"We can help with that cost." Mrs. Seeger nudged Shaw. "Right?"

Shaw grimaced. "How much will that cost?"

"Probably several thousand dollars on the low side. It's all a function of how long it takes." Janae made a quick note. "My client and I can get that started this week."

The back-and-forth continued for half an hour before Carter raised his hand. It was adorable even as she wanted to kiss him for being sweet enough to not interrupt anyone. "If I may, I think there's an option we haven't considered that would appease everyone." Mrs. Seeger stiffened at his words, but he hurried on. "Assuming we can fill in the missing information, how about a partial sale? The museum is a half owner and Mrs. Seeger and the other heirs are a half owner. All the provenance documents are corrected to reflect the true ownership history of the painting once we finish the research, and it stays on display at the Elliott."

Mrs. Seeger's frown deepened, but Mr. Shaw leaned over and

whispered in her ear. She sighed. "I will consider it and take it to the other heirs. What amount are you considering?"

"The fifty million dollars you originally put on the table is too high. But it's possible we can collect fifteen million."

She inhaled sharply and turned to Shaw. "We will discuss it. And you promise to fix the history?"

"Absolutely."

Thirty minutes later Jarod Shaw and Mrs. Seeger walked out with a printed outline of the proposal. The moment they exited the building, Carter picked up Janae and spun her in a circle. "You did it!"

"We did it." She relaxed as his arms tightened around her. She could lean in to this moment and welcome the completion. "But we still have work to do." Quite a bit of it.

He lowered her slowly and his grin grew. "I just realized the museum won't be your client for long. We'll just be on retainer." He waggled his eyebrows at her. "That means I can finally do something I've wanted to for a long time."

Electricity pulsed between them, the kind that drew her to him and wouldn't let her look away. She found she didn't want to.

Then he lowered his head, pausing when he was inches away. She could feel his breath on her cheek, and when she didn't pull back, he eased even closer.

"A very long time."

Then his lips grazed hers—at first a whisper touch, then he leaned in and her arms slipped around his neck. She stretched to her tiptoes, and he pulled her closer. She couldn't breathe and was flying at the same time.

Janae sank into the moment, embracing the promise of what was possible.

When she was about to run out of oxygen, she eased back. "We aren't quite done. There's more to accomplish, sir."

He leaned his forehead against hers. "We also have to figure out the history of your paintings."

The weight settled back on her shoulders. "Yes, but without a thread to pull on, we're stuck."

"Then let's pull on the whole ball."

"How do you suggest we do that?"

"Instead of waiting for the Art Loss Register report, I have a virtual appointment set with one of their researchers tomorrow. We can show them the paintings and see what they've found so far."

Janae could feel her lungs tightening and tried to sip air through the constricted airway. "What if they think my grandma and I have done something wrong?"

"When did you discover the paintings?"

"November thirteenth and twenty-second."

"And when did you submit your request on the first?"

"December thirteenth."

"Most important, when did you find your grandpa's journal?"

"I found it at the end of November, but we didn't read it until December twelfth and thirteenth."

"If you were the defense attorney, what would you say?"

"That we responded as quickly as we could." She leaned into him. "Maybe you missed your calling and should be an attorney."

"No, I'm quite content leaving that to you." He tucked her closer to his side, and she loved how they fit together. "But I won't leave you to handle this alone. We'll find the way to honor his change of heart and do the right thing."

She nodded against his side, not sure how that would happen, but trusting that together they could find a way.

Chapter 41

Friday, December 23

THE BUTTERFLIES WOULDN'T LEAVE HER alone as Janae walked to the Elliott. It might be cold, but she needed the exercise to lower the nerves that had made her unable to sit still all morning. Carter had suggested they take the call from his office since the paintings still resided in the Elliott's safe. With the call set for the end of the day in London, and for an early lunch in the States, the administrative wing should be empty, so she'd agreed.

All Grandma knew was that she had a call regarding possible next steps on determining ownership of the paintings.

If this didn't work, then the next step would be to contact the FBI's Art Crime Team, but she truly hoped they could learn enough to avoid something so public. Regardless, she was committed to doing the right thing no matter the personal cost. And she would do everything in her power to protect Grandma.

With the Elliott's crisis on the road to settlement, she'd spent the previous night focused on rectifying her grandpa's thefts. The challenge was, without a title for the paintings, it was difficult to search the INTERPOL and FBI stolen-art databases. There hadn't been a Bruegel listed on the FBI's National Stolen Art site, and the Rembrandts hadn't matched the one she had. She couldn't access the INTERPOL site without an account, but with a quick download of its ID-Art app, she was able to scroll through pictures of stolen Rembrandts. However, there were still no Bruegels, and the Rembrandts, while including a few portraits of old men, didn't match the one she had uncovered.

She'd done the due diligence possible for her without help to discover if someone had reported the pieces as stolen. She also wasn't sure that the paintings would have been reported as stolen. If Grandpa had taken them during the war and immediately after, as his journal stated, then there was a strong chance the owners had never reported their disappearance because the owners either hadn't survived the war or had assumed the paintings hadn't. However, exploring the FBI website gave her the hope that she could partner with law enforcement to identify the owners if she couldn't solve the mystery with Carter's help.

Carter opened the side door when she arrived. He pulled her into a hug, and she settled into it, feeling something inside her relax at the realization she didn't have to figure this out alone. Instead, she had a good man who would walk with her through the process. She hadn't realized how her commitment to doing everything on her own had placed heavy burdens squarely on her shoulders. Sharing the concern really did make it bearable.

"You ready for this?" Carter's gaze searched her face.

She wanted to relax and nod but knew she couldn't get all the way there. "I'm nervous."

"Remember, this is the next step in trying to find the owners." He rubbed his hands up and down her arms. "It might not work, but it's necessary. Then we'll look for a second and third if needed."

"I did a quick search of the FBI's site and INTERPOL app last night. I didn't find anything."

"See, you're already doing the next right thing."

"I couldn't find anything with Bruegel."

"There are other places and ways to search." He led her to his office, and she noted he already had the paintings out, sitting on top of their bubble wrap. "Need anything to drink?"

She pressed her hand against her stomach and shook her head. "I don't think I could keep anything down right now."

He took her hands and squeezed. "Can I pray?"

"Please."

"Father, guide this conversation and give us wisdom on how to proceed. Help us find the owners and the history of these paintings."

"Amen." It hadn't been a long prayer, but her nerves began to settle. "Thank you."

Carter ushered her to a chair in front of his desk, then moved his computer and monitor around so he could sit next to her and they could both be in the view for the call. He clicked a couple of buttons, and they waited to be let into the online room. A few moments later, a studious woman about Janae's age appeared. Her dark hair was pulled back in a messy bun, and she had glasses perched on her nose.

After Dr. Petra Brumm introduced herself, she launched into her findings. "So far, I have not found much on the painting."

Janae cleared her throat. "There are actually two." She swiveled to grab the Bruegel. "There's this one, but also another that looks like a Rembrandt."

The woman squinted and leaned closer to her camera. "Can you hold them closer to the camera? One at a time?"

"Yes." Janae held up the Bruegel and gave Dr. Brumm plenty of time to examine it.

"The block letters in the left-hand corner definitely match what we would expect to see from a Bruegel." She made a few notes. "And the other?"

Janae switched paintings.

Another couple of quiet moments passed. "Without more in-depth exploration, I cannot make a definitive declaration, but I would say you have accurately identified that these are, at a minimum, from the workshops and schools of these great artists. I have examined the catalogue raisonné available for Bruegel and have not found one like yours. It is distinctive with the lapdogs yet is similar to the one with two monkeys. Without a record, we can submit it to our database and others owned by various police agencies and see if anyone claims it and can support the claim with valid provenance."

Janae made rapid notes. "What do we do with it in the meantime?"

"Where was your grandpa when he took it?"

"I'm not sure." She hesitated then plunged forward. "I can send you a copy of the journal pages where he talks about it."

"That could be helpful if you are willing to share."

Janae glanced at Carter, and he nodded. "It won't hurt to share that history."

"I can scan and send it by tomorrow."

"Good. Then I would tell you to protect the work until someone steps forward, but recognize that could happen tomorrow or never."

The words settled on Janae with weight. "So act as a bailee for the actual owner." She made a note. "That's heavy. We'll need insurance and security."

"You could lend it to a museum. Then some of that burden would fall on it." The woman gave a small smile. "I'm sure we could find some in Europe, but it sounds like you have one right there."

Carter held his hands up. "I'm willing to help, Janae, but you and your family will have to make the decision."

Janae nodded. "What about the Rembrandt?"

"The Rembrandt is more difficult, yet easier. There is every reason from a quick inspection to think it is real. However, it will take a search and some work to ascertain whether it has been submitted somewhere." She gave a small shrug. "I would suggest you complete the paperwork, pay the fee, and I will start the work."

"Yes, ma'am. I guess I wanted to see if anything came up with the Bruegel first. I'll get that filed tonight. I haven't seen anything on the FBI or INTERPOL sites that looks like it."

"That is a good start, but there is more I can do." After a few more minutes of discussion, she leaned back. "Is there anything else?"

"No. Thank you for your help."

"You are welcome."

The screen went blank, and Janae collapsed against the chair. "Wow."

"You have some decisions to make."

"No, Grandma does. These are hers." She looked at Carter. "Will you help me talk to her tonight?"

"Absolutely." He glanced at his watch. "I have to pick Andrew up from school in a couple of hours first. Now that he's back, I'm trying to get used to the school routine again." He grinned. "It's so good to have him back home where he belongs and to know he's safe."

That night, Carter arrived at Grandma's stone house with Andrew right after supper. Mom and Dad sat at the table with mugs of decaf coffee, and Grandma didn't settle into a spot but flitted around like a hummingbird desperately looking for nectar.

Andrew bounced into the kitchen with a big grin. "Anyone have cookies?"

Carter groaned, but Grandma stilled long enough to pull out a container. "Of course. Oatmeal chocolate chip I made this afternoon." She took the lid off and extended the container to Andrew. "You may have two, young man."

"Thank you." He grinned at her and snuck a third.

"Why don't you watch a video on my phone?" Carter handed the device to his nephew, and then Andrew walked into the living area and sat in a chair. Carter turned to the rest. "Now we can talk without interruption."

"I heard that."

Janae gave a startled laugh. "Maybe." Then she reached for Grandma as the woman hurried past. "Have a seat, Grandma. We have some information on the paintings."

Grandma's hand fluttered to her throat, and then she sank onto a chair. "I don't know that I can handle this."

"You can, because we're here supporting you, Mom." Janae's mother looked around the table. "This isn't any one person's burden. We'll handle it together."

"Carter and I talked with an investigator at the Art Loss Register. She agrees that you likely have a Bruegel and a Rembrandt. She hadn't done any research on the Rembrandt because we showed that to her today." Janae considered how to best explain what would come next. "There's no clear owner claiming either, based on what I've found. If she agrees, then we can approach the FBI Art Crime Team and see whether it can help. Until then we need to decide what to do with the paintings."

Carter nodded. "They're valuable and will need insurance and security."

"Oh my." Grandma placed a hand over her heart as she collapsed against the back of her chair. "And to think one was sitting in my carriage house and the other in the basement."

"Yes, but no one knew they existed. That won't be the case now."

His phone vibrated in his pocket, and he glanced at his watch. "Huh."

"What?"

He tugged out his phone and read the text. "The marshal just texted. The Italian thugs were arrested at La Guardia trying to board a plane to Rome. He said a news alert will be coming out soon. Police have arrested Stanley for the murder of local attorney Mark Ashby too."

Janae hurried to his side and read over his shoulder. "Stanley killed Mark? Why?"

"Says here police have evidence he killed him over a painting." Carter shook his head. "He admitted that Mark was supposed to stop Mrs. Seeger from filing the lawsuit, and when she switched attorneys, wouldn't share what he knew."

"That's a terrible reason to kill someone. What a mess."

"The flash drive helped connect the records related to the mafia and show the money trail connecting Stanley to the Botticelli." Carter sighed as he slipped his phone back in his pocket. "I really hoped it would provide some answers related to Charlotte's death."

"I'm sorry it didn't. You might never know." Janae leaned into his side.

Carter nodded, wrapping an arm around her. "I'm just glad this is over."

There was a knock at the door, and Andrew jumped up. "I'll get it."

Grandma waved a hand. "Thank you, young man."

Janae glanced at Carter. "Is Stanley okay?"

"The marshals assure me he is."

The door opened, and there was a shriek. "Mom!"

Carter pushed to his feet and moved toward the front door. A stunning woman with dark hair and bright green eyes stumbled in the door and clung to Andrew.

"Charlotte . . . ?" Carter moved toward her as if he were in quicksand. "You look different."

She reached up to touch her hair. "I had to alter my appearance a bit." She held fiercely to the young boy as she buried her face into Andrew's arms around her neck. Then she looked up and mouthed to Carter, "Thank you."

"What are you doing here? How?"

"I used the Find My app. Remember, we put those on each other's phones years ago."

He paused, hands on his hips. "So you could track me, when I couldn't track you."

She nodded and then kissed the top of Andrew's head. "I needed to know he was safe."

"But . . . where have you been? We . . . we buried you," he said, visibly trembling.

"I had to disappear or it would have happened for real. I also needed Andrew far away while I worked with the FBI on a case."

Carter's color rushed back. "Dukes."

Charlotte nodded. "Yes, in a way, but he was a small fish—well, until he decided to kill a local attorney over the Botticelli. Can you believe he thought that was a forgery?" She shook her head. "But we also got the big fish he was working with. In addition to a certain someone who decided tailing Mom and Dad was a good idea." She pulled Andrew even closer as he clung to her leg. "With Dukes locked up, you'll be looking for a new board chair."

"I can't say I mind." Carter walked to Charlotte, and the three of them formed a circle, reunited again.

Janae watched, a big smile growing on her face.

"Well, that's something." Grandma hustled to the front and waved everyone back to the kitchen. "I'll get hot water going. Janae, put the cookies on a plate."

When everything calmed back down, Janae settled into the crook of Carter's arm. "What do you want to do with the paintings in the interim, Grandma?"

"Let's leave them where they are. I can loan them to the museum because I trust you to do the right thing, Dr. Montgomery. That will take care of the insurance and security, right?"

"And you can label the provenance as unknown but under investigation."

"Yes. We'll get them to the right owners if we can discover who they are."

"And until then, the public can enjoy them." Janae shrugged. "Maybe the publicity will help."

She looped her arm through Carter's and leaned against him. "You must be in shock to have her back."

"I am, but in the best way. I didn't want to be Andrew's caregiver because he needed his mom. Over the last year, he's become a big part of my life. But now she's back—and I can't imagine what that means."

She looked up and watched a flood of emotions play across his face. She wrapped her arms around him and held on tight. "It's a miracle."

He nodded. "Yes."

A few minutes later, Charlotte and Andrew walked to the front door. "He's so worn out. I'll drive him to your house."

Carter shook his head and then slipped from Janae's side. "Our house. You can both stay as long as you like. I've gotten used to having him around."

She grinned and squeezed Andrew against her side. "Thank you."

Janae followed Carter onto the porch, and together they watched until the taillights disappeared down the drive. Then Carter pulled her against him, and she sank into the circle of his arms.

"We've done pretty well."

He nodded, his chin against the top of her head. "We have." Then he pulled back enough to look into her eyes. "And now we can step into our future. Explore what we have."

"I'd like that. Very much."

His head dipped down, and he kissed her, a promise conveyed from his heart to hers.

In that moment her last concerns about whether she'd made the right choice to return home vanished. She was right where she wanted to be, expectation unfolding inside her.

As long as Carter stood beside her, she couldn't wait to see what tomorrow held.

Author's Note

WHEN I STARTED WRITING THIS book, I had a vague idea. It's a little terrifying to look back now and realize just how vague it was—I had Janae, and I had the series idea. I had just researched and written the novella for *We Three Kings*, which meant I had immersed myself in research related to art, the Monuments Men, World War II, and the days immediately after the war. Along the way I collected an assortment of research books that had my mind spinning with ideas. With art on my mind and knowing that the big what-if needed to relate to the law, I'd wanted to play with an art provenance issue since writing *Shadowed by Grace*. There are so many ongoing legal issues related to art ownership after the widespread art theft that occurred during World War II.

Because the art markets are largely unregulated, it's also an area ripe for abuse, which became the foundation for Charlotte's story in *Art of Deception*. Art sales are often used by organized crime for money laundering purposes, which is utterly fascinating in its own way. Then add in the complicated nature of art hoaxes, forgeries, and so much more, and I had *a lot* of material. I went from not having more than a few sentences of an idea to a mind that was a carousel of what-ifs and possibilities.

I made charts and spiderwebs as I tried to track what could happen. I read cases and researched to see what the legal arguments might be related to ownership and more. I had to figure out how to compress a legal case that lingers in the courts for years into a sequence of events that might take two months in this novel. All with an eye and commitment to keeping it realistic and true to procedure and facts, while at the same time recognizing that this book is a work of fiction.

One of the grand challenges of being a novelist who also loves research, history, and learning is finding the sweet spot of sharing enough to keep the story real without turning it into a master class on the topic. I hope I've hit the right balance. If not and you're eager to learn more, then I have a long list of books I can recommend.

The art tour that Janae's grandfather guarded is based on a real tour that the actual Monuments Men did not support. They demonstrated their lack of support through the Wiesbaden Manifesto, a process I included in "Beauty Bright," my novella in the *We Three Kings* collection. You can learn more about the tour through *The Berlin Masterpieces in America: Paintings, Politics, and the Monuments Men*, a book from the Cincinnati Art Museum (2020). The Art Loss Register also publishes handbooks and, in volume 1, has a chapter on restitution of Holocaust-era looted art (2021). There are many more I could include, but one that was fascinating for the diversity of examples it included was *The Art of the Con: The Most Notorious Fakes, Frauds, and Forgeries in the Art World* by Anthony M. Amore. Published in 2015, it highlights in part the dark aspects of the art world, including just how far people will go to convince themselves that they are buying a real master even when everything indicates it has to be a fake or forgery. It would be easy to write a dozen books set against the backdrop of the art world in all its diversity and variance, and I've greatly enjoyed setting several books in and around it this past year.

I truly hope you've enjoyed the reading journey with me.

Acknowledgments

It has been a delight working with everyone at Kregel. Many thanks to Janyre Tromp for being an enthusiastic supporter and encouragement when I wasn't quite sure where this series would land. It has been such a joy to work with you on this novel, and I can't wait for the future books. You are a great brainstormer, and I love the way you trusted me when we had to pivot at the eleventh hour. Many editors would have panicked to hear a writer say, "I think we need to change the order of the series," but you listened, and I'm so pleased with this book. It was scary, but we made it work in a way I'm so proud of. Thank you!

Catherine DeVries, Katherine Chappell, Rachel Kirsch, Julie Davis, and the rest of the team at Kregel: thank you so much for being wonderful to work with. It's been a delight to share this part of my writing journey with you. Thanks for your enthusiasm for my stories!

Rachelle Gardner, thank you for coming alongside me and being a champion for me when I needed one. I've enjoyed working with you at the ACFW conference for years. It's been fun getting to know you as my agent over the last eighteen months.

Beth Vogt, while you didn't edit this book, you created time in your schedule to edit *Art of Deception*, the prequel to this book, which I wrote after this one. THANK YOU! The book is so much stronger thanks to your loving care. And my writing journey is so much richer thanks to your friendship.

My family continues to be my biggest cheerleaders. Thanks for encouraging me and being so understanding in a year that included writing two novellas, a full-length novel, plus a 55,000-word prequel. Y'all are the best, and I'm so grateful for you! Here's to a more deliberate pace in the coming year.

Finally, thanks to my students and colleagues who find it intriguing and maybe slightly fun that in addition to teaching law and ethics, I write novels. I truly hoped to write one book that would be published. This is book forty—dreams can come true. Never forget that. Just be willing to turn off the TV and do the work.

About the Author

SINCE THE TIME SHE COULD read Nancy Drew, Cara Putman has wanted to write mysteries. In 2005 she attended a book signing at her local Christian bookstore and met fellow Indiana writer Colleen Coble. With prompting from her husband, Cara shared her dream with Colleen, who encouraged her to follow it. Ever since, Cara's been writing award-winning books.

Cara is an active member of ACFW and gives back to the writing community through her service on the executive board. She has also been the Indiana ACFW chapter president and area coordinator.

Cara is also an attorney, a full-time clinical professor at a Big Ten university, and an all-around crazy woman. Crazy about God, her husband, and her kids, that is. She graduated with honors from the University of Nebraska–Lincoln (Go Huskers!), George Mason Law School, and Purdue University's Krannert School of Management. You can learn more about Cara at www.caraputman.com.

Facebook: https://www.facebook.com/cara.putman
Twitter: https://twitter.com/cara_putman
Instagram: https://www.instagram.com/caracputman
Bookbub: https://www.bookbub.com/authors/cara-putman
Goodreads: https://www.goodreads.com/author/show/939004.Cara
   _C_Putman

Join Cara Putman alongside authors Angela Ruth Strong and Crystal Caudill in *We Three Kings: A Romance Christmas Collection*, as they craft tales that will warm your heart and kindle the festive spirit.

KREGEL
PUBLICATIONS